THAT SUMMER

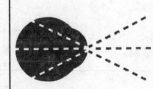

This Large Print Book carries the
Seal of Approval of N.A.V.H.

THAT SUMMER

LAUREN WILLIG

THORNDIKE PRESS
A part of Gale, Cengage Learning

GALE
CENGAGE Learning

Farmington Hills, Mich • San Francisco • New York • Waterville, Maine
Meriden, Conn • Mason, Ohio • Chicago

BOCA RATON PUBLIC LIBRARY
BOCA RATON, FLORIDA

GALE
CENGAGE Learning

Copyright © 2014 by Lauren Willig.
Thorndike Press, a part of Gale, Cengage Learning.

ALL RIGHTS RESERVED
This is a work of fiction. All of the characters, organizations, and events portrayed in this novel are either products of the author's imagination or are used fictitiously.

Thorndike Press® Large Print Core
The text of this Large Print edition is unabridged.
Other aspects of the book may vary from the original edition.
Set in 16 pt. Plantin.

LIBRARY OF CONGRESS CATALOGING-IN-PUBLICATION DATA

Willig, Lauren.
    That summer / Lauren Willig. — Large print edition.
        pages cm. — (Thorndike Press large print core)
    ISBN 978-1-4104-6970-0 (hardcover) — ISBN 1-4104-6970-0 (hardcover)
    1. Inheritance and succession—Fiction 2. Antique dealers—England—Fiction. 3. Large type books. I. Title.
    PS3623.I575T48 2014b
    813'.6—dc23   2014015301

Published in 2014 by arrangement with St. Martin's Press, LLC

Printed in the United States of America
1 2 3 4 5 6 7 18 17 16 15 14

BOCA RATON PUBLIC LIBRARY
BOCA RATON, FLORIDA

To Madeleine

ONE

New York, 2009

"Someone's left me a house," said Julia. "In England."

It was a Sunday morning and her father was ensconced in his usual place at the kitchen table. It was the Cadillac of kitchen tables, blond wood, worth more than Julia's rent for the month. A woven mat held a vase of flowers, three white lilies against a spray of ferns, deceptively simple.

Visiting her father's apartment always made Julia feel as though she were stepping into an illustrated spread in *Town & Country*. Her ancient blue jeans and button-down shirt were decidedly incongruous against the silver appliances and careful flower arrangement.

"Your aunt Regina's house," said her father without hesitation.

"Aunt who?" Julia didn't have any aunts, or at least none she knew of. Her mother

7

had been an only child and her father might as well have been. She was vaguely aware that he had a half sister — or maybe a half brother? — in Manchester, but they'd never had anything to do with that part of the family, not so much as a Christmas card.

"Your mother's aunt," said her father briefly, shaking out a section of the Sunday paper. "Regina Ashe."

He didn't meet Julia's eyes. Well, that was par for the course, wasn't it? In all these years, they had never spoken about England, about that gray prehistory that Julia revisited only in nightmares.

Sometimes, she dreamed of it still, the flash of lights, rain on a windshield, heard the screech of tires and her own cries. She would wake up trembling, her arms wrapped around her shaking body, crying for her mother.

"Am I meant to know who that is?" Julia kept her voice carefully light, trying to hide the way her hands trembled. She wandered over to the percolator on the counter, giving herself time to compose herself, striving for normal, the normal she had so carefully cultivated over the past twenty-five years. "That was the name on the letter. Regina Ashe."

"She was your mother's guardian," said

her father.

His voice was very clipped, very British. Rather than diminishing over the years, her father's accent had become even more pronouncedly BBC the longer they stayed in the States. He groomed it as one might a well-tended head of hair. Julia couldn't blame him. There was a peculiar status accorded to Englishmen in New York.

It was distinctly annoying, particularly because her childhood accent had had the reverse effect on her peers. She had wasted no time in shedding it.

Transference, the psychiatrist Julia had seen in college had called it, and a long string of psychobabble that would probably have made more sense to her if she had taken the intro psych course like her roommate. The basic gist of it was clear, though. She had sloughed off that old self, that little girl who had lived in London, who answered to "Julie," who lived with both parents in a flat with a garden, and become an American girl named Julia. It was a coping mechanism.

Julia had nodded politely and hadn't gone back. She didn't need someone to tell her the obvious.

"Right," Julia said. "Her guardian."

The Sunday *Times* crinkled as her father

turned the page. From the counter, all Julia could see was the back of her father's head, gray, carefully cropped, the tips of his ears, the wire rims of his glasses.

Her mother had a guardian who had a house. It sounded like something out of a French exercise. *Avez vous la maison de la tante de ma mère?* But Julia didn't want the house of the aunt of her mother. All of that was over, done, a long, long time ago. She was American now, as American as yellow cabs and gum on the sidewalk. Her life was here, and had been ever since that awful October they had picked up and moved lock, stock, and barrel to New York.

Julia opened the glass-fronted cabinet, helping herself to a mug from a neatly stacked row. The mug was white, with blue flowers, very Swedish, very modern. Everything in her father's kitchen was very Swedish and very modern, except for those items that were very Danish and very modern. The coffeemaker was silver, bristling with more buttons than an international space station. There was something soothing about its belligerent modernity.

"I thought it was one of those Nigerian bank account things," Julia said, trying to make a joke of it, wishing it were a joke.

"The house isn't in Nigeria," said her

father, turning and giving her one of those looks over his spectacles, the look he gave to particularly dim doctors-in-training. "It's just outside London."

"I know that," said Julia irritably. "It's — oh, never mind."

If her father didn't know what a Nigerian bank account scheme was, she wasn't going to explain. As far as she could tell, his grasp on e-mail was limited to dictating his correspondence: at work, to his secretary; at home, to Helen, Julia's stepmother.

Julia had remarkable respect for Helen. The fact that she'd managed to cater to Julia's father's whims for nearly fifteen years now without emptying the coffee carafe over his head was a miracle in and of itself.

Julia took her cup back around to the table, setting it down carefully on one of the woven mats thoughtfully provided for just that purpose.

"Assuming this is for real. . . ." she began.

Her father raised his brows over the tops of his glasses. "Assuming? You haven't contacted them?"

Julia stared down into her cooling coffee. The surface was rapidly scumming over. That would have been the logical thing to do, wouldn't it? Due diligence. It was so easy these days; just a few clicks on a

11

keyboard and you had names, addresses, details.

Instead, she'd left the letter sitting on her kitchen table, in the limbo that was her life these days, in between a box of Cheerios and a three-month-old stack of magazines.

"I get a lot of junk mail," she said defensively. "People send all sorts of crazy things."

"Julia —"

"I know," she said sharply. "I know, okay? I would have followed up if I'd thought it was anything serious." If anyone had bothered to tell her that she had an aunt Regina or that that aunt Regina owned a house. "I wasn't aware I was in line for an inheritance."

Her father ignored her sarcasm. "How long has it been?"

"Only a week." Or two. The weeks blurred together. It had been in the pile of junk mail, in between a credit card come-on offering her cheap cash — only 18 percent interest for the rest of her life! — and an invitation to the NYSPCC's summer party, jungle themed, sarong optional.

Once, she would have taken care of it in five minutes. Once, she had rushed through her day, propelled by adrenaline and caffeine, the hours racketing into one another like bumper cars, never enough space between meetings, always running late, always something more she should be doing.

That was before she had lost her job and time had stretched out like taffy.

She hated that phrase, "lost her job," as though she had accidentally misplaced it somewhere between her desk and the ladies' room. She hadn't lost it. It had been ripped away from her, another casualty of the subprime crisis, the tanking markets, the recession.

Julia tugged at the elastic that held her ponytail, pushing it more firmly into place. "I'll call them on Monday."

"Call who?" Julia's stepmother let herself in by the service entrance on the far side of the kitchen, dropping her keys in the pewter bowl that sat on top of the washing machine. From her arm swung a Dean & DeLuca bag, smelling deliciously of fresh bread.

Helen had the hard-won slimness of late middle age, her hair dyed to that particular shade of Upper East Side ash blond. Not too blond — that would be trashy — but just blond enough. It was a shade that went admirably with camel-colored pants in winter and brightly colored print shifts in summer.

Helen had been a lawyer once, in-house at Sotheby's, but she had quit when Jamie

13

was born. Julia wondered what Helen did with her days. There was a cleaning lady who kept all that glass and chrome sparkling and Jamie and Robbie were well past the age of needing constant care, unless one counted picking up their sneakers, which seemed, whenever Julia was in the house, to multiply and scatter themselves over broad areas.

Julia wondered whether time stretched out for Helen the way it did for her, whether Helen found herself inventing errands or drawing out trips to the grocery store, just to give herself something to do. She couldn't ask, though. They didn't have that kind of relationship.

Her father spoke without preamble. "Julia's inherited a house."

"Supposedly," Julia added quickly. "It might still be a scam."

"It isn't," said her father with assurance. "I remember that house." In case she might read anything of memory or nostalgia into that statement, he followed it up bluntly with, "It's probably worth a fair sum, even in this market."

"That's nice." Helen bent to give Julia the obligatory kiss on the cheek, checking out the contents of her cup on the way up. "Your father gave you coffee?"

14

Julia lifted her stained cup in illustration. "Any more and I'll be bouncing off walls."

Helen looked suspiciously at the coffeepot. "Shouldn't that be decaf?"

Her husband ignored her. Julia suspected it was deliberate. Since the last stent, her father was meant to be on a low-sodium, low-caffeine diet — or, as her father put it, low on everything that made life livable. He had a surgeon's contempt for the prescriptions of lesser medical professionals. If it couldn't be cured by cutting and slicing, it wasn't worth noticing.

Her father nodded smugly at the paper on the table. "I bet that's put Caro's nose out of joint."

"Who?"

"Your mother's cousin. You played with her children when you were little; don't you remember?"

"No," said Julia slowly. "No, I don't."

She had been told it was natural, after a shock, for the mind to circle wagons, erecting a wall against unpleasantness. But was it natural for it to continue to do so, a quarter of a century on?

Julia covered her confusion with bluster. "Either way, I don't see what this house in Hampstead has to do with me."

15

"Not Hampstead," said her father. "Herne Hill."

Julia shrugged. "Same difference."

"Not really," said her father, and there was something in his eyes that Julia couldn't quite read, as though, for a moment, he was somewhere else, long ago and far away. He picked up the discarded real-estate section. "If it were in Hampstead, it would be worth more."

Julia gave him an irritated look. "Thanks, Dad."

He gave the paper a shake. "You'll have to go over there and do something about it," he said, as if she were one of his dogsbodies at Mount Sinai, one of the legions of residents who hopped to when he called. "It'll probably take some time to clean out."

"I can't just pick up and go," Julia protested.

"Why not?" he asked, adding, with casual cruelty, "It's not as though you have anything else to do, is it?"

Julia stared at him, white lipped. "That's not fair."

He'd never forgiven her for not following him into medicine. Particularly because she had the grades for it. When she'd told him she was going to business school, he'd carried on as though she had suggested a fine career in pole dancing.

"Am I wrong?" he asked, and she could hear the implied *I told you so* beneath his words.

Julia bristled. "Do you know what the jobs statistics are like right now?" It wasn't like she was just sitting flat on her ass at home. She had sent off enough résumés to paper a small home. At least, at first. Before inertia and depression had set in. "Everyone's firing; no one's hiring."

"My point precisely." Her father neatly folded the paper. "There's no reason for you not to go to England. It's free money, just sitting there."

"Would anyone like more coffee?" said Helen, with a second wife's instinct for defusing tension. "Julia, there's skim milk in the fridge, or cream if you want it."

Julia bared her teeth in a simulacrum of a smile. "No, I'm fine."

She wasn't fine. She hated that she had nowhere to go during the day and that her savings account was steadily dwindling, eaten up by the mundane necessities of living. She hated that her father was right.

Nine months of hanging around her apartment in Winnie the Pooh pajamas eating peanut butter out of the jar hadn't done much for her. She didn't have anything else to do, not right now. The job hunt, such as it was, could be conducted long-distance.

Even so, she disliked the casual assumption that she could just pick up and go.

"My apartment —" she began.

"We'll keep an eye on it," said her father. Julia caught Helen's eye. They both knew what that meant. Helen would keep an eye on it. "It's not going anywhere."

"Yes, but I don't know why you think I should," said Julia in frustration. "My home is here."

Her father had made very sure of that. Her UK passport had been traded in for a US one; she still had that first US passport in a drawer somewhere, a little girl with taffy-colored hair in braids and eyes made glassy by the flash of the light.

Her father snorted. "A studio?"

"That's a junior one-bedroom, thank you very much," said Julia tartly. "It may not be on Fifth, but I happen to be fond of it."

Her father, like most self-made men, was big into status symbols. Like this apartment. And Helen.

Julia could still remember when they'd lived in a high-rise in Yorkville, with paper-thin walls and the smell of burnt food perpetually in the air. Her father had shed all that like it had never been. To hear him

18

now, you would think he had always lived on Fifth, always brewed his coffee in chrome splendor, rather than a battered old plastic coffeepot that smoked when it heated.

"Well, I think it's wonderful," said Helen quickly. "The house, I mean. Like something out of a novel. Maybe you'll have ghosts."

"Great," said Julia. "Just what I needed."

"Isn't there a saying about looking a gift house in the mouth?" said Helen lightly, rummaging in the cupboards. She dropped a tea bag delicately into a cup of hot water. The pungent smell of mint filled the kitchen.

"What about Greeks bearing gifts?" retorted Julia. "I don't remember that turning out well for anybody."

Helen gave an unexpected chuckle. "I don't think you'll have a house full of Trojans." When they both looked at her, she said apologetically, "Jamie just made a diorama of it for his Latin class."

Julia grinned reluctantly. "You mean you made the diorama?"

Helen looked apologetic. "You know how he is with glue."

"It was Greeks in the horse, not Trojans," Julia's father said dismissively. He looked at Julia over his spectacles. "Don't be a fool,

19

Julia. Houses don't come along every day."

"Mom?" Jamie's voice echoed down the hallway, cracking the tension like a marble against ice. "Moooooommmm? Have you seen my —"

Whatever he was missing was lost somewhere in the sounds of electronic explosions from the den.

"Robbie!" barked Julia's father. "Turn that bloody thing down!" just as Helen called, "Just a minute, Jamie!"

Julia unobtrusively slipped out of her chair and went to set her cup in the sink, uncomfortable at being caught in the crosshairs of someone else's family life. Jamie had been all of two months old when Julia had left for college; Robbie hadn't even existed yet. They were both bright, good-natured, pleasant boys, but they'd never felt quite like hers. They were part of her father's second life, like the blond pine table, like the blue and white dishes, like this apartment, acquired after Julia had gone off to college, a new start for a new life, a new wife, new children.

Helen cast Julia a quick apologetic smile. "I'll be right back. There are croissants if you want one. Just help yourself. I know I don't have to tell you that."

Helen slipped out of the kitchen, in pursuit of Jamie's iPod or gym shoes or the stray wing of a model plane.

Julia looked over to find her father looking at her.

"Caroline would probably buy the house off you if that's what you want," said her father quietly. "You wouldn't have to go back."

Julia leaned against the counter, the taste of cold coffee sour on her tongue. Her anger evaporated, leaving her feeling nothing but tired, tired and confused. "I'm damned if I do and damned if I don't, aren't I?" she said. "There's no good way to deal with it."

She didn't understand why this unknown great-aunt would pass up the cousins on the spot for a great-niece who didn't even remember her name. Memory stirred — fresh-cut grass and the heavy scent of flowers and the cool of water against her fingertips — and was gone again.

"Dad?" Her father looked up from the paper. Julia levered herself away from the counter, the hems of her jeans, always too long, brushing against the tiled floor. "Why would this aunt . . . Regina leave the house to me?"

She half-expected him to shrug, to punt the question. Instead, he folded the paper meticulously, setting it down on the side of the table, exactly aligned with the grain of the wood. "Your mother grew up in that house," he said. He cleared his throat. "Your aunt always used to say it would be your mother's someday."

His eyes met Julia's. They were gray, like hers. They had the some coloring, or had once. Her father's hair had long since gone gray, while hers was artificially enhanced with lighter highlights. Underneath, though, it was the same pedestrian mid-brown.

Her mother's hair had been black, her eyes a vivid blue. She was everything that was alive and lively. Until she wasn't.

When Julia tried to remember her mother, all she could scrounge up was an image from an old picture, the colors faded with time, her mother, in a garden, a kerchief tied over her black hair, laughing up at the camera. All around her, the trees were in bloom. There was a lake or a pond somewhere in the background, just the vaguest impression of a shimmer of water.

The picture had stood on her father's nightstand. It had gone into a drawer not long after their move to New York. Julia had never quite had the nerve to ask her father what he had done with it. Their mutual grief was a palpable silence between them.

"And I was the next best thing?" Julia

hadn't meant it to come out sounding quite so sour.

"Either that," said her father drily, "or Regina was looking to put Caroline's nose out of joint. There was no love lost there."

Julia tucked her hands into the pockets of her jeans, fighting against the urge to curl into a ball like a porcupine, all defensive prickles. She missed the familiar armor of her job, that relentless whirl of work that meant she never had to think about anything she didn't care to, pushing it aside with the excuse of being too busy.

But she wasn't busy now, was she? And she needed the money. It had been nine months already since Sterling Bates had let her go, with crocodile tears and false condolences. They had fired her, as was their charming practice, the day before bonuses were announced, reducing her take for the year to a third of what it would otherwise have been. Her severance would run out soon, but the bills were still coming in: mortgage, health care, groceries. She had no idea what property sold for in Herne Hill, whether it had been hit anywhere as hard as the market in the United States, but either way one looked at it, it was an unexpected windfall. She'd be an idiot to turn her back on it, all because of something that had happened a quarter of a century ago.

The past is a distant country, one of her art history professors in college had said. If Julia thought about it like that, maybe it wouldn't be so bad. The England she and her father had left didn't exist anymore. It was gone; the house was just a house, and there was no reason to let misplaced misgivings get in the way of a tidy profit.

One month, maybe two. Surely it wouldn't take longer than that? It would be irresponsible to sell the house without seeing it first. And it was really rather idiotic, all these years later, to still tiptoe around the topic of her mother. It had been a quarter of a century. People grieved, dealt with it, moved on.

Julia had been in England since, to London, for work. Surely this wouldn't be all that different. This would be work, too, not some sort of sentimental pilgrimage.

"I'll see what I can do," she said. It was the closest she could come to a concession, to admitting that she had nothing better to do.

Her father nodded, slowly. "Strange . . . After all this time . . ." His eyes looked past her, towards the half-open door of the den, where the shadows of Robbie's electronic monsters could be seen playing out against the wall. "Your aunt always said your mother was the only true heir to the family legacy."

Julia cocked her head. "What does that mean?"

Her father looked back at her, his lips twisting wryly. "I have no idea. No idea at all."

TWO

Cornwall, 1839

"Are you quite certain, my love?" Despite the mildness of the day, Imogen's father had two blankets tucked around him, the edges overlapping, trailing onto the gravel and moist dirt below his bench. "I wouldn't want you to feel rushed or constrained by —"

"No," said Imogen quickly, heading off her father's words. She hated it when he spoke of death. Yes, he might be a little frail, the winter had been hard, but it was spring now, or almost spring, and he would get better, he would. "I don't feel the least bit constrained."

On this first warm day of March, Imogen had brought her father out to his favorite spot in the garden, in the little wilderness next to the rectory. She had hoped it would make him feel more like himself again, put some color back in his cheeks.

Not so very far away, she could hear the faint and omnipresent roar of the sea and smell the salt tang in the air. Penhallow was a small village. Officially, the inhabitants made their living by fishing, but if the sea sometimes swept up a bounty in the form of bottles and lengths of silk the local authorities turned a blind eye. Imogen and her father had lived in Penhallow for nearly as long as she could remember. This garden, with its paths lined by crushed shells, the well-worn arbor with the stone bench below, had been her haven since she was old enough to evade her nurse's eye.

Imogen knew this village in her blood, in her bones, even though she and her father were, in local parlance, foreigners still. She had had the run of the village from the time she was old enough to walk. She remembered nothing of the world they had left behind, the parish in Gloucestershire, the houses of her cousins. She knew, because she had been told, that her father's older brother was a baronet, Sir William Hadley of Hadley Hall, and that her father had been meant to have the living on that estate. She knew also, from the curl of her father's lip when he spoke of his brother, that he found the loss of his companionship no great burden.

It was her mother's health that had driven them from Gloucestershire to Cornwall. Sea air was meant to be good for frail constitutions, so, when Imogen was just old enough to toddle, her father had found this parish in Cornwall, a small parish, far from anything the world deemed fashionable. The sea air hadn't had the promised effect on her mother's health, but they had stayed in Cornwall all the same, in this pleasant, sleepy village with the smell of the sea in the air.

It might, perhaps, have been a little bit lonely, but Imogen had never wanted for occupation. As soon as she was old enough to read, she had helped her father with his studies, marveling over the tiny figures painted into illuminated letters, careful not to rip manuscripts gone frail and brittle with age. By the time she was six, she could read the cramped Latin hands of late-medieval scribes as easily as she could the printed pages in her primers. There had been no question of her going to the village school — she was the daughter of the vicar, of a different order than the village children — so her father had taught her himself, making geography and history come alive with his tales of tormented kings and defiant queens, of knights and ladies and impossible quests.

It wasn't all knights and ladies and fantasy. All of the responsibilities of the lady of the parish had quickly devolved to her. The villagers came to her father for spiritual consolation, but it was Imogen who tended to their more practical needs, bringing soups and jellies to the poor, reading to the elderly, making sure they had enough wood for the winter.

Through the shrubbery, just down the hill, lay the church where her father preached every Sunday, or had preached, before the cough had settled in his chest and his lungs. Hard by the little village church, in the shadow of the steeple, she could see the grim shapes of tombstones, one after the other.

A touch of sun, Imogen told herself staunchly, that was all that was needed. Warm weather and good food and her father would be right as rain again.

"Truly," Imogen said, tucking in a corner of the blanket next to her father. "I want to marry Arthur — Mr. Grantham."

She stammered a bit over the name. It was so new still. She wanted to hug it to herself, to whisper his name in private, to marvel over it like a bit of sea glass found on the beach, something rich and strange and rare.

Impossible to think that only three weeks ago she'd had no idea such a man existed and he no notion of her. There they had been at opposite ends of the world until fate had brought them together.

Arthur, she repeated to herself. In public he could be Mr. Grantham, but she had the right to call him Arthur.

It was her father's illness, ironically, that had brought her and Arthur together. As the winter had grown colder and her father had grown sicker, he had begun to fret about money. There had never been terribly much. What little they had her father spent on books. That hadn't mattered, so long as he had his parish, but with his death Imogen would lose her home and what little income there was. There was nothing saved away, nothing salable, except for her father's beloved fifteenth-century Book of Hours.

Against Imogen's protests, he had put it about, through select channels, that his book, his precious book, might be available for sale.

She had expected the purchaser to be someone of her father's age, another elderly antiquarian, with a lined face and thin hands, someone as pale and fragile as the old parchment he coveted.

Instead, it had been Arthur.

30

He came riding in, like his namesake, like a knight of old, albeit in a sensible traveling chaise rather than on a charging destrier. Imogen didn't hold that against him. It would be rather hard to ride a galloping steed all the way from London, particularly given the state of the roads in winter.

He had appeared on a blustery February day, bringing with him the tang of the outside world, like the orange her father always gave her at Christmas, tart and sweet and strange. Arthur's long ginger whiskers, the cut of his clothes, the shape of his hat, all spoke of a world well outside their cloistered village.

He was not a man of fashion, Arthur had told her apologetically, just a widower, a scholar, a man of quiet tastes and quiet habits.

He had found her in the garden that first day, on this very bench. Her father had fallen asleep over his papers, and Mr. Grantham didn't like to wake him. Ought he to wait, or to return to the inn where he was putting up? He would, he said with a polite bow, enjoy more of her father's conversation; it was a pity such a learned man was retired so far from his peers, from the men who might benefit from his knowledge. Arthur himself was engaged in attempting to create a comprehensive catalog of late-medieval devotional manuscript art.

Was he limiting himself to any geographical area? Imogen wanted to know. Or was it a comparative project?

He settled himself on the bench, his hat balanced on his knees, and began describing his work, the manuscripts he had seen, the ones he still hoped to find, his methods of classification and analysis, while Imogen asked questions and proposed refinements to the scheme.

Had he considered a comparative study of Northern and Southern European manuscript art?

The negotiations over the Book of Hours had stretched to two days, to a week. Imogen suspected both men were enjoying it. Every day, Mr. Grantham walked down the lane from the Cock and the Hen, the village inn. For an hour, he would sit with Imogen's father in his study; through the window, Imogen could see them, heads bent over her father's papers. Then, as her father dozed, Mr. Grantham would join her in the frost-crisp garden, on the bench, their cheeks red with cold, telling her tales of the places he had visited, the wonders he had seen. Venice, Florence, Bologna. Paris, Avignon, Tours. The very names sang.

"And did you see . . . ?" Imogen would ask, and he would steadily, patiently paint pictures in words for her, of this painting or that statue or the particular fall of light on an autumn day behind the ruined towers of a Cathar castle.

Two weeks, then three. He had family waiting for him at home, he told her regretfully, family who would be expecting his return. A daughter, and his wife's sister, who kept house for him. Since his wife's death . . .

His wife was dead?

Yes, seven years ago, the same age as his little girl. Since his wife's death, he had spent most of his time away from home, traveling the world, collecting treasures. But now that Evie was of an age to miss him, he owed it to her to return to his own hearth.

"Although," he added in a low voice, "had I known what wonders awaited me in Cornwall, I should have journeyed this way long since."

"You would have had little luck then persuading my father to relinquish his Book of Hours," said Imogen practically. Her father's real interest was in the secular literature of the High Middle Ages, the chansons de geste and courtly tales, but the Book of Hours had been a gift from her mother and was prized as such. "It is his greatest treasure."

"It was not of the book I was thinking," said Mr. Grantham.

It took Imogen a moment to catch his meaning. She looked at him in surprise, in confusion, doubting her own understanding. He was sitting where he always sat, beside her on the bench, but his eyes were steady on her face and there was a look she had never seen in them before.

"You look like a Madonna," he said. "Wrapped in serenity."

Imogen felt anything but serene. She could not think of anything to say, so she said foolishly, "I had thought the Madonna was meant to be blond."

"Only in the common way," said Mr. Grantham, with a connoisseur's scorn for the common. "Some men cannot see past the glint of gold."

Imogen touched a hand to her own dark hair. It was parted in the center, pulled smoothly back, not bunched and frizzed in the current fashion. There had never been any need to take pains with her dress; she was neat and tidy and that was all.

Mr. Grantham leaned back, studying her with an intensity that made her drop her eyes to her folded hands. "You remind me of a Madonna I saw in a little church outside of Florence. The painter was a man of no name, but his work has survived him. The Madonna's hair was pulled back just as yours is, her hair as dark, her skin as fair. There was a haunting loveliness about her. I would have bought it," he said, with a deprecatory smile, "had it not been fixed to the wall."

"I can see," said Imogen, speaking too high and too fast, "why they would not wish to part with their treasure. It should leave a rather large blank space on the wall."

When she looked up, Mr. Grantham was still looking at her, steadily. His eyes were a cloudy blue, like the sea on an overcast day. "I should like to take you there. To see it."

Her heart beating very fast, her fingers trembling in her lap, Imogen had said directly, honestly, "I should like to see it."

It was then that he had kissed her for the first time.

He had been very apologetic afterwards, excoriating himself for abusing her father's hospitality, for betraying her innocence, but Imogen had gone through the rest of the day in a cloud of wonder, touching a finger to her lips where his lips had touched. She had studied herself in the mirror trying to see what he had seen but saw only her own face, pale skin against dark hair, deep-set brown eyes, features too strong for fashion.

But if Arthur saw loveliness there . . .

"He is so much older," murmured her father. "I should have liked someone younger for you, someone closer to your own age."

Imogen squeezed her father's hand, trying to ignore how it quivered in her grasp, how frail and thin his fingers had become. "What are a few years? You've always said I was an old soul." She made a face. "I've certainly more to say to Ar— to Mr. Grantham than to anyone my own age."

Not that she knew many people her own age. The boys in the village were shy in her presence; they pulled their caps and shuffled their feet. As for the Granvilles, who lived in the great house, they were seldom in Cornwall, spending most of their time in London. Their boys were six and ten, still in the frogs and stones stage.

"I have kept you too much secluded," her father said, more to himself than her. "You ought to have had some exposure to society . . . to young people of your own kind. . . ."

"I have never missed it," Imogen said truly.

"Your uncle . . ." her father said, half to himself. "He would take you in, at Hadley

Hall. Even after — Your uncle wanted to marry your mother. Years and years ago, when we were all young. He was furious when she chose me, instead."

"Yes, yes," said Imogen. She had heard the story before. Right now, she had no interest in old scandals; it was the present that concerned her. Arthur had tactfully returned to the inn, leaving her to wrangle her father's blessing. "But, Papa —"

Her father continued, "Even so, you are still a Hadley. And it has been so long. . . . I should have written to William months ago. I have been selfish, foolish."

Imogen bristled. There was nothing that appealed to her less than the idea of being a pensioner in her uncle's home. The idea of going from mistress in her father's household to an oddity in her uncle's was distinctly unpleasant.

"Uncle William wouldn't know me from — from that rock in the garden. Why should I be bundled off to him like an unwanted parcel?" She added unhappily, "I thought you liked Arthur. I thought you would be happy for us."

Her father roused in his seat, the blankets rustling. "I do. But it's a very different thing to like a man over a glass of port than to wish him married to one's only daughter."

His thin lips pressed together, wobbling at the edges. "I wish I had more time. I wish your mother were here."

He had been speaking of Imogen's mother more and more recently, speaking of her as though she were only a room away, near enough to call.

Fear made Imogen reckless. "Mama would have understood. She chose you over Uncle William, for all that you were a younger son. She chose you because she loved you."

There were deep furrows between her father's eyes. "Your mother and I had grown up together; we had known each other from childhood. This Grantham —"

"I love Arthur, Papa," said Imogen boldly. "Truly, I do. What does three weeks or three years or three decades matter? Would it have taken you that long to know that you loved Mama?"

Her father's hands trembled against the rough wool of the blankets. "I had not thought," he said heavily, "that when I offered up one of my treasures, I should find myself losing the other as well."

Imogen scented triumph. She asked eagerly, "Does that mean you give us your blessing?"

She wished he looked happier about it. "I haven't much choice in the matter, have I?

38

The thought of leaving you, all alone in the world . . . I have left you so ill prepared."

"You have given me everything I ever wanted," said Imogen passionately.

"No," said her father. "I have given you everything *I* ever wanted. It is not the same thing."

Imogen brushed that aside. "You will come to London with us, won't you?" she said. "Arthur has a little house, he says, outside the city. There is a garden and almond trees. . . ."

And a seven-year-old daughter. The thought gave Imogen a moment's unease. She brushed it determinedly aside. This would be her family now, her daughter, her husband. It might be a bit strange at first, but surely the little girl would come to be used to Imogen in time, and she would have Arthur, Arthur there by her side.

She could imagine them in the years to come, in the library he had described to her so vividly, surrounded by rich, leather-bound volumes, a fire crackling on the hearth, working together on his grand compendium in perfect companionship. Charitably she sketched Arthur's little girl into the picture, lying on the hearthrug with an illustrated book of fairy stories. And, perhaps, a baby, too, a baby in a cradle by the hearth.

"Yes," her father began. "But —"

"And the books, Papa!" Imogen added quickly before her father could think to raise other objections. "A whole library full of treasures. Just think of the *books*. Why, you could spend years just on a shelf of it!"

Fondness and concern warred in her father's face. "There is more to marriage than books," he said.

Stolen kisses in the garden, eyes full of admiration, professions of love. "Yes, manuscripts, too, and quartos and folios," Imogen said. "We'll be as happy as two birds on a bough. What does age matter to that?"

It still amazed her that out of all the women in the world, all the women Arthur must have met, older women, fashionable London women, he had chosen her. He made her feel special, treasured, rare.

"Rare." That was a word he used frequently to describe her. *Have you any idea how rare you are?* he would say, and Imogen would shake her head and demur, hoping that "rare" wasn't really just another term for "odd."

Her father coughed, a horrible hacking cough that wracked his whole body. When he put his handkerchief away from his mouth, the white linen was stained with red.

"I don't have the strength to argue with you," he said unevenly. "All I want is your happiness. If Arthur Grantham will make you happy . . ."

Imogen remembered the expression on Arthur's face, the reverence in his voice. *You look like a Madonna.* The memory warmed her like sunshine, pushing away all doubts and fears.

"He will," Imogen said with all the assurance of sixteen. "You'll see."

She pushed aside the image of the rust-stained handkerchief. Surely a change of air . . . Her father was old, it was true, but he had been old for as long as she could remember. She had been a last-chance child, born long after her parents had given up all hope. Her father was susceptible to colds and fevers. Admittedly, never one as bad as this before, but . . . No. Nothing bad could happen now.

Standing in a rustle of petticoats, she lifted her face to the watery spring sun, breathing deep of the familiar salt-stained air. Soon she would have a new home, a new garden, a new family.

"Come with us to Herne Hill," she said, holding out her hands to her father, "and you'll see how happy we can be."

41

Herne Hill, it turned out, was indeed a hill. A very steep one.

Julia lugged her bags from the train station, sweating in the June heat. Too much to hope that Aunt Regina's house would have air-conditioning? Probably. The wheels of Julia's suitcase scraped against the pavement, and the strap of her computer bag dug into her shoulder. She could feel the sweat creeping down under her shirt, long sleeved, button-down. Heat rose off the red and black graveled road in waves, adding the stench of tar to the strong scent of overripe foliage.

For some reason, she had assumed England would be chilly.

To be fair, she hadn't really given it much thought. She had deliberately avoided thinking of it as she went through the motions of subletting her apartment, packing her things, meeting with various friends for good-bye drinks before she left for the summer. Just for the summer. That was what she kept repeating to everyone. Her apartment was rented out through the middle of September.

It was, when she looked back on it, a little unsettling how easy it had been to pack up her life in New York, her entire existence post-college reduced to a suitcase and a sublet. Her work friendships had disappeared along with her job; sure, they'd all pledged to stay in touch, to meet for drinks, but they had quickly scattered, absorbed into their own private lives without the physical confines of the office to hold them together. Her apartment had been easy enough to clear out for a tenant. Books and clothes and mementos had been bundled into boxes at the back of the bedroom closet. The books mostly dated back to college; ditto for the pictures.

Shouldn't she have something more than that to show for the past eight years?

The one person she would really miss in the city was Lexie, her college roommate — but even there they saw each other, what? Once every month? If that. Lexie was a fifth-year associate at a firm, with two children under the age of four. Somehow, she'd managed to do what Julia hadn't. Lexie had built something real and solid for herself. Julia was beginning to suspect that everything with which she'd surrounded herself had been nothing more than a cardboard stage set, convincing until you gave it a shove and watched it all topple over.

She didn't really miss her job — financial analysis had never really floated her boat —

but she missed what it represented.

Okay. That was enough of that. Julia gave her suitcase a wrench as it caught in a crack. That was jet lag talking. Or maybe the heat. She'd been in transit since ten o'clock New York time last night, which made this the technical equivalent of an all-nighter, thanks to a seatmate with particularly sharp elbows and strong perfume. Julia had dozed a little on the plane, but they had been strange, unsettling dreams. She was following her mother through a garden, but the garden was tangled and overgrown, thorns ripping at Julia's clothes, catching in her hair. Somewhere, through the foliage, she could see the gleam of water; somewhere, just past the thicket, dragonflies skimmed over the surface of the lake and butterflies danced on brilliantly yellow blossoms; somewhere, her mother had a picnic laid out for her by a gazebo gleaming with white paint; Julia could hear her laughing, somewhere, just out of reach, but the thicket held her fast.

She had woken with a pounding headache and the cloying scent of flowers in her nostrils, thinking very nasty thoughts about people without the common courtesy to go light on the perfume before a seven-hour flight. It was no wonder she had dreamed of gardens. Of gardens and of thorns.

44

Julia paused, swiping the sweat off her brow with the back of one hand. Up ahead she could see a small commercial oasis, the striped awnings of shops a welcome break in the otherwise unbroken residential terrain.

Shouldn't she be at the house by now? Number 28, the solicitor's letter had said. What he hadn't bothered to specify was that the numbers on the hill ran backward, highest to lowest, with the hundreds down in the shallows by the train station and the PizzaExpress. Up and up the road ran, past Victorian terraced houses, recently refurbished, if the smell of paint was anything to go by. That boded well for real-estate values in the area, if not for Julia's calves, which were protesting the unexpected exercise.

She probably could have used some of the past six months of idleness to reacquaint herself with the gym. But in the beginning, she had just assumed this was all temporary. After all, she'd made the responsible choice out of college; she'd turned her back on the chimera of grad school and gone, instead, lemming-like, into consulting. She hadn't been quite sure what consultants actually did, other than fly around and look harried and important, but it paid well and, more to the point, it was about as far as she could get from med school.

From McKinsey it had been easy to stumble along the well-trodden track from consulting to business school, and from business school to a position as an equity research analyst at one of the big banks.

Telecom didn't precisely consume her soul — all right, if she was being honest, half the time it bored her silly — but there was a certain kick to being one of the few women in a man's world. She'd proved that she could play with the boys.

There was a time when that had mattered to her. Right now, she wasn't quite sure why. Either way, it had brought her where she was now. Kind of ironic that after all these years, after all her work, all her degrees, here she was, back in England, unemployed, alone.

So much for doing everything right.

Julia bumped her suitcase past a restaurant, a dry cleaner, a grocery store. Good to know there was somewhere to get sustenance around here; the bottom of the hill was a long way down and she didn't have a car. There was even a wine shop, suitably Yuppie-fied, to go with the newly refurbished Victorian brick houses, and a real-estate agent, with tantalizingly touched-up pictures of glossy wood floors and souped-up washing machines in the windows.

Number 28 was just across the way.

Julia's steps slowed as she approached. She wouldn't have known it but for the numbers on the gateposts, 26 on one side, 28 on the other. The house took up two plots, although it was hard to tell if there even was a house back there. The trees had grown thick in the yard, blocking whatever lay beyond. In the bright sunshine the yard lay in shade, the light crowded out by the thickly clustering trees.

Julia rested her computer bag on top of one of the gateposts, the one that said "26," the "6" listing slightly to the side where a nail had come loose. There was no actual gate, just a four-foot gap between the gateposts. The wall was brick, modern, and ugly. It looked as though it had been thrown up merely to serve as a nominal barrier, a sign to the uninvited to keep out.

Not that it was needed. The close-grown trees, the general air of dilapidation and decay, were deterrent enough. The houses on either side seemed very far away. It was hard to tell how far the plot went back. Some ways, she guessed. She could just make out the chimney pots above the trees, four of them. Ahead of her, a walk twisted its way to what she presumed was the house, the bricks cracked and overgrown.

Julia had a sudden image of that same path in autumn, red and orange leaves slick under her feet, as she hopped from brick to brick in a complicated pattern of her own devising. There was someone holding on to her hand; she knew that even though all her attention was focused on the pattern of the bricks beneath her patent-leather Mary Janes. Just ahead, up a small flight of stairs, the door of the house opened, spilling out light and warmth and —

The sun was shining painfully into her eyes. Julia blinked, hard, and the illusion vanished. It was just jet lag, that was all. Nothing more. Her contacts were practically glued to her eyes from sleep deprivation; it was a wonder she could see anything at all.

Yanking her computer strap higher on her shoulder, Julia hauled herself and the bags through the gap in the gate. Her wheelie skittered and bumped on the uneven surface of the walk, wheels catching on bits of cracked brick. It seemed longer than it was, twisting and curving coyly through hedges that might once had been decorative edging but had since run amok, catching at her ankles, prickling against the hems of her jeans. For a moment, she remembered her dream, the thorns pricking at her as she fought her way through.

Just a dream, Julia told herself, and shook her ankle free, marching down the path with a little more force than necessary. Some people liked old houses. Somewhere, surely, there would be someone who would want to take this one off her hands, preferably for a satisfyingly large amount of cash.

Up close, the house was larger than she had realized, covered in a muddy stucco that might once have been white but had darkened over time to a sort of dun. It was a tall house: three main floors, an attic floor, and what looked to be some sort of basement area, the top of the windows just visible from ground level. The front door was up a flight of stairs, flanked on either side by long windows, draped in dirt and damask. The sun couldn't compete with the thick growth of foliage around the house; it was almost chilly in the shade, chilly and very quiet. It seemed odd that the road was just a few yards back, smoking in the July sun. Just down the block people were buying lottery tickets and picking up their dry cleaning. But here all was still and silent.

Julia marched up the stairs, hauling her wheelie with her, wincing as it clunked against the old stone steps. The door had once been painted, but the paint was gray and peeling, the panels of the fanlight grimed with dirt.

The solicitor had sent the keys, in a package padded around and around with tape that had taken forever to pick off. Julia wished she had more confidence that they might work. There were five in all. Three had small tags attached reading "front door: lock," "front door: bolt," "back door." The last two were unlabeled.

That was going to be fun, trying to figure out what they belonged to, if they belonged to anything at all.

She was stalling, she realized, reluctant to open the door. Really, what did she think was going to be on the other side? Dracula? Frankenstein's aunt? Julia mocked herself, digging in the pocket of her computer bag for the keys. At worst, she might face a bad smell. She hadn't thought to ask the lawyer if anyone had remembered to empty the fridge. Assuming there was a fridge and not just an icebox, or whatever it was. No, that was silly. People had been living in this house more recently than that.

Her mother had lived in this house.

Ignoring a wave of light-headedness, Julia fumbled the key out of her bag. It was a normal key, cheap and flimsy, not a baronial clunker. The bottom lock turned without a protest; the bolt squeaked slightly, then gave way.

Julia pushed the door cautiously forward, feeling as though she were intruding, as though, at any moment now, someone was —

"Hello?" It seemed silly to be speaking to an empty house, but Julia did it anyway, feeling slightly sheepish.

She nearly fell down the stairs when she heard someone answer, "Yes?"

THREE

Herne Hill, 1839

"Who is *she*?" The stairs creaked as a woman stepped out onto the landing, a candle held aloft. She looked at Imogen with visible consternation and no little surprise. "Arthur?"

Spattered with the mud of a fortnight of travel, unsteady with the sudden cessation of the motion of a coach, Imogen looked from the woman on her stairs to her husband. "Arthur, didn't you —"

Evading her eyes, Arthur leaned past her, waving at the man with their baggage. "Yes, bring it through there. Cook will see you're fed in the kitchen." That dealt with, he lifted his cane in greeting to the woman on the stairs. "Ah, Jane! Meet my bride."

"Your bride," the woman said flatly, without leaving her perch at the head of the stairs.

Imogen tried to muster a smile, but her

body ached with travel and the expression on the woman's face made her feel like a tradesman who had wandered in by the front door.

The woman on the stairs was perhaps a decade older than Imogen, her fair hair worn in an elaborate coiffure of curls and braids. There was a brooch at her throat, a large cameo, framed in gold. Her dress was a deep purple, in a fabric that shimmered in the light, banded in an intricate pattern of gold braid, perfectly fitted to her narrow, fine-boned form. The richness of her raiment made Imogen feel even more battered and travel stained.

This wasn't how she had imagined her arrival at her new home.

In her imagination, it was daylight, flowers blooming all around and Arthur's daughter running forward to greet them, face alight with excitement. Instead, they had arrived at Herne Hill hours later than expected. Spring rains had turned the roads soggy and rutted, the wheels of their hired chaise mired in mud. Imogen's first view of her new house was by torchlight, the lanterns of the coach sending strange shadows along the walkway and walls. There was a smell of spring in the air, of grass and growing things, but she could see none of it through the mist and the fog.

A maid reached out to take Arthur's hat and cloak. "Welcome home, sir," she said, with a bobbed curtsy.

"Thank you — er," said Arthur. It was clear he couldn't remember the maid's name, but he beamed genially all the same.

"That will be all, Anna," said the woman on the stairs, and the maid retreated, with a curious backward glance at Imogen, still in her coat and bonnet.

Imogen took a step forward, her damp cloak heavy against her shoulders. "You must be Miss Cooper," she said as engagingly as she could. Arthur had mentioned her in passing, his wife's sister, who had kept house for him all these years. "I have heard so very much about you."

Imogen's husband's sister by marriage gave her a narrow-eyed look. "How curious. I heard nothing at all about you."

Imogen directed a quick, quizzical glance at her husband. She had assumed he had written, just as she had written to her family — what little family she had — to inform them of her and Arthur's nuptials.

Arthur drew Imogen forward, gently but firmly relieving her of her cloak. "Imogen, my love, this is Jane Cooper, who has been keeping house for me since my Emma left me." He spoke to Imogen, but he addressed himself to Jane. "I do not know what I would have done without her these many years."

"Eaten cold stew and overboiled potatoes," said Jane tartly. "You are too soft. People take advantage." Her eyes raked over Imogen's shabby traveling dress, her black gloves. "I had thought you went to find a book."

"I found the book and my Imogen, too," said Arthur easily. He dropped Imogen's gloves and bonnet on a table topped in dark marble. "We were married a month since."

Jane Cooper's lips were very thin. "This is certainly . . . unexpected."

Embarrassed for her husband, Imogen said quickly, "I am so very sorry. The letter must have been lost along the way. We had meant to tell you, but my father —" Imogen's throat closed around the words.

Her father had lasted long enough to see her married, but not much after. Word had reached her and Arthur on the road, at a dreary coaching inn somewhere in Devon. Her father had been found two mornings after her wedding, at his writing desk, his beloved books and papers around him, a miniature of Imogen's mother in his hand.

It was for the best, Imogen had told

55

herself. He was with her mother now.

But Imogen missed him all the same.

"I see," said Miss Cooper, her lips narrow and tight. Turning to Arthur, she said, "She is very young."

"Like Proserpina, Imogen brings with her the spring," said Arthur poetically.

It was, Imogen thought, a lovely compliment, but not very much to the point, especially given that it had rained all the way from Cornwall to London. Imogen put her chin up and her shoulders back. "I managed my father's household in Cornwall. For many years."

Miss Cooper descended the stairs in a crinkle of crinoline. "Cornwall," she said, as though Imogen had said *Mongolia.* "I assure you, you shall find this very different from Cornwall."

"I expect I shall," said Imogen warily, put off by the hostility in the other woman's voice.

For a moment, Imogen fancied that she saw her father's face. She could hear his gentle voice, counseling her, as he so often had, to compassion. Wouldn't she be furious, too, if a strange woman were to show up on her doorstep and announce herself mistress of the house? As a dead wife's sister, Jane Cooper had no real place in the

56

household; she was neither blood relation nor employee. It wasn't the least bit surprising that she should resent Imogen's appearance.

In an effort at conciliation, Imogen said, "I have been very much looking forward to meeting Evangeline."

"Evangeline is long since asleep," Miss Cooper said coolly, and turned to Arthur. "I have kept your correspondence for you in your study —"

"Admirable, Jane!" said Arthur, nodding and smiling at Imogen as though Jane were a pet who had performed a particularly clever trick.

Miss Cooper cast Imogen a smug look. "— but there was one letter I had thought a mistake." There was a pile of cards on a silver tray on the marble-topped table. Jane rustled through them, retrieving a sheet of paper folded and sealed in the old style. She held it out to Imogen, by the tips of her fingers, as though holding something diseased. "This must be for you."

It was addressed to Mrs. Arthur Grantham. It took Imogen a moment to remember that was she.

"I assumed it was a mistake," Miss Cooper said to Arthur. "I had meant to give it to you when you returned home."

The writing was unfamiliar. Imogen broke the seal. "It is from my aunt," she said in surprise. "Lady Hadley."

Imogen supposed it wasn't all that odd that Aunt Hadley should have written. Imogen had, directly after the funeral, penned a hasty letter to her uncle William at Hadley Hall, informing him of her own marriage and her father's death, the one so sadly on the heels of the other. Imogen had apologized for the hasty nature of the funeral arrangements and provided them with her new direction.

Some expression of condolence was to be expected, even if her memories of Hadley Hall were hazy with time. Her father and uncle had corresponded irregularly, but Imogen had seen nothing of her aunt, uncle, or cousins since her father had taken to living in Cornwall.

Miss Cooper raised a brow. "Grand relations you have."

Imogen shook her head in demurral. "The name is an old one, but not particularly distinguished. It is only a baronetcy."

"Only a baronetcy," echoed Jane. "Well. I suppose we must seem like nothing to you after that."

Imogen glanced at her in confusion. "Not at all." She wasn't quite sure how she had offended, but she felt it important to set it right. "This is far grander than anything Hadley Hall can boast. My uncle has always cared more for his stables than his house."

"Hadley Hall," murmured Miss Cooper, and looked significantly at Arthur.

Arthur placed a hand on Imogen's arm. "What does your aunt say, my love?"

Imogen glanced down at the creased sheet of paper. "She says —"

Not condolences, or, at least, not the sort Imogen had expected. The letter was a triumph of malice and poor grammar. They had made discreet inquiries, wrote her aunt, and their man of business had informed them that Arthur Grantham was nothing more than the son of a wine merchant; indeed, he actively pursued the business himself. Imogen had, so far as they were concerned, put herself beneath all notice by marrying so far beneath herself. Imogen should expect them to have nothing more to do with her. They hoped she would be happy with her tradesman, and it was really no more than was to be expected after the haphazard way her father had raised her. If he had heeded their advice and —

Imogen hastily folded the letter before she could read further. She didn't need to. Of all the nasty, snobbish, vile —

To say such horrible things, about Arthur, cultivated, scholarly Arthur, and, even worse, of her own dear father, scarcely cold in his grave. And to do so in such a splotched, uneven hand, rife with blots and misspellings and language straight from the stables — she didn't care if Aunt Hadley had an earl for an uncle and the best seat on a horse in five counties; she was still a crude, unlettered old hag and Arthur was worth twenty of her, however much his father might have been in trade. A fishmonger would have more in her of true gentility than Imogen's Aunt Hadley had.

"Well?" said Miss Cooper. "Or are we not fit to hear?"

Imogen drew in a deep, uneven breath. "My aunt wishes us felicitations on our marriage," she said steadily. "And condolences on my father's death."

There was no need for Arthur to know the horrid things Aunt Hadley had said; it would only hurt him, and needlessly.

On an impulse, Imogen reached out and took his hand, squeezing it with all the emotion in her heart. Arthur was her family now, all the family she needed.

" 'With one drooping and one auspicious eye,' " Arthur quoted soulfully, if inaccurately. Lifting her hand to his lips, he brushed her knuckles with an airy kiss. Imogen saw Jane stiffen and look away. "From this sad beginning, my love, shall come many happy years. Whatever may have been past, this is your home now. Jane will show you about."

"Oh, no," said Imogen quickly. "I shouldn't wish to put anyone out. Tomorrow is more than time enough."

Tomorrow, when she was less worn with travel, she would sit down with Jane and make her see that it was all quite all right, that she hadn't the slightest notion of displacing her. Tomorrow, in the light of day.

"In that case," Arthur said, framing Imogen's face in his hands, "you must have a tray in your room and go straight to bed."

In this strange house, with the candlelight flickering off the smug faces of the painted lions lining the tops of the walls?

"Not unless you come with me," said Imogen firmly, "You are quite as worn with travel as I am."

For a moment, Imogen thought he might demur, but his face softened and he said, in a voice intended only for her, "You know, my love, that I can deny you nothing."

"Your correspondence —" said Miss Cooper shrilly.

"Can wait for another day," said Arthur.

61

He linked his arm through Imogen's. "Come, my love, and let me show you to your room."

It was petty, Imogen knew, but hard not to feel a little flicker of triumph. She looked back over her shoulder at Miss Cooper's pinched face.

"Good night," Imogen said as warmly as she could.

The other woman did not return the sentiment.

"I am afraid we have offended Miss Cooper," Imogen murmured to Arthur as they ascended the stairs. There were candles lit in sconces on the wall, beeswax candles, and the carpet beneath her feet was something finer than the usual drugget, far finer than anything she had been accustomed to at home.

Trade, Imogen could hear Aunt Hadley sniff.

"It is late," was all Arthur said, as if that explained everything. As he pushed open a door the hinges protested as though they had not been used in a very long time.

The heavy drapes were drawn, blocking the faint light of the stars, and the air was heavy with the scent of dusk and damp. Arthur's candle cut an uneven path through the darkness, revealing rosewood furniture draped in flowered pink brocade.

It ought to have been pleasant. Once, it might have been. The bed and dressing table were both of rosewood, carved in gentle curves. The paintings on the wall were all floral in theme, delicately framed in gilt. The two long windows were shrouded in heavy drapes in a color that must once have been rose, like the bedspread, but had faded to an ashy pink.

"This room has not been used in many years," Arthur said apologetically.

He set the candle down on a dressing table, next to the miniature of a woman propped on a small, gilded easel. The woman looked a little like Miss Cooper, but her features were softer, rounder, her hair in a froth of blond curls around her smiling face. She was young, as young as Imogen. The candlelight flickered off the painted features, lending an uncanny illusion of life to those painted blue eyes.

There was no doubting who she was, or to whom this room must have belonged.

In the mirror over the dressing table Imogen could see her own face reflected back at her, pale and drawn, her hair dark and drab about her face, loose, limp locks straggling free of their pins, nothing like the pink and gold loveliness of the woman in the picture.

In the candlelight Arthur suddenly seemed a stranger, this man whom Imogen had known only a little more than a month, on whom all her happiness depended.

Impulsively Imogen put her hand on Arthur's sleeve. "Do you miss her? Your —" She couldn't quite bring herself to say *wife*. "Her?"

For a moment he seemed almost puzzled, and then his eyes followed Imogen's to the miniature on the mantelpiece. Arthur lifted the picture of his wife, regarding it as if viewing a stranger.

"It was a very long time ago," he said almost apologetically. And then, as though he were examining any work of art, "It is a good likeness."

Imogen didn't want it to be a good likeness. She wanted it to be rank flattery, for the real Emma Grantham to have been squint-eyed or hunch-backed or have a laugh like an unoiled door hinge.

In a subdued voice Imogen said, "It was too bad of you not to give Miss Cooper any notice of my existence."

Setting down the picture of his first wife, Arthur held out both hands to Imogen. "You are too precious to share."

Next to the miniature of his wife Imogen

felt anything but precious; she felt large, clumsy, and gauche.

Imogen nestled her hands in Arthur's, drawing reassurance from his touch, trying to hold on to the memory of their time together in Cornwall, that enchanted courtship in the garden, when Arthur's eyes had been for her and for her only.

Naturally, everything seemed gloomy now, late at night, with the rain dripping down the shrouded windowpanes, but the morning would dawn sunny and bright and they would begin their lives here together just as Arthur had promised they would, working together in perfect companionship and harmony.

But she couldn't quite stop worrying away at the uncomfortable realization that Arthur hadn't bothered to let anyone know at home about his new wife.

"She was very cross," said Imogen. "And she had every right to be."

"Once Jane knows you, she will love you, just as I do." Imogen felt the pleasure of his words warm her like sunshine until Arthur added thoughtfully, "She will be a great help to you as you learn to get on."

"I did manage my father's household for a great many years," Imogen reminded him, wishing she felt more confident that the one translated to the other. Miss Cooper was right; London was a very long way from Cornwall. Imogen tilted her head up at her husband. "And I thought it was I who was meant to be a help to you. With your work."

"Oh, yes, that," Arthur said vaguely. He touched a finger to her cheek, skimming the surface as if it were a treasured relic. "I didn't bring you here to use you as a clerk. I shouldn't want my wife weighted down with dreary old papers."

Imogen laughed up at him. She was on more stable ground here. "You know I don't find them the least bit dreary. Your compendium —"

"Certainly doesn't call for such diligence from a new bride as that," said her husband indulgently. "Besides, there is nothing here that would interest you just now, just dull correspondence and business matters. I was away too long and there are matters that await my approval."

"Of course," said Imogen, trying to look as though she understood. She knew that Arthur still, nominally, ran his father's import operations. She knew nothing of such things, but she could learn. "Perhaps I might help you? Two hands make light work."

"That is what my clerks are for." Arthur

looked at her dark dress, at the cheap fabric, the fall of the skirt. "Talk to Jane about buying some fabric for new dresses. I like to see you in pretty things."

Imogen almost opened her mouth to protest — but what was there to protest in being offered a new dress? It was all reasonable enough. He was right; she didn't know anything about the import of amontillado, and it would be foolish for her to make a mess of his correspondence when he had clerks for that. Once his pressing business was dealt with, there would be time enough for them to resume work on his compendium of medieval religious art.

In the meantime, she still had a house to explore and a new stepdaughter to meet. Imogen had only just arrived. There was plenty of time for all the bits and pieces of their new life to fall into place.

"I am so happy to be here at last," she said huskily, sliding her arms up around Arthur's neck. "In your home."

"In *our* home," he corrected her. "It is your home now, too."

And as he leaned forward to press a kiss against her brow, and then her closed eyelids, she heard a floorboard creak outside.

As though someone were listening.

"Is someone there?" Julia's voice sounded very small and tinny in the dark hallway. Get a grip, she told herself, and called out, more forcefully, "Hello?"

Her fingers fumbled for a light switch and found it. It was gummy, but it worked. Two bulbs blinked into life high above her head, encased in elaborately chased frosted glass. The pale light they produced only dusted the edges of the gloom. The hall wasn't particularly large, even to her city-bred eyes, but the ceiling seemed to go up and up, the light fixture hanging from an elaborate, if dusty, plaster roundel.

A staircase, carpeted in red patterned with what might originally have been blue, rose up in front of her, turning sharply towards a landing.

Footsteps pattered down the stairs, accompanied by a voice calling, "Sorry! It's just me."

Julia's hands, which had tightened around the strap of her computer bag — burglar knocked out by PC! — relaxed. The voice wasn't familiar, but it certainly didn't sound threatening. It was a woman's voice, husky, and unmistakably British.

"Is that Julia?" The owner of the voice passed the curve of the stair, the worn treads squeaking as she cantered down the final flight, one hand on the banister, the other flapping for balance. She stopped, breathless, at the bottom, sweeping her long hair out of her face. "Hi."

Her hair was a darker brown than Julia's, expertly streaked with lighter highlights. Over a pair of designer jeans she wore one of those floaty chiffon tops that only the very tall and very thin can wear. She was both.

What was a fashion model doing in her front hall? The lawyer hadn't said anything about anyone being in residence. The word "empty" had been used quite distinctly.

Julia dumped her computer bag on top of her wheelie. "Yes, it is Julia," she said cautiously. "And you are — ?"

"Oh, sorry." The stranger came forward, hand extended in welcome. Even in ballet flats, she was a good four inches taller than Julia in her high-heeled loafers. "It's Nat," she said, and, when Julia looked blank, tried again. "Natalie? Your cousin? I've haven't seen you since — well. Yonks."

Julia forced a smile. Not very polite to admit she had no recollection of Natalie, no recollection at all, so instead she said, "It's been a while."

She didn't ask, *What are you doing here?*

but the question must have been implied, because Natalie laughed lightly and said, "Crenshaw told my mother that you'd be in this week, so I thought I'd pop by, make sure the lights worked and the loo wasn't stopped up. I didn't mean to scare you, though. They hadn't thought you'd be in until tomorrow."

Natalie was smiling, smiling brightly, but her eyes didn't match her lips. Or maybe that was just the half-light of the hall, creating shadows, distorting perception.

Next to the other woman's casual trendiness Julia felt even more dirty and disheveled than she had before, painfully aware that her jeans and shirt had been with her since New York. They had the accumulated stains on them to prove it. Her hair was coming out of her ponytail and she could feel the waves of dirt coming off herself like Pig-Pen in the old Charlie Brown comics.

It put her at a distinct disadvantage.

"That's very sweet of you," said Julia cautiously. It seemed rude to ask how Natalie had gotten in, but Julia wasn't sure she liked the idea of cousins popping in and out at will. If Natalie was a cousin. "Does your mother have a key?"

Natalie wafted Julia's question aside. "That kitchen door never closes properly."

70

Good to know. She'd have to find the local equivalent of Home Depot and install a bolt.

"Besides" — Natalie leaned forward confidingly, bringing with her the slightly chemical scent of expensive shampoo — "I wasn't going to leave you all alone in the chamber of horrors."

"I was thinking more House of Usher," admitted Julia. "Are there any other lights in here?"

"It wasn't as bad when the foliage was trimmed," said Nat, casting a dubious look around the hall. "There used to be some light from the windows. Not exactly cozy, is it?"

"I don't know. A bit of Windex, some hedge trimmers, a can of gasoline . . ." Hmm, she probably shouldn't joke about arson, not to someone she didn't know. Julia massaged her aching shoulder. "Do you live around here?"

Nat gave an exaggerated shudder. "Hardly." From her expression Julia gathered that her question was a social solecism. "Would you like the tour?"

What she would really like was an hour of privacy to settle in and get her bearings. But Nat didn't seem to be going anywhere fast. Was this normal? Julia had never had any family before, or none that she remembered. It was hard to know where the boundaries were meant to be. She and her father had adopted the New Yorkers' creed of keeping to oneself.

"Sure," said Julia. "But first — a bathroom?"

"This way." Natalie led the way to a tiny bathroom tucked away under the stairs, just a toilet, a sink, and a mirror. The toilet was the old kind, with a wooden seat and a tank hanging from the ceiling, chain dangling down. "It's a bit primitive, but it works. Mostly."

There were times when it was an advantage to be on the smaller side; Julia's head just cleared the sloping ceiling. The wallpaper was covered with bits of verse. *I have wasted time, and now time doth waste me. If you neglect time, like a wilted rose, it withers. Tempus fugit.* Cheerful stuff.

Julia made a mental note to repaper the bathroom before showing the place to prospective buyers. Constant reminders of one's own mortality weren't exactly bathroom fare.

Despite Natalie's dire predictions, the toilet flushed and the water, after a few moments, ran clear. Julia splashed her face with cold water, blotting it with a limp towel hanging from a ring in the wall. Looking up at herself in the streaked mirror, she was astounded by how normal she looked. Mid-brown hair pulled back in a ponytail, wet wisps clinging to her cheeks. Her cheeks were flushed, her eyes a little bleary from jet lag but more awake than half an hour ago. There was nothing like being scared out of your wits to wake you up.

Looking on the bright side of things, she decided, rubbing ineffectually at a water splotch on her shirt, Natalie's appearance had scared her other ghosts away, at least for the moment. Jet lag, she told herself. Heat and jet lag. With another person in it, the house was reduced to exactly what it was: a large, elderly establishment that had the stale smell that comes of being shut up for too long.

Natalie wasn't in the hallway when Julia let herself out of the bathroom.

"Nat?" Julia looked around, trying to figure out where she might have gone.

There were doors on either side of the front hall. A narrow hallway ran past the stairs, branching out into more hallways, more doors. From the outside, the plan of the house looked like it ought to be fairly simple, but it stretched farther back than Julia had thought, with hallways darting off at odd angles.

She pushed open the door to her right, directly across from the bathroom, and found herself in what must have been Aunt Regina's rumpus room. The furniture was chintz and worn; there were piles of crossword puzzles on the floor next to the couch and a surprisingly large flat-screen television standing uneasily on a table that looked too small for it. She had obviously enjoyed James Bond movies. A box set of them sat next to the DVD player, with a gap where one had been pulled out.

It looked as though Aunt Regina had just stepped out for a moment. Her spectacles were still on the corner table, next to the lamp. There was still a tray table, one of the cheap, portable kinds, open in front of the couch, holding a placemat, an empty mug with something caked on the bottom, and no fewer than three remotes.

Why me? Julia wanted to ask her, but Aunt Regina wasn't there to answer. The glasses sat where they were on the side table, the lamp dark.

It was a slightly unnerving feeling. Julia hurried across the room, pushing open one of a pair of double doors, coughing at the dust. Somehow, she didn't think that Aunt Regina came in here much, whatever it was.

The room smelled dank, and in the dim light from the study Julia could just vaguely make out windows shrouded in heavy drapes.

The switch was one of the push kinds. Julia pressed down on it. Blinking in the sudden light from the crystal chandelier, she found herself face-to-face with a woman on the wall.

For a second, the dark hair, the pale skin, the flowers, made Julia think of her mother, of that faded image in an old snapshot.

But there was nothing faded about this picture. Even dimmed with dust and neglect, there was a vibrancy about the painted image that drew the eye like a magnet. It shouldn't have. There was nothing particularly exotic about it, just a woman sitting in a garden, trees flowering all around her, roses twining as if reaching for her hand, the sun catching the gold lettering on the book that lay beside her, abandoned on the bench.

The woman's clothes made Julia think of the cover of her high school volume of *Jane Eyre,* a tight-waisted dress in a deep, dark blue, with a modest white collar and cuffs. Her dark hair was uncovered, parted in the middle, pulled down smoothly to cover her ears, then looped and knotted in the back.

Just another society portrait.

Except for her face. She was looking up, lips parted as though about to say something. The serenity of her hair and gown was belied by the turmoil in her face. She looked, realized Julia, as lost as Julia felt. The contrast between the woman's restrained clothing, her carefully arranged hair, and the wildness in her eyes struck a powerful chord with Julia. She felt a kinship with this unknown woman, whoever she might be, with the confusion and frustration all bottled into that prim exterior.

Whoever the artist was, he was pretty darn talented to have conveyed all that, just in the tilt of a head, the slightly parted lips, the luster of the eyes. Julia took a step forward, feeling as if, if she only got close enough, those lips might whisper secrets to her. She could practically hear the buzz of expectancy in the air around her. Even the dust motes seemed to have paused to listen.

A door opened on the other side of the room, and the mood shattered.

"There you are!" It was Nat, slightly breathless. "I just went to make sure I'd closed the back door. Hideous room, isn't this? It smells like someone died."

FOUR

Herne Hill, 1842

"Arthur?" Imogen hovered in the doorway of Arthur's study, a candle in her hand.

The linen of her nightdress billowed around her, the fullness of the fabric seeming to emphasize the emptiness beneath. Her abdomen felt hollow without the baby who should have been rounding it.

The first time Imogen had miscarried, she had scarcely known she was with child before she had lost it. This time, she had felt the tingling in her breasts, had seen her nipples darken and change. Her stomach had barely started to round, but she had known the child was in there all the same. She had felt it quicken, the smallest flutter of sensation, but there nonetheless.

Until it wasn't.

Imogen pushed the door a little farther, stepping tentatively over the threshold into Arthur's domain. It was less a study than a gallery, crammed with rare and precious objects of beauty. The light of her candle glinted off the stained glass of the window, off the richly polished wood of the shelves and paneling, off the gold illumination in her father's Book of Hours, which lay open on its very own stand at the far end of the room.

Imogen seldom came here; Arthur had a way of hurrying her out again, in the nicest possible way but just as definitively for all that. Argument and entreaties alike were blunted against his smiling courtesy.

"Arthur?" she said again, and he looked up, blinking a bit.

"Yes, my dear?" He was still at his desk, impeccably dressed in jacket, cravat, and dark trousers. "Did you want something?"

She wanted to turn back the clock, to their courtship in Cornwall, to the way he had looked at her then, to the promises he had made her.

Somehow, ever since she had come to Herne Hill, nothing had gone quite as it ought. Instead of drawing closer to her, Arthur had retreated ever more into his own business, business that didn't concern her. The door to his study was closed to her; the manuscripts he had once so vividly described to her were wrapped away in their own special casings and jealously guarded. There would be time enough for that, he had told her indulgently, once she had adjusted herself to her new life. Wouldn't she be more comfortable in the morning room with Jane?

Jane hadn't wanted Imogen in the morning room any more than Arthur had wanted her in the study. The only place in which Imogen had found a welcome was in Evie's nursery. She had persuaded Arthur to allow her to sack Evie's worthless governess and let Imogen take on the task. Those hours with Evie, reading with her, taking her through the rudiments of French grammar and basic mathematical equations, were the only times that Imogen felt truly useful.

It was only temporary, Imogen had told herself. Once the household was accustomed to her . . . once Arthur had dealt with the most pressing of his business . . .

Why did it all sound more and more like an excuse? It had been three years now, and, but for Evie, Imogen still felt nearly as much a stranger at Herne Hill as the day she had arrived. More so. Then she had been wrapped in the comfort of Arthur's love, never knowing that he would grow more distant day by day until even his visits to her room by night became a rarity rather

79

than a commonplace.

Didn't he love her? He said he did; he paid her formal and flowery compliments on those occasions when their paths should chance to cross.

So why did it feel as though he was slipping away?

Imogen looked at Arthur, sitting behind his desk, and felt as though she were looking at a stranger. The thought filled her with a deep and nameless fear.

Nonsense, of course, all of it. It was natural to be prone to melancholia after the loss of a child; that was what the doctor had said, prescribing a horrid draught that Imogen poured into her slop jar when the nurse wasn't looking.

"It is late," Imogen said, trying to sound as though she called on her husband in his study in her nightdress every night. "Shouldn't you come to bed?"

To her bed. If she could feel his arms around her, perhaps she wouldn't feel quite so alone, so lost.

"Presently," Arthur said, his eyes already straying back to the papers in front of him. Since she had lost the baby, he seemed to look past her rather than at her. "Presently."

A small painting of a Madonna and child stood on an easel on Arthur's desk. The

Madonna's cloak was impossibly blue; the colors glowed as though it had been painted yesterday. The mother's expression, as she gazed down at her child, felt like a personal reproach.

Imogen took a step closer, encroaching onto forbidden territory. "You work so very hard."

It wasn't a ledger open in front of him but a periodical of some sort. Arthur hastily closed it, looking up at her with a smile that was slightly strained around the edges. "Did you need something, my dear?"

Companionship. Affection. "I had thought we might take a picnic," she suggested. "If the weather stays fine."

Arthur's brow furrowed with concern. "Should you overtax yourself with such excursions, my dear? You need your rest."

"I have done nothing but rest!" The words cracked out with more force than Imogen had intended. She took a deep breath, gentling her tone. "I had thought it might be . . . pleasant. Like our afternoons in Cornwall."

"Yes," Arthur said abstractedly, fingering the edges of the papers on his desk. "Yes, that would be a capital idea — but I fear I have business in town."

Was it her imagination, or did he sound

relieved?

"Some other time, perhaps," he said, and Imogen realized, sinkingly, that it wouldn't be any other time at all, just as there was never the time to show her his manuscripts or take her to visit the collections of his friends. "Was there anything else?"

"No," she said in a small voice. "Nothing that signifies."

Unless he could tell her where she had failed him. She had tried, so very hard, to conform to whatever it was Arthur wanted her to be, wearing the dresses he chose for her, calling on the ladies he deemed suitable. But it hadn't done any good, had it? He was sitting behind the desk, and she was standing barefoot in her nightdress, abashed and rebuffed and more alone than she had ever imagined she could be.

Don't you love me? she wanted to ask. But the words stuck in her throat. She wasn't sure she wanted to know the answer.

Arthur pushed back his desk chair, standing in a clear indication that the interview was over. "You shouldn't be out without a shawl," he said reproachfully. "Not when you have been so unwell."

"Unwell." A bland enough euphemism for the loss of their child.

How could he paper it over with platitudes? They had never discussed it, never grieved together; he had only patted her on the cheek and hurried from the sickroom. Away on his business, whatever that business might be. Imogen suspected it was with a comfortable chair at his club.

The bitterness of the thought stopped her cold. Surely she shouldn't be thinking that, not of her husband, the man whom she had pledged to love above all others.

"Arthur —" she began, and stopped, not sure what she meant to say. She looked at him, at his bland, smiling face, the whiskers so carefully trimmed, the hair combed just so, and none of it betraying the slightest hint of any kind of emotion.

"We don't want you to catch your death of cold," he said, moving her in the direction of the door.

"No," said Imogen blankly. "That was foolish of me."

"You must go directly upstairs and make sure Anna brings you a hot brick for your bed."

Her bed, not his.

Arthur tapped a finger gently against her cheek. "And don't frown so. We don't want furrows to mar that pretty face."

"No," said Imogen numbly. "Of course not."

She knew she should stand her ground, pour out her doubts, her unhappiness — but something told her that it wouldn't be any use. Arthur would just squeeze her hand and ask her if she wanted Anna to fetch her medicine, or tell her that she would feel better in the morning. Arthur didn't like displays of emotion; she had discovered that when her father died, and had bottled her grief as best she could.

At the time, she had told herself that it was merely that no bridegroom wished to be burdened with a weeping wife in the first week of marriage. She had told herself that it was a sign of his delicacy of feeling, respecting her grief by avoiding bringing up a topic that might cause her more pain.

Unless it wasn't anything of the kind. Unless it was simply that Arthur didn't care for anything that didn't directly concern Arthur.

Arthur ushered her gently but firmly to the door. "Good night, my love."

"Good night, Arthur." Imogen's voice sounded strange and flat to her ears, but Arthur didn't seem to notice. She shouldn't have expected that he would.

The door clicked quietly shut behind her, leaving her alone in the hallway, with nothing but closed doors to all sides. She was still holding her candle, and the flame flickered with the trembling of her hands. She felt numb, from her head to her toes, numb and cold, in a way that had nothing to do with her lack of a shawl.

Desperately she scrambled to recall the early days of their courtship, the giddy joy of those halcyon days in her father's garden. But even her most treasured memories felt flat and stale. When she thought of him on the bench beside her, it was always Arthur talking about Arthur: his journeys, his observations, his acquisitions.

No, that wasn't entirely true. She clung to the memory of the compliments he had paid her, the touch of his hand, they way he had gazed into her eyes.

But even those memories had lost their savor. Beautiful, he had called her, and rare, but he might just as well have been speaking about her father's book or the chalice in the hall; she had seen him handle both with as much reverence and just as nonchalantly tuck them away.

With a sinking feeling, Imogen remembered her father's warnings. At the time, she had dismissed them as so much croaking. She knew love when it presented itself. But was it love? Or simply infatuation? She had been so convinced that theirs was a meeting of minds, but now, three years later, she wasn't sure she had ever known Arthur's mind at all.

And what she did know of it she wasn't entirely sure she liked.

The thought filled her with a wordless dread. Imogen pressed her eyes shut against the burning light of her candle flame. Maybe Arthur was right; maybe she was overtired.

Or maybe she had made a horrible mistake.

And if she had? What then? There was nowhere for her to go. Even if her relations hadn't disowned her for marrying Arthur, she was a married woman now; under the law, she was one person with her husband, her identity subsumed in his. There was no means of dissolving the marriage short of death.

There was a tread in the hall, and Jane appeared, holding a tray on which a pot of tea steamed.

"Arthur is working," Imogen managed. Some remnant of pride prompted her to add, "I don't believe he wishes to be disturbed."

Jane gave her a pitying look. "You should be in bed," she said, and calmly opened the study door.

Imogen only heard Arthur's words of appreciation: "Tea! Just what I was wanting!" before the door closed behind Jane, leaving Imogen on the wrong side.

Herne Hill, 2009

"What a horrid place." Natalie's cut-glass tones cut through the atmosphere in the room, reducing it to just a room, old and unused.

"It *is* a little dank," admitted Julia. Or a lot dank. The dust had clotted and clumped into a brownish haze. She wondered how the portrait would look after a cleaning, whether brightening the colors would somehow brighten the mood of it. She doubted it. It wasn't anything in the palette but something in the woman's face.

"A little?" Natalie raised her perfectly manicured brows. "I don't think anyone's been in here since before Thatcher. Aunt Regina always used the other room, back there."

"Yes, I saw it," said Julia absently. She pointed to the fireplace. "That portrait — who is she?"

"Goodness, that *hair.*" Natalie stood back to squint at the painting with a practiced gallery goer's stare. "Was she auditioning for a spot as Princess Leia?"

87

"That was the look at the time." Julia prowled around the base of the painting, looking for a plaque, a date, a signature. The curved and gilded frame was stubbornly uninformative. "Mid-nineteenth century?"

"I shouldn't be surprised," said Natalie noncommittally.

The woman had smooth wings of hair parted in the middle and coiled on the side and a dress with a high-buttoned basque.

"Eighteen-forties, maybe?" Catching Natalie looking at her, Julia shrugged and said brusquely, "It's the hair and the dress. Who do you think she is?"

"An ancestress, I imagine. Otherwise I doubt she'd be on the wall. One of the ancestrals was a collector of sorts, but anything good was sold off ages ago. At least, that's what my mother says."

There was a slight edge to Natalie's voice when she mentioned her mother. Or maybe the edge had more to do with the family treasures being sold.

"Your mother was my mother's cousin?" said Julia, trying to get the family tree into order. She remembered what her father had said, back in New York. "Caroline?"

"Yes." Natalie didn't seem interested in pursuing that line of discussion. She nodded to a portrait on the far wall. "Do you think that's your portrait's father on the wall over there?"

On the far wall, over a faded sofa upholstered in rose and cream silk, hung a portrait of a man whose features were muffled in an exuberant display of facial hair, from bristling sideburns to even more prominent whiskers. The ginger of his hair was liberally streaked with gray and the buttons of his jacket strained over his waistcoat in proper prosperous middle-class Victorian fashion.

He had been painted in his study, or in the artist's fantastical re-creation of one, with his hand resting on a stand on which a vividly colored Book of Hours lay open, the pages looking as though someone had just turned them. Julia would have wagered money that it had been painted by a different artist; the draftsmanship was impeccable, but there was something mannered and flat about it. If there was any character in the man's face, she couldn't find it.

Julia glanced back at the woman, her smooth face and haggard eyes.

"Or her husband," said Julia. "They married them young back then."

"What do you mean, 'back then'?" asked Nat, dropping onto a droopy, silk-upholstered sofa. A cloud of dust rose into the air, and she batted at it, coughing. "Half of my friends are dating fifty-year-olds. My mother says —" She broke off, lips compressing.

Julia perched on the edge of a chair that seemed to have fared slightly better in the dust department. "Trust me, the New York dating scene isn't much better."

"Are you seeing anyone?" asked Natalie.

"I'm between men at the moment." Technically true, if slightly misleading. She had gone on a few dates since losing her job, mostly at the instigation of her college roommate, but none of them seemed to last long. "What about you?"

Natalie shrugged her thin shoulders, looking down at her pricy shoes. "A few contenders, no one in particular at the moment. Frittering away my time, Mum calls it. As if it were that easy!"

Julia kept her voice dry. "Mothers do say the most charmingly helpful things, don't they?"

Not that she would know.

It had been the right thing to say. Natalie's face broke into a genuine smile. "God, yes." Impulsively she leaned forward. "Would you like to go get something to eat? There are a handful of places not far from here — and we could get out of this wretched house."

At the mention of food, Julia's stomach growled loudly. "I think the last time I ate was somewhere over the North Sea."

Natalie hauled herself up from the couch, shaking dust off her extremities. "It's not exactly an oasis of civilization, but we should be able to find something to feed you." Glancing back over her shoulder, she made a wry face. "If I'm being honest, this house gives me the willies!"

Julia rescued her shoulder bag from where she'd dumped it in the front hall, then, on second thought, dug out her wallet instead. No point in lugging everything out with her. This was, after all, home base for the next few weeks.

Sticking her wallet in her jeans pocket, she looked up at her cousin. "The willies?"

Natalie shrugged. "Just — you know. Shall we go?"

She already had one hand on the door-knob. Julia glanced back over her shoulder through the open doors of the drawing room, at the beautiful, tortured face of the woman in the portrait. She'd take another look later. Without Natalie.

"Sure," Julia said, and dug Aunt Regina's keys out of her pocket. "Let's get some dinner."

FIVE

Herne Hill, 1849

Arthur hadn't told her that there would be guests for dinner.

Imogen paused in the doorway of the drawing room, her skirts belling gently around her legs. The sound of voices alerted her even before she approached, male voices, raised in spirited conversation, interspersed by Evie's high, lilting laugh, a little too high and a little too lilting. Male company wasn't something they had often, not in the quiet house on Herne Hill.

It was Evie who saw Imogen first, her pretty young face lighting up. Breaking off her conversation, she raised a hand in greeting to Imogen, and the two men to whom she had been speaking turned with her. One was tall and fair, with a carefully maintained mustache. He was dressed in the height of fashion in a tight-waisted frock coat and a waistcoat of a dull but expensive fabric. The other was shorter, with long, waving locks, a buff coat, and a cravat knotted in a tight bow at the neck, the very caricature of an artist.

There was another man in the back of the room, in quiet conversation with Arthur. His back was to Imogen; all she saw was close-cropped dark hair.

They must be more of Arthur's protégés. He collected people as he did manuscripts, trading them off when he grew bored.

Imogen felt a moment of malicious amusement. Three male guests for dinner, and none of them announced. Jane must be down in the kitchen, cajoling Cook into stretching the soup and shredding the hens into timbale. The table would be unbalanced, but Arthur never cared for things like that. Jane did, but Jane would never naysay Arthur. Jane was, Imogen had realized years ago, quietly and painfully in love with Arthur.

And Arthur was simply Arthur, imperturbable and entirely self-absorbed.

Belatedly aware of his wife's presence, he turned, holding out a hand to her. "Imogen, my love. Come and greet our guests."

What a misleading word, that *our.* It pleased Arthur to pretend that she had some role in the household, as gracious chatelaine, if nothing else. It masked the fact that her only task was to be ornamental, to smile at him with the feigned echo of the love she had once believed she bore him.

Sometimes she thought back with astonishment to that sixteen-year-old girl she had been, poor, naïve sixteen, still dreaming of knights in shining armor, convinced that Arthur was the embodiment of all her maiden dreams.

The years had been kind to Arthur, but there was no disguising the fact that he had broadened and settled into comfortable middle age. His once ginger hair had faded in parts to gray; the whiskers she had once found so dashing had grown bristled and bushy. He looked more and more like the portrait of his father that hung above the mantel, a prosperous merchant with a merchant's mind, smug in the constant counting of his treasures.

Of which she, for some reason, was one, acquired and cataloged like the porcelain in the cabinet or the books on the shelves.

She supposed it was better than being a pensioner in her uncle's home. That was what she told herself, and there were times when she even believed it.

Arranging her paisley shawl more securely around her shoulders, Imogen moved gracefully across the room, taking her husband's proffered hand, letting him tuck her arm through his. Arthur liked to show her off, she knew, just as he liked to display the Book of Hours in the study, or the fifteenth-century triptych in the hall. Outside, it was dark already, the early dark of February, but the firelight reflected prettily off the purple poplin of her dress, picking out the richness of mother-of-pearl buttons and silk braid.

"Gentlemen," she said, her smile nicely calculated to include them all, while marking no one in particular. Over the years, she had become very good at playing Arthur's hostess, at showing the face he wished for her to show. "Welcome."

"We are now," said the man with the wild dark curls, flashing her a smile intended to be dangerous. Imogen couldn't help but be amused by it, the dash and bravado of it all, a little boy playing at Casanova.

"My love," said Arthur, leading her forward like a visiting dignitary, "I should like to present to you Mr. Rossetti."

The man with the careless cravat and the tousled curls pressed his hand to his heart.

"Mr. Fotheringay-Vaughn." Blond and elegant, the second man essayed a languid bow. He had cultivated the look of perpetual ennui that went with his tightly tailored

95

waistcoat and carefully tied cravat.

"— and Mr. Thorne." That was the third man. He inclined his head in greeting but made no move closer. He put Imogen in mind of a jungle beast, quiet and alert. "They have come to visit our collection."

There was no need to specify which collection; there was only the one that counted, Arthur's medieval objets d'art, carefully selected and enlarged over time. Imogen could see lying open on the card table Arthur's pride and showpiece, her father's Book of Hours.

"You must have a powerful love of antiquities to venture out on such an inclement day," said Imogen lightly. The rain had been hissing and spitting down all day, the sky the color of sleet, the ground an unappealing blend of mud and slush. "Are you also collectors, then?"

"Call us admirers, rather," said Rossetti. His teeth flashed in a smile. "We haven't the tin. Our pockets are to let."

The blond man, Fotheringay-Vaughn, looked pained. He fingered his expensive enamel watch fob. "Yours, perhaps."

Thorne made no response. Alone of the three, he stayed clear of the female presence, withdrawing with Arthur to the table by the window.

96

"These gentlemen are all artists, Mama."
Evie hastened to fill the gap. "They have
come for *inspiration.*" She spoke the final
word with touching conviction.

"And have you found it, then?" Imogen
asked.

"Most certainly," drawled Fotheringay-
Vaughn. His eyes were on Evie, frankly admiring.

Evie's cheeks went pink, her eyes as wide
as saucers.

Imogen looked pointedly at Arthur, but
Arthur was deep in conversation with
Thorne, their heads bent over the Book of
Hours as Thorne sketched something in a
notebook with a quick, sure hand.

Not that Arthur would be any use; Imogen
had warned him, time and again, that he
was keeping his daughter too close, that she
needed to be allowed to try her charms on
the inoffensive sons of neighbors, under the
watchful eye of half a dozen earnest mamas.
She would be an heiress when the time
came. Not a great heiress, not the sort who
made waves in society and elicited articles
in the *Illustrated London News,* but she
would have a tidy enough sum to bring to
her future husband. Especially for an artist
with pockets to let and expensive taste in
watch fobs.

Kept close as she was, Evie was likely to be easy prey for the first plausible fortune hunter who came her way.

As you were, my dear? Arthur had chucked Imogen under the chin and laughed a little laugh to show that he was joking.

The idea, of course, was risible: the fortune was his; she had been all but penniless when he married her. Jane had certainly remarked upon it often enough. And yet . . . And yet. Imogen wondered if the arrow had fallen quite so far from the mark as he had intended. He might not have married her for money, but she had been gulled by him all the same, had, in her naïveté, believed him something quite other than what he was.

She was determined that Evie shouldn't make the same mistake; when Evie married, it should be for some form of real and lasting affection, not on the strength of a compliment and an illusion.

Sometimes Imogen thought that those years in the schoolroom with Evie were all that had kept her from packing a bag and slipping out a window in the middle of the night. Their lessons had been no great success. Evie would never make a scholar; she hadn't the interest or the dedication. She had a facile, if shallow, intelligence, but she made up for it with the exuberance of her affection.

Evie was the closest to a child that Imogen was ever likely to have, and Imogen wouldn't let her throw herself away on a scoundrel.

"Goodness, how interesting," said Imogen loudly. "It is so seldom one gets to see real artists at work."

She crossed carefully between Evie and Fotheringay-Vaughn, sliding her arm through her stepdaughter's, ranging herself between them. She was taller than Evie by half a head; if she didn't entirely block her stepdaughter's view of the older man, at least she impeded it.

She squeezed Evie's arm affectionately. She was so slight, so unprotected, her Evie, as unaware of the vagaries of the world as Imogen had been. In its own way, Herne Hill felt as far from London as Cornwall.

"You must tell me more of your visit," Imogen said to Rossetti. "Was there anything in particular in my husband's collection that you came to see?"

"Anything!" said Rossetti, with a sweeping gesture. "Everything! It has been a revelation." The word must have pleased him, because he repeated it. "A revelation! I had seen the works of such painters before only in crude, printed copies. To see the originals . . ."

"Was a revelation?" Imogen provided with a hint of a smile.

"Like a heavenly vision," said Rossetti extravagantly. "Did you know that in all of our National Gallery there is only one work painted by an artist prior to Raphael?"

Fotheringay-Vaughn rolled his eyes.

Imogen found Rossetti's enthusiasm rather charming. Had she been like that once? Yes, a very long time ago, when she had thought she would help Arthur in his work and they would immerse themselves in medieval manuscripts together. Such a utopian vision and so very far from the life she now led. The study door had been courteously but firmly closed to her. "I must confess. I was unaware of that. There are several lovely Reynolds, however."

"Sir Joshua Reynolds!" Rossetti was deeply indignant. "Sir Sloshua, more like! His meaningless rules have stifled generations of English painters. There is no life in his paintings, no color. Do you know that he has decreed that all landscapes must be painted in shades of *brown*?"

Imogen felt her lips relax into a smile. "I fear that does seem to be the color of our countryside at present."

"Yes, but think of May!" said Rossetti passionately. "Think of the sun gilding the fresh, green grass and the roses unfurling their first velvet petals. There is a world of color and light just waiting to be captured on canvas."

Despite herself, Imogen was moved by his words. "I am sure that if anyone can, you shall, Mr. Rossetti," she said.

"Not if the Academy has its way," said Mr. Rossetti darkly.

"The Academy does its best." It was Thorne, who, with Arthur, had come to join them. Imogen didn't miss the warning look Thorne sent his friend. "I wouldn't say ill of them."

His voice was deep and rich, with the hint of a regional accent he made no attempt to hide, the vowels flattened, the consonants soft. He was older than his peers, closer, Imogen imagined, to her own age than Rossetti, who looked to be scarcely older than Evie. The sun had burned Thorne's skin brown and etched lines on his lean face.

Imogen found herself intrigued by what it was he wasn't saying. "What would you say of the Academy, then, Mr. Thorne?"

"Oh, Thorne is one for painting, not for talking," said Rossetti merrily. "He believes in saving his breath to wield his brush. He

101

leaves the grand manifestos to the rest of us."

"Have you a grand manifesto then?" asked Evie breathlessly. The question was for Rossetti, but her eyes were on Fotheringay-Vaughn.

"This lot do," said Fotheringay-Vaughn indolently. He fixed his gaze on Evie. "My only creed is to paint beauty where I find it."

That, decided Imogen, was quite enough. Leaning down to put her mouth to the girl's ear, she murmured, "Evie, dearest, would you go and see what's keeping your aunt Jane?" She deliberately made her voice droll. "I should hate to think she's been kidnapped by Cook."

"Yes, Mama." Evie always made a point of calling her mama.

For a moment, Imogen fought against a wave of bleak despair. What was she to do when Evie was gone? Well, she would face it when she faced it. She just needed to see Evie happily settled, with someone who appreciated her for her many excellences of spirit, not for the money Arthur had settled in the Funds.

"If you will excuse me?" Evie's words were painfully dignified, stilted even, but her voice betrayed her youth. She still curtsied like a schoolgirl, awkwardly, her eyes darting up for approval. "I must see to supper."

The gentlemen made the appropriate polite noises. Rossetti picked up immediately where he had left off, saying something about throwing off the shackles of artistic constraint. Imogen wasn't quite listening. Neither was Fotheringay-Vaughn. His eyes followed Evie as she left the room.

The other man, Thorne, was watching Imogen.

She caught him watching her, watching her watching Fotheringay-Vaughn, and there was recognition in Thorne's eyes, as though he knew exactly what she was about — as though he knew and was watching her as one might a caged beast in a menagerie! His eyes ought to have been black, with that coloring, but instead, they were a pale brown, the color of amber, or of aged sherry, light and bright and far too observant.

Imogen bit back the angry words that rose immediately to her throat. Instead, she adopted her most painfully proper expression, pushing the anger, the indignation, down, down, down, and away, down beneath her stays, compressed into a tiny little ball as shiny and hard as a locket, a locket with a picture in it no one could see.

What right had he to judge her? It was no business of his, no business at all.

"How fascinating," she said politely to Mr. Rossetti, and turned her face away from the other man's disturbing amber eyes.

Herne Hill, 1849

The Granthams set a lavish table.

There had been turbots in sauce and lamb cutlets and saddle of mutton and asparagus and fresh peas — asparagus and peas, in February! — and other dainties Gavin didn't even recognize.

The chair in which he sat was awkwardly shaped and uncomfortable, the seat slippery, the back elaborately carved with knobs and curlicues that dug into his back when he leaned back too far. Bad on him for letting himself slouch; no wonder the ladies of the house had such good posture. Miss Cooper — Miss Grantham's aunt? — looked as though she had swallowed a ramrod and found it tough going. Her mouth was permanently pursed in an expression of displeasure, but at no time more so than when her gaze happened to land on her guests.

They looked all wrong in this lavish room, with the light of the candles reflecting off mahogany and cherrywood. Gavin knew that. Even Augustus in his expensive cast-offs (oh, yes, they were cast-offs, for all the other man's airs) looked out of place, too flash, too fast. Only Rossetti looked comfortable, his elbows on the table, his cravat carelessly tied, fingers curled around the stem of his wineglass, but Rossetti was one of those men who were at home anywhere, from a tavern to a palace; his opinion of himself and his own abilities was that high.

Gavin would have been far happier supping on bread and cheese in his own studio. But he didn't need Augustus to tell him that this was part of how the game was played, Augustus, who had no interest in antiquities and had only come, so he said, in the hopes of wrangling a commission from a rich bourgeois who might be tickled at having his portrait painted by a rising society painter. An artist needed patrons, and Grantham certainly had money enough and connections with those who dabbled in art and criticism.

So Augustus had said, but watching him, Gavin wondered if his object was rather more than that. Augustus was being far too obvious in his pursuit of Grantham's pretty daughter. A daughter and an only child. Gavin could practically see the visions of guineas dancing in Augustus's head.

The daughter liked it well enough, but the other ladies of the house didn't, Gavin could tell. As for Grantham . . . it was hard to tell what Grantham saw or didn't see. A cool customer, that one. He gave the impression of vague geniality, but he noticed more than he let on; those blue eyes were shrewd in that carefully bland face.

Or maybe that was just a trick of the light, a trick of good candles reflecting off silver and crystal. No tallow here, but pure beeswax, with wicks carefully trimmed, more of them than Gavin used in a week.

Augustus had been right; a man who could afford those candles could certainly fling a commission to an artist without missing the tin. Gavin hated the idea of bowing and scraping, but there was no denying that canvas and pigments didn't come cheap and, as much as he would have liked to pretend otherwise, success in the Academy was seldom won by merit alone.

Gavin watched as Augustus played his game. Oh, he did it well, there was no denying it. He was buttering up the girl right proper, just a little bit of butter at a time, but the very richest and the best, full of cream.

Gavin wasn't the only one who had noticed. More than once, Mrs. Grantham had changed the subject, deftly moved the conversation back to Rossetti and art, diverting the girl's attention away from Augustus.

"It must be very dull for you," Augustus was saying to Mrs. Grantham, idly reaching into the bowl of nuts that sat hard by his place, "all this talk of the Middle Ages."

Gavin didn't miss the slight waspishness in his colleague's tone. Augustus didn't react well to women who didn't succumb immediately to his charm.

Nor was Mrs. Grantham in Augustus's style. He liked pink and white society beauties. If Miss Cooper was a Rembrandt sketch of a purse-lipped Dutch housewife and Miss Evangeline Grantham a Dresden shepherdess, all pink and white, and yellow curls, Mrs. Grantham was something else entirely. In the candlelight she was ebony and ivory, the dark waves of her hair accentuating the strong bones of her face.

"Not at all," Mr. Grantham answered for his wife, casting her an indulgent look across the length of the table. "My wife's father was a scholar as well. And she has some small interest of her own in the period."

"I have always found that era particularly engrossing," said Mrs. Grantham, and there was an echo of something beneath her words that Gavin didn't quite understand.

"It's all very romantic, isn't it?" drawled Augustus, who had, in Gavin's opinion, drunk too freely of Grantham's wine. Augustus winked at Grantham's daughter, who giggled in return. "Chansons de geste, courts of love. . . ."

"Gallant nights and noble ladies," Rossetti finished for him. Unlike Augustus, there was no sarcasm in Rossetti's voice. His eyes were dreamy in the candlelight. Whatever one might say of Gabriel, he believed his own fantasies, and not by halves. "Poetry and pageantry and doomed loves."

Miss Evangeline shivered at that *doomed*. "Must they all end unhappily?"

"You have a soft heart, Miss Grantham," murmured Augustus. "It does you credit."

"Much as it pains me to disagree, I find very little romantic about the Middle Ages." Mrs. Grantham's voice was low and husky. "Yes, Mr. Rossetti, the poetry is beautiful — inspired, even! — but beneath the romance of chivalry one finds plague, poverty, lawlessness, and the depredations of constant warfare."

Rossetti rose to her words. "Isn't it in times of strife that one needs beauty all the more? Perhaps times of turmoil provide the impetus for great art."

"Art from the dung heap?" said Augustus skeptically. He sketched a bow down the table. "With apologies to the ladies."

"But ought we to shy from a mention of a midden?" The reflection from the wine brought color to Mrs. Grantham's pale cheeks. "That is just the difficulty! I believe that to live under such conditions required a form of strength that we feeble creatures have long since forgot. Can you imagine any of us riding off to a Crusade like Eleanor of Aquitaine or defending a castle against siege as did the great chatelaines of the fourteenth century? We are weak creatures in comparison with those who came before us."

"My dear." Grantham's voice was gentle, but it acted as a reproof all the same. "You are too harsh on our modern age. I should not wish you to have to defend our home against invaders."

They all laughed politely at the very idea of it, but, privately, Gavin wasn't quite so sure. For a moment, he could have imagined the woman across from him wielding a sword, wearing a man's breastplate and gauntlets.

Mrs. Grantham lifted her glass to her lips but didn't drink.

"I, for one," said Miss Cooper, "am grateful that we live in a civilized age, one with comforts and conveniences." She gestured to the waiting maid to refill the gentlemen's glasses.

Mrs. Grantham's eyes were on the maid. "Comforts and conveniences for some, but not for all."

Miss Cooper made a noise dangerously like a snort. "Not that book again?"

"What book?" asked Rossetti, with interest. Any form of printed matter was irresistible to him. Gavin admired and envied Rossetti that, his easy facility with words, his ability to bounce them about like a master juggler. "Might I have read it?"

All eyes were on Mrs. Grantham. *"Mary Barton,"* she said. "It is a novel by a Mrs. Gaskell."

"Mrs. Gaskell, indeed," said Miss Cooper tartly. "If she were any sort of proper woman, she would be tending to her family, not courting scandal and poking about in matters that don't concern her."

Mrs. Grantham lifted her chin. "What does it matter who calls attention to such ills, man or woman, so long as someone does?" She looked pointedly at Miss Cooper. "We live in such plenty here that it seems positively selfish not to pay heed to

110

those who are suffering."

Mr. Grantham wagged a finger at her, a gentle simulacrum of a scold. "Such accounts are exaggerated for effect, my love. It is a novel, after all."

"That's what you get for reading such nonsense," said Miss Cooper triumphantly. "What have we to do with mill workers in Manchester? I shouldn't be surprised if most of it were pure invention."

To his own surprise, Gavin heard himself speaking, his own voice echoing in his ears, filling the large room. "Like a painting, a novel may arrange elements to most effective advantage, while still drawing them from the life."

They all looked at him, candlelight glinting off eyes and teeth and hair.

Gavin cursed himself for the strange impulse that had driven him to Mrs. Grantham's defense. What had he thought to accomplish? He'd learned long ago knight-errantry was a luxury too rich for the likes of him. There was no point in alienating a potential patron, not when Gavin needed every honest coin he could earn. He'd learned to keep his mouth shut and his brush moving.

What business had he feeling pity for the likes of Mrs. Grantham? Her dress alone cost more than he earned in a year.

Augustus shifted in his chair, leaning lazily back. He subjected Gavin to a long, assessing look. "You would know all about that, wouldn't you, Thorne?"

"What does he mean?" asked Miss Cooper, looking back and forth and back again.

"Thorne grew up in Manchester," said Augustus maliciously. "Didn't you, Thorne?"

This, Gavin knew, was payback, payback for some half-imagined slight, a painting left uncovered, a return to the studio too soon. Augustus resented Gavin for knowing the real nature of his finances, resented him and needed him. As for Gavin, he only wished to be left alone to paint.

"I left Manchester many years ago." That much was true. He'd been out like a shot, as soon as he was able. As soon as — well, there was no point in thinking of that now. It was all over now and done. "I am afraid I know far less than Mrs. Gaskell about the current conditions in the city. But I did," he added, "read her novel with interest."

With interest and more than a pang of recognition. Mrs. Gaskell had only skimmed the surface. There was more he could have told her about life in the meaner parts of town — but that was a life he had put aside long ago, when he had begged and borrowed his way to London, his entire being directed on winning a place in the Academy. He hadn't Augustus's pretensions, but one thing Gavin knew: he'd never live like that again. They'd lived worse than rats, rats in the gutter.

The rich trappings of Grantham's table, the pearls and gold at Mrs. Grantham's ears and throat, seemed to mock him.

"You surprise me, Mr. Thorne!" It was young Miss Evangeline, flushed with her own daring at entering the conversation. "I hadn't thought gentlemen read novels."

"But of course we do!" Augustus leaned confidingly towards Miss Evangeline, and the attention passed away from Gavin. Mercifully. "Or else what would we find to discuss with you ladies?"

Miss Evangeline Grantham giggled and turned her blushes towards her glass, which contained lemonade rather than wine.

"Miss Grantham does not read such novels," said Miss Cooper stiffly. "Nor do I see any reason why she ought."

Gavin didn't miss the look that passed between Miss Evangeline and her stepmother. "Oh, no, Aunt," said Miss Evangeline Grantham solemnly. "Only the improving ones."

Mrs. Grantham was angelically silent. Gavin would wager that the two ladies had very different ideas as to the meaning of "improving."

Not that it was any of his lookabout, or so Gavin reminded himself of that on the long, cold walk home, Augustus trudging along beside him, lost in his own thoughts.

Rossetti had gone off, whistling, on an errand of his own. The rain had stopped, but the temperature had dropped. The air was crisp and biting, the ground hard with ice beneath their booted feet.

They chose their footing carefully as they crossed over the Thames at the Waterloo Bridge. The Bridge of Sighs, it was called, for all who had used it to take their plunge off this mortal coil into the icy water below. Below, the watermen still plied their trade and the light of the gaslights danced off the cold waters of the river. Gavin's feet felt like lumps of ice in his boots. It was a good two hours' walk from Herne Hill to the studio on Cleveland Street and neither of them had the blunt to hire a hack.

Not that Augustus would ever admit such a thing. No, it was "the air clears the mind after a heavy dinner, don't you agree, Thorne?"

It was no matter. Gavin was used to it. There had been winters, at home, when there had been no money for coal at all, nothing that could be broken up to use for firewood. They had gleaned twigs where they could, but mostly they had huddled for warmth together beneath a ragged blanket, the five of them, in a basement smaller than Arthur Grantham's dining room.

Compared to that, Gavin's own small studio was a luxury and a cold walk home of little matter.

A wealthy patron would mean more coal on the fire, and commissions led to commissions.

Augustus's voice was half-muffled by the high collar of his coat. "The daughter would do very well. Not society, of course, but she's certainly easy enough on the eyes." He spoke as though to himself, his eyes fixed on the reflection of the lights in the water. "She seemed docile enough. And then there's the inheritance. . . . Forty thousand pounds. If the old man doesn't fritter it all away on manuscripts and reliquaries."

So that was why Augustus had been so eager to come along. He must have made inquiries beforehand.

"It's no matter to you if he does." Gavin's

breath inscribed pale circles in the cold air as he said, "Be careful how you go there. Grantham may be all that is affable, but he won't see his daughter throw herself away on you."

Augustus bridled, yanking at the edges of his impractical silk scarf, an imitation of the ones worn by grander men at better occasions than these. "Who says it would be throwing herself away?"

Gavin was too tired to stroke his colleague's ego. "Don't play games, Alfie."

Augustus shot him a quick, fierce look. "I told you not to call me that." Brushing Gavin aside, Augustus returned to his brooding perusal of the river. "Grantham is just a petty bourgeois. He'd be lucky to have a cousin of the Earl of Vaughn for his daughter."

Gavin held his peace. Augustus had half-convinced himself of his own fictions. Like a sleepwalker, it was dangerous to wake him.

Augustus puffed out his chest. "The daughter likes me well enough. And she is a prime piece. A bit of polish and who knows where she mightn't be invited?"

A prime piece? Gavin couldn't see it. Miss Evangeline Grantham had been as light and sweet as the lemonade in her glass, entirely charming and by no means out of the ordinary.

Mrs. Grantham, now. She was made of another metal entirely. It wasn't just the striking lines of her face, her features too strong boned, her coloring too stark, for fashion. No, there was something else there, a reserve, a simmering of strong emotions just barely held in check.

His fingers itched to paint her, to take up a brush and try to plumb her mysteries in the only way he knew, through paint on canvas. His fingers were wiser than he was. They saw and conveyed subtleties that his waking wits weren't quick enough to catch. What a challenge it would be, to portray the shades of emotion playing across that seemingly serene face.

Not that it would ever happen.

Gavin caught himself up short, before he could fall too deep into reverie. They were across the bridge now. By the streetlamp, two streetwalkers, rouged and dyed, their skin blue beneath their tattered wraps, plied their dubious wares. These were the women who posed for their paintings, not the Mrs. Granthams of the world, not respectable matrons in their ruffled, gilded homes.

And what was he doing, romanticizing the woman? He was as bad as Gabriel. She was just another pampered rich man's wife, made momentarily interesting by an illusion created by wine and candlelight. She played at sympathy as a parlor game, having never seen true suffering, true poverty.

"Put them from your head," Gavin told his colleague. "We'll not be invited to that house again."

Augustus adjusted his scarf with a satisfied air. "Would you care to wager on it?"

Six

Herne Hill, 2009

"Why does the house give you the creeps?"

The place Natalie suggested turned out to be a jazz café. The tables were small and round, the lighting low. On a Sunday night, the small stage was dark and quiet and only one of the other tables was occupied, by a middle-aged couple who addressed the one waitress comfortably by name.

Natalie and Julia had no trouble securing a table by the window. From her seat, Julia could just about see the tangle of trees that marked the edge of Aunt Regina's property. Her property now. She kept forgetting that. For all that the keys were wedged uncomfortably into the pocket of her jeans, she still felt like a guest in a home from which the hostess was unaccountably absent.

Oh, well. It wasn't likely to be hers for long. Clean and sell, that was the plan. The lawyer — solicitor? — she had spoken to long-distance from New York had assured her that that wasn't likely to be a problem. Property values in the area were good, despite the general recession.

On the other hand, if there were ghosts . . .

"Oh, no, nothing like that," said Natalie quickly. She curved her hands around her cup of black coffee. "Mother dragged us there every Sunday for years. Duty visits. Dead boring."

From the way her eyes shifted, Julia suspected there was more to it than that, but she was too tired to pry. In the quiet of the jazz café, jet lag had come crashing down. Julia stifled a yawn as the waitress brought her a triangular piece of quiche lightly fringed with assorted greens.

"No restless spirits, then?" she said, giving the corner of her quiche a quick, exploratory probe. "No specters clanking chains and going bump in the middle of the night?"

Natalie's perfectly manicured eyebrows rose. "I've never been there in the middle of the night. Andrew, my brother, did claim he saw something in the garden once."

"What kind of something?" Julia asked indistinctly, around a mouthful of quiche. Whatever their jazz was like, the restaurant certainly had gotten the café part right. The taste of food reminded her that the last time she'd eaten was somewhere over Ireland, cardboard croissants and long-life jam.

Natalie shook her head. "Nothing, really. It was all rubbish, just telling himself stories. He said he saw a man, in old-fashioned clothes, down by the old summerhouse." She shoved a lump of Gorgonzola out of the way with her fork, scooping up a quick bite of plain greens. "Probably just a tramp."

"Or a bit of underdone potato?" murmured Julia, having images of Marley posing as Scrooge's door knocker.

Natalie frowned at her. "What?"

"Nothing. Dickens. Never mind." Julia scrubbed her hands over her eyes. Jet lag always made her slaphappy. "Tell me about Aunt Regina," she said quickly. "What was she like?"

Natalie's fork paused over her salad as she considered. "She was a photojournalist back in the forties and fifties," she said finally. "Hanging out of helicopters, taking pictures of war zones, all that sort of thing."

Julia's image of the feeble old lady puttering away with her crochet hook underwent a quick revision. "Wow," she said inadequately. "She sounds fascinating."

"She was . . . outspoken." Natalie drove her fork into a wad of arugula. "My mother always thought it was unfair she was left the house when she was the only one of them that didn't have a family."

Julia looked up from shoveling down the remains of her quiche. "She never married?"

"You'd have to ask Mum." Natalie poked at her salad. "There was some story about someone when she was younger, someone unsuitable." She made a face over the word, making a joke out of it.

"Standards were different then?" Julia hazarded.

"Don't say that to my mother. Hers haven't changed. In any event," Natalie added quickly, pushing her plate out of the way, "Aunt Regina lived there alone as long as I knew her. From the way she carried on about the old place, you'd think she had a Rubens hidden away among the clutter; she was that possessive of it."

And was that what Natalie had been looking for when Julia arrived?

No, that was too ridiculous. It wasn't fair to dislike someone just because she looked like she'd stepped off the cover of *Vogue*.

"Do you think she did?" Julia asked cautiously.

Natalie lifted her hands in a quick, helpless gesture. "She might at that. Goodness only knows. She was rather paranoid in her old age. She thought people were trying to sneak in and steal her treasures."

"You mean like those piles of old newspaper clippings?" said Julia drily.

"And that grim portrait in the drawing room. Poor old you. I say sort it all right into the bin."

Julia hadn't found the portrait grim. She'd felt a strange kinship with that unknown woman, whoever she was.

"I don't know," said Julia slowly, feeling her way along as she spoke. Her brain felt slow with food and fatigue. "It could be interesting. It's like an archeological dig, layers of history all crammed together. I don't know very much about our family."

The words felt odd on her lips. *Our family.* She'd been thinking of this as just another task, clean out an old house, put it on the market, but there it was, that strange, unexpected sense of ownership, of belonging.

"Well," said Natalie practically, "if you need the help, just ask. I've a brother who can be put to work."

"Does he know you're offering him up?"

"Details, details." Natalie signaled to the waitress for the check. "Besides, his oldest friend is an antiques dealer. We can drag him along, too. Maybe he can tell us who that portrait of yours is."

At the word "dealer" Julia's hackles immediately rose. "I don't want to put anyone out."

"No, it will be fun!" protested Natalie. The waitress set down a black plastic tray with the chit on it. Natalie put down two twenty-pound notes and waved away Julia's fumblings for her wallet. "My treat. It's not every day I get a cousin back from the States. In any event," she added as they got up from their seats, Julia's scraping back against the hardwood floor, "I'll ring Andrew and tell him to ring Nicholas. Saturday?"

"There's really no need," said Julia, following Natalie out through the door. After the air-conditioned café, the July evening air felt hot and sticky. Twilight had fallen, obscuring the landscape, playing tricks with Julia's eyes. There were cars in people's yards, lights in the windows. Next to it all, Aunt Regina's house looked particularly isolated. Julia fell in step with Natalie as they walked down the block. "Honestly, there's a lot of pure garbage tossing that needs to happen before I get to anything like appraising."

And if she was going to have appraisals, she'd be the one picking the person. It wasn't just her New York–bred cynicism

124

coming to the fore; she didn't like other people interfering in her private business. Even if they genuinely meant well. Whether he had meant to or not, her father had raised her to be independent.

Maybe a little too independent?

Natalie turned back with a winning smile. "Oh, not like that," she said. "I just thought you might use the manual labor. It will do them good," she said innocently. "Especially Nicholas. Put them to work, get up a sweat."

There was something about the way Natalie pronounced the name that gave Julia her clue. "This Nicholas," she said. "Have you known him long?"

Natalie feigned indifference, but there was no hiding the sudden light in her eyes. "He's been Andrew's friend for yonks. They were at school together. Harrow," she added importantly.

"Mmm," said Julia noncommittally. They had come to Aunt Regina's gate. In the twilight, the entrance to Aunt Regina's house looked even more forbidding, shadowed, and overgrown.

"This is me," said Natalie, pointing down the street at an SUV parked half a block away from the house.

"Okay." The two of them stood there awkwardly. It felt, thought Julia with a tinge of amusement, like an awkward blind date. "Thanks for dinner. And for coming to help me get settled in."

Natalie's eyes shifted away and she made a quick, fluttery gesture with one hand. "It was nothing." Looking from Julia to the house, she said awkwardly, "Are you sure you'll be all right there on your own? My flat doesn't stretch to a spare bed, but there is a rather comfortable sofa. . . ."

Julia was touched by the offer, although she couldn't think of anything she would like less than sleeping on a stranger's couch. When it came to the trade-off, Julie would rather have the odd family ghost and a room with a door. She imagined that Natalie wanted to have her just about as much as Julia wanted to be there.

"I'll be fine," Julia assured her. "It's really sweet of you to offer, though."

Natalie looked uneasily over her shoulder at the long, winding walk down to the old house. "The offer stands if you change your mind." She gnawed on her lower lip, clearly still feeling guilty. "I'd come in with you and see you settled, but I'd better be going. Work tomorrow morning."

She grimaced expressively, and it hit Julia, with a jolt, that this was the first time work had come into the conversation. At home, that was the first thing anyone asked: *What do you do?* As though it were the sum total of one's worth.

"No, no, that's fine," said Julia, stifling a yawn. With her belly full of food, her body was making a desperate bid for a bed. Or any flat surface, really.

"If you're sure . . ." Natalie brushed her cheek against Julia's in a quick, practiced embrace. Julia thought inconsequentially of Japanese rice paper, silky and scented. Over her shoulder, Natalie called brightly, "I'll see you on Saturday?"

Saturday? The door had closed on the SUV before Julia could tell her not to bother.

Herne Hill, 2009
Julia spent a satisfying week sorting through old papers and throwing out moth-eaten sweaters.

The house wasn't quite as unmanageably large as it had originally appeared to her apartment-bred eyes. There were only six rooms on the main floor, although an ancestor at some point had knocked through a wall to make room for a conservatory, which bulged from one side of the house like a large glass mushroom, filled with ancient rattan furniture, droopy cushions, and

127

dispirited potted plants. On the second floor were four bedrooms, although it seemed a good guess that the large bathroom with its claw-footed tub had once been a fifth. The floor was dotted with odd little nooks and cubbyholes, dressing rooms and linen closets and doors to narrow staircases that led up into the attics or down into the basement.

The attic wasn't properly an attic, at least not as Julia understood attics. One-half of it had been knocked into a single large room. A nursery? There were colored tiles around the fireplace, decorated with images from fairy tales: Cinderella and her slipper, Rose-Red and her bear, Rapunzel letting down her long, long hair. Someone had used the room more recently than that. There was an easel in one corner, and a pile of art books next to it, a dried-out palette sitting on top of the books.

Julia had skirted around the easel without lifting the linen draping over it. Later, of course, she would have to — but she was starting with the rooms downstairs, she had already decided. This was just an exploratory mission, to get the lay of the land.

The other rooms in the attic, small and dormered, were all heaped with detritus from downstairs: old furniture, piles of clothes, steamer trunks, and cardboard boxes. Had no one in the family ever thrown anything away?

Still, it was better than the basement. That was a damp space with large stone sinks, a rusted coal stove, and a series of dark and faceless pantries, all crammed with obsolete kitchen equipment dating from roughly the origins of the house up to decrepit 1950s mix-masters in molding cardboard boxes. The original kitchen must have been down there once. Julia sincerely pitied the poor domestics who had had to work down there. The only windows were well above their heads. Forget light; the ventilation must have been terrible, especially with that old stove belching coal smoke, even in the height of summer.

It really did make one think twice about the good old days.

Still, Julia couldn't deny the fascination of it all, of sinking her hands into the detritus of the past: cloche hats and crumbling newspapers, buttoned boots and letters that began with phrases straight out of an Edwardian manners manual. By the end of that first week, her days had begun to fall into a pattern. Coffee in the morning, from the surprisingly good stock and sleek coffeemaker Aunt Regina had left behind, and

129

then off to the room of the day, to empty closets and sort drawers into three stacks: throw away, give away, keep/sell?

Many of the throwaways were easy — clothes so moth-eaten that not even the charity shop would want them, shoes with the heels worn down, broken coffeemakers — but the other two categories tended to slide back and forth. The china pug with the horrible bow around its neck could easily go on the giveaway pile, but what about the rosewood sewing box with the hidden compartment on the bottom? Not that Julia sewed, but there was something rather neat about it, and about the stack of ancient magazines from the 1920s and '30s, a little yellowed but still perfectly readable.

Aside from some treasured pictures and a tattered collection of books from college, there was very little in Julia's apartment that wasn't immediately functional. Some of it she blamed on being a consultant for all those years; it didn't make sense to haul family heirlooms around from posting to posting or to acquire large and bulky souvenirs. She had lived light; her last move had taken ridiculously little time to pack. But now she found herself suddenly seized with unreasoning cupidity. What was she going to do with a rocking horse with a missing tail, or with piles of photo albums filled with sepia pictures of people who had been dead before she was born?

She didn't know, but she wanted them anyway.

Maybe just a few things, she told herself, and let herself squirrel the photo albums into the keep/sell pile. And the sewing box. She knew enough to know that she had no idea what she was doing; at some point, a real appraiser would have to be called in. But, right now, Julia was finding the whole process oddly restful. She should have felt isolated, but she didn't, at least, not yet. In the evenings, bone-weary and content, she would take her glass of plonk (four pounds per bottle at the liquor store down the block) out onto the patio and collapse into a deeply uncomfortable old specimen of lawn furniture. Sometimes, she would call her best friend, Lexie, catching her between meetings at the office; other times she would just sit and sip her wine and look out over the tangled expanse of lawn stretching out in front of her.

The garden — although "garden" was far too grand a word for the wilderness she could see from her bedroom window — stretched out the length of a full city block. As she sat there, the world felt very far away.

Sometimes, if the windows were open and the wind was right, she could catch a faint snippet of someone else's television or dinner table conversation. But mostly, it was just the sound of crickets and the wind in the leaves of the trees. From the patio behind the house it might have been a hundred years ago, a world without cars or Internet or electric lights.

"Are you sure you're all right out there?" her father asked when she called him four days in.

"Fine," she said. "Why wouldn't I be?"

Somehow, it seemed disloyal to admit that she was actually enjoying herself, enjoying the hauling and the sorting, and the absence of the grinding self-doubt that came of sitting idle in her own apartment, waiting for the phone to ring with job offers that didn't exist. She'd been in the rat race for so long. She felt as though she'd stepped not only out of her own life but somehow also out of time.

The contents of the drawers and cupboards aided her on that. Friday night, she stayed up way too late reading through a pile of an old magazine called the *Tatler*, from the 1920s and '30s. It was better than reading the headlines of the supermarket tabloids. Good Lord, had people actually lived like that? Socialites bolted to Kenya, viscounts eloped with Gaiety Girls (Julia gathered that Gaiety Girls must be the 1920s equivalent of exotic dancers, from the way the magazine went on), and debutantes were caught in compromising positions with members of the Russian ballet. It was fascinating. Also, strangely addictive.

Julia slept through her alarm on Saturday morning and woke up with a 1920s tabloid hangover. She'd meant to explore the garden today. . . . But first coffee. Pulling her unbrushed hair into an untidy ponytail, she pulled on ancient shorts and tank top — the few 1970s window units scattered around the house didn't do much to condition the air — and stumbled downstairs to the blessed chrome coffeemaker.

She'd only just dumped milk into the miraculous life-giving brew when the buzzer rang. It took Julia a few moments to realize that it must be the front door.

Who in the hell would be on her doorstep on a Saturday morning? Neighbors, complaining about the amount of garbage she'd been dumping out front? Jehovah's Witnesses? Did they even have Jehovah's Witnesses in England?

Coffee clutched firmly in hand, Julia opened the front door, prepared to tell off whoever it might be.

Natalie stood on the steps, a male person in tow.

Julia resisted the urge to swear. She had forgotten about Natalie. It didn't improve Julia's mood that she'd been caught in ancient Yale shorts and a tank top with holes in the hem. Natalie, in contrast, was wearing a yellow linen sundress. There were matching sandals, with delicate ribbons that tied around the ankles.

The man beside her looked like he was trying to be anywhere but where he was. Next to him, Natalie looked little and dainty — which put Julia at somewhere near pigmy status. His sun-streaked blond hair suggested ski vacations and tropical getaways.

Julia wished they would. Go away, that was. They looked very pretty together. And she needed more coffee.

"Hi," Julia said shortly, trying to remember when she had last washed her hair. Yesterday? At least, she thought it was yesterday. She took another slug of her coffee. "So — you decided to stop by!"

"We've come to help you," Natalie said brightly, then turned to the man standing next to her with a swish of her blindingly clean hair. "Welcome to the old family homestead. I know it's not anything like your old family homestead. . . ."

"You mean the flat in Fulham?" he said drily.

Natalie gave a tinkling little laugh. "You know it's not."

Julia stood in the doorway, feeling decidedly superfluous. Was it really necessary for them to come all the way to her doorstep to have this conversation? Or to make her watch? Her coffee was getting cold and her greasy hair was making her head itch. She repressed the ignoble urge to slam the door on them and go in search of more coffee.

"Would you like to come in?" she said ungraciously.

Natalie flashed her a quick, apologetic smile. "This is our cousin Julia," she said to the blond man.

Julia held out a hand. "Current owner of the old family homestead," she said. Just in case anyone was wondering.

The man ignored her outstretched hand. "You're American."

Julia let her hand drop. "My passport agrees with you," she said pleasantly.

"Julia grew up in the States," said Natalie apologetically.

"New York," added Julia entirely unapologetically. Let him put that in his pipe and smoke it. The shade of Helen, the ever gracious, prompted Julia to add, "You're welcome to stand on the doorstep if you like, but there is coffee in the kitchen."

"Did I hear someone offering a coffee?" Another man bounded up the stairs. He was more casually dressed than the others, in jeans, sneakers, and a striped rugby shirt. His hair was the color of an old penny. "Sorry I took so long. I've parked somewhere in the Outer Hebrides." He turned to Julia. "You must be Cousin Julia. I'm Andrew, Natalie's brother."

Did one say *nice to meet you* to someone one might have played with as a child?

"Good to see you again," she said instead, and Andrew smiled at her, a broad, open smile. She could see the resemblance to Natalie, now that she was looking for it, but on Andrew the features had been rounded out by the proper amount of poundage, not honed to razor thinness.

Julia turned to the blond man, who hadn't bothered to introduce himself. "And you are?"

Natalie jumped in. "This is Nicholas. Nicholas *Dorrington.*" The last name did sound vaguely familiar, but Julia couldn't tell whether that was because she'd actually heard it somewhere or because Natalie said it as though she was meant to know who he was. "He knows everything there is to know about antiques."

Nicholas the Wonder Man pooh-poohed Natalie's praise. "Hardly." Somehow, the supposedly modest comment sounded more arrogant than any amount of puffery. "I have a shop, that's all."

"A gallery," corrected Natalie, for Julia's benefit. "In Notting Hill."

It just got better and better. "Are you a cousin, too?" Julia asked him.

She seemed to have acquired a superfluity of them recently.

"Oh, no," said Natalie quickly.

"We went to school together," put in Andrew. "Shared a room for four long years." The two men grimaced at each other in what Julia assumed was a male expression of affection.

"The smell of your socks nearly drove me out," said Nicholas.

"My socks? Your rugby kit." This was clearly an old argument. Andrew was grinning broadly. He slung an arm around the other man's shoulders. "Don't mind him, Cousin Julia. His pong is worse than his bite."

"I don't pong," protested Nicholas.

"Not now you don't," said Natalie archly. "But wait until we have you sorting a few

137

cubic meters of rubbish."

"We"? What "we"? This was Julia's house, not anyone else's. Not at the moment, anyway.

"There's no need for anyone to sort rubbish, cubic or otherwise," Julia said with a stiff smile. "If you'd like some coffee . . ."

"Don't be silly," said Natalie indulgently, brushing past her into the hallway. "We're here to help." To Nicholas, she said, "You can't imagine what's piled up. The family has been here since the dawn of time."

"Or about 1800," murmured Andrew. Julia decided she liked Andrew. She liked him even more when he said, "What can we do?"

"Yes, let's get on with it," said Nicholas, detaching himself from Natalie's determined attempt to give him a tour of the highlights of the family estate. "I have a lunch to get to at one."

Julia didn't miss the way Natalie's face fell.

She was tempted to consign both Nicholas and Natalie to the basement and the hard labor of carting out ancient electronics and unidentified pieces of rusty something-or-other. After all, weren't old irons considered antiques and collectibles these days?

That would be petty. And, besides, it looked like Nicholas was just as much a victim of Natalie's good intentions as Julia was. He wanted to be here about as much as she wanted him here. Julia swallowed her pride and summoned up her better self.

"There are a number of sideboards and cupboards in the dining room I haven't gone through yet," she said briskly. She turned to Nicholas. "Would you mind going through and sorting out the good stuff from the mediocre stuff? I can tell Sèvres from Woolworth, but that's about it."

"I live to serve," murmured Nicholas Dorrington.

Yep, and she was Richard III. Julia ignored him and turned to her cousin. "Nat—"

"I can help Nicholas," Natalie volunteered. Julia felt an unwilling pang of sympathy for her. That kind of crush was so painful. Both to experience and to observe.

"No need," said Nicholas, and Natalie's happy mask dropped for a moment. Julia couldn't tell whether Nicholas was being brutally oblivious or just brutal. "It shouldn't take me long."

Implication being that there was nothing there worth spending time on. Charming.

Julia turned her back on Nicholas and concentrated on being extra-nice to Natalie. She didn't believe in kicking the wounded. "Would you mind taking the desk in the conservatory? There are some family papers and photos in there."

"What about me?" asked Andrew, presenting himself gamely for duty.

For the first time, Julia's stiff social smile relaxed into something genuine. "I've been trying to go through the bedrooms upstairs. Want to tackle one of those for me?"

"Happily," said Andrew gallantly.

"I'm off to the conservatory, then!" Natalie said loudly. Just in case Nicholas wanted to know where to find her, Julia surmised. Natalie looked archly over her shoulder at Nicholas. "I'll call you if I find anything interesting."

Nicholas made an uncouth snorting sound. "I wouldn't expect to find any treasures."

Ouch. Julia might have said the same herself, but it was quite another thing to have this Nicholas person do it.

"You never know," Julia said tartly. She dredged up Natalie's phrase from the weekend before. "There might be a Rubens hidden away in here."

And with that Julia marched away upstairs, the remains of her coffee grimly clutched in one hand. Screw him. It would serve him right if they did find a Rubens.

Hell, she'd settle for a Rembrandt.

SEVEN

London, 1849

"You mustn't expect to find any treasures," Arthur told her as their hired hack pulled up as near to the National Gallery as it could manage. "Sir Martin says it's a sorry lot this year."

Imogen pulled her gloves up on her wrists. "I know," she said, with a forced smile. "He says that every year."

Arthur was terribly proud of his acquaintance with Sir Martin Shee, the president of the Royal Academy, although the acquaintance was little more than an exchange of nods and a vague recollection of their names.

It was through the good offices of Sir Martin that Arthur had acquired his tickets to the Private Viewing of the Royal Academy's Summer Exhibition. Arthur and, it seemed, half of London. The area around Trafalgar Square was mobbed with the carriages of the fashionable, the already-soot-stained stone of the National Gallery half-eclipsed by the tall hats of the gentlemen and the wide skirts of the ladies as they made their way up the stairs to the East Gallery, pausing to hail acquaintances, speaking of this week's on dits and last week's scandal.

Arthur stepped out first, handing out first Imogen, then Evie, wide-eyed and thrilled at being included in this opulent scene, peopled by so many of society's favorites whose names appeared in the illustrated papers.

The Granthams weren't part of that world, but it tickled Arthur to pretend to be, for this one day a year. There was something rather pitiable about his gratification at the connection.

But, then, what did that make her? If Arthur was a hanger-on to Sir Charles, she was little more than an extension of Arthur. It was a distinctly lowering thought.

There was no one in the crowd whom Imogen recognized, except for the familiar, rail-thin figure of John Ruskin in his blue coat, engaged in conversation with two men whom Imogen imagined to be critics from the cuts of their coats and the rather dilapidated quality of their hats. The Ruskins had once lived rather near the Granthams at

Herne Hill, and Arthur had made John free of his collections. They still dined together, once or twice a year.

"How grand," breathed Evie, her eyes on the gowns, the hats, the carriages with crests.

"Wait until you see the art, my dear," said Arthur, shooing his daughter towards the wide stairs. If there was just a hint of reproof, Evie didn't seem to notice.

As he handed Imogen a copy of the exhibition booklet he leaned a little forward to murmur in her ear, "You were right, my dear."

Imogen looked at him in surprise, the ribbon of her fashionable new bonnet teasing the corner of her eye.

"About Evie." Imogen's husband sighed a sigh that went deep down past the buttons of his waistcoat. "I have been selfish in keeping her so much at home."

He showed their tickets to the man at the door.

"Perhaps not so much selfish," said Imogen guardedly, "as protective. Who would not be so?"

Arthur pressed her hand gently and then released it. "I must attend to your counsel more often."

Imogen looked quizzically at her husband.

"It was only what anyone so close to her would see."

They were through the doors now, surging along with the tide of humanity into the first of the exhibition rooms.

"Perhaps," said Arthur, smiling whimsically. "But not her old father. Ah, Evie! What have you found there?"

Using his walking stick to part the crowd, he stepped forward to take Evie's arm before she could disappear entirely into the maelstrom of humanity. Imogen followed along more slowly, hating herself for the small pleasure Arthur's words brought her. Again and again, they had played this same farce. She had told herself, years ago, that she had given up seeking Arthur's good opinion, that she had given up on any hope of true companionship. And then, out of nowhere, he would make some small overture, and for the space of those few minutes she would be sixteen again, sixteen and desperately yearning for his affection and his approval.

She despised herself for her own weakness, especially now that she knew Arthur for what he was, not the prince of her imaginings but a limited man of limited imagination and small ambition.

But that was churlish. Imogen watched

144

Arthur's back as he took his daughter's arm, directing her attention to the high-piled paintings on the wall, stacked one on top of the other, hung so close their frames brushed. Whatever his flaws, Arthur had a genuine appreciation for beauty, even if his first impulse was to purchase it and then lock it away.

As he had Imogen.

She smiled to herself, a little wryly, and took a firmer grip on her exhibition catalog. Would she really have been better off otherwise? It was a game she played with herself from time to time, wondering what would have happened had she heeded her father's advice and refused Arthur's offer for her hand. She did not know that she would have been any happier as a pensioner in her uncle's home than she was at Herne Hill. Would she have become the perpetual poor relation, like Jane Cooper, alert to any petty change in status, constantly jockeying for place and position?

Perhaps. Or perhaps Imogen might have formed a genuine attachment, an attachment to someone who would speak to her without that gentle edge of reproof in his voice, who would admire her for something other than her fine skin, who would treat her as a person and not as a figurine to be set in a glass case and shielded from the world and her own impulses. There were times when she wanted to rail at Arthur for stealing her away from all that, for stealing her youth, made all the worse by the fact that she knew that he believed he had not so much stolen as saved her and that she ought to be grateful — perpetually, grovelingly grateful — for all that he had so generously conferred upon her: collars of gold that clutched at her throat, rich dresses that pinched her waist, opulent meals that caught in her throat, a surfeit of luxury and no air to breathe.

It was hot and close in the exhibition rooms, the ladies' skirts belling out across the floor, the people pressing in around her like the endless parade of seasons from the window of her room in Herne Hill.

Spring and summer and fall and winter, spring and summer and fall and winter . . .

Imogen pressed her lips tightly shut and resolutely took hold of her exhibition catalog. There were pictures to be viewed. Compressing her broad skirts, she managed to navigate a channel around a group of ladies who had taken refuge on the chairs provided in the center of the room. Between the ladies' extravagant bonnets and the gentlemen's high hats it was impossible to pick out Evie or Arthur, so Imogen wiggled her way closer to the wall instead, opening her exhibition catalog, the paper pages sewn together with string.

For now, for the next hour, she was free, entirely by herself amid the throng.

In the East Room, she was promised *The Real Scenery of the Bride of Lammermuir,* by J. Hall; a view of the Carnaervon Hills by another artist of whom Imogen hadn't heard; *Henrietta Maria in Distress,* by the unfortunately named Mr. Egg; and a series of portraits of various worthy but largely unattractive souls.

Imogen decided to take her chances with the Middle Room. *The Return of the Prodigal . . .* Oh, dear, not another one. *A Scene from the Lady of the Lake.* Not bad, but a little overdone. Imogen's eye was caught briefly by a *Lorenzo and Isabella,* by a Mr. Millais. The bright colors and medieval raiment pleased Imogen, but why was Isabella's brother sticking out his leg at that odd angle? It looked most uncomfortable.

She was about to attempt the Octagon Room when her attention was caught by the painting next to *Lorenzo and Isabella.* It had been hung on one of the coveted places on the line; as opposed to the paintings stuck up by the ceiling or down by one's knees, it was right at eye level. Which meant that Imogen had an excellent view of her own sewing box.

It was quite definitely her sewing box. There was the corner of a book, sticking out of one side where she ought to have kept embroidery threads instead, and the chip on one corner, where she had accidentally knocked it over that time.

As Imogen examined the painting in growing indignation, she realized that it wasn't just her sewing box that had been appropriated for display. There was Arthur's chalice . . . his triptych . . . her father's Book of Hours. All around her, the crowd eddied, gossiping, considering, judging, but Imogen stood stock still, transfixed at the indicia of her private life impaled on canvas like a butterfly on a naturalist's screen, hung up at the Royal Academy's Summer Exhibition for all to see.

The subject was a woman, a woman standing by a window — the stained-glass window from Arthur's study, a detached part of Imogen's mind noted — her body posed in such a way as to convey yearning and longing. One hand reached towards the glass, almost, but not quite, touching it.

The pain in her face, the balked desire, took Imogen's breath away.

How many times had she stood by the window, in just such a pose, waiting, yearning, for something, something, something to happen, something to change, watching the raindrops drip, watching the leaves blow, watching the seasons change around her? And there, there was her own sewing box by the woman's feet, Imogen's own Book of Hours open on the table in front of her. Imogen sucked in a deep, hard breath, fighting against the pressure of her stays, fighting for composure, trying to fight the conviction that someone had snuck into her most private places in the middle of the night and looted not just Arthur's treasures but also her own soul, plastering it onto canvas for all to see.

No. That was ridiculous. It was a model in the painting, her dress a costume, a re-creation of a medieval gown, long and flowing, clinging to the contours of her form in a way that was causing several gentlemen to elbow one another appreciatively. The woman didn't even look like Imogen. Any similarities were purely superficial. Her hair was several shades lighter than Imogen's and unmistakably red, her features less pronounced, her mouth and nose smaller.

Mariana, read the small plaque embedded in the frame.

The exhibition catalog dangled almost forgotten from Imogen's hand. She opened it, hastily leafing through, her fingers clumsy in their gloves, the paper tearing at her touch.

Mariana in the Moated Grange, read the full title. And there, beside it, the artist's name.

Pale eyes, watching her across Arthur's drawing room. Knowing eyes, seeing too much. Imogen felt herself tingling with a powerful wave of anger and indignation, that this man, this man Arthur had invited into his home, had made himself so bold — had dared —

She ought to have known who it was, even before she saw the name. But there it was, in black and white in the exhibition catalog: *Gavin Thorne.*

Herne Hill, 2009
Julia left Andrew in one of the smaller back bedrooms, merrily tossing twenty-year-old bank statements and obsolete grocery bills into what he referred to as "the bonfire pile."

"We'll have a jolly one," he said, with a pyromaniac gleam in his eye.

Julia left him to it and went to tackle the room next door. She would have killed for another cup of coffee, but Natalie and Nicholas were downstairs and she had no particular desire to encounter either of them. Of course, it was her own fault; she'd forgotten Natalie's offer of housecleaning help. Or, if she'd remembered it, she'd assumed that it was one of those polite nothings, like *let's get together soon!* when you run into an old acquaintance in the street, neither of you with the slightest intention of ever following up.

Julia hadn't reckoned with the Nicholas factor. Because that was clearly what this was about. Not a sudden desire to rekindle cousinly ties. Natalie was trying to impress Nicholas — with what? A musty old house that had belonged to a great-aunt Natalie didn't even like? Her dubiously ancient ancestry? Either way, it wasn't working. Julia would have felt sorry for Natalie if it weren't all so damned annoying.

Oh, well. On the plus side, Julia was getting free labor out of it.

That was what she wanted, wasn't it? Julia told herself stridently as she let herself into the room next door. To clean up and get out?

Somehow, that didn't sound as attractive a prospect as it had a week ago.

Julia set her coffee cup down on a dusty desk. She hadn't been through here yet.

Like the drawing room, this room had the musty smell of long disuse. The walls must once have been a pale blue — or maybe lilac? — but had faded over time to a gentle bluish gray, punctuated with woodwork that had been white a very long time ago, before the grime began to accumulate and the paint peel. There were two tall white bookshelves against one wall, one on either side of a narrow window looking out on to an alley, each crammed with a collection of tattered paperbacks and untidy piles of papers. There was a narrow bed, with a white metal bedstead, a chest of drawers, and, making up for the lack of a closet, a massive wardrobe, the heavy mahogany incongruous against the rest of the cheap, white-painted 1960s-era furniture. The wardrobe looked as though it had been there for a very long time; no one would want to try to navigate that monster out through the door.

It was a smallish room, but that was more than made up for by the view from the two windows on the far wall. The windows looked out over the garden, all the way down to the neglected orchard that bounded the fence on the far end of the property. Even now, unweeded, neglected, the garden looked like a scene out of a fairy tale: the peeling peaked roof of the summerhouse, surrounded by a tangle of wild roses, over-grown paths of yew hedges, dotted with rusted iron benches. Forty years ago, with the summerhouse freshly painted, with water in the birdbath and bright blossoms in the overgrown flower beds, it must have been glorious.

There was a small painting hanging between the two windows, a watercolor. It was the same view but in spring, the trees a mass of white blossoms, the sky a perfect, celestial blue. Julia didn't need to look at the signature at the bottom to guess who must have painted it.

Her mother had been in art school when Julia's father met her.

It was one of the few things Julia knew about them. It was why her father had looked so grimly pained when Julia had majored in art history, why she knew, without ever discussing it, that it would cut him to the bone if she followed through and went for her PhD.

Julia turned slowly in a circle, taking in the details of the room, the sketchbooks on the shelves, the slightly grimy Princess phone. There was no doubt about it; this must have been her mother's room. Forty years ago, in another world, her mother might have sprawled on that bed, phone cord stretched across the room, speaking in hushed tones to Julia's father, muffling her laughter so Aunt Regina wouldn't hear.

At least, Julia assumed her mother and father must have laughed together. Once.

From far away, Julia seemed to hear her father's voice, raised in anger; a female voice, answering back; the slamming of a door. She could feel the prickle of a carpet beneath her bare knees. She was crouched under something, a table, listening to her parents arguing.

Where in the hell had that come from?

Julia's hand was on the knob of the door before she realized that she had retreated, step by step, ready to duck out and shut the door. She laughed shakily. Great. Metaphor made action. Her English professors in college would have loved that. Shut the door and shut the door. Just like she had been shutting the door all these years.

Julia's knuckles were white against the old brass doorknob. This was insane. Insane. What was she so afraid of? What was she was so afraid of remembering?

Maybe she was just afraid she would miss her. Her mother.

The answer came unbidden. It was so much easier to pretend her mother had never been, that Julia had always lived in an apartment in New York with her father, easier not to remember anything warm or tender, because warm or tender would hurt and it was easier just to be angry, to be angry at her mother for leaving them. Somehow, despite the fact that it had been an accident — the word "accident" had been emphasized over and over again — Julia had never been able to shake the conviction that it had been a willful desertion. Her mother had left her, had left them.

Maybe it was her father's refusal to talk about it that had cemented the idea, his tight-lipped pain when her mother's name was mentioned. It wasn't just grief; there was anger there, too. Small as she was, Julia had gotten the message. Mummy was to blame for leaving and the only way to deal with it was to shut her out entirely, to pretend she had never been.

Julia leaned back against the door, feeling the sweat prickling through her tank top. She'd done a pretty thorough job of it, hadn't she? She'd blotted out every memory of their life in England. But for that one old picture, she wouldn't even remember her mother's face.

Maybe it was time to start remembering.

Maybe. Later. Julia took a slug of her cold coffee, trying to ignore the way her hands

155

were trembling. One step at a time. Not running out of her mother's room and slamming the door would be a good start. It wasn't precisely heroic, but it was a beginning.

Julia yanked the elastic up on her ponytail and decided to tackle the wardrobe first. It was less personal than the bookshelves, the desk, the bureau. Baby steps, she reminded herself, and tugged open the door to the wardrobe. It took a fair bit of tugging. It wasn't the catch; it was the wood itself, warped with damp and age. There were drawers all up and down one half, but the other half of the wardrobe was one big rectangle, with a bar across the top for hanging clothes, sweaters and pants piled on the bottom.

The clothes in the wardrobe were her mother's, decades old, with the musty smell of old wool. Turtleneck sweaters, plaid skirts with high waists, minidresses and maxidresses. Slowly, Julia began transferring them from the wardrobe to the bed.

It seemed like an awful lot of clothes to leave behind at the premarital home, but Julia recognized that her own perceptions might be skewed. Just because she had cleared out entirely when she left for college, when Helen and Julia's father bought the new apartment, didn't mean that everyone did. She had friends who still had full closets at home, a good decade after college. And her mother had been fairly young when she married Julia's father, a good decade younger than Julia was now. Twenty-one? Twenty-two? Something like that. Her father could tell her, but Julia didn't want to ask.

Where had they lived when she was little? Not here, she assumed. This was a teenager's room — and besides, Julia couldn't imagine her father submitting to being a kept man in the spousal familial home.

"A garden flat." The phrase came out of nowhere. She could hear it, someone saying it, with a little laugh as though it were a joke, one of those adult jokes she didn't quite understand. Beige walls and glass sliding doors and a concrete patio with a wire table and chairs. There was a cat, too. Their cat? A neighbor's cat?

She could see its tail disappearing between two potted plants, just out of her eager grasp. *Mummy, kitty!*

The image disappeared with a pop, leaving Julia blinking at the pasteboard back of the wardrobe.

It had seemed so real, that child's-eye view, but that didn't mean anything at all. It was too easy to manufacture memories, to stitch together bits of books and stories and convince herself that they were real. Only the solid, the physical, held any true security. The scratchy wool of her mother's old skirts, that was real. So was the heavy wood of the wardrobe, although the back didn't look quite so solid as the front.

Julia leaned forward, into the now empty wardrobe. The back wall was a totally different color, a discolored beige rather than a rich mahogany. When she poked it, the whole panel shifted. Whoa. Instinctively Julia snatched her hand back. If the wardrobe was going to collapse on her. . . .

But that wasn't part of the wardrobe. That wasn't even wood. Cautiously, Julia stuck her head back in, feeling around the edges of the panel. It was some kind of heavy cardboard, or something similar, cut to fit the dimensions of the back of the wardrobe.

Tentatively, Julia jiggled the pasteboard panel. When tentative didn't work, she gave it a good yank. Whoever it was had stuck the false back in good and hard. The panel popped free, Julia staggered back, and something plopped heavily into the cavity of the wardrobe, raising a heavy cloud of dust.

Coughing, Julia went to investigate. It was

a rectangular parcel, wrapped in layers and layers of linen, linen yellowed by age. With difficulty, Julia extracted the bundle from the wardrobe. It was nearly as wide as the wardrobe itself, made even wider by the layers of padding. Whoever had constructed the hiding place had fixed it to fit the dimensions of this parcel.

Slowly, Julia began unwrapping the layers. The linen smelled faintly of lavender, the fabric strange to the touch, not at all like the synthetics to which she was accustomed. Julia felt a prickle of excitement. This wasn't her mother's, whatever it was. This had to be older, far older. These sheets had never seen a factory. They had been hemmed by hand, the stitches small and neat — amazingly small and neat — but without the perfect sameness of machine stitching.

It was too ridiculously Nancy Drew.

"The Mystery of the Old Wardrobe," Julia murmured to herself, but her hands were quick to strip the old sheets, only to encounter a layer of plain brown paper wrapping tied in twine. Tied in twine because there had been no tape?

She was going to be really disappointed when it turned out to be an old pile of magazines or someone's large cutting board. It was the right size and shape for a cutting board, but not quite heavy enough.

The knots in the twine had hardened to glue-like consistency with time. Julia gave up on trying to untie them and wiggled the cords off along the sides, feeling like a child trying to get at a prissily wrapped Christmas present. Finally, the brown wrappings fell away.

It was a painting. Not a copy or a print, but a genuine oil painting, stretched out over matting but unframed. Julia lowered it onto the bed with an ungraceful thump. Freed from its wrappings, the colors glowed amazingly bright, the brushwork as fresh as though it had been painted yesterday.

And she was looking at it upside down.

Julie turned it right side up, scooping old sweaters and skirts ignominiously out of the way. She knelt before the bed, entirely entranced. It wasn't a portrait, or a land-scape, or someone's beloved pug dogs. It was a story scene, knights and maidens and feasting. At the center, the king dined at the high table. Julia cleverly deduced his position from both his seat at the center of the table and the rather conspicuous circlet on his brow. He was surrounded by fawning courtiers, all leaning towards him.

In the foreground, however, a man and a woman stood in a window embrasure, the only ones not paying attention to their monarch. Their focus was fixed on each other, their eyes yearning, while their hands were locked around a golden goblet they held between them. Although they were off to the side and the king's trestle table in the center, the artist had worked it cleverly so that the attention was immediately drawn to the clandestine couple — including the king's. His goblet was raised in a toast, but his eyes had slid sideways. He was watching the man and woman and didn't like what he saw.

It was all pure Pre-Raphaelite, the stained-glass windows, the pennants flaring from the beams, the colorful doublets of the courtiers. The lady wore a long gown with a dropped waist in a rich sapphire blue. Her hair wasn't the usual Pre-Raphaelite red but a dark, dark brown, nearly black. It fell unbound to her waist, held only by the golden circlet at her brow.

There was something very familiar about the woman.

"Julia?"

She caught at the edge of the bed as someone called her name. How long had she been kneeling here? Her knees had gone numb and her neck was stiff.

"Julia?" It was Andrew, popping his head

around the door. "I thought you might want to see — What's that?"

Julia lurched to her feet, fighting the urge to step in front of the painting, to hide her discovery.

Like Gollum with his Precious, she thought in disgust, and stepped aside. "I found this in the back of that wardrobe. Pretty neat, no?"

Andrew's eyes widened as he started at the canvas on the bed. "I'm no judge of art, but whatever that is — it looks real." He grinned at her, his open face lighting up. "Maybe you've found that Rubens."

Julia put out a hand to stop him. "I'm sure it's not —"

But Andrew was already shouting down the stairs. "Nick? Nick! Come up here! You'll want to see this."

"It might be a copy of something," said Julia hesitantly.

But it wasn't; she was sure of it. Copies didn't look like that. They didn't have that firmness of brushstroke. They didn't glow with life.

Julia heard the *click-clack* of Natalie's heels on the stairs.

"What is it?" Natalie asked her brother grumpily just as Nicholas came up behind her, bracing one hand against the doorjamb.

"This had better be good," he said. "You've taken me away from a cow creamer for this."

"This," said Andrew, and pointed at the painting on the bed.

For a moment, everyone in the room just stood and stared. And then —

"That isn't a Rubens," said Nicholas.

EIGHT

"No shit, Sherlock," said Julia.

"It *is* a painting," said Andrew helpfully.

"Brilliantly spotted," drawled Nicholas.

Julia gave him a look. "I'm going to go out on a limb and guess Pre-Raphaelite," she said. "It's got the right . . . feel to it."

Maybe if she'd stuck with art history she'd have the technical terminology to elaborate on just what those details were that made her so sure. It was something about the colors, about the subject matter, the quality of the light. She hadn't taken any classes on the Pre-Raphaelites back in college — they were considered vaguely déclassé by the art historical establishment at Yale when she was there — but they'd been standard dorm room decoration. In her own room she'd had Dicksee's *Belle Dame sans Merci*, Millais's *Ophelia*, and Waterhouse's *My Sweet Rose*, all courtesy of the poster collection at

164

the Yale Co-op.

But those had been prints. This was the real thing.

"You're right," said Nicholas, surprising her. "Is there a signature?"

Their heads narrowly escaped collision as they both leaned over the painting at the same time. Julia's arm brushed Nicholas's, damp with sweat in the un-air-conditioned room. Andrew had been wrong; there wasn't any pong about Nicholas. He smelled of soap and laundry detergent and the slightly musty odor of old books.

"Well?" said Natalie impatiently from behind them.

Julia's eyes met Nicholas's. They were blue, but not a pedestrian, workaday sort of blue; his eyes were like stained glass limned in sunlight, the blue tinged a translucent green.

"*PRB.*" Julia's voice was breathless. Three little letters, such a small thing to make the hair on her arms prickle like that, to send a chill down her spine. Julia used the edge of the bed to lever herself back up to a standing position. "You saw it, too, didn't you? On the bottom right. The initials *PRB.*"

"Who's PRB?" asked Natalie.

"Not who, what," said Julia before Nicholas could. "The Pre-Raphaelite Brotherhood. They were a group of painters in the mid-nineteenth century. Mad, bad, and dangerous to know. But they painted beautiful things."

"Postcard art," said Nicholas, rising to his feet. Standing, he was considerably taller than she was, placing her eyes somewhere on a level with the top button of his shirt.

Julia refused to be loomed over. "Tell that to the Met," she retorted.

"Or the Tate," said Nicholas blandly, and she realized he'd been deliberately winding her up. To Natalie he said, "The art community is always suspicious of anything that's too popular with the masses."

"Is there a name, or just those initials?" asked Natalie, placing a proprietary hand on Nicholas's shoulder. Julia took a step back, feeling, strangely, chastened. "Do we know who painted it?"

"I'm not seeing a signature," said Andrew, hunkering down by the painting. "Not that it means there isn't one," he added hastily.

"Even if there isn't one," Nick said slowly, "I think we can narrow it down. If I'm right."

"How?" asked Julia.

His eyes met hers, the glint in them belying his reserved tone. "It was a small movement. It wasn't just anyone who used the

166

initials *PRB.* It was only members of the original brotherhood and only at the very beginning of the movement. They dropped the use of the initials — I don't remember exactly when. Within the first few years. Early enough."

That would be easy enough to find out; she could Google it once they were gone. Julia's head swam with possibilities. The idea that this painting, sitting here on the bed, might be a genuine Pre-Raphaelite, that it might not have been seen since it was first painted . . . Someone, 150-odd years ago, had dipped his brush into paint and produced *that.*

The mind boggled.

"I wouldn't get too excited," Nicholas warned her. "There were a few of those early Pre-Raphaelites who were non-starters. They weren't all Rossetti and Mill-ais."

Julia ignored that. "So you think it's real," she said. "I mean, a real Pre-Raphaelite, not just a copy or an imitation."

"I don't know."

"Don't know or don't want to say?"

Natalie quickly stepped between them. "Really, there's no need —"

Ignoring Natalie, Nicholas said abruptly, "Look. Would you let me take this into my shop? I know a person or two who might take a look at it, tell us what it is."

Natalie clapped her hands together. "Didn't I tell you? Just like *Antiques Roadshow*!" She linked an arm through Nicholas's. "What would we have done without you here?"

"Taken it to a real expert?" Disentangling himself from Natalie, Nicholas turned to Julia. "What do you say?"

Julia found herself oddly reluctant to relinquish the painting. "Won't some snapshots do just as well?" She scrounged for a plausible excuse. "Hauling it back and forth can't be good for it."

"It's been sitting in the back of a wardrobe for the better part of a century," Andrew pointed out. "Hardly archival preservation."

"Do you have a digital camera?" Nicholas asked.

Julia looked at him in surprise. "Yes. Hang on. I'll go grab it."

She hurried out towards her own room, hoping that the camera was actually at the bottom of the second pocket of her suitcase, where she usually forgot it for months at a time.

Her own room was diagonally across the hall. As she bent over her suitcase, scrabbling for the camera case, she heard Natalie ask, "Why not take the painting with you? Wouldn't that be simpler?"

"And risk losing it over lunch?" said Andrew laughingly. "Or getting egg mayonnaise on a lost masterpiece?"

"No one's going near this with any kind of food." Julia returned, breathless, with the camera. "Okay. Who wants to play photographer?"

Miraculously, there was actually still some battery life left in the camera. The three of them stood by while Nicholas photographed the canvas from every possible angle, with particular attention to those three entwined letters: *PRB*.

Julia couldn't resist asking, "Whose do you think it is?"

"I don't know enough to make an educated guess," he said. "The subject matter is reminiscent of Millais, but the color palette looks more like Rossetti. My friend Anna will be able to tell you."

"Anna?" said Natalie, arching an eyebrow.

Nicholas was oblivious. "A lecturer at Cambridge. This is her area. She'll know." He set the camera down on the desk, his eyes fixed on the painting, incongruously nestled among Julia's mother's old skirts and sweaters. "It might be a copy."

"Of course," murmured Julia. And she

169

might be Genghis Khan.

"But if it were a copy," said Andrew, "wouldn't they have copied something more familiar?"

"Andrew," said Julia, "I love you."

Andrew jostled her arm affectionately with his elbow. "Anything for a cousin. Weren't you meant to be going, Nick?"

Nicholas glanced at his watch and swore. "Bugger. I'm late for lunch." Turning to Julia, he said, "You'll remember to e-mail me those files?"

There was one slight problem with that plan. "I don't have my camera cord with me. Just take the camera with you. There's nothing else on it right now anyway." She hoped. Not without malice, she added, "Natalie can always get it from you for me."

"The gallery *is* on my way from work," chimed in Natalie.

"That's that sorted," said Nicholas. He gave Julia an oblique look. "I'll ring you by Monday and let you know what I've discovered. What's your number?"

It was only after he'd gone that Julia realized that none of them had asked the real question: what in the hell was a Pre-Raphaelite painting — imitation or original — doing hidden in the back of her wardrobe?

As if through a fall of water, Imogen heard the whisper of skirts, the chatter of voices, the clatter of heels on the marble floor as the exhibition goers moved on their varied courses around her. Her hands felt damp in her kid-leather gloves.

There she was, on the wall, for the world to see.

No, not her. A model. A model with long, red hair. Painfully, Imogen forced herself to step back, to look at the painting critically, trying not to feel as though she'd just been stripped bare in the middle of the Academy.

So what if it was her sewing box, her Book of Hours? They were just objects, nothing to do with her. Anyone else looking at the painting would see only a scattering of items, part of a scene, a scene from a poem, depicting something very long ago and far away. No one would think to ask to whom the individual items might belong. They were simply props, like the pasteboard crown in a Shakespeare play.

She should, Imogen told herself firmly, admire the technical skill of the work. The colors were rich and glowing, making the composition stand out among the duller shades of the paintings hung above and beside it like a robin in a field of wrens. The window, in particular, shone as though light were streaming through the glass. It had the same pure, clear tones as the best sort of medieval-manuscript miniatures.

And her deepest, darkest feelings staring out at her from a stranger's face.

"Mrs. Grantham!"

The sound of her own name started her out of her reverie. She turned, surprised, and her exhibition catalog fell, splayed open on the floor.

Mr. Rossetti gallantly scooped it up for her before it could be trampled. His disordered curls had been brushed for the occasion, but his cheeks still had the proper air of artistic pallor.

"I see you're admiring Thorne's work," he said as Imogen received the catalog from him with a murmur of thanks.

"Mr. Rossetti." Imogen forced herself to sociability. "Where is your work?"

Rossetti shrugged with feigned nonchalance. "Not here, I'm afraid. I exhibited at the Free Exhibition in Hyde Park this year instead. I didn't want to risk my *Girlhood of Mary Virgin* being hung all the way up by the ceiling with the cobwebs! As you can see, Thorne got one of the good spots."

"Yes," murmured Imogen. "Yes, he did." On the line, they called it. Hung conveniently at eye level for all to see.

Rossetti said easily, "But I'm sure you'll be wanting to see Thorne to congratulate him."

"No, really, there is no need —" began Imogen.

"There is every need," said Rossetti. "Honest admiration is good for the artist's battered soul. Particularly once the critics have been at one. There he is, with Millais. Thorne!"

Rossetti raised a hand to the other man, who was standing a little bit away, in a group that included another man, with a high forehead and fair, tousled hair, and the ubiquitous John Ruskin. Seeing them, Thorne murmured something to the others and started in their direction.

Imogen adjusted her sweat-sticky gloves and pasted a polite smile on her face.

"Mr. Thorne." Her greeting was all that was politely condescending. "I have just been admiring your work."

"Admiring" wasn't at all the word she would have preferred to use.

"Mrs. Grantham." His deep voice with its regional accent sounded particularly out of place against all the high-pitched chatter around them, something from a different, more rough-and-tumble sort of world, for all that his words were everything that was correct. "It is a pleasure to see you again."

"You seem to have taken much from your visit to us," Imogen said, trying to keep her voice light.

Thorne's brows rose at the acid note in her voice. "Your husband was kind enough to allow us to sketch anything that caught our interest. I was given to understand it would not be an intrusion."

Of course, Arthur would say that, thought Imogen bitterly. It wasn't his soul being bared on canvas.

Her sewing box, that was. Not her soul. Mariana in her moated grange was nothing to do with her.

"I am surprised by your choice of subject," she said, her voice just a little too loud. "Don't you find Mariana a rather dull character?"

"You've read the poem, then?"

Read it and chafed at it. She had despised weak, whiny Mariana — and despised herself even more for the sense of kinship that came to her through those lyrical, despairing words. Perhaps that was why the poem had annoyed her so much, annoyed her enough that she had flung the slim volume aside and sought solace in her garden, in the honest work of digging and planting and tearing out weeds. She knew how it felt to be caught in a cage, waiting, constantly waiting.

And for what? She had learned long ago that there were no such things as knights in shining armor. And if such a being did come to bear one away, it was inevitably to one's doom, or so the stories would have it.

"The mirror crack'd from side to side. . . . Singing in her song she died."

But that was another poem, also by Mr. Tennyson, beautiful and disturbing and with a heroine just as ill-fated.

"Mr. Tennyson," Imogen said tightly, "has a wonderful way with words but a rather dreary choice of subject."

"You find Mariana dreary?"

"She calls herself dreary." Imogen's voice was sharper than she would have liked. In exaggerated tones, she quoted, " 'Then said she, "I am very dreary, / He will not come," she said; / She wept, "I am aweary, aweary, / O God, that I were dead!" ' There you have her, condemned from her own lips. One cannot have it on better authority than that."

"Would you say that we are the best judges of our own characters?" He was looking at her far too intently. "We delude ourselves as much as we do others."

"Save for the eagle eye of the artist?" Imogen said acidly.

"I'd hardly say that." To her surprise, he laughed, a low, rough laugh, his eyes crinkling around the corners. "We painters, we're — there's a French term for it. Knowing idiots? We wield the brush, but we only see the half of what we convey."

"The wise fool." She knew better than to be fooled by a show of false modesty. Imogen countered, "But isn't it true that a fool who knows himself is no fool?"

Mr. Thorne held up his hands in surrender. "You're too sharp for me by half, Mrs. Grantham."

She couldn't tell whether it was meant as a compliment or an insult.

"Yes, she is that, isn't she?" said Arthur, coming up beside her and taking her arm. "I had wondered where you had got to, my dear. Mr. Thorne. I see you've put our little collection to good use."

"I cannot thank you enough for your generosity." They were speaking man-to-man now and Imogen had faded back into the background, just another ornament, as insignificant as Mariana in her moated grange. "It's the details that make the difference. Having a proper model, even for the smallest things — it brings a scene to life."

Arthur regarded the painting thoughtfully. "Yes. Yes, I do see what you mean. There is a clarity to it, an immediacy. No more blurry backgrounds for you, eh?"

Mr. Thorne's face was set and stubborn. "If there's a daffodil, I want to paint a real daffodil, not just a generic imitation of one; if there's sky, it will be the sky as I saw it, myself, with my own eyes. I won't pay my viewers in false coin."

"Honesty in art . . ." Arthur turned the idea around, prodding it gently. "It's an interesting idea, although some would say it's a contradiction in terms."

"There's truth in fiction, sometimes, sir," said Mr. Thorne, "and I mean to keep my fictions as true as they can be."

"A little too true." Imogen hadn't meant to speak the words aloud. As both men looked at her, she laughed awkwardly and gestured at the painting. "So much emotion — it's almost uncomfortable to see."

Her husband regarded her thoughtfully. "Do you know, Thorne, I might have a proposition to put to you." Turning to Imogen, he said, "We had spoken of having your portrait painted."

Yes, they had spoken of it — a portrait to

match the portrait of Arthur that hung in the drawing room — but it was one of those projects that were always delayed to some indefinite time in the future. As for herself, Imogen was largely indifferent. It didn't particularly matter to her whether she hung on the wall of Herne Hill for posterity. What difference would it make to her, once she was gone? Like Arthur's poor first wife, forever immured in a miniature in a back bedroom, laughing at a world she had never lived to see.

But of one thing Imogen was quite sure: she didn't want to be painted by Gavin Thorne. If Arthur must have her painted, let it be by someone safe and stodgy, someone who would translate her features to canvas and leave her emotions alone.

"There's really no need," she said quickly. "Besides, I shouldn't wish to take Mr. Thorne away from his other compositions. There are all those individual daffodils to be painted, after all."

"Nonsense," said Arthur genially. "It's a rare artist who isn't in want of a commission. Don't tell me I'm wrong."

"We mustn't presume —" Imogen began quickly, but Arthur cut her off with a quick gesture of his hand.

"You're right, sir," Mr. Thorne said to Ar-

178

thur. "I would be glad of the work. And, of course," he added, "grateful for the chance to paint someone so lovely as Mrs. Grantham."

The gallantry sat ill on his lips. Imogen pressed her own lips tightly together, saying nothing. What could she say? She would only sound churlish if she were to protest.

"Good man," said Arthur genially. "We shall expect you at Herne Hill — shall we say next Monday?"

The question wasn't directed at Imogen. And why should it be? There was no activity in which she might engage that Arthur couldn't rearrange for his own convenience.

"Yes," said Mr. Thorne, and he looked again at Imogen. Imogen felt the color rise in her cheeks for no reason. She wondered if this was how a butterfly felt, pinned to the table of a naturalist, splayed, defenseless. "Next Monday should do very well."

NINE

By the time mid-afternoon on Monday rolled around, Julia made herself shut off her cell phone. Just so she would stop checking it.

It wasn't that she was so eager to hear from Mr. Nicholas Dorrington, King of the Art World, she told herself self-righteously. He had clearly been tagged Property of Natalie, whether he knew it or not. If it mattered, which it didn't. But Julia would like to know more about her painting, and he was her best bet.

She had done more than a little bit of scrounging around on her own, but the Internet was staggeringly uninformative. Of the seven original members of the Pre-Raphaelite Brotherhood, she only recognized three of the names: Dante Gabriel Rossetti, John Everett Millais, and William Holman Hunt. One of the seven was Rossetti's older brother, added in to make up the numbers. That left three other artists, all unknown to her.

The painting itself wasn't much more helpful. No matter how she looked, she couldn't find a signature, not worked into the rushes on the banqueting floor, not hidden in the embroidery in the train of the lady's gown. There was nothing on the back, either. The canvas had been stretched over a wooden frame. It all looked quite old to Julia's unpracticed eye, but she vaguely remembered that the experts had their own ways of determining dates, something to do with the types of paints and canvas.

She knew enough of Arthurian legendry to be fairly sure that the scene represented in the painting was Tristan and Iseult, the doomed lovers who cuckolded the middle-aged King Mark of Cornwall. The king was appropriately middle-aged, his ginger hair and whiskers laced with gray. There was something rather sad about him, about the expression on his face as his eyes shifted sideways to his young wife and his nephew.

Googling "Tristan and Iseult" and "Pre-Raphaelites" yielded several images, but none were anything like Julia's painting. Waterhouse had done one and so had Edmund Blair Leighton, but both were dated much later and neither portrayed the scene as her unknown painter had, with as much detail and action. In both of the others, the lovers trysted alone; only her version had King Mark watching them from the corner of his eye.

That had to be a good thing, didn't it? If her painting was a copy, there would have had to have been an original off of which to copy, and if there was such an original, Google didn't have it in its image cache.

And if it wasn't in Google . . .

By this point, Julia had had a great deal of coffee and was beginning to feel more than a little bit slaphappy.

Julia closed the lid of her laptop with a click. She had propped the painting up against the back of a chair, eye level.

"You couldn't have come with a museum plaque?" she demanded of the painting.

The painting didn't presume to answer.

So much for all of her art history professors talking about paintings speaking to them. From long ago and far away Julia dredged up the memory of those classes, of "reading" a painting the way she now read financial reports, picking apart and decoding the smallest details. Somewhere, somewhere in the details of the scene, a real expert could find some clue as to the identity of the artist — not just the style and brushwork, but props that had been used elsewhere, costumes, a familiar model.

According to Julia's reading, the artists tended to model for one another, at least in the early days when money was scarce. The man, lean and dark, might have been one of the Brotherhood himself, hard to tell when most of the pictures online were of the men much later in their lives, grown old and respectable, with bushy eyebrows and exuberant facial hair. She had found an early sketch of Rossetti, ringleted and romantic. She thought he might be one of the banqueters, sitting at the side of King Mark, but she wasn't entirely sure.

Julia turned to the woman instead. Funny to think how radical this all must have been at the time and how incredibly stereotyped it looked now, the willowy woman in the pseudo-medieval dress, all that flowing hair. Julia had seen the equivalent of that same woman in a dozen dorm rooms. La Belle dame Sans Merci, fair Rosamund, Guinievere . . .

But those had all been redheads, and this woman was dark. Her features had the dramatic angularity associated with the great Pre-Raphaelite models, but, somehow, the more Julia looked at her, the more she seemed wrong, as though Julia had met her somewhere else, in quite another guise, like bumping into a work friend only seen inside the office in tailored suits on the sidewalk in jeans and a T-shirt.

If Julia imagined the hair up, instead of down, traded the gown of sapphire silk for a white collar and cuffs . . .

It was the woman in the drawing room.

No. It had to be a mistake. Respectable Victorian matrons didn't just pose for paintings, at least not paintings that weren't portraits, and the woman in the drawing room was very respectable indeed, buttoned up to the chin and down to the wrists. Julia was imagining things, that was all. Too many hours of peering at minuscule thumbnails of Pre-Raphaelite paintings on the Internet.

But it couldn't hurt to check. Just to take a look.

Carefully, Julia swathed the painting in its linen wrappings and maneuvered the clumsy bundle down the stairs, taking extra care not to bash the edges into the walls. It was gloomy in the drawing room, even in the middle of the afternoon. The shrubbery had grown too wild to admit much light through the grimed old windows. Julia made a mental note to buy hedge clippers and clicked on the electric light.

It wasn't much of an improvement, but it was enough to see by. She set down her bundle on an old card table and gently peeled away the wrappings. Over the mantelpiece, the lady with the Princess Leia hairdo and the buttoned basque looked away into space, as though disclaiming any responsibility.

Same cheekbones. Same chin. Same nose. Hairstyles changed, but basic features didn't, at least not in those days, before plastic surgery and discreet little doctors on Park and 73rd.

Julia looked from the portrait to the painting. Prim respectability. Wild abandon. One of these things was not like the others. But which? Which was the real story and which was the aberration?

There was something so prim and stuffy about that parlor, about the white woodwork and the careful swags of the draperies, as prim and stuffy as the white lace collar and cuffs of the lady in the portrait, the carefully modest hairstyle that obscured even her ears. It was impossible to imagine an artist's model living here — unless, of course, she had been an artist's model before her marriage and then married into a stuffy bourgeois family.

The more Julia thought about the theory,

the more she liked it.

"That would explain why you were in the closet," she said to the painting.

Painting: still not talking.

Julia began to wonder if being alone for such extended periods of time was quite good for her. If she kept this up, she'd have to get a dog. Talking to dogs was generally considered more socially acceptable than talking to paintings and avoided the stigma of "crazy cat lady."

There was one person she could talk to. . . .

Julia's hand hovered over her cell phone. It was a very off chance. He probably wouldn't know anything. All the same . . .

She turned the phone back on and waited impatiently as it warmed up.

No new messages. Surprise, surprise.

The display on her phone read: 4:13, which meant that it was just a little past eleven in the morning at home in New York.

She started, automatically, to type in her father's number at Mount Sinai, then hastily hit the End Call button. It was late July. Her father and Helen would be at the Hamptons house. The idea of her father taking a full two weeks away from the hospital was mind-boggling — when she was little, a weekend felt like a boon — but, somehow,

Helen had managed it. Every summer, they went out to East Hampton for the last two weeks of July, while the boys were away at camp.

From what Julia gathered, while out there they pretty much replicated exactly what they would have done at the apartment on a Sunday at home: Helen read mystery novels, Julia's father read medical journals, and they drank fresh-ground coffee out of blindingly white mugs.

They had invited her up, again and again, but she had always found an excuse to stay away. She had told herself it was because the idea of her father in swimming trunks was too horrible to contemplate.

Taking a deep breath, Julia punched in the Hamptons number. It was Helen who answered. She professed herself delighted to hear from Julia. That was one of the nice things about Helen: she always did sound genuinely pleased. There were times when Julia felt a bit guilty for not having been more of the daughter Helen so obviously wanted and would have been happy for her to be.

Easy to see that now, at thirty-one; it had been less easy at sixteen.

They covered the usual social niceties — the weather here, the weather there, the boys' bulletins from camp — before Julia asked, "Is Himself around?"

"I'll just get your father for you." Julia's sense of humor sometimes left Helen a little flustered.

"Hello?" Julia's father picked up the phone with that brusque bark that pretty much typified his bedside manner. It was, she had always thought, a good thing he was a surgeon, not a GP. He'd scare his patients right out of the office. On the other hand, he was brilliant with people out cold on an operating table.

Julia got straight to the point. If she was going to ask a silly question, she might as well ask it fast.

"Dad . . . what do you know about my mother's side of the family?"

Herne Hill, 1849

When Gavin arrived at the house on Herne Hill, a portable easel uncomfortably bundled on one shoulder, a maid directed him to the garden.

He would find Mrs. Grantham in the summerhouse, the maid said. When Gavin asked after Mr. Grantham, he was informed that the master was not at home but had left instructions for Mr. Thorne to be served tea, alfresco. Or, as the maid pronounced it, all fresho.

He could tell that the maid didn't quite know what to make of him. As a journeyman painter, he wasn't quite a gentleman, he wasn't to have his hat reverently taken from him and be received in the drawing room, but he wasn't one of the lower orders, either, to be received in the kitchen and offered a slice of bread and dripping. So the maid afforded him his "mister" but left him to make his own way into the gardens.

Gavin felt as though he had slipped into a little bit of Eden. The ground sloped steeply down behind the house, so it seemed that there was nothing ahead of him but trees and flowers and birdsong, stretching down as far as the eye could see, lazy bees drowsing in flowers and tree branches frothy with white blossoms that released their own heady scent into the drowsy spring air. It was the sort of day in May that justified poets' pay, the sun gilding the grass, the breeze enough to cool but not to chill, and the first buds of flowers opening their cautious petals to the sun.

Who would have imagined that such loveliness existed, tucked away, within walking distance of London? It was a world away from the squalor of Cleveland Street, the squawk of the hawkers' cries, the stench of human and animal offal rotting in the gutter, trod down into the spaces between the cobbles. Unbidden, the image of the cellar where he'd spent his youth rose into his mind, the effluvia of the gutter sinking through the stones and fouling the floor, the damp that marred the walls even on the sunniest of days. He'd sketched to escape it, drawing pictures with a stick in the dirt, imagining landscapes such as this.

The summerhouse was a small, white building, the roof pointed, the sides open to the sun. Rosebushes, not yet in bloom, grew in profusion around the base, all buds and thorns, like Sleeping Beauty's briars. In the middle of it sat the princess in her tower, her wide skirts billowing around her, a book in her hand.

Gavin stood for a moment, like a pilgrim at a shrine, caught by the play of light and shade, the curve of pale fingers against the red morocco cover of a book, the tilt of her head, the elegant angle of her neck. The sunlight picked out hidden veins of red in her dark hair. In his imagination, the summerhouse became a stone tower, the blue gown a flowing robe of sapphire samite. There would be a gold circlet around her brow. . . .

"Mr. Thorne." Mrs. Grantham shut her

book with a snap, setting it aside, and the spell was broken. It was just a simple whitewashed building, and he was a disheveled and slightly dusty painter, overly warm from his six-mile walk and a cravat that wilted loosely around his neck.

"Mrs. Grantham." Gavin bowed, stiffly, encumbered by his parcels. Was there a protocol to such meetings? Was he meant to ask her, formally, to sit for him? With models, one simply told them where to go and what to do, but this wasn't a model; he was the employee in this relationship, not the employer. He ought to have asked Augustus. Augustus would have laughed and looked down his nose, but he would have been more than glad to air his own expertise.

Gavin's own inexperience irked him, and it didn't make it any easier that Mrs. Grantham was looking at him as though he were a bug who had landed on her tea cake. The devil of it was, he couldn't afford to offend her. She could glower all she liked, but he was the one, at the end of the day, who needed to be paid.

"My husband suggested you paint me here, in the garden." If Mrs. Grantham had any opinion as to her husband's choice, she gave no sign of it. Her expression and voice were as bland as her dark blue dress. "The weather appears inclined to cooperate."

Gavin deeply hoped that Grantham realized that a portrait wasn't painted in a day. "I had meant to take some sketches today. Before we begin in earnest."

Mrs. Grantham inclined her head. The white line of her parting looked strangely vulnerable. "You are the expert, Mr. Thorne. Where would you like me?"

"If you wouldn't mind moving just a little to your right, where the light falls better . . . Yes, there." He added awkwardly, "Thank you."

Mrs. Grantham smiled stiffly. "Nonsense, Mr. Thorne. You must be frank with me and tell me what I must do. I shouldn't wish to impede your task."

Clumsily, Gavin set up his easel. In his studio, his hands were swift and sure. Here, they fumbled on the slats of the frame. The wood made a hideous scraping noise against the plank floor of the summerhouse. Mrs. Grantham looked away, her expression polite, detached. Had his journey been difficult? Wasn't the weather lovely? Gavin made the requisite replies, fumbling his chalks from his satchel, until even that poor excuse for conversation trailed into awkwardness.

"If you would just turn your head a little to the left . . ." Somewhere, a bird squawked, strident. Gavin's chalk scraped clumsily against the page.

If Mrs. Grantham noticed, she made no sign; she sat perfectly still, her spine straight, her expression blank.

The lines of her face were easy enough, but the character eluded him. Gavin threw back a precious page and started again, but his skill, what small skill he might have, was blunted by her reserve and his discomfort. If they carried on like this, her portrait would look more like a death mask than a living, breathing woman.

"You've a pleasing prospect here," Gavin ventured, trying to elicit some response, any response.

Mrs. Grantham inclined her head slightly in acknowledgment. That was all. Not even a one-syllable response. As if he weren't even there.

For a penny he'd have packed up his paints and left. But he couldn't, and it galled him. It galled him to be dependent on the whims of wealthy matrons, singing for his supper, fighting for the handful of coins that separated him from the fate of his father, his family. He looked at her pale, protected profile and thought of his sister, as he'd last seen her, her features mottled and disfigured, her poor, work-worn hands lying slack in death. Gavin's fingers tightened on his chalk.

"I'm sorry this seems so painful for you," he said, and there was an edge to his voice that made Mrs. Grantham turn and look at him, really look at him, for the first time. The glint of surprise in her eyes was the first flicker of emotion he had seen since he arrived.

She settled herself on the bench, like a bird smoothing its plumage. "I am quite comfortable," she said coolly.

"That's not what I meant." No point in beating about the bush. Gavin cleared his throat and took the situation by the horns. "If I'm to be frank with you, Mrs. Grantham," he said, and the accents of his youth roughened his voice, made it come out too load and coarse, "you must be frank with me. I've offended you and I'm not sure why."

"Not at all." Mrs. Grantham's words were as stiff as her limbs.

"At the Exhibition —" Gavin persevered; Once he had gone this far, it made no sense to pull back in polite retreat — "my painting displeased you."

He had struck home there. Mrs.

Grantham's lips pressed tightly together. "I was simply taken aback to see my — my husband's possessions hanging on the wall at the Royal Academy. It was as though one's laundry were hanging in a public field."

The homely simile surprised Gavin into a bark of laughter. "The Academy frowns on airing the washing." He'd like to see Sir Martin's reaction to that.

Mrs. Grantham wasn't smiling. "But my sewing box was perfectly acceptable. With my book in it."

She was quite serious, and, in the face of it, Gavin felt his own amusement fading.

"I'd no notion there was anything private there. Mr. Grantham told us to sketch what we liked." Medieval artifacts from the collection of a collector. And most of what Gavin had sketched had been. But the sewing box had been there, too, the perfect, homely touch to ground Mariana's mythical past in some sort of reality. He had seen it and he had sketched it, as he had the chalice and the Book of Hours, because he had needed one for the picture and because it was there. He hadn't thought of the sewing box as belonging to anyone in particular. The book sticking out of one side, that was simply a nice touch.

Would it perturb him if his shaving kit were to appear in one of Rossetti's pictures? Probably not. He'd been painted in as a reveler in Millais's *Lorenzo and Isabella* and cast as a slightly cranky Roman soldier in Hunt's *Rienzi.* But Gavin was used to the notion that anything — and anyone — was a potential model for the painting of the moment. Mrs. Grantham wasn't.

"I will confess," Gavin said honestly, feeling more than a little abashed, "I'd not been thinking of those objects as someone's personal property."

Mrs. Grantham raised her dark brows. "Radical notions, Mr. Thorne?"

He was digging himself in deeper by the moment.

"I was wrong to use your sewing box. But as for the artifacts . . ." Gavin set down his chalk, trying to sort his feelings into words. "What I ought to have said was I'd not been thinking of them as belonging to this time. To me, they were the possessions of the people who had them in the time when they were made. Putting them into the scene felt like . . . well, like returning them to the time in which they belonged."

"Displayed like animals in a menagerie," said Mrs. Grantham in a low voice, "hung on the wall for all to see."

"No," said Gavin emphatically, and his chalk scraped against the page with the force of his emotion. "It's quite the contrary. I've put them back where they're meant to be. None of those objects were intended to be displayed as curiosities, set on a table against a velvet backdrop. Once they were practical, useful — even that Book of Hours was the object of someone's private devotions once. We look at those illustrations and think only of the artistry, but someone used that once, to real purpose."

It was a longer speech than he was accustomed to making, and he felt a bit sheepish, all the more so because it was true and not something he would otherwise have thought to share. Rossetti might go about baring his feelings to all and sundry, but Gavin preferred to put his emotions into paint and paint alone.

But it had been the right thing to say. He had her attention now. "A lady," said Mrs. Grantham softly, "kneeling at a prie-dieu, her book in her hand."

Gavin sketched furiously, trying to catch that elusive hint of emotion. *Stay like that,* he wanted to say. *Don't fade away again into pale reserve.*

"When I lift that chalice," he said rapidly, trying to catch her before she could slip away again, "I wonder whose hands have held it, whose lips have sipped from it. Did they drink in celebration? In despair? It's not just an object, to be put on a pedestal and admired for the quality of the craftsmanship. It's the embodiment of the thoughts and feelings of the people who used it."

"One doesn't see it with a cup of course," Mrs. Grantham said, her hands folded tightly in her lap, as though she were afraid of giving too much away, "but in the manuscripts there are so often bits of writing in the margins, little windows into the souls of the people who held and read them. In one book, at the very beginning, someone — oh, centuries ago! — crossed out the former owner's name and wrote below it: *Non est elus liber, est meus liber.*"

"*Non est — ?*"

"It's not his book, it's my book," Mrs. Grantham translated.

Gavin looked up from his work in surprise. "You read Latin, then?"

The question was a mistake. Mrs. Grantham's features rearranged themselves into stiff, social lines.

"My father was a vicar." The answer was a polite evasion. He had accidentally trodden on forbidden territory.

"I envy you that," Gavin said, keeping his voice carefully matter-of-fact. "My education didn't stretch to the classics." Both true and less than the truth. His education hadn't stretched to much of anything at all. "I should have liked to have learned."

"It's not too late," Mrs. Grantham said, and, for a moment, Gavin thought he was seeing the real person beneath, before she added, her face a study in indifference, "I imagine you haven't the time for it now, though."

Gavin made a droll face. "It's more that I'm afraid I would prove a poor pupil. I'm too big to be caned." Gavin felt as though he were coaxing a wary bird out of its nest. "Your father's parish. Was it near here?"

Mrs. Grantham looked out over the glossy vines twining along the slats of the summerhouse, the neat boxwood hedges, and the ranks of almond and apple trees below, and an expression of inestimable sadness crossed her face. "Farther than you can imagine."

Gavin had the impression that she was speaking of more than a physical distance.

Briskly she added, "It was in Cornwall. At the outer edges of the earth. I doubt you would have heard of it." She straightened in her seat, saying, with evident relief, "Evie!

Did you need me?"

Gavin turned and saw Miss Grantham hurrying down the slope, flounces fluttering in the breeze, one hand holding on to the light shawl that threatened to slip from her shoulders. He had been so focused on Mrs. Grantham that he had failed to hear the sounds of Miss Evangeline's approach.

"Mr. Thorne." Miss Grantham ducked her head in greeting. She grabbed at her wrap as it threatened to slip from her shoulders. "I do beg your pardon for the interruption, Mama, but Aunt Jane says we're to remind you that we're to call on the Misses Cranbourne at four."

On the verandah behind the house, Gavin could see a shadowy figure watching. Aunt Jane, he presumed. The one who didn't like the works of Mrs. Gaskell.

"Is it already that time?" Mrs. Grantham rose with an alacrity that belied her words.

Miss Grantham made a face. "Yes. I tried to make Aunt Jane believe I had the plague, but she was most unsympathetic."

"You're short a few boils," said Mrs. Grantham, but there was a depth of warmth to her voice that Gavin wouldn't have expected of her. The corners of her lips turned up in a suspicion of a smile.

He wouldn't have suspected her of having

a sense of humor, either, but there it was, hiding away in the corners of her lips, in the light in her eyes.

Gavin wondered what her first name might be. Something mundane like Anne or Jane? Neither suited her at all. Elizabeth, perhaps. Something queenly. Or Ophelia, Shakespearean and tragic. But that wasn't quite right, either.

His fingers itched to crumple the sketches on his easel and start again. A dozen Mrs. Granthams stared out at him in red and black chalk: Mrs. Grantham cold, Mrs. Grantham haughty, Mrs. Grantham wistful, Mrs. Grantham wary, but nowhere was there the slightest hint of amusement. He felt as though he were looking at a palimpsest, a medieval manuscript overwritten in crisscrossed layers until the original message was all but lost beneath the confusion of text.

This commission might be a more interesting project than he had envisioned.

"It is a very subtle form of plague," protested Miss Evangeline.

Mrs. Grantham shook out her crumpled skirts. "Come along," she said to her stepdaughter. "Best to face the inevitable with fortitude."

"Eliza isn't inevitable; she's unpleasant,"

complained Miss Evangeline.

"Inevitably," murmured Mrs. Grantham, and there it was again, that glimpse of wry humor, until she turned to Gavin and the cool composure settled again over her features like a layer of thick-painted varnish. "I must crave your pardon, Mr. Thorne. I fear our time together is at an end."

More relief than fear, he would have guessed, and wasn't sure whether to be offended or intrigued. Or, perhaps, just a little bit of both.

"For this week," Gavin said.

TEN

Herne Hill, 2009

"I should have anticipated that being back there would raise some questions." Julia's father's voice was heavy. "What do you want to know?"

At least he hadn't hung up the phone. Julia wondered what he was afraid she might ask. All those *tell me about my mother* questions she should have been asking ten years ago? It wasn't, she realized, that her father had ever actively refused to speak about her mother. It was just that he had looked so unhappy, turned so into himself, when Julia had cried for Mummy in those first, horrible months that they had gotten into the habit of not speaking of her, a conscious absence, like the shiny tissue of a scar.

Julia could understand that, now. But it had been long enough now, long enough that they should be able to speak of her, with more curiosity than pain.

But not now. Now Julia had other fish to fry.

"Nothing too recent," said Julia, and could practically feel her father's relief across the line. "I've found an old painting and I'm curious about the provenance. We're talking mid-nineteenth century."

"Oh, if that's all . . ." She heard the creak of a chair as he relaxed back against the cushions. Wicker and chintz, if she knew Helen. "There's not that much I can tell you. Your mother" — there was that little pause, that little pause that always followed those words, like a hiccup in time — "your mother wasn't particularly interested in that sort of thing. That was never one of her vices."

Julia wandered over to the heavy old draperies, twisting a dusty tassel around her finger. "That sort of thing?"

"Lineage. Family pride. 'Our people are better than your people.' Your mother believed in taking people on their own merits, good or bad. That her family had been planted in the same place for a hundred years meant very little to her, one way or the other."

Julia was fascinated by the faint note of fondness in her father's voice, by this window into her mother. If she pushed too hard, though, she risked having her father clam up again, so she said as matter-of-factly as she could, "So she never said anything about any old family stories or family scandals?"

"Not really." For a moment, there was silence on the line, silence and a faint exhalation of breath that made Julia think of the stirring of air in old, long-closed vaults, heavy with old memories and old regrets. "Your aunt Regina was the one for family stories, usually of the saltier variety. She didn't have much respect for sacred cows."

That lined up with what Natalie had said over dinner that night. "Unfortunately, she isn't here," Julia pointed out.

Which really was a pity. From what everyone said, Julia had the feeling she would have liked her tremendously.

Her father took a swallow of something, probably coffee. He was supposed to be cutting down, but he generally managed to get around Helen's attempts to switch him to decaf or, even worse, herbal teas, which he regarded with the general scorn of the hardcore caffeine addict. "If you want the official family line, you'll have to ask Caroline. Your mother's cousin."

Julia wiped dust from her hand onto her

shorts. "Natalie and Andrew's mother?"

"Was that their names? I remember you played with them a bit when you were little — not so very much. Caroline didn't approve of our postal code." Julia's father's voice was dry, but there was a real edge underneath it.

Well, then. "They've been over, helping me out — Natalie and Andrew, I mean," Julia clarified. "They came with a friend last weekend to help me go through some of the stuff in here."

Nicholas Dorrington, who still hadn't called.

Julia banished the image of Nicholas, sweaty and intense in the back bedroom, and concentrated on the vague static on the phone line.

The cushions creaked again. "If they're anything like their mother, I'd check the fillings in your teeth when they leave."

Julia blinked at the acid in father's voice. "I take it you and Cousin Caroline didn't get along?"

There was a long, weighted pause. "No."

Alrighty, then. Julia persisted. "But it's Cousin Caroline you think I should talk to about the family history?"

Her father sighed. "Caroline had a family tree made up, going all the way back to the

Conqueror. Some of it might even be true." He paused for another swallow of his beverage. "Not that you'll get anything interesting from her. It was all how great and good and successful the family all were." His voice was heavy with sarcasm. "If you're looking for scandal, you'll have to look elsewhere."

"Paragons of virtue one and all?" said Julia sweetly. "Now we know where I get it from."

"Brat," said her father affectionately. Julia heard the rustle of paper in the background. "By the way, before I forget, it seems I'll be in London in August for a conference. May I take you out for dinner?"

Family reminiscence hour was officially over.

"Sure. That would be great." Julia noticed he didn't suggest coming to the house. "I think I can clear the space on my exceedingly busy social calendar."

There was a brief silence from the other end of the line, then, "You're not too lonely out there?"

Julia found herself strangely touched by the gruff question. Her father liked to talk about emotions the way she liked having her teeth drilled. Without Novocain. From him, this was a major expression of concern.

"I'm fine," she said gently. "Actually, I kind of like it out here." As the words came out, she realized how her father might take them and added quickly, "It makes a nice break from my real life."

"All right," he said, and she was grateful to him for not voicing whatever misgivings he was obviously feeling. She really didn't feel up to a lecture on the state of her job hunt right now. "As long as you're managing."

"Thanks, Dad," Julia said, and meant it. She was about to say her good-byes and hang up when something else struck her, something she had meant to ask. "Dad, when I was little, did we live in a garden flat?"

Her father was taken aback by the question. "A — well, yes. I guess you could say so. It was really just a basement flat, convenient to the hospital, but your mother put out a couple of potted plants and called it a garden flat. Why?"

The concrete patio, the rickety metal table, the kitten.

"No reason," said Julia. That odd flash of memory the other day, her mother's voice, laughing. "I just wondered."

If that had been a real memory, and not her imagination, then what else did she remember? Voices raised in anger, her father's hard and clipped, the linoleum floor of the kitchen hard and cold beneath her knees, the sound of crockery smashing.

"Dad —" She didn't even know what to ask. She was saved by a tiny electronic beep. "Oh, damn, that's my call-waiting."

"I'll talk to you soon," said her father with obvious relief. "Think about August."

And he was gone, with a click. Julia didn't know whether to curse or be grateful.

She jabbed the tiny flash button. The number on the screen was unknown, a UK number.

"Hello?" she said shortly.

"Julia?" The voice was British. Male. More than a little Jeremy Irons–esque.

Julia put on her best professional voice. "Speaking," she said briskly. Always best to sound busy, as though one were efficiently handling multiple international trades instead of hanging out in shorts and tank top in a dilapidated Victorian mini-mansion.

"This is Nick. . . . Nick Dorrington," he elaborated when his initial introduction was followed by blank silence. "Andrew's friend."

"Oh, right! Hi." No need for him to know that she'd been waiting for his call like an overeager teenager.

"On that painting" — the dryness of Nicholas's tone suggested he knew exactly what she was doing — "I believe I've got something for you."

Any embarrassment Julia might have felt was subsumed in a tingle of pure treasure-hunting excitement. This, she thought, this was why people went on *Antiques Roadshow* and scoured flea markets for hidden treasure, this thrill of discovery. "Do you have the name of the painter?"

"Possibly." Nicholas was the very model of professional caution. "Do you have a — *bollocks.*"

Julia choked on a laugh. There went professional. She manfully restrained the urge to say, *No, no, I don't.* At least not if bollocks were what she thought they were. England and America, divided by a common language.

In the background, Julia could hear the tinkling of a bell and a high-pitched female voice raised in an extended and breathless monologue.

"Just a moment, Mrs. Cartwright," said Nicholas with false heartiness. "I'll be right with you. Would you mind terribly leaving Fifi outside? You remember what happened last time."

A sharp bark illustrated Fifi's feelings on

the matter, but the discordant jangle of the bell suggested that her owner had complied.

Lowering his voice, Nicholas said to Julia in confidential tones, "My assistant is out today, so it's just me minding the fort. Look, I know this is a bit of cheek — but would you mind terribly coming to the shop? I can show you what I've found." There was a pause, and then, "It's more effective with illustrations."

Curiouser and curiouser.

"Sure," said Julia. She ought to mind being dragged out, but it had been — how many days? — since she had left Herne Hill. Besides, she was curious about this shop. Natalie made it sound like a cross between Christie's and Sotheby's with a dash of the Frick Collection thrown in. "Where is it?"

"Are you driving?"

Do you drive? would be the more pertinent question. She had no desire to ever get behind the wheel of a car, and, growing up in Manhattan, she hadn't had to. "No."

"Wise," said Nicholas briskly. "The shop is in a cul-de-sac off Portobello Road." He reeled off the address in a professional monotone that suggested he'd been through this same routine many times before. "Either Notting Hill Gate or Ladbroke Grove will do you equally well. Yes, Mrs. Cartwright!"

"Great," said Julia. "See you there." And then, because she couldn't resist, "Have fun with Fifi!"

She clicked the END CALL button before Nicholas could respond and went to go explore her suitcase to see if she could find any of her more respectable summer clothes. Preferably something without sweat stains.

Who knew? She might even shower.

Herne Hill, 1849

It was raining the following Monday when Mr. Thorne came for his appointment.

"We'll have to be in here, I'm afraid," said Imogen, ushering the artist into the drawing room. "Would you like a cup of tea? A cloth to dry yourself?"

Mr. Thorne looked wet to the bone, rain dripping from the brim of the hat he held in his hand, soaking his jacket. The hat didn't appear to have done him much good; there was water matting his dark hair and trickling down his face.

He looked ruefully down at the hat in his hand. "The latter, if you don't want me to drip on your carpets."

Imogen cast a disparaging glance at the red cabbage roses Jane had chosen two years ago. She wasn't sure they could be hurt by it. But she only said, "I'll tell Anna."

Imogen might not mind mud in the carpet, but Jane would, and when Jane minded she could make life very tedious.

Imogen watched as the artist toweled his face and hair dry, damp strands clinging to his cheekbones and forehead like streaks of wet paint. With his hair plastered to his head by the rain, he looked like a statue of a Roman emperor, the bones of his face strong and stark, his lips thin and mobile. He made the shuttered room feel small, crowded, and close.

Imogen hastily looked away as Mr. Thorne caught her staring. He must have thought the cause was something else entirely, because he hastily finished his ablutions and, handing the cloth back to Anna, said, "Is there anywhere else we might — ?" Catching himself, he said quickly, "I don't mean to sound particular. It's the light, that's all."

"Or the lack thereof?" In the rain, the drawing room looked even gloomier than usual, the heaving drapes weighing down the windows, the dark, textured paper brooding on the walls. But the morning room was Jane's province and the study forbidden territory without explicit authorization from Arthur.

"I am afraid not," said Imogen apologetically. "But I can light the lamps."

She set about the room, suiting action to words, adjusting the wicks, coaxing the small flames into life.

Mr. Thorne eased his bundles off his shoulder, onto Jane's cabbage roses. "This is the first time I've painted a portrait. I want to get it right."

Imogen paused in the act of fussing with a wick. "I was under the impression you'd painted a great many people." The image of Mariana's tortured face rose unbidden before her, Mariana, leaning yearningly towards the window, her whole body a pattern of longing.

"Those were models," said Mr. Thorne. As Imogen watched, he unpacked the apparatus of his trade, setting up the easel with an easy skill that made his clumsiness of the week before even more remarkable. From the corner of her eye Imogen watched his hands, swift and sure, anchoring his canvas to the frame. "Women who are paid to play a role."

Imogen fingered the stiff fabric of her dress, the dress that Arthur had insisted she wear. Arthur had decreed every aspect of her appearance for her portrait: where she was to sit, what she was to wear, how she was to arrange her hair. It was Arthur who had insisted it be in the summerhouse, "Since you are so often there, my dear." She was to be immortalized as he designed, frozen into paint as the surface image of the wife he wished to display to the world.

"Is there such a difference?" Imogen said wryly.

Mr. Thorne's amber eyes fixed upon her face, hawk-like in the gently diffused light.

All he said, though, was, "If done properly, there ought to be."

"You are an idealist." Her voice came out too dry; she licked her lips to wet them.

"No," he said, and she could feel him watching her, assessing her, as if he could peel her away, layer by layer. "I simply strive to paint what I see."

See a little less, she wanted to say, but she was interrupted by the sound of heels clacking against the marble floor of the hall.

"Imogen?" It was Jane in the doorway, her skirts taking up the width of the frame, blotting out what light there was from the hall. Her eyes darted to Mr. Thorne, behind his easel, and back to Imogen again. "Cook can't find the keys to the pantry."

"Cook has most likely left them where she always leaves them," said Imogen pleasantly. "Buried in the flour."

Jane shrugged. "Be that as it may." She

made no move to leave. Instead, her starched petticoats rustled briskly as she bustled into the room, planting herself firmly down on a chair by the lamp. Imperiously she said to Mr. Thorne, "Will you be long?"

Imogen winced at Jane's rudeness. However she might feel about this portrait, Mr. Thorne was a talented artist; he didn't deserve to be treated like a delinquent chimney sweep. Imogen's eyes met Mr. Thorne's; his lips quirked at the corners, as though he understood, understood and sympathized. Biting her lip, she looked away.

Patiently, he said to Jane, "I shall endeavor to work as briskly as possible."

Jane sniffed and took up her sewing, effectively blocking out the light of one of the lamps.

Imogen felt her temper rising.

So she was to be chaperoned, was she? Never mind that this painting was at Arthur's wish, Arthur's insistence; never mind that the door had been left, appropriately, a good foot open; never mind that she had never, in a decade of marriage, given the slightest cause for suspicion or reproach.

"I thought Cook needed her key," Imogen said, keeping her voice low and pleasant. "Oughtn't you make certain she has it?"

Jane looked at Imogen with narrowed eyes. Imogen held her gaze.

Jane jabbed her needle sharply into her embroidery, making a small, displeased noise. Dropping her embroidery hoop onto a side table, she stood abruptly, her skirts belling around her. "If you will excuse me, Mr. Grantham will be home shortly. Someone has to see to supper."

And with that parting shot she rustled her way out the door, pausing only for a pointed look at Imogen.

Was she meant to rise and excuse herself, too? Was that what Jane wanted? It was absurd, and all really quite unnecessary. Jane could perfectly well see to supper by herself. It wasn't as though she had ever welcomed Imogen's interference in her housekeeping.

Was it the intrusion of a male in the drawing room Jane minded, or that it was Imogen who would hang there rather than she?

Mr. Thorne kept his eyes on his paper and his voice neutral. "Miss Cooper is Mr. Grantham's cousin?"

"His wife's sister. His first wife's sister." Hastily, eager to change the subject, Imogen said, "Do you have enough light?"

Mr. Thorne's eyes were still on the doorway, where the sound of Jane's displeasure vented itself in the weight of her footsteps against the floor, each one an exercise in indignation. "It will have to serve."

"But it doesn't really?" Imogen said, to say something, to draw attention away from the slap of Jane's footsteps against the floor of the hall. Imogen settled herself down on the stool that was meant to serve as the placeholder for the bench in the summerhouse. She shifted uncomfortably. There was a hard lump in the center, unfortunately apparent even through the multiple layers of skirt, petticoats, and pantalets.

On the verge of a polite demurral, Mr. Thorne shook his head abruptly. "It's not the same, you see," he said. "There's light and there's light. Even with all the lamps lit, lamplight casts a very different tone from sunlight, just as the sun at noon is different from the sun at dawn."

"I had never thought of it," Imogen confessed. She had been taught to sketch, indifferently, as a girl, and had produced the usual sorts of clumsy watercolors, but she had never had the eye for it, or the patience.

"It changes the nature of the picture." Mr. Thorne paused, considering. He looked at Imogen, his eyes intent on her. "When you sit in the summerhouse, the light falls across you in a certain way. It changes every surface it touches; it lights your face and shadows your chin; it creates swirls and eddies in your skirts." His hand rose, sketching the path of the sunbeam, and then fell. "No artificial light could replicate just that angle, just that touch."

Imogen swallowed hard, breathing in against her stays. Even halfway across the room, that gesture had felt like a caress.

Nonsense, of course.

Sharply she said, "But don't many artists work from their studios?"

Mr. Thorne dropped his eyes to his canvas. "They do, and so do I. But those are often a different sort of scene. Indoor scenes. Or the finishing touches on a painting that's already begun."

His words were terse, as though he regretted his earlier volubility.

"Is it all artists who are so careful?" asked Imogen curiously.

The question seemed to relax him. "No, not all," he said. His chalk moved against the canvas even as he spoke. A bit displeased him and he rubbed it out. "Most aren't. But my friends and I — we want to be as true to life as possible."

A strange notion from men who painted works rooted in myth. "Isn't the purpose of art to improve upon the mundane?"

"That's only if you find the world as it is mundane."

Nostalgia stirred, for the cliffs of Cornwall and the scent of the sea, the beauty of the patterns in the waves. " 'Sweet are the uses of adversity,' " quoted Imogen, " 'Which like the toad, ugly and venomous, / Wears yet a precious jewel in his head . . . / Finds tongues in trees, books in the running brooks, / Sermons in stones, and good in everything.' "

She could remember when she'd felt that way, a very long time ago.

The corners of Mr. Thorne's eyes crinkled. "I haven't painted any venomous toads, but I've a friend who lost days on a painting because he wanted a water rat in the foreground and wouldn't rest until he'd found a real one as a model." A swift smile transformed Mr. Thorne's saturnine features. "You'd be surprised at how hard such rats are to come by."

Half-jokingly, Imogen said, "Is it the object alone or the circumstances as well that must be exact? For example, must the water rat be in the proper place on the riverbank to be painted?"

Mr. Thorne gave her question serious consideration. "It depends on whom you're asking. I think that might be a bit much to ask of a rat, to expect him to stay as still as a model, but, if it were possible . . . yes, that would be preferable to seeing him through the bars of a cage."

Imogen could feel the boning of her stays pressing against her sides, digging into her ribs, contorting her into the shape society found pleasing. "I imagine few things are entirely themselves in captivity."

Something about her voice must have caught Mr. Thorne's attention, because his gaze lifted to hers, searching.

Imogen said hastily, "Have you thought at all of your painting for next year's exhibition yet?"

Mr. Thorne returned to his painting. "All of my friends appear to be working on religious subjects," he said. "Rossetti is painting an Annunciation, with his sister as the Virgin Mary, Hunt has his early Christians persecuted by Druids, and Millais tells me he means to paint Christ in the house of his parents."

"But what of you?" Imogen asked. "I hope you don't mean to take on one of the more gruesome martyrdoms."

"No. Next to the others, it seems sacrilegious, but . . ." Mr. Thorne shrugged. "It's only an idea yet."

"Yes?" Imogen found that she was genuinely curious. Just so long as it didn't involve her sewing box. "Not more Tennyson, I hope."

Diffidently, Mr. Thorne said, "I've been thinking of Tristan and Iseult. Not exactly on the same order as the Annunciation, is it?"

"No," said Imogen sacrilegiously, "far more interesting than that."

"And your father a vicar." Mr. Thorne's voice was serious, but she could see it now that she knew to look for it, the little twist at the corner of his lips.

"My father would have been delighted by the notion." And so he would have. His religion had been deeply felt but not a Sunday chapel sort of piety. His wonder at the workings of God had expanded to encompass all of God's creations, even the more secular ones.

Especially the more secular ones.

For a moment, Imogen felt her father's presence as though he were there beside her. But not, as in the past, with a sense of loss, but with all the warmth of his love.

Imogen shook herself back to the present. "Which bit of the legend do you mean to paint?"

Mr. Thorne's brush moved busily. "That's just it. There are too many possibilities."

Almost shyly, he said, "What I'd really like to do is a whole cycle of paintings, the whole story from beginning to end — but that would take too long, and the Royal Academy will only let me exhibit one. If they take that one, that is."

"If your one is successful, why not a cycle by and by?" The idea caught Imogen's imagination, fired it. She clasped her hands together in her lap, seeing the panoply of images playing across the wall, like the tapestries in a great lord's hall. "They used to tell stories so, picture by picture, why not now?"

Her enthusiasm caught him aback, made him choke on a hasty laugh. "One picture at a time, Mrs. Grantham!" But his eyes were bright, as if her excitement were mirrored in his own. "Rome wasn't painted in a day."

"Yes," said Imogen demurely. "First things first. Have you considered a banqueting scene?"

Mr. Thorne paused with his paintbrush in the air. "The lovers together with King Mark looking on?" He seemed genuinely intrigued by the idea.

"Or perhaps," Imogen offered, "the introduction of Iseult to the king, with Tristan standing by." That would certainly provide scope for emotion, cupidity on the part of the aging king at the sight of his beautiful young bride, Iseult's veiled reluctance, Tristan's unvoiced agony.

Mr. Thorne's eyes were unfocused, looking past her at a scene far away. "I could paint them on the ship, with the potion, in that first moment of falling in love. . . ."

"Or later," Imogen suggested, "when they flee the stronghold of King Mark. Can't you just picture it, his hand on his sword, her backward glance over her shoulder? No matter how she loved Tristan, she must have had some second thoughts. Or not second thoughts, precisely. Fears, more like."

Mr. Thorne nodded his assent. "It's no small thing to cuckold a king."

"Taking refuge in rhyme, Mr. Thorne?" Imogen raised her brows in gentle mockery. "My father's parish was not far from King Mark's keep at Tintagel. He took me there when I was little. On pilgrimage, one might say."

"I should like to see it someday," said Mr. Thorne. "Tintagel."

He spoke the name reverently, imbuing it with untold layers of majesty and magic, bringing it vividly to Imogen's memory, the ruined walls with the ivy creeping through the stones, the fallen arches in the Great

Hall where once banners had flared and knights exchanged bragging tales of their own daring.

Imogen smoothed her broad skirts. "It is all tumbled down now, but you can stand among the stones and imagine King Mark banqueting there and hear Tristan's harp among the wind in the trees."

Thorne leaned forward. "Is it true King Arthur sleeps below the rocks, waiting only for the right moment to wake and rise again?"

"I never stumbled across him." For honesty's sake, Imogen added, "Although not for want of trying."

"Perhaps," said Mr. Thorne, his eyes meeting hers over the top of the easel, "you simply were not looking in the right place."

In the silent room, the tapping of the trees against the windowpane, the hiss of the wind and the rain, seemed very loud, the room very small and isolated, wrapped in the peculiar gray-yellow glow of a rainy day. Even with the door open, the silence from the hall lent to the sense of seclusion. Imogen was suddenly very aware of being alone with Mr. Thorne, with nothing but an easel between them.

"Will you —" she began, just as he said, "If one were to —"

The clock on the mantel chimed shrilly, pinging six times. Imogen rose from her stool, shaking out her skirts, her limbs heavy and stiff. She had been sitting there for two hours. It had felt like ten minutes.

"Mr. Grantham will be home shortly," she found herself saying. "And supper . . ."

"Of course," said Mr. Thorne, setting aside his palette. But he disarmed her by adding, "You've left me with much to think on. I'll confess, I'm eager to return to my studio and sketch out some of your ideas."

"You will have to let me know how you get on," said Imogen, and was surprised by how much she meant it. She hadn't realized how starved she was for this, for the discussion of those familiar places and familiar stories.

Mr. Thorne began packing up his things quietly, efficiently. "I'll bring you the sketches and you can tell me if my Tintagel matches your memories."

"My memories are half myth," Imogen said apologetically. "It has been so long."

Mr. Thorne's lips crinkled. "So are the stories. It's only in setting them down on canvas that we make them seem real."

Imogen raised her brows, unable to resist saying, "I thought you only painted what you believed to be true? The daffodil as daf-

226

fodil, as it was? Or the water rat as water rat?"

Mr. Thorne paused in the act of slinging his satchel over his shoulder. He looked at her with unfeigned admiration, and Imogen felt herself expanding under his regard.

"Perhaps," he said slowly, "it's the truth of the emotion that lies underneath the myth that we seek to capture, whatever may have actually occurred. But," he added with a crooked smile, "I should prefer to believe that Tristan was Tristan and Iseult Iseult."

"And that the king sleeps under the mountain," agreed Imogen. She preceded Mr. Thorne through the door, stepping aside to let him make his own way through the hall.

Outside, the rain had lightened to a mist and the first hints of light were beginning to peek through the crowds.

"Until next week," said Mr. Thorne.

"Yes, next week," said Imogen vaguely, and realized, with surprise, that she was looking forward to it.

ELEVEN

London, 2009

Nicholas Dorrington's shop wasn't entirely what Julia had anticipated.

From the reverent way Natalie had uttered the word "gallery," Julia had been expecting something more like the galleries she knew from New York, glass doors and white walls and track lighting, like a hospital waiting room crossed with a futuristic minimalist aesthetic out of a low-budget seventies movie.

Instead, the building to which he'd directed her was a two-story redbrick building that looked like it might have been a carriage house in another life, sandwiched between a garage and a rummage shop. Rather than immaculate sheets of plate glass, the windows were made of thick, old glass that gave a distorted, murky appearance to the items within. Both bow windows were filled with a jumble of china lamps with molting, feathered shades, cracked satin slippers, and low stools with tufted, embroidered cushions.

Julia tried peering through the jumble, but it was no use; the interior of the shop was tantalizingly out of sight, blocked by merchandise and blurred by the old glass.

It was kind of clever, in its own way. No window-shopping here; anyone who was the least bit intrigued would inevitably find their way into the shop.

Julia straightened the belt on her pale blue cotton shirtwaist dress, last summer's favorite dress, purchased in the anticipation of the sort of alfresco brunches and drinks on roof decks that everyone always talked about but that never seemed to happen. Not, of course, that she'd dressed up for Nicholas Dorrington. But this was her first time back in London since arriving at Herne Hill. She had felt it deserved a bit of fanfare, or at least something other than ratty shorts and a tank top.

She'd forgotten there was a reason she never wore this dress. After her excursion on the train and the Tube, there were permanent wrinkles in the skirt and a distinct feeling of damp under the arms.

Keeping her arms close to her sides, Julia tentatively pushed open the heavy wooden

229

door. A bell jangled above her head.

"Hello?" she called. The shop appeared to be empty, aside from the faint sound of Baroque music, harpsichord and horns.

With the smell of must and old leather in the air, she felt as though she'd stumbled back a hundred years or more, into Dickens's old curiosity shop, or a Harry Potter–esque slip in time. The jumbled look was deceptive; whoever had organized the place had done so in a series of set scenes, little domestic groupings. There was a Victorian parlor, neatly re-created, with rose-spattered china set out on a heavily carved walnut table drawn up by a matching red velvet upholstered settee; a Jacobean dining room, with a fantastically carved sideboard and cane-backed chairs; and a Georgian library, complete with globe and a bookcase with a delicately carved top.

All of the objects were rich and rare and in the best condition, the gilded frames of mirrors reflecting the light, rosewood and mahogany glistening with lemon oil, but, despite it all, the place felt oddly cozy. Homey.

If one's home were in a *Doctor Who* episode jumping through time periods.

A door opened in the back of the store, bringing with it both a Handel fanfare and a rumpled-looked Nicholas.

He raised a hand in greeting. "Julia. Thanks for making the trip. Sorry to drag you out here."

He wore a blue Oxford cloth shirt, with the sleeves rolled up past his forearms, and a pair of wire-rimmed glasses. It was amazing how different a pair of glasses could make a person look. He seemed more boyish, somehow. More approachable. Although that might also be the rolled-up sleeves and the ink stain on his wrist.

"Nicholas." Julia resisted the urge to tug on her skirt. "It's no problem. I was curious to see your shop. I mean, gallery."

"It's a shop," he said with a grin that brought out an elusive dent in his left cheek that might have been a dimple. He shoved his sleeves up his arms. "And it's 'Nick.' Only my grandmother calls me Nicholas."

And Natalie. Julia decided to let that slide.

"Nick," she said. She let her eyes wander around the shop, not bothering to hide her admiration. "This place is great," she said honestly. She gestured to the Georgian library. "I feel like George the Third is about to step in for a cup of tea."

Nick raised his brows. "You have a good eye," he said. He gave the globe an affectionate pat. "This is all late eighteenth century."

"I spent a lot of time in museums growing up," said Julia offhandedly.

With her father working crazy hours, there hadn't been much lure to coming home to an empty apartment, so she'd used his membership card to spend hours in the Met, checking her heavy backpack in the Great Hall and wandering unencumbered through the familiar marble halls. The galleries of European paintings, straight up the main stairs, had been her favorite places, but the period rooms, with their wealth of eighteenth-century furniture, had also been regular haunts.

Sometimes she would imagine herself taking up residence in one of those rooms, like the runaway children in *From the Mixed-up Files of Mrs. Basil E. Frankweiler.* Not that she would have, of course. Both the museum administrators and her father would have taken a dim view of that.

"No surprise, then, that you pegged that painting straight off," said Nick.

"Well, it was pretty obviously not a Rubens," said Julia, deadpan.

A pained expression crossed Nick's face. He pressed his eyes briefly shut. "Look, I owe you an apology. I was being a bit of a shit on Saturday. I shouldn't have taken it out on you."

Taken what out? He didn't seem inclined to go on, so Julia said neutrally, "If it makes matters better, I wasn't exactly being a queen of graciousness, either."

Nick held out a hand. "Truce?"

His clasp was warm and firm. He wore a battered gold ring on one finger. Not a wedding ring, a signet, the crest worn to almost nothingness.

"Truce," Julia agreed, and tried to smother a slight sense of unease. If Nicholas Dorrington, arrogant and annoying, was attractive, this new, friendly version was deadly.

Not that it mattered. Their relationship was purely professional. Julia shook his hand more briskly than necessary, just because.

Ushering her farther into the shop, he said, "If it helps to make amends, I have a date for you on your painting, or at least an approximation of one." When Julia looked at him expectantly, he went on, "It was painted no earlier than 1848 and no later than 1850."

Julia cocked her head. "No earlier than 1848 because that's when the brotherhood was founded and no later than 1850 because that's when they stopped using the initials?"

Nick's face relaxed into a grin. "You've

been doing your research."

"Wouldn't you?" Researching painters sure beat tracking down financial reports. She'd forgotten how much she missed this sort of thing. "What did your friend have to say? The art historian?"

"She has a name for you." Slipping past Julia, Nick turned the store sign from Open to Closed and flicked the latch on the door. "Gavin Thorne."

It wasn't as though she'd really been hoping for a lost Millais. . . . But Julia couldn't help feeling a little disappointed all the same. Gavin Thorne?

"I've never heard of him," she admitted.

The corners of Nick's lips quirked. "If it helps, I hadn't, either. He was one of the original group, along with a few other blokes who didn't make the *Dictionary of National Biography.* Only three of them stuck it out."

"Rossetti, Hunt, and Millais," Julia supplied for him. Oh, well. It really would have been too much to expect her painting to be by one of them. But there was something about it, something so vivid and compelling. It was hard to believe that whoever had painted it hadn't attained any kind of professional renown. "On the phone, you mentioned something about illustrations?"

Nick was all business. "I can't tell you much about Thorne — there doesn't appear to be much out there — but I did get hold of copies of his extant oeuvre. He's definitely our man." Nick gestured towards the half-open door at the back of the shop. "The pictures are in the office. Care to take a look?"

That was a silly question.

Good manners forced her to say, "If you have time . . ."

"My plans are the opposite of pressing." When Julia looked at him quizzically, he clarified, "Takeaway and televised snooker."

There really was something about that smile . . . Julia told herself to get a grip.

"I don't know," she said, following him as he led the way into the office. "I'm not sure I can cope with the guilt of tearing you away from snooker."

Nick raised a brow. "I'm sure you'll find a way to live with yourself."

His office wasn't the bland, modern variety but a cozy den, with a sofa upholstered in tattered chintz and a scarred old desk that Julia guessed was probably early twentieth century. The walls were crammed with books, a haphazard collection of reference books, binders, glossy coffee-table books of antiques, and a healthy selection of popular history and biography. A globe stood in one corner of the room, by a battered metal file cabinet.

Nick flipped open the lid, revealing a series of bottle tops. "Drink?"

"How could I say no to that?" There was something rather endearing in his obvious pleasure in his toy, like a little boy with a new battery-powered car. "Very cool bar."

"It's a repro, but it means I don't have to feel guilty if I slosh scotch on it." Nick held up two bottles. "Scotch or wine?"

"I'll take the scotch." She'd learned in business school that she had a tolerance disproportionate to her size. There were few things more entertaining than drinking large men under the table.

"A wise choice." Nick grabbed two mismatched glasses from a shelf that also held a collection of mugs, a coffeemaker, and a scattering of old sugar packets. "That wine was left over from our last open house. It wasn't particularly good then and it's probably even worse now."

"Thanks." Julia took the glass from him. Scotch. Straight up. He didn't offer water or ice.

"Cheers," he said briskly. He clinked his glass briefly against hers, then reached out to pull over an oversized folder that was sitting on top of the debris on his desk. "Behold. The collected oeuvre of Gavin Thorne."

Nick's hands dealt out colored prints like playing cards, fanning them across the desk, one after the other.

"*Ulysses . . . Locksley Hall . . . Mariana in the Moated Grange . . . Lancelot Denied the Grail . . .*" Nick stepped back, gesturing Julia forward. As she leaned over the printouts, he added briskly, "All in chronological order. *Ulysses* is currently at the British art center in New Haven, *Locksley Hall* is at the Delaware Art Museum, *Mariana* is at the Tate, and *Lancelot* is in the hands of a private collector."

Women in clinging gowns, men in knightly garb, rich colors, elaborate details. They all looked pretty Pre-Raphaelite to her.

Ulysses was the only one that struck a note of "one of these things is not like the others." The faux Grecian garb looked awkward on the model, and the details of the background scene, presumably a Greek island, based on the amount of sand and what Julia supposed were olive trees, were less well realized than in the later paintings, where the painter had fallen into his stride with a medieval landscape that seemed to come much more naturally to him.

In all of them, however, there was a general overarching air of loss: Ulysses staring off to sea while his shipmates partied around him, the soldier turning away from the gates of his old home, Mariana at her window, Lancelot veiling his eyes as the Grail was borne away from him.

"All of Thorne's mature works represent themes of isolation and loneliness," proclaimed Nick importantly. Dropping the *Masterpiece Theatre* voice, he added, "I quote from the Art Institute exhibition catalog where these were last displayed. You can read into them what you will."

Julia hadn't read that into her painting, her *Tristan and Iseult*. Loneliness? No. Quite the opposite. In that one, the lovers were bound together — emotionally, by the intensity of their gaze, and physically, by their twined hands around the base of the cup.

Speaking of that cup . . . Juliana pointed at the printout of *Mariana,* at the table by the window. "That's the same cup from my painting."

She could feel Nick's breath on her hair as he leaned over her shoulder to see. "They often reused props. The early Pre-Raphaelites were especially keen on only painting from actual examples. That narrowed the field a bit for them."

"More Art Institute exhibition catalog?" said Julia, glancing up at him.

"No, Wikipedia," he said, straight-faced.

"Uh-huh. Sure." Julia turned back to the pictures fanned out across his desk. "What about Thorne's other paintings?" Nick had only shown her the four that had been gathered for that one exhibition. "Where are the rest of them?"

It took Nick a moment to answer, and when he did she could hear the change in his tone. "These are the rest of them. There are only four works extant, all four dating between 1848 and 1850."

When Julia looked up at him in surprise, he added, "By the spring of 1850, Gavin Thorne had disappeared never to be heard of again."

Herne Hill, 1849

"We missed you last week."

When Gavin arrived at the summerhouse, Imogen Grantham was already there, as she always was, a book in her hand and a plate of tea cakes next to her. The day was a warm one and the rosewater icing on the cakes was already beginning to melt, but Gavin felt his spirits lift all the same, as they did whenever he saw her.

239

No matter how long and dusty the road, in the garden there were cakes and the scent of flowers. And Imogen.

Imogen. Aloud he still called her Mrs. Grantham, as she called him Mr. Thorne, maintaining all the formal niceties, but in his head she was Imogen, as he had heard Miss Cooper call her. There could be no impropriety in it, so long as he never took the liberty of addressing her so. It was just a way of fixing his mind on her personality for the portrait, that was all. The name suited her. "Mrs. Grantham" sat upon her like an ill-fitting suit of clothes.

As spring warmed to summer, they had fallen into a regular pattern in their sittings. Every Monday, Gavin would make his way to Herne Hill, where Imogen would be waiting in the summerhouse, with a plate of cakes ostensibly for her but really for Gavin. She had discovered, somewhere in the first month of their acquaintance, that Gavin had a taste for sweets, and first currant cakes and then jam-filled sponge had appeared with increasingly regularity on a china plate on the bench beside her.

It had been nearly two months now. Two months of Mondays, and tea cakes, and conversation, two months of the heady scent of flowers and the gentle drone of the bees in the rosebushes. There was a leisurely, enchanted quality to these Mondays, as though they might go on forever, just the same.

But, of course, they wouldn't. Summer wouldn't last forever, and neither would this commission. The portrait had been coming along well. Too well. Gavin had wrestled with her face and her expression — longer, perhaps, than he ought, ascribing his diligence to professional pride. Grantham was paying him a pretty penny, after all. But the hardest part was long since done and only the journeyman work remained. The leaves on the trees behind her, the planks beneath her feet. Much of which could, realistically be completed back in his studio.

He should tell Mr. Grantham so. But he hadn't.

It was mid-July already. Within a week, two at most, the portrait would be done. The thought of it filled him with something approaching physical pain.

"Yes, last week," Gavin said, and busied himself unpacking his paints and his palette. "Mr. Grantham received my note?"

"Yes, he did, and he quite understood." Imogen tilted her head, her expression quizzical. "The garden felt very empty without you. I had to eat all the tea cakes myself."

241

More likely, she fed them to the birds. He had a sudden image of her, leaning over the railing, scattering crumbs to the birds gathered around her, graceful and solitary.

Gruffly Gavin said, "I'd other work to get through, and the press of time —" True enough, as far as it went, but not the whole truth.

He'd stayed away to see if he could, like a prospective martyr holding a finger over a flame to steel himself to bear the full force of the fire.

"Other portraits?" Imogen grimaced comically, but there was a hint of wistfulness beneath it. No matter how easy they were with each other, no matter how many Mondays they spent together, there was always a bit of herself she held in reserve. "Have I set a new pattern for you?"

"No other portraits. Augustus is the portrait painter, not I." Gavin debated telling her the truth. It wasn't something widely known, and certainly not something that would do him any good on his goal to eventually become an Academician someday. "I draw pictures for the penny dreadfuls. Story pictures."

Imogen's face brightened with interest. "I've never read one, although I've seen Anna with them." She leaned forward, sending the pattern of light and shades playing along the folds of her skirt shifting. "Do you mind it? The time away from your painting?"

Gavin mixed his colors together, shades of gray for the weathered boards beneath her feet. "When I've an idea making my fingers itch and not enough time to paint it? Then I mind it. But the penny dreadfuls pay for the paint and canvas. Besides that . . . It's a challenge, getting so much emotion into such a little space, and doing it without color. Everything has to be in the force of the lines."

Imogen nodded, considering. "It's a bit like the idea of a story cycle in paintings, but writ smaller."

"And cruder," said Gavin ruefully. The last one he had done had involved a high-wayman who met a particularly gory end.

Imogen waved a hand in dismissal. "Let us call it 'bolder.' Is it a great deal of work?"

It was more time-consuming than he would have liked it to be, but it paid. They all had their ways of making ends meet. And it was good to know that he could make his living purely by his brush. His father had mocked and cuffed him, but here he was, *Mr.* Thorne, with his own studio and his name listed in the Royal Academy exhibition catalog for all to see. For that he would have done far more and far worse. "I don't mind being busy. I'd mind more not."

"Yes," Imogen said, and he saw sadness pass across her face like the shadow of the leaves on the summerhouse floor. "I never understood why boredom was a disease until I found myself afflicted with it. It's pure self-indulgence, of course. I keep reminding myself that it's a privilege to have the luxury to be bored."

"What would you do if you could do it?" Gavin studiously kept his eyes on his painting, giving her space to answer, if she would. She spoke without reserve of books and ideas, her face lighting with interest, but personal questions tended to drive her back behind her shell.

Not that he ought to blame her. He shied from questions about his own life as much as she did hers.

Imogen scuffed the toe of her leather shoe against a scratch on the floorboard. "Surround myself with dusty manuscripts and write dry books about the Middle Ages, I imagine." With a shrug and a smile she changed the subject. "While you were away, your friend came to call."

"Rossetti?" He would have thought Gabriel too much occupied with scribbling nonsense for his new magazine, *The Germ,* meant to be the mouthpiece of their movement but, really, just an excuse for Gabriel to avoid getting on with his Annunciation.

"No, the other one," said Imogen. Her voice made eminently clear what she thought of him. "Mr. Fotheringay-Vaughn."

"He's not my friend," said Gavin brusquely. "We share a studio, that's all."

Augustus was seldom there. Unlike Gavin, who lived in the apartment attached to the studio, Augustus had lodgings elsewhere, paid for, Gavin suspected, by one of the many ladies of a certain age whom Augustus flattered in paint and squired so assiduously about town.

From long ago, in the frost and cold, he could hear Augustus's voice, saying, musingly, *A prime piece.*

He'd hoped Augustus had forgotten about Evangeline Grantham, had found some greater heiress to pursue. Apparently, he had been wrong.

"I thought as much," said Imogen matter-of-factly. "He claimed he came to see the Book of Hours, and then spent a full hour making eyes at Miss Grantham."

Damnation. And damn Augustus, too. He'd known Gavin wouldn't be at Herne Hill, would have his head down over his illustrations, more than enough time to work some mischief.

Gavin only hoped that was all Augustus had been doing.

Should he warn Imogen, tell her what Augustus really was? Not that Gavin knew for sure. It was all just suppositions, mere gossip and guesswork. He didn't know what to say, so he merely said brusquely, "She should be careful of him."

And you should be careful of me.

The words stuck, unsaid, in his throat. Ridiculous, too. Why should she be careful of him? She had no thought of him except as her portraitist. And, perhaps, if he was very fortunate, as a friend. Every confidence, every bit of herself she shared, no matter how small, felt like a minor triumph. He wanted to unravel the layers of her mystery, to get to the very heart of her — not for the portrait, but for himself.

And that, he realized, was a very dangerous idea.

"I'd gathered that. I've sense enough to know a rotten apple when I see one," said Imogen wryly, and it took Gavin a moment to remember that she was talking about Augustus. "What I don't know is how to be rid of him." Her voice caught. "He's stuffed Evie's head full with his grand friends and his aristocratic connections."

Aristocratic connections all of Augustus's own devising. Gavin almost spoke the words, but old habit kept him silent.

Imogen went on, her hands gesturing expressively. "You should have heard him at tea last week! It was all heavy hints about the title that would have been his but for cruel, cruel fate. He's half-convinced Evie that he's the lost heir of a Gothic drama." She tried to make a joke of it, but the worried lines between her brows betrayed her true emotions. "Jane would say it was my fault for letting her read novels. Miss Cooper, I mean."

Her hands knotted tightly together in her lap, the knuckles showing white against the stuff of her dress. Gavin remembered Imogen, watching Miss Grantham, the night of the dinner party, stepping between Miss Grantham and Augustus, protecting her as best she could.

What right did Augustus have to Gavin's loyalties?

Abruptly Gavin said, "It's not true. None of it. His aristocratic connections, that is." Some residual sense of fairness prompted Gavin to add, "The popularity of his portraits is real enough. He's a dab hand at bringing out the best in his subjects. He'll go far, they all say."

If he didn't find himself at the receiving end of a rightfully indignant husband's bullet first.

"So he's not the unacknowledged son of Lord Vaughn, then?" Imogen picked up a tea cake but didn't bite into it. Butter-rich crumbs flaked beneath her fingers, sifting along the folds of her skirt.

"Oddly enough, no," said Gavin. "That's not even his right name. He added it in the hopes of drawing more custom."

It had worked, too. Gavin didn't quite understand it, but it had. It bothered Gavin, deep in his bones. A man should stand on his own merits, on the merits of his work, not on trickery and lies.

"I had thought as much," said Imogen quietly. She set the cake aside, her face averted, her teeth worrying at her lower lip. "Even Jane was half taken in by his story."

"And Miss Grantham's father?" Gavin couldn't bring himself to say *your husband.*

Imogen shook her head, her face abstracted. "He has no idea of it. He is . . . not often at home." She looked directly at Gavin, her eyes dark and clear. *All that's best of dark and bright . . . .* The words flitted nonsensically through Gavin's mind. "The last thing I want is to see Evie fall prey to a fortune hunter." Imogen looked away, her fingers threaded tightly together in her lap. "She is so very young."

There was a wealth of love and fear packed into that simple phrase. Gavin didn't see that Miss Grantham deserved it — she struck him as a flighty, shallow thing, ripe for the Augustuses of the world — but Imogen loved her, and that was all.

What would it be like to have Imogen speak of him as she did of Miss Grantham, with that sort of depth of emotion, all the stronger for being so carefully concealed?

"If I tell you this," he said slowly, "it goes no further."

Imogen's back straightened. "I have no truck with gossip. At least, not about people who haven't been dead for several hundred years."

There was a forlorn gallantry about her words that tore at the last of Gavin's resolve.

In brief, terse sentences, Gavin said, "Augustus's real name is Alfred Potts. His father was a dustman. His mother is — or was — a governess before she married, which is how Augustus, Alfie, got his education. He claims she was some connection to the Vaughns, a poor cousin or the like."

Sometimes Gavin thought that the reason Augustus was so convincing in his adopted role was that he had half-persuaded himself of his own story, that he wasn't the dust-man's son at all but a changeling, the child of his mother and the Earl of Vaughn, with secret marriage lines hidden away like a lost prince in a story.

"I see," said Imogen thoughtfully.

Gavin looked at her, in her expensive brushed silk, in the quiet of her garden, and said quickly, "Not that there's any shame in that. It's the lying that's the shame, not his parents, whoever they might be." A bitter laugh rose in his throat, harsh and ugly. "I've certainly no right to throw stones. My own people make Alfie's look right grand."

A dustman would have looked down his nose at them, and rightly. There hadn't been dustmen in their part of Manchester. The refuse had collected in the streets, pounded into the dirt, seeping through the stones of the basements where men lived like rats.

Imogen took her time in speaking. "At the dinner that night," she said carefully, "you said you grew up in Manchester?"

Gavin could feel his hands tense on his brush. He couldn't make himself meet her eyes. "Yes."

"And yet you made your way to the Academy." Something in her voice made Gavin look up. There was no condemnation in her face, but softness and a kind of wonder. She sat in shade, but her face seemed to glow like a hundred candles. "You made your way to the Academy by nothing but your own talent and determination."

Talent and determination and coins filched from the pockets of his betters. He'd never meant to, never wanted to, but hunger drove one to strange things. He'd lived on the streets those early days in London, swiping apples from carts, pouncing on dropped coins.

Her admiration shamed him.

"I've lived in ways you can't begin to imagine," Gavin said hoarsely.

"Everything you have you won for yourself." Her voice vibrated with quiet passion. Her hands balled into fists in her lap, she leaned forward, setting her pearl earbobs swinging. "Do you realize how rare that is? I would be proud, *proud,* to have done what you have done."

He didn't know how to make her understand just how low he had been, just how loathsome. "To have scrounged and scrabbled and — and scavenged?"

"No," Imogen said. Her eyes caught and held his. "To have a talent such as you have and the will to use it."

There was magic in her eyes. He couldn't

251

look away. In them, as in a scryer's bowl, he saw himself not as he had been but as he might be, as she believed him to be. It was heady and exhilarating and utterly terrifying.

"Whatever you were, it is nothing to what you are now." Her lips moved, uttering words that Gavin only half-heard. He was caught by the shape, the color, the texture, of them, the way she tipped back her head as she spoke, the vibration of the delicate blue-veined skin of her neck. "That is the difference between you and Augustus Fotheringay-Vaughn. He seeks to take the easy road, by trickery and lies, trading on a past that never was — whereas you, you are all that is honest and honorable."

Gavin was seized by a sudden mad desire to press his lips against the hollow of her throat, just there, where her words still reverberated. He wanted to sink his fingers into the shining dark mass of her hair and shake it free of its pins until it tumbled like silk around his hands, to draw her close and stop her mouth with his, kissing and kissing her until the world swirled in dizzy circles around them and the chirping of the birds blurred to nothing beside the frantic beating of their hearts.

The force of it staggered him, leaving him

stunned and gasping, so barely in control of himself that his hand trembled on his brush and his body burned with unimaginable desires.

Honest? Honorable? He shamed both her and himself.

"Forgive me," he said, stepping back so abruptly that he almost overset the easel.

The urge for flight overwhelmed all else, trampling on common courtesy and common sense. He couldn't stay. If he stayed . . .

That wasn't to be thought of. She was his patron's wife. His friend.

Gavin clutched at words, words that eluded him, syllables disintegrating on his tongue, chasing away from his disordered senses. "I — An appointment — I had misremembered — I must go back to town. At once."

Imogen stood up abruptly, her skirts belling around her legs. "Mr. Thorne? Are you quite all right?"

The concern in her eyes nearly undid him. Oh, God, to be able to come by that honestly, to be able to put his head in her lap and feel her fingers in his hair, her lips against his brow.

"Quite," he managed, clumsily piling his supplies back into his satchel. He had never felt more wrong, hot and cold as though in

253

the grip of a fever, wracked with guilt and longing. "Forgive me." And then, again, helplessly, "Forgive me."

And then he strode away across the garden at a pace that felt suspiciously like flight.

TWELVE

London, 2009

Disappeared? He had to be pulling her leg.

"You're making that up," said Julia. She picked up her scotch from its perch on top of a Sotheby's catalog. "Aren't you?"

Nick shook his head. "A bit of exaggeration for effect, perhaps, but in substance it's all quite factually true. Thorne dropped off the map. Quite literally. There's no word of Gavin Thorne after the summer of 1850. According to Anna, it was strange enough that a bunch of his mates in the PRB found fit to mention it in their letters." He considered for a moment. "Not that it bothered them for long."

Maybe it was that loaded word, "disappeared." It conjured up images of dark fates and foul play.

Julia sat down slowly on the old chintz sofa. The hollowed-out upholstery sagged

255

beneath her. "What happened to him?" she asked.

Nick looked down at her, his eyes crinkling around the corners. "You look like a little girl waiting for a bedtime story." When she scowled at him, he said, "It's thought he might have immigrated to New South Wales. That *is* on his Wikipedia page," he added blandly.

There was an exposed spring digging into Julia's hip. She shifted to one side. "Thought? They don't know?"

Nick perched on the edge of his desk. The office was small enough that his knees practically brushed hers. "It wasn't like now. You didn't have Facebook tracking your every movement. People fell off the grid, disappeared. Rather refreshing, that, when you think about it. Move someplace new, assume a new identity . . . and, voilà! New life."

"Yes, but why leave if you're just in the middle of building a career? The Pre-Raphs would have been just taking off in 1850. Why go off to — to —"

"New South Wales," Nick provided. "Sheep farming. It wasn't a smooth, upward trajectory. They all had some tough times in those early years. Thomas Woolner ran off to Australia to join the gold rush. Another one of the original seven gave up and joined the priesthood. Rossetti almost abandoned painting to write poetry full-time. It's entirely plausible that our man Thorne threw his brush in and decided to try something more immediately lucrative. Although . . ."

"Although?"

Nick absently pushed an art book out of the way and settled himself more firmly on the desk. "One of the few facts I did find was that Thorne sold his *Mariana* for one hundred and fifty guineas. Not pounds, guineas." Julia wasn't sure what the difference was, but from Nick's tone she gathered that meant something bigger and better. "That was big money in those days. Not retire to Tahiti type money, but enough to keep a fledgling artist going for quite some time."

"Maybe he took the money and cashed it out for a sheep farm in New South Wales?" Even to herself, Julia didn't sound convinced.

"Or diamond mines in South Africa? There were a thousand ways for men to lose money back then and all sorts of corners in the earth in which to lose themselves."

Julia looked down at her scotch. "This is going to sound silly, but it seems like a shame. To have talent like that and then just throw it away."

Out of nowhere, she thought of the grad applications she had never sent in, the ones for the PhD programs in art history. Her advisor had been so disappointed when she had told him she was taking the McKinsey job instead; he'd told her if she changed her mind he'd be there to make calls for her.

But that was silly. It wasn't at all the same thing as Gavin Thorne throwing in the brush to raise sheep. His was a true, creative gift. Her talent, such as it was, had been analytic rather than creative. Did the world really lose out by having one fewer art historian?

The world might not have lost out, but she was beginning to wonder if she had.

Shaking her thoughts back to the present, Julia gestured towards the pictures on which Nick was half-sitting. "Even from those, you can just see this Thorne getting better and better. Can you imagine what he might have produced if he had stuck it out?"

"Or he might have burned out," said Nick. The words were cynical, but his tone was sympathetic. "Burned out or sold out. He might have hit a big success and just gone on painting more and more mawkish variants of the same. The Pre-Raphaelites started out as a revolutionary movement, but most of them ended up as establishment and found they enjoyed it."

"True." The scotch burned the back of Julia's throat. She remembered those pictures of bearded patriarchs she had seen on the Internet, prosperous Victorian bourgeois with gold watch chains straining across their chests, so different from the sketch she had seen of Rossetti in his youth, hollow cheeked and passionate, long curls tumbling around his shoulders. "Still. Better to age than not. Are there any pictures of Thorne?"

If Nick noticed the abrupt change of topic, he didn't comment on it. "There might be. They all seemed to spend half their time sketching themselves and each other. I can ask Emma. She might know." He set down his glass next to him, precariously balanced on a pile of invoices. "There doesn't seem to be much on Thorne at all. Biographically, I mean. According to my sources, it's because his career was so short. With only four paintings, he didn't generate enough of an oeuvre for anyone to expend serious time studying him."

Only four paintings. "Five now," said Julia. The mind boggled. "Assuming we can verify it."

"I wouldn't be surprised." Nick's eyes met

259

hers, a brilliant blue-green behind his glasses. "You do realize what this means. If it is genuine, that painting marks a whole different direction for Thorne. Everything anyone thought they knew about this man is going to have to be reevaluated. It's not exactly headline of *The Times* stuff, but a number of learned academics are going to have their knickers in a twist."

"If it is genuine," said Julia. Deep in her heart of hearts, she had no doubt it was. The only question was proving it. In a weak attempt at humor she said, "I think I need more scotch."

She was joking, but Nick topped up her glass anyway. "It will help if you can find anything to trace the provenance," he said, sliding the bottle back into its slot in the globe. "Any contemporary reference — or any reason it might have turned up in your house."

Julia tapped her fingernails against the side of her glass. "There might be a connection. . . . There's a portrait in the drawing room of the house that looks just like the woman who's posing as Iseult in the painting. I'm pretty sure they're the same person."

"Not to sound too skeptical" — Nick readjusted his glass — "but what would an artist's model be doing hanging in the drawing room?"

Julia took another swig of her scotch. "My theory is that she was an artist's model first and then married into respectability later. That would explain why she made it into the drawing room."

A wry expression crossed Nick's face. "That sort of thing has been known to happen a time or two. But why stow the painting away in a wardrobe?"

Julia curled her legs up beneath her. "Maybe her husband wanted to suppress evidence of her former career? That would explain why we found it hidden away."

She could see Nick trying to find fault with her theory. "It's an idea," he said cautiously.

With repeated application of scotch her idea was looking better and better to her. "Admit it," she said. "It's a great idea."

Nick swallowed a grin. "I'll give you 'plausible.' Do you have any idea who the woman in the portrait is?"

Julia shook her head. "An ancestress, presumably. My father thinks I should talk to my cousin Caroline — Natalie's mother."

Nick grimaced. "Better you than me." Remembering himself, he frowned at his scotch. "You didn't hear me say that. It was the scotch talking."

Julia bit her lip on a grin. "What else does the scotch have to say?"

Nick regarded the amber liquid in his glass. "Not much more or I won't be able to drive home. Can I offer you a lift?"

It took Julia a moment to realize it was a dismissal. She glanced quickly at her watch. Oh, hell. How it had been over two hours? No wonder Nick was trying to get rid of her. It was a Monday night. The poor guy was probably dying to get home. Not to mention starving.

Hastily she set down her empty glass and began to struggle her way out of the sagging old sofa. "That's really sweet of you, but I'll be fine on the train."

No one had warned her that the couch was a Venus flytrap. Sagging down in the middle, it resisted her puny efforts to free herself.

"Need a hand?" Grasping her hand, Nick hauled her effortlessly to her feet. Julia landed on her feet with a little bounce. Instead of letting go, he said, "Are you sure about that lift? It sounds like it's pouring out. And it's really no bother."

For the first time, Julia realized that there was rain drumming against the tiny window behind the desk. It was hard to see much through it, narrow and barred, but what she could see looked far too gray for seven o'clock on a summer night.

Julia looked down at her impractical linen dress, her open-toed sandals.

"If you're sure it's really no trouble . . ."

"I wouldn't have offered if it were." Nick dropped her hand and began shuffling papers into place, loading a silver laptop and assorted folders into a worn brown leather computer bag. "I'm parked just down the block. You don't have an umbrella, have you?"

An umbrella? In England? That would have been way too sensible. "I'm afraid not."

Nick hauled his bag up on his shoulder. "Neither do I." There was an Indiana Jones–esque glint in his eye. "We're just going to have to run for it."

As it turned out, running didn't do much good. The rain was coming down in sheets. Julia was soaked before Nick had pulled down the grille of the shop, her dress plastered to her body and her hair hanging in long, lank strands around her face.

"Just a little mizzle," said Nick cheerfully, beeping the car doors open.

Julia stuck her tongue out at him and slid into the passenger seat. "Sorry for dripping all over your upholstery," she said as he climbed in on the other side.

"Stop apologizing." Reaching out, he switched on the CD player. Not Handel this time, but vintage Depeche Mode. It seemed to suit the rain running in rivers down the window. Rubbing his glasses against the hem of his shirt, he glanced at Julia, his lips twitching in part amusement, part sympathy. "Do you need the heater?"

Great. She must really look like a drowned rat. Unfairly, the rain had only darkened his fair hair to the color of the scotch they had been drinking and flattened his shirt against a chest that bore out either some sort of sport or a good gym membership. Did hauling antiques around count as weight lifting?

"I'm fine," said Julia hastily. She lifted her hands, twisting her hair to try to get some of the wet out. It had the unfortunate effect of relocating the trickle of cold water right down her back. It had also, she realized, following Nick's appreciative gaze, placed various aspects of her anatomy in a rather suggestive position. Julia hastily dropped her hands. "All that booze is keeping me warm."

"There was a reason the Scots invented the stuff," said Nick agreeably. The car swung smoothly around a corner, through a maze of tiny streets. "Better than central heating."

"I wouldn't go that far," said Julia. She turned in her seat. While she had a captive antiques expert on hand . . .

A captive cute antiques dealer. Not that that was the least bit relevant. He was property of Natalie. Or at least Natalie thought he was.

She really shouldn't have had that third glass of scotch.

"So." Julia swiped wet hair out of her eyes. "About the painting. I gather establishing provenance is the next step?"

"That would be the major hurdle," said Nick. "The ideal would be a receipt for the painting, preferably with Thorne's signature on it."

"Possible," said Julia. "Unlikely, but possible. I don't think my ancestors ever threw anything away." And she had the trash bags to prove it.

Nick's eyes were on the road, providing Julia with a view of his profile. "If you like," he offered, "I can do some digging around on my end, find out if there's any mention of the painting in other sources, if it was ever exhibited."

"Really?' That was unexpectedly generous of him. "Are you sure? That would be great."

His eyes flicked briefly in her direction. "How often does one get a chance to rearrange the artistic canon?"

"In your profession?" said Julia. "Probably not infrequently."

"It's rarer than you'd think," said Nick. "Whatever the *Daily Mail* may claim, there are a limited number of old masters tucked away in attics — and half of those are fakes." He dodged neatly around a homicidal cab. "If you tackle your cousin Caroline about the possible family connection, I'll follow up on Thorne on my end."

Julia smoothed her wet skirt over her knees. "It's a deal — although why do I feel like I just got the short end of the stick? Hey. Stop smirking."

Nick held up one hand. "I didn't say anything."

Julia burrowed back into her seat. "Anyway, I like my theory about the mystery model. If you look at the portrait in the drawing room, there's something incredibly tragic about it." Julia struggled for the right words. "Yearning. As if she's trapped and doesn't know how to get out."

She caught Nick's eye in the rearview mirror. He raised a brow at her.

"What? This is what my art history professors used to call reading a painting." Julia wafted a hand. "You'll have to take my word on it."

"Do I have to take your word on it," said Nick drily, pulling up by the sidewalk in front of Aunt Regina's gate, "or do I get to see the actual portrait?"

Julia hadn't realized they were already there. The neighborhood looked disorientingly different from the inside of a car, with the rain dripping down the windows around them.

It also hadn't occurred to her that Nick might want to come in.

Julia turned in her seat. "What about your snooker and takeout?" she asked. The scotch had hold of her tongue. At least, she preferred to blame it on that. "Or did you just offer me a ride home so you can come in and see my paintings?"

She could see the glint of amusement in Nick's eyes. In the background, the engine idled. "Is that what they're calling it these days?"

His voice was velvety and smooth, with just a hint of suppressed humor. It sent ridiculous little tingles down Julia's spine.

Julia did her best to keep her tone light. "There's nothing wrong with a little art appreciation."

"As much as I'd like to see your paintings" — from his voice it was impossible to tell whether he was serious or not — "I have

267

an early meeting tomorrow morning."

Well, that showed her.

"Anyway, thanks for the drive," Julia said quickly, reaching for the door handle. Just a little harmless flirting, that was all. What was it her guy friends at the office used to say? *No harm, no foul.* She flashed a quick, meaningless smile over her shoulder as she pushed the door open. "Enjoy your snooker."

"Wait." Nick's voice stopped her, one leg in, one leg out. "What are you doing on Friday evening?"

Surprise shocked her into honesty. She swung her legs the rest of the way out. "Cleaning the attic?"

Nick leaned over the gearshift, one hand holding her door open. "Can I suggest a counter-proposal?"

After her little art appreciation gaffe, Julia wasn't taking any chances. "What did you have in mind?" she asked warily.

"Art appreciation," said Nick blandly.

Julia's eyes narrowed, but before she could think of a suitable retort Nick went on, "Your place, Friday night. If you provide the paintings, I'll bring the takeaway curry." He raised a brow. "Do you prefer rice or naan?"

"Still working away, Thorne?"

Gavin looked up from his painting to find Augustus standing in the doorway of the studio. It was early in the morning, early for Augustus, at any event. The other man looked as though he hadn't been to bed; he was wearing evening clothes, a top hat in his hand, a white scarf hanging carelessly around his neck.

Gavin reached a paint-spattered hand to massage a sore muscle in his own neck. What day was it? For the past few days he had been painting around the clock, burning precious candles, working like a fury to get Mrs. Grantham's portrait done before the following Monday.

Mrs. Grantham. Never Imogen. Gavin reminded himself of that with every stroke, trying to exorcise the longing, the crazy yearning.

He had tried to tell himself that that moment in the summerhouse had been an accident, an aberration, but once he'd started thinking of her that way he couldn't stop. He'd dreamed of her last night, her long, dark hair unbound and streaming around her shoulders. She'd been dressed in nothing but her shift, the tie at the top undone, the fabric sliding down over the curve of her shoulders as she bent over him, her long hair hanging around them both like a veil. "Shh," she whispered to him, and leaned sweetly forward, her lips warm against his ear, his throat, his chest, and then lower, lower still.

He'd woken up in a sweat, his fingers clutching the sheet in a death grasp, elated, aroused, and horrified all at once.

He pulled on his trousers, yanked on a shirt, lit a candle, and padded through the door to the studio, fighting the waves of light-headedness and headache, as though by finishing the portrait he might put an end to his feelings as well, this horrible, heady mixture of lust and tenderness.

He'd felt desire before, yes, but not like this. That had been carnal, pure, and uncomplicated. This . . . Gavin didn't know what he wanted. He didn't know himself. He wanted to sit with her by a fire and feel the soft weight of her head in the hollow of his shoulder and rub his cheek against the silk of her hair. He wanted to hold her hand when it was grown old and gnarled, her skin as wrinkled as the peel of an old apple.

He'd been fighting against it for days, fighting it the only way he knew how, with a brush in his hand, but there it was, waking or sleeping: he'd fallen in love with Imogen

Grantham.

It was madness. Madness and foolishness. If Grantham had the slightest notion what Gavin was thinking, he could ruin him and the world would account him justified. A word in the ear of Sir Martin Shee and Gavin's painting would be set in the lowest, darkest corner of the Academy show or, simply, not accepted at all. All his work, all his ambitions, gone for a bit of passing emotion.

That was all it was, he told himself firmly. Passing emotion. And friendship. He owed Imogen — Mrs. Grantham — that. And, as her friend, there was at least one thing he could do for her.

Setting his brush carefully down on the palette, he said to Augustus, "I heard you've been calling on Miss Grantham."

Augustus didn't like that. He straightened slowly, rising to his full height. "What business is it of yours if I have?"

Gavin shrugged. "Mr. Grantham has been very good to me."

Augustus looked narrowly at Gavin, pursing his lips suggestively. "Are you sure it is *Mr.* Grantham who's been good to you?"

"He has been very generous with his collections," said Gavin stiffly.

Augustus leaned back against the wall,

arms folded across his chest. "And do those collections include his wife?"

Alarm sliced through the fog of Gavin's fatigue, turning his body tense with wariness. "I don't know what you mean."

"Don't you?" Augustus's smirk was a miracle of suggestiveness. "There's no point in coming over all high-and-mighty with me. You can pretend to be all pure and high-minded, but do you think I haven't guessed what's been going on?"

"Spare me your lurid imaginings," said Gavin tersely. The idea of Augustus thinking of Imogen that way —

"Lurid, is it?" Augustus strolled across the room, pausing to flick a speck of imaginary dust from the surface of a painting. "Tell me, how many times have you tupped the wife now? Is it an extra part of your fee?"

Gavin had Augustus up against the wall, his hands wrapped around Augustus's throat, before he was even consciously aware of moving. Rage surged through him, like a red haze. He shoved Augustus back against the wall, hard, making the candlesticks on the tables rattle. "Take that back."

Stunned, gasping, Augustus managed a choked laugh. "Or what? You'll throttle me? You couldn't paint in Newgate."

Gavin pushed away, so abruptly that

272

Augustus staggered. He leaned over, his hands on his knees, fighting a wave of nausea. Would he really have done it? Crushed Augustus's windpipe, and for words?

Augustus massaged his sore throat with an air of innocent injury. "Do you think I don't know what you've been doing — alone with her?" He readjusted his cuffs, tugging the folds just so. "She's not bad looking for a woman that age."

Gavin breathed in deeply through his nose, fighting the urge to slam his fist into Augustus's smug face, to pound those arrogant features into a pulp. He wouldn't let anger turn him from a man to a beast.

Clinging to self-control by a very short straw, he said brusquely, "For the love of God, Augustus. We've been in public, the whole time. In full view of the house. Trust me, the proprieties have been observed."

Mostly. In summer, the shrubbery grew thickly around the summerhouse and the leafy branches of the trees shielded the interior from the view of the house. In his mind's eye, he could see Imogen drawing the pins from her hair, undoing the mother-of-pearl buttons that fastened her collar and cuffs, beginning, one by one, to start on the long row of buttons that ran down her bodice from neck to waist. His fingers itched to undo them, to peel away the layers of fabric, to watch the play of light and shadow across skin and bone, bared in that glorious circle of seclusion among the shielding leaves of the trees.

One movement forward, one moment of encouragement . . .

And farewell to all his dreams of being an Academician someday.

"Have you seen that summerhouse?" Guilt made Gavin crude. "Do you really think I'd rut in a wicker cage for the amusement of every passing housemaid?"

"I don't know." Augustus's heavy-lidded eyes regarded him shrewdly. "It depends on just how badly you want the lady. Or," he added delicately, "how badly the lady wants you."

"You impugn her good name," said Gavin roughly. "You speak of a lady."

Augustus raised a brow. "And my future mama, if all goes my way." Almost gently, he added, "Don't go all Knight of the Round Table on me. That's the fantasy you paint on your canvas. Real life isn't like that. And you know it as well as I."

"You can keep your so-called real world." The phrase tasted sour on Gavin's tongue; he spat it out like rotten fruit. The world was what a man made of it, good or bad. Gavin would take his "real" over Augustus's any day. Even if it balked him of his dearest desires. "And stay away from the Granthams."

Augustus looked at him pityingly. "I don't care what you do with the older one — but I intend to marry the younger one, before the year is out."

He meant it, too. Gavin looked at him incredulously. "You're mad."

"Not mad, just ambitious, and a rich young wife will serve me well." Augustus's face hardened, steel beneath the sleek, social exterior. "Don't cross me in this, Thorne, or you'll see just how determined I can be."

THIRTEEN

London, 2009

In the end, Julia didn't have to call Cousin Caroline. Cousin Caroline called her, with an invitation to tea that felt more like a royal command.

Or, if not a royal command, at least a suitably regal one.

Out came the blue shirtwaist dress again, somewhat the worse for its recent dunking. That's what she got for buying "dry-clean only." But it was the only respectable outfit she'd brought with her and she didn't think Cousin Caroline would take well to shorts or jeans. Something about the way Caroline had said *tea* had conjured up images of large hats and extended pinky fingers.

A train, a Tube, and a bus ride later, Julia was making her way through the iron gates of an alarmingly well-maintained redbrick house in Richmond. She felt that she had, at last, achieved a comprehensive overview of the British public transportation system. And she wasn't looking forward to doing it again in another hour or so.

There would be no Nick to offer her a lift this time.

She'd really gotten the wrong end of the stick with him at the house last weekend. Unless, of course, that had been the right end of the stick and the sudden surge of cheer and goodwill towards men had more to do with her suddenly being in possession of a potentially interesting painting.

Much as the conspiracy theorist in her liked that idea, she didn't think the painting was worth that kind of money. It was more that it was a mystery, a matter of curiosity — and curiosity didn't attract men with a bottom line in mind. It was possible that he really had just been in a crappy mood the previous weekend, had gotten snippy, was feeling guilty, and was trying to make amends. Or he could be an asshole of the highest order.

She'd just have to see what happened when he showed up on Friday. She'd put in an order for chicken tikka masala, onion naan, and a mango *lassi* and refrained from asking whether he came with the meal.

He might just be a decent guy doing a favor for the cousin of a friend.

Or not. It was always safest to assume the worst.

Ahead, in the house, a curtain twitched. Cousin Caroline, watching for her from the bay window? The house looked like Aunt Regina's on steroids: instead of a cracked old brick walkway, there was an entire courtyard of large, interlocking pinkish-red bricks. The house was also brick, a modern architect's take on traditional architecture, everything just a bit too big, too sleek, too polished. When Julia pressed the bell, a series of sickeningly sweet chimes rang out.

Cousin Caroline matched her house, just a shade too carefully put together. Like Helen's, her hair was an assisted blond, but where Helen's ash blond managed to look natural, Cousin Caroline's was chopped and styled and her tailored pantsuit was just a bit too much for tea at home.

Her verbal style matched her clothes. She was so frightfully sorry; she'd meant to welcome Julia before, but, of course, Julia understood how it was; one was just so *busy*. All the same, it was wonderful to see Julia after all these years and such a pity she had stayed away so long. Such a tragedy, all of it.

"Your poor, dear mother." Caroline's voice was syrupy with pity. "She and I were so very close. Practically sisters."

The sort of sisters who didn't like each other much?

From very far away, Julia could hear her father saying, *I don't know why you let her treat you like that,* and another voice, a female voice, saying lightly, *Oh, it's just Caroline. You know how she is.* And Julia's father, grimly, *No. I don't.*

Memory? Or imagination? Julia shook the echoes aside and trotted out her best schoolgirl manners. "It's so nice to see you again. Thanks so much for having me over."

Caroline led the way into an overstuffed living room. The carpet bore the tracks of recent vacuuming. There was a tea tray on the table, the china a familiar pattern of roses and gilt. It made Julia think wistfully of Helen's restful Danish modern.

Caroline indicated that Julia was to seat herself on the sofa. "Well, *naturally.* It was *the least* I could do. It must have been such a shock for you, inheriting the house, when you hadn't even known Regina."

Beneath the italics and faux sympathy was a distinct air of pique.

"It was a bit of a surprise," said Julia cautiously. "But I'm enjoying getting to know more about the family."

She seated herself carefully on the rigid

279

cushions of the chintz sofa. For something so billowy it was a surprisingly uncomfortable piece of furniture. Julia sat on the edge, her legs crossed at the ankles, her hands folded in her lap.

Cousin Caroline looked at her with obvious condescension. "I can't imagine you know much about it, living as you have." She made it sound like Julia had been raised in a grass hut in the Ubangi. "The family has lived in that house for *generations.*"

And now, Cousin Caroline's tone implied, it had fallen to the barbarians. Or the Americans, which was much the same thing.

"Yes," said Julia demurely. "I gather my mother grew up there. I've spent some time in her old room." Before Cousin Caroline could muster her guns, Julia said quickly, "I was hoping you might be able to tell me something about the family history. I asked my father, and he said you were the one to ask."

The tactic worked. Cousin Caroline patted her too-blond hair. "Of course, *your father* wouldn't take any interest. People with no family themselves . . ."

Julia took a hasty sip of tea to stop herself from swinging back with *my father is too busy saving lives to bother with genealogy.* Her father didn't need defending. He was an internationally renowned surgeon, and, yes, she might have her personal quibbles with him — sometimes he had all the emotional sensitivity of a fossilized starfish — but he certainly didn't need to be justified to a suburban snob in a polyester pantsuit.

Not like she was a little touchy or anything.

By an act of will Julia kept her social smile in place. That was twelve years of all-girls school for you; she could do nicey nicey phony phony with the best of them. "Dad mentioned that you had a family genealogy?"

Her father was right; Caroline did have a genealogy and she was only too happy to share it — all part of impressing on Julia that she was the degenerate and degraded branch of an otherwise illustrious family history.

The genealogy was one of those vanity affairs ("Just send 29.95 now!"), on faux parchment, with lettering in red and gold, going all the way back to the Conqueror, or, at least, to the Conqueror's second cousin once removed. It got fuzzier and more fantastical the further back it went. Julia suspected that there was a strong element of fiction and wishful thinking going on. No one had that many monarchs in their family tree. And, yes, Charles II had fathered many bastards, but hadn't most of them been recognized and given titles? She sincerely doubted that he'd taken the trouble to pop out an extra just to give Cousin Caroline a claim to connection with the Stuarts.

Although, given Charles II's infamous amatory proclivities, who knew?

Cousin Caroline was more interested in the earlier, fictional portions of the family tree — which made sense, since it all became more prosaic the further it went. The earliest plausible ancestor was a Josiah Grantham, a wine merchant or, as Caroline put it, a purveyor of fine spirits. Julia thought that was rather like calling a janitor a custodial engineer, but she held her tongue. She had other fish to fry.

"There's a portrait I'm particularly interested in putting a name to," said Julia, making an effort to divert Caroline's attention from the fourteenth-century Beaufort bastards to the nineteenth century. "It's the one in the drawing room —"

"I am quite familiar with that drawing room," put in Caroline loftily.

"Then you'll know the one I'm talking about. It's the woman in the blue dress with the" — Julia refrained from saying *Princess Leia hair* — "dark hair."

"You must be thinking of Imogen Hadley." Caroline pointed one immaculately lacquered nail at a line way down towards the bottom of the chart. "She married Arthur Grantham in 1839."

Eighteen-thirty-nine sounded way too early. The Pre-Raphaelites hadn't even gotten going until nine years later. Julia was looking for a marriage that had taken place in 1849 or later. "Are you sure it was 1839, not 1849?" she asked hopefully.

Caroline looked down her nose at her. "We have all the documentation." She looked away. "At least, your aunt Regina had."

Which meant that Julia now did. Somewhere.

Julia set her cup carefully down on her saucer. "Was this Imogen Grantham an artist's model before she married?"

Caroline looked like she had discovered something unpleasant on her shoe. "An artist's model? No. She was the niece of a baronet." Julia gathered she was meant to be suitably impressed by this. "Where would you get an idea like that?"

"No reason," murmured Julia. She didn't want to tell this woman about her painting.

Natalie knew, of course . . . but Julia was beginning to understand those barbed comments Natalie had made about her mother. Poor Natalie. Julia was beginning to feel a tardy appreciation for Helen. She scrabbled for an excuse. "It's just that picture in the drawing room. It looks so . . . professional."

"Oh, is that all?" Caroline gave a tinkling little laugh that sounded unnervingly like Natalie's. "For a moment you sounded so like Aunt Regina. She was always trying to invent scandal. She said it added spice to an otherwise dull family tree. Such foolishness!"

Julia deeply regretted having missed out on Aunt Regina. "What sort of scandal?" she asked hopefully.

Caroline waved a hand. "Oh, this and that. All nonsense, of course."

Grrr. Well, at least she had a name to put to the portrait, although she was resistant to the idea of relinquishing her beautiful artist's model theory. Eighteen-thirty-nine, 1849, all it would take would be one smudged number. She would have to start digging through the house for that documentation that Caroline had mentioned, whatever it was that Regina had possessed. Somewhere in the recesses of the old house there had to be something.

"Biscuit?" said Caroline, holding out the plate. The chocolate-covered biscuits had been arranged in a fan pattern.

Julia took one; her hostess didn't. Having a mouth full of chocolate and biscuit put one at a distinct disadvantage.

Finally swallowing the gummy mess, Julia offered, "Natalie and Andrew have both been a huge help."

Caroline set the biscuit plate back down on the tray. "Naturally, they take an interest."

Feeling like she was steering a sinking ship, Julia said, "They came over last Saturday to help me sort through everything. And their friend Nick."

"Nick? Oh. You must mean *Nicholas*." Caroline sat a little straighter in her chair. "Such a lovely boy. And so modest, considering."

"Considering?" Considering that in a pair of wire-rimmed glasses he exuded a strange sexual magnetism? Somehow Julia didn't think that was what Caroline meant.

Caroline took a small sip of her tea. "They don't use the title anymore — such a silly technicality — but by rights it should be his."

Julia tilted her head, feeling like she'd lost the plot somewhere. "Title?"

"Viscount Loring." Cousin Caroline rolled the name lovingly on her tongue. "There was an estate in Hampshire, but the National Trust has that now. Still. It's an old, old family." She looked coy. "Nicholas and Natalie . . . well, enough about that. More tea?" She lifted the gilt-rimmed pot.

Julia put a hand out over her cup. "No. Thanks." Nicholas and Natalie what?

Caroline set the pot down again. "Andrew has always been like a brother to him, so, of course, it was only natural. . . . Well." She smiled tightly at Julia, making sure her point had been driven home. "Is there anyone special in your life?"

A long-dead artist?

And an Indian food date that probably wasn't. Funny, Nick hadn't said anything about being betrothed to Cousin Natalie. Julia wondered if he knew or if Cousin Caroline was just planning on bashing him over the head and marching him to the altar.

On second thought, bashing wasn't really her style. She'd probably just slip something into the tea.

Julia didn't know whether to be flattered or pissed off that Caroline had felt the need to warn her off.

"Right now," said Julia, matching Caroline smile for smile, "I'm just enjoying my

house. Thank you so much for the tea, Cousin Caroline; it's been really lovely. Can I help you clean up at all?"

Herne Hill, 1849

Imogen knew that something was wrong as soon as she spotted Mr. Thorne coming down the slope from the house.

He didn't have his easel slung over his shoulder, nor the leather satchel in which he carried his palette and paints. Instead, he was carrying a large bundle in his arms, wrapped up in brown paper. He didn't look up as he approached, didn't hail her and wave as he usually did. Instead, his eyes were firmly planted on the ground, his head bowed against the sunlight.

Setting her book aside, Imogen stood, raising her own hand in greeting.

"Mr. Thorne," she said as he climbed the three steps, those well-worn three steps to the summerhouse. When he returned her greeting with nothing more than a nod, she indicated the cakes beside her. "I had thought you would be in want of refreshment after your long walk from town."

"Thank you." His words were as brusque and abrupt as the first time they had met. He said heavily, "You are very kind."

"Not kind." Imogen looked at him quizzi-

cally. They hadn't observed any of the polite commonplaces for weeks now, and certainly not in the matter of cakes, which were a regular part of their weekly ritual. "Is there something the matter? Are your pigments not behaving as they ought?"

"Quite the contrary." Mr. Thorne set down his parcel, with a thump, on the bench, leaning one end against the wall. Quickly, with the air of someone getting done with a bad business, he said, "I have something for you. Your portrait. It's done."

"Done." The word was like a knell. Imogen supposed she had remembered, dimly, that the purpose of his visits was the production of her portrait, but they had not, since that first sitting, discussed it. It was just part of the backdrop of their visits, like the bees droning among the roses or the one branch that kept tap, tap, tapping against the roof of the summerhouse. She hadn't stopped to contemplate what it would mean when the portrait was done.

Done, all their conversations, all their comfortable colloquy, all wrapped up in brown paper, reduced to nothing but oil on canvas and hung on the wall of the drawing room.

She felt suddenly cold in the sunshine, even in her heavy dress.

Imogen drew in a deep breath, gathering her composure around her like a shawl. "Well, then," she said. "May I see it?"

Mr. Thorne nodded tersely. There were lines on his face she hadn't seen before and marks of sleeplessness beneath his eyes. His fingers fumbled on the string holding the wrappings together, and Imogen was reminded, with a pang, of the last time she had seen him so clumsy, at their first sitting, before they had known each other.

"Let me," Imogen said, striving for normalcy, for the easiness that had, until so recently, existed between them.

Her ungloved fingers brushed Mr. Thorne's as she reached for the string. He snatched his hand away, as though burnt. Imogen took a step back, winding her hand in the folds of her skirt, unsure of what to say or do.

"Are you — unwell?"

"No," he said, and turned back with a will to yanking at the string. The knot on the parcel appeared to confound him; he struggled with it, his profile to Imogen, so familiar and yet suddenly so foreign, closed to her now, like a book set out of reach.

Perhaps he really was ill, ill from overwork or the heat of the long walk from town. She had never seen him moody before; abstracted, yes, but not like this, not reserved to the point of rudeness, treating her like a stranger, as though they hadn't shared two months of conversations and confidences.

Everyone had their testy days.

"It is very warm today," she ventured, to see if she might get some response, any response, something to break through the wall around him to the man she knew, or thought she knew.

"Yes." Thorne fished in his pocket, abstracting a penknife, and slashed through the bindings holding the wrappings together. Imogen winced at the controlled savagery of the motion.

Mr. Thorne brushed the cut bits of string aside, pulling away the brown paper. Imogen knew better than to try to help. She stood a little bit away, watching as the wrappings fell away from her portrait.

"There," he said, and stepped aside.

Imogen glanced uneasily at his face, but it told her nothing. He was looking, fixedly, at her portrait. Or, rather, the portrait that was meant to be her.

There was no denying that it was a beautifully executed piece of work, the colors deep and strong. Every leaf had definition; every floorboard was just as it was, down to the small knots and burls. He had caught the subdued opulence of her gown, expense and restraint all in one, the fabric rich but not too shiny, the full sleeves, the modest neck, the discreet expense of pearl earbobs and cameo brooch.

The woman in front of her was buttoned and boned and stayed, her hair coiled sleekly on either side of her head, her skin smooth and pale. The world around her was bursting with life, the sunlight limning the leaves on the trees, the redbird on its branch, but where was the color in her? She had worn the dark blue dress Arthur had commanded, with its white collar and cuffs, but she had never expected to find herself as colorless as the fabric.

Was this what she had become? All around her was summer, but she was shades of winter, bark and frost.

Her chest ached with a strange pain, a fear she couldn't quite name. What had happened to that girl in Cornwall, the one who had run barefoot along the cliffs? She was there somewhere, immured inside a porcelain shell.

"Is this really how you see me?" she said in a small voice.

This was worse than Mariana. Mariana, at least, had leaned yearningly towards the window, her body supple, her hair tumbling

down over her shoulders, fierce in her longing, while this woman, this woman with
Imogen's face, was caught in a brittle still-
ness that was less yielding than any tower.

Perhaps that was the face she showed to
the world, but Mr. Thorne? After all these
weeks, she had thought he knew her better.

"I painted what I was told to paint," he
said gruffly, and Imogen felt something
inside herself wither, like an autumn leaf.

"It is a very accomplished composition,"
Imogen said carefully.

What was there to say? Mr. Thorne had
said it all. He had painted the picture he
had been paid to paint. She felt as though
the slightest movement would make her
crack, shattering into a thousand sharp-
edged shards.

She took a deep breath. "Mr. Grantham
will be very pleased."

Mr. Thorne made a quick, instinctive
movement of negation. "It's all wrong."

The words were deep and hoarse,
wrenched from the depths of his chest.

"If I were to paint you properly," he said,
his eyes never leaving hers, "it wouldn't be
like this. I would paint you with the sea
behind you and the waves crashing on the
sand. I would paint you in a gown that
doesn't crackle when you move. I would

paint you with your hair flowing free, not bunched and bundled. This" — he indicated his own painting with scorn — "this isn't you at all. It doesn't even touch the surface."

"It is a very elegant picture," said Imogen in a voice she didn't recognize as her own.

Mr. Thorne shook off her praise, saying passionately, "It's a lie, that's what it is. If I were to paint you properly, it would be as a wood nymph or a warrior maiden or a —" He broke off. In a voice so low, she could hardly hear him, he said, "I can't do this."

"Paint me?" Imogen grasped at the pretense, at the possibility of extending their time together. "If you are unhappy with the painting, we can start again, try another pose, another place. . . ."

"No."

That was all, *no,* as though the thought of another day with her was too much for him to bear.

"Have these past months been such a hardship?" Imogen tried to stop the hurt from leaking out, tried to keep her voice steady, but it came out anyway, corrosive and painful. "I am sorry you have been forced to endure my company for as long as you have."

More fool she for forgetting that they were painter and subject, not, as she had allowed herself so carelessly to believe, friends. He had been passing the time with her because he had been paid to do so.

Mr. Thorne stared at her as though she had grown a second head. "How can you think — Christ." He scrubbed his fingers through his hair, shaking his head helplessly. "I had never intended — I meant only to spare you —"

"Spare me?" His mouth was moving, forming words, but the words had no sense in them, no meaning. She straightened her back, slowly and painfully. "I do not need anyone to spare me anything."

"To spare myself, then," he said, and there was something in his voice that made her look at him, really look at him.

His eyes were rimmed with deep circles, bloodshot from lack of sleep. He'd missed a patch while shaving; there was a swathe of dark stubble on his chin. His eyes were wild, like a painting she had seen once, of John the Baptist in the wilderness, the eyes of a man driven past endurance.

Rapidly he said, "This portrait ought to have been finished three weeks ago. But I have let myself drag it out, week after week, stroke by stroke and leaf by leaf, all for the indulgence of being able to sit here across from you for a few hours each Monday."

Imogen stared at him dumbly, her mind failing to grasp just what he was saying, even as a tingling began to spread across her palms, a strange sense of anticipation and elation that had nothing to do with sense.

"I can't sleep at night for thinking of you," Mr. Thorne said harshly. She could see his fingers digging into fists at his sides, his whole body tense. "You've become a fire in my blood and I can think of no way to put it out but to run as far and as fast as I can before I burn us both."

His words ought to have evoked pity or horror, but they didn't. Instead, Imogen was filled with a burning joy, a mad, triumphant joy that had no name and no explanation.

It was beautiful and wonderful and horrible all at once, and she didn't want him to stop; she wanted him to keep speaking, to keep saying these things, to say them again and again until she could be sure she had heard him, that it was true.

"I can't sit here, across from you, week by week, and pretend it's nothing more than another sitting, just so many hands, eyes, lips conveyed from brush to canvas. It's — I —" His shoulders sagged, like a man dealt a mortal blow. "It's done. That's all. It's done and I'll go back to town and you'll stay here and maybe our paths will cross at the RA show and you'll be kind enough to praise my next work and I — I —"

Imogen leaned forward, her stays constricting her breath. "Yes?"

"And maybe," he said bitterly, "by then, I will be able to smile and nod and bow over your hand without dishonoring myself or you."

Taking his hat, Mr. Thorne jammed it down on his head. It was a dilapidated thing, battered and shapeless, the brim sagging. The sight of it filled Imogen with an almost unbearable feeling of tenderness. She wanted to commit him to memory as he had committed her to canvas, every crease of his cheek, every wrinkle of his jacket, every gesture of his hands.

"Mr. Thorne —" she began, but he was already retreating, his hand on the rail.

"There. That's all. I've said more than I intended — more than I ought. I'll be off now before I can embarrass you further." Mr. Thorne's voice was bleak. "I trust you will forget I said any of this and remember me — remember me kindly."

He was turning, leaving, his hands jammed in his pockets, his head bowed.

Beside Imogen, the plate of cakes still sat untouched on the bench. It felt like hours, days, but it had only been minutes, minutes for the world to turn upside down and everything to change. It seemed obscene that the birds should go on chirping, the sun shining, when they all ought to be frozen in their course, as frozen, as confused, as she.

No. He couldn't leave. To leave now — after what he had said, after what he hadn't said — it was unthinkable, as unthinkable as the prospect of never again seeing him walk whistling down the slope, his easel over his shoulder.

She didn't stop to think what it meant if he stayed; all she knew was that she couldn't let him go.

The words burst out of her. "Don't go."

FOURTEEN

Herne Hill, 1849

Imogen's words stopped Gavin in his tracks, clenching around his heart like a fist.

Her voice behind him was unsteady, shaking. "How can you simply turn and walk away after *that*?"

Gavin knew he shouldn't turn around. Leaving and leaving quickly was the only option open to him. But he turned anyway.

"After that," he said, his voice low, "how could I stay?"

Imogen's face was very pale, but for two patches of color high on her cheeks. "So you'll just take the coward's way out? Speak and run and leave me here behind?"

Frustration crackled through him. "And if I were to stay, what then? Tea cakes and polite conversation?"

Imogen made an impatient gesture. "I thought you liked the tea cakes!"

"I do!" Good Lord, were they really arguing about tea cakes? They stood facing each other, panting as if they'd just gone a round in the ring. Or a bout in bed. Gavin pressed the heels of his hands against his temples. "It's not the bloody tea cakes."

He saw her eyes widen. Had no one sworn before her before? Good. Let her see what he really was and be warned. He wasn't one of her polished gentlemen; he'd come from a place where people grabbed and scrabbled.

"For the love of God, Imogen —" He hadn't meant to call her by her name. It just slipped out. Gavin ground determinedly on. "I don't see any other way. To sit here and be near you and see you smile and yet not be able to touch you — It's more than flesh can bear. It's more than I can bear."

He didn't know how else to say it, how to make her understand. His feelings for her weren't honorable and courtly. They were messy and raw and very, very carnal.

"I don't trust myself with you," he said. "You shouldn't trust me with you."

Instead of moving away, Imogen took a step towards him, the wide skirts of her gown brushing against the toes of his boots. Her face was pale and set, her eyes dark and wide.

"I do not want to lose you," she said.

Gavin pressed his eyes shut, hating himself for hurting her, hating himself all the more for not being able to simply walk away. He had thought to spare them both pain, but this only made it worse.

"You will forget me," he said in a constricted voice. "The portrait will hang on your wall and become dingy with soot and you will forget all about the man who wielded the brush."

Even as he said it, he knew he lied. He didn't want her to forget him. He wasn't noble enough for that. He wanted her to long for him as he longed for her, to dream of him at night, restless and unsatisfied.

"Can you really believe that?" Imogen's skirts swished against her legs as she moved in agitated circles around the summerhouse. "You cannot know, you cannot imagine, how much these past months have meant to me, to know, every Monday, that you would be here. To speak together, to really *speak* together, as if you care what I have to say —"

"I do care." Gavin knew he shouldn't say it, but he couldn't lie. "I have shared with you things I have shared with no one else."

Imogen looked up at him, her teeth digging deep into her lower lip, hard enough to draw blood. "The thought of your leaving

300

— that you might never return — is like a little death."

Gavin told himself that she couldn't know the slang meaning of that term, couldn't know what it implied. But he did, and the image left him shaking with desire and shame.

"Death if I leave," he said, through white lips, "but dishonor if I stay."

"Honor," Imogen repeated bitterly. " 'I could not love thee, dear, so much, / Loved I not honor more.' Men always call it honor when they would rather be somewhere else."

Gavin had gone two strides forward, her hands clenched in his before he realized what he was doing. His hands were on her wrists, her forearms, her shoulders. He gave her a slight shake. "Do you really believe that there is anywhere else I would rather be?"

She was tall for a woman, nearly as tall as he. She barely had to tilt her head back to look him in the eye.

"Gavin," she said breathlessly, and the sound of her name on his lips undid him. "Gavin."

They stared at each other like drowning men sighting land, drinking in the sight of each other, her skirts enveloping her legs, the buttons on her basque pressing into his chest, her breath warm on his lips.

Gavin wasn't sure who moved, but Imogen's arms were around his neck and his around her waist, pulling her close, pressing her to him as though he could make her part of his flesh, her skirts billowing around his legs, as they kissed deeply, hungrily, all the frustrated desire of the last months taking shape in that burning, endless kiss, his blood singing wildly in his ears, every nerve of his body alive, alive to Imogen, Imogen . . .

Gavin pulled back, breathing heavily. He felt as though he'd just pounded back a pint of gin, his wits gone, his lungs burning. Imogen's lips were rosy, her hair mussed. He'd never seen anything more lovely or more desirable.

Lovely and desirable and quite definitely married. Married to the man who had hired him to paint her portrait. In her husband's garden by her husband's house.

"Your reputation —" Gavin managed, the words coming out in pants. "Your husband —"

Imogen's hair had come loose from its pins. She shook it back, her color high and her eyes bright. "Why would he miss what he does not want?"

"You can't mean —"

She didn't shy from the question but met him eye to eye, a wealth of bitterness in her voice. "It has been years since he has touched me so."

A wave of possessiveness washed over Gavin, tenderness mixed with a fierce anger against Grantham, for having Imogen and not appreciating her.

"The man's a fool," Gavin said roughly. "Or incapable. There's no other reason for it." He struggled to put his feelings into words. "It's not just the way you look — it's the way you move, the way your expression changes as you speak, the way your lips curve when you smile."

There was so much passion in her, all buttoned and locked away, and he wanted to be the one to free it, to feel the force of it all directed at him. He'd avoided entanglements all these years, concentrating on his art. But when he was with Imogen — it didn't seem like a choice of one or the other.

"I want you so much that it scares me," he said baldly. "And if you have any sense, you'll take the portrait and send me packing."

With a deliberate movement, Imogen slid the palms of her hands up his chest to his shoulders.

"Stay," she said, her voice thick with emo-

303

tion. "Stay."

And that was all.

Her lips blotted out reason. Thought was replaced by sensation as they slid slowly to the ground together, shielded by the walls of the summerhouse and the rosebushes that twined around and encircled them.

Herne Hill, 2009

Nick showed up eight o'clock sharp on Friday night, takeout in hand.

Julia came to the door in jeans, flip-flops, and a button-down shirt. She'd meant the flip-flops as a sign that this was just a casual evening at home, not anything special, but she'd underestimated the height differential.

Nick looked at the spot where he'd expected to find her, then down. "You've shrunk."

Julia waggled a foot. "No heels." She cocked a brow. "Unless it's just your extreme loftiness. Why didn't you tell me I'm supposed to curtsy when I see you?"

For a moment, Nick looked blank. Then he mustered a heartfelt groan. "Oh, Lord. Caroline."

Julia closed and locked the front door behind him. "She hasn't quite set up a shrine to your family name, but she's getting there." Julia decided not to tell him that

304

he was also apparently betrothed to her cousin Natalie. That might sound like she was fishing. "I was informed in no uncertain terms that your lineage be both old and venerable."

"It's not nearly as illustrious as she thinks it is." Nick held up two paper bags. Orange liquid was beginning to stain the bottom of one. "Where shall I put these?"

"Kitchen. This way. Cousin Caroline would probably have a heart attack if she knew I was using you as my takeout delivery boy." Julia waved Nick forward, down the twisting corridors that had become so familiar during her month in residence. They passed the formal dining room, an afterthought of a breakfast room, and a butler's pantry lined with glass-fronted cabinets, with all the latest in 1930s mod cons. "Have you ever seen that old show *Keeping Up Appearances*?"

"Hyacinth Bucket?" Nick choked on a laugh. "God, you're right. They're sisters under the skin."

"I could tell she was itching to plump the pillows the second I sat down on them. I'm pretty sure she thinks I have cooties." Julia flicked on the kitchen light, a bulbous 1960s fixture with stylized metal leaves and large glass balls. It was a cozy room, obviously a later add-on to the house, with mustard yellow appliances and cheerful pine cabinets. "The afternoon wasn't a total loss, though. I did find out who our mystery woman is."

"Who?" Nick set the bags down on the kitchen table as Julia went to fetch plates from the cupboard. They were Aunt Regina's old dishes, once brightly patterned with gaudy yellow flowers, now faded to a comfortable pastel. Julia suspected that Aunt Regina had ceased investing in housewares around the same time bell-bottoms were just coming into style.

Julia doled out two plates, two sets of forks and knives. "Her name was Imogen Grantham and she was married to the son of the guy who first bought this house. The dates don't work, though."

"How so?" Nick began uncrating the food, entirely at home in Aunt Regina's old kitchen. He was wearing another button-down shirt, this time with jeans. The casual outfit suited him. He didn't look like a viscount; he looked like a J.Crew ad.

Julia realized he was waiting for her to speak. She dumped a pile of soupspoons in the center of the table. "According to the genealogy, Imogen married Arthur Grantham in 1839, which makes it way too early for her to have posed for Thorne

306

before she married Grantham."

Nick opened the rice and offered it to her first. "You wouldn't expect to see a respectable bourgeois matron posing for an artist." In male fashion, he bypassed the spoon and dumped lamb vindaloo on his plate by the simple expedient of upending the container. "Do you think the date's off? On the genealogy."

"Possible," said Julia, judiciously spooning chicken tikka over her rice. "Cousin Caroline claims that Aunt Regina had documentation —"

"The marriage license?"

"— but I haven't come across anything that early. All the papers in Aunt Regina's desk seem to be recent stuff."

Nick leaned his elbows on the table, nudging the rice container out of the way. "Any chance there are earlier papers elsewhere?"

Julia traced patterns in her rice. "The attic," she said. "It looks like later generations just shoved everything they weren't using up there willy-nilly." She looked up at him. "It's a huge project. There are metric tons of boxes."

Nick grinned at her and ripped off another piece of naan. "I don't have anything else to do tonight, have you?"

Julia tucked a strand of hair behind her

ear. "What, no snooker match tonight?"

Nick leaned forward. His tone was low and intimate. "I'll let you in on a secret. I only watch snooker when I'm legless."

When he turned on the charm, even in jest, it packed a potent punch. Julia speared a chunk of chicken, trying to maintain a respectable air of sangfroid. "Does that really improve it?"

The corners of Nick's mouth twitched. "You'd be surprised."

"Yes, yes, I would be," said Julia, and felt foolishly pleased when Nick laughed. "Wait, so how did you come to own an antique store? Instead of becoming a professional snooker watcher."

For a moment, she thought he might fob her off, but then his shoulders relaxed into a shrug. "Accident, really." He tore off a large piece of naan. "I'd been several years at Dietrich Bank, mostly in M and A. That is —"

"I know," said Julia. "I'm an equity research analyst. Was an equity research analyst. Anyway. You were all on track to be extremely boring and very wealthy —"

"When my great-aunt died and left me her flat." He indicated the appropriate irony of this with a raised brow. "She was the most tremendous pack rat. When the family gave the house to the National Trust — I'm sure Caroline mentioned the house."

"Lovingly," Julia assured him.

"The family had been told they could take what they liked of their favorite personal effects. Aunt Edith interpreted that very broadly."

His expression was so droll that Julia couldn't help laughing.

Nick held up a hand. "Don't laugh! She must have hired a couple of thugs and gone in with a lorry. It wasn't just paintings and whatnots. There was an eighteenth-century pianoforte and a rather baronial bed and a massive seventeenth-century bust of Charles the Second. Charles's nose, I am sorry to say, had been chipped in transit and Aunt Edith appeared to have made an attempt to mend it with sticking plaster."

Julia set down her cup with a shaky hand. "Please," she said. "You're going to make me get soda up my nose."

"You think you're shocked? Imagine my feelings when I walked into the place! It was a five-room flat and every inch of it was crammed with Aunt Edith's loot." He looked thoughtful. "I shouldn't wonder if she would have taken more if she'd only had an extra room."

Julia was laughing hopelessly. "I can just

see it. So you took her loot . . ."

"And opened a shop," Nick finished for her. "The proceeds from selling the flat paid for the lease on the shop."

"Do you ever regret it?"

"On the days when I meet with my accountant? Yes. Otherwise? No." For a moment, he let the glib façade drop. "All of these objects, they have stories to them, histories. You never know what you might find shoved at the back of a drawer or in the space between a canvas and a frame. And," he added lightly, "the hours are much better."

Julia wondered if he'd gotten any flack from his family, if his parents had minded his throwing in a promising job in finance to run an antiques shop in Notting Hill. Or was that just the American reaction? She hadn't had the guts at twenty-one to tell her father that what she really wanted to do was look at paintings for a living; she couldn't imagine how he would have reacted to her opening a shop.

Of course, her father thought anything that wasn't medicine was one step away from pole dancing, so he was his own special case.

Nick set his fork down on his plate and dropped his napkin next to it. "You promised me paintings?"

Sharing time was clearly over.

Julia took a final sip of her soda and pushed back her chair. " 'Promise' is such a strong word . . . but since you brought the curry, yes."

Nick glanced back at her over his shoulder as he carried his plate to the sink. So cute, thought Julia, and apparently house-trained, too. "What would I get if I brought dessert?"

"Indigestion?" Julia quipped, and led a quietly chuckling Nick back down the corridor, her flip-flops an anachronism against the old hardwood floor.

She had to remind herself that he was here for professional purposes. It would be far too easy to let the false intimacy of dinner delude her into reading more into the evening than she should.

"I brought the Thorne painting down to the drawing room," she said, flipping on the drawing room lights, "so you can look at both together."

The drawing room looked even more dingily pink than usual. Nick squinted up at the fixture. "You'd probably get more light if you cleaned those globes," he said. "That looks like a few decades of grime."

Julia switched on a table lamp. It helped a

bit, but not much. "I get the feeling that Aunt Regina didn't use this room much. Anyway, that's the portrait of Imogen Grantham over there." She gestured to the lady over the mantelpiece.

Nick moved to stand in front of it, locking his hands behind his back. "I see what you meant," he said soberly, "about her expression. She looks . . ."

"Lost?" offered Julia.

"Something like that. It's an amazing portrait. Much better than that one." Nick nodded towards the gentleman with ginger whiskers. "That one's flat, conventional, the background muddy. This one . . . The detail is incredible." He turned abruptly. "Where did you say the Thorne painting was?"

"Here." Julia had cleared the top of a table of its clutter of vases and knickknacks, propping the painting up against the wall.

She waited as he examined both, prowling back and forth from one to the other before saying finally, "You're right. It's the same woman."

"Don't sound so surprised," said Julia lightly. "It doesn't take a PhD to spot a face. Although it is nice to have confirmation. I was beginning to wonder if I was imagining things."

Like all those bits and fragments of memories that kept bubbling up, bits of old conversations, sensory impressions. Sometimes it made her wonder if being alone out here was making her lose her grip on reality.

"It's not just the same woman; I'd lay money on it that it's the same painter," said Nick, prowling back and forth between the two paintings. There was an air of suppressed excitement about him, like an electric current. "There are certain similarities in style. If you compare your Imogen portrait to the other portraits in the room . . ."

"Yes?" prompted Julia.

Lost in mid-sentence, Nick was staring at the portrait of the man with the ginger whiskers. Looking slowly from the portrait to the painting, he let out a low whistle. "Now, isn't *that* interesting."

Julia was beginning to feel like she was losing the plot. "Isn't what interesting?" she asked impatiently.

Nick snapped out of whatever trance he'd fallen into. "Your Imogen Grantham isn't the only person in the room in that painting." He pointed to the portrait of the ginger-haired gentleman on the far side of the room. "Look closely. That portrait's not great, and Thorne's shaved his whiskers and

313

given him a beard, but if you can look past that . . ."

Nick was right. Take off the whiskers, add a beard, and there he was, the ginger-haired man, front and center, smack in the middle of the banqueting scene, a gold circlet around his brow, his eyes narrowed as he looked out over the trysting lovers.

"Oh," said Julia. How in the hell had she not seen that before?

" 'Oh,' indeed." Nick folded his arms across his chest, looking more than a little bit smug. "There's your King Mark."

Julia felt a strange chill down her spine as though someone had just breathed down the back of her neck. A goose walking over her grave, the old saying went. She wasn't quite sure, but . . .

"You mean Imogen Grantham's husband."

Nick's eyes met hers. "If that's her husband, then who's Tristan?"

Fifteen

Herne Hill, 1849

"Go on," said Imogen, dropping down onto a convenient fallen log. She'd learned to recognize the expression on Gavin's face that meant he'd spotted a particularly intriguing bug on a branch or quirk of the light. "I don't mind sitting while you sketch — so long as you don't sketch me."

Gavin squinted at the sky. "Nah, it's passed," he said, and folded himself down next to her, nudging her to make room. He slid an arm around her waist and she leaned comfortably into him, the contours of his body already a familiar landscape. His fingers traced a pattern along the curve of her waist. "Why do you so dislike being drawn?"

Imogen gave a little shrug, leaning her head against his shoulder. At her feet, the grass was already beginning to turn from green to brown. It felt so natural and easy being together that it was a constant effort to remind herself that their time was finite, that it would be foolish to let herself feel too much.

"You see so much of me," she said, at last. "It is not always comfortable."

Gavin rested his cheek against the top of her head. "But all of it beautiful," he said quietly.

The simple words made Imogen's heart ache. "You find water bugs beautiful, too," she said determinedly. "And frogs."

"It's not quite the same thing," said Gavin drily. Pulling back, he flicked a finger against her cheek. "Your gills aren't nearly so green."

"Honeyed words," said Imogen mockingly.

She made as if to rise, but he caught her hand and tugged her back down. "Shall I tell you it's your spirit I find lovely, then, and not your skin? As charming as that is," he added, with a hint of a grin.

It made her uneasy when he spoke so, uneasy because part of her so wanted to hear it.

Imogen wrinkled her nose at him. "There's no need to try to seduce me. You already have. Come," she said, imperiously holding out a hand. "Shall we sit or shall we walk?"

Since the portrait session had ended, Imogen had developed a habit of long walks, an eccentricity entirely in line with her character. Jane attributed it to Imogen's ridiculous rural upbringing; Arthur made no comment at all, except to remark that it was nice to see some color in her cheeks again.

Two, sometimes three times a week, Gavin would fall into step with her just past the orchard gate and together they would roam the still rural reaches down along the dale of the Effra, a million miles away from the world. Here there were no prying eyes, no sniping tongues. Arthur's set, when they left the hill, departed by carriage, taking only the well-traveled roads. They would never have thought to climb over stiles or risk their shoes in the mud of the damp ground by the tributaries of the river. Sometimes a heron would be startled into flight by her and Gavin's passage; other times their progress would be regarded by the liquid eyes of grazing cows. Otherwise, they might have been the first man and the first woman, alone in their innocence.

Not that their walks together were always innocent.

There were days when just the touch of his gloved hand against hers was enough to set her skin burning, when a picnic blanket might become an impromptu bed, more luxuriant than the softest goose down swathed in linen.

There were other days when it was enough just to be together, walking easily side by side, the ground sucking and sinking beneath their shoes, the smells of autumn all around them in the rich loam of the earth, the first tinge of coal smoke in the air.

" 'Season of mist and mellow fruitfulness!' " quoted Imogen, lifting her face to the late-afternoon sun.

Tucking her hand under his arm, Gavin said with mock seriousness, " 'Think not of the songs of spring.' "

"I believe you mean, 'Where are the songs of Spring? Ay, where are they? / Think not of them,' " said Imogen loftily, although she knew that Gavin knew the poem better than she.

It was Gavin who had introduced her to Keats, quoting verse after verse, each line an offering, a gift from him to her. For a man with little formal education he had a store of poetry and stories, and something about the way he savored them, the way he rolled them on his tongue, reminded Imogen that such tales were originally meant to be spoken aloud, to be shared, not confined and hoarded between the leather covers of a book.

He found beauty everywhere and, finding it, showed it to her, even in the bruised side of a fallen apple, or a path trodden by dusty feet. When she was with him, colors were brighter, scents sharper; she felt as though she had awakened after a long sleep into a world she was learning again, piece by piece.

There was no one to interfere with Imogen's outings. Arthur was always away from home, and Evie had struck up a friendship with one of the Misses Cranbourne, which kept her busy with teas and picnics.

"I thought you couldn't stand Eliza Cranbourne," said Imogen idly, picking up her embroidery frame as she joined Evie in the drawing room before dinner one evening.

"People change," said Evie enigmatically. She was, noticed Imogen, looking particularly pretty, her cheeks pink and her hair arranged in a new style. It made her look, thought Imogen with a pang, practically grown-up. "We were such children then!"

"Elderly at seventeen," Imogen teased, but she wasn't moved to inquire further. Even Jane had nothing to say about the Cranbournes, other than that they seemed to be quiet, well-bred girls and it was a pity they hadn't an older brother rather than a sickly little six-year-old one.

Fotheringay-Vaughn hadn't called again, and Imogen allowed herself to hope that he had been called to greener pastures or greater heiresses.

On a day when he knew Fotheringay-Vaughn would be out, Gavin took Imogen to his studio.

"At last!" she said. "The Bluebeard chamber."

Gavin slanted a sideways glance as he let her in through a narrow entryway, up a steep flight of narrow stairs. "You know I'd have shown you sooner, but for Augustus."

"A convenient excuse," Imogen teased. "I expect a scene of the utmost decadence."

"Mess, perhaps," said Gavin, opening a door at the top of the stairs, "but hardly decadence."

"Orgies of dust?" Imogen poked her head around the door. "Goodness."

There seemed to be bits of paper everywhere. Sketches, scattered wantonly along a long table, curling at the edges, spilling over onto the floor. Gavin hadn't been joking about the dust; she could see the dust motes dancing in the light from the uncurtained windows. A strong smell of charcoal and paint scented the air.

One corner of the room had been roped off into a makeshift dressing room by the simple expedient of hanging a piece of cloth from a string. Imogen had known, intellectually, that he and his friends believed in painting only from specific examples, but it was one thing to hear it said and quite another to see the pile of theatrical doublets and pasteboard swords, glass gems, and pieces of fabric of every type and color imaginable.

"You never told me that it was Aladdin's cave," Imogen said. Imogen lifted up a sapphire blue gown, a needle still stuck through a corner of the sleeve. The seams were all sewn in the simplest of basting stitches, the trim tacked on with more of the same. "Is this your handiwork?"

Gavin held out his hands in acknowledgment. "I can't afford a seamstress to make my costumes."

"It's beautiful." The fabric was cheap, the trim tawdry, but Imogen could see it as it would appear, transmuted in paint, the sleazy blue silk something rich and rare, the ha'penny trimmings trappings for a queen.

"It's for the Tristan and Iseult painting. Your painting," Gavin added. He insisted on crediting her with the inspiration for it.

His lips quirked as he saw the way she was looking at the gown. "Put it on. I designed it with you in mind."

"It won't hurt it?" Imogen found she wanted to put it on, very much.

"My stitches aren't pretty, but they generally hold." Gavin bundled the fabric into her hands and pushed her lightly towards the screen. "Go on."

Behind the curtain she found a straight chair and a washstand with basin, both currently empty of water. Her own dress wasn't difficult to shed. The basque buttoned down the front, as did her corset. Her petticoat, stiffened with horsehair, would have to go, of course — Iseult's gown wasn't designed for such things — but Imogen hesitated over her pantalets and chemise.

In for a penny, in for a pound. She felt as though she were sloughing off a second skin. Petticoat, pantalets, shift, stays, all piled on the ground, leaving her feeling light and free as she slid Iseult's gown over her head, feeling the whisper of the silk against her naked skin, following the curves of her body, flaring gently from waist to hip.

Her shoes and stockings joined the pile of underclothes. Modern and practical, they would never do for a Cornish queen.

On an impulse, Imogen reached up and

pulled first one pin from her hair, then another. When she raised her arms, the silky fabric of the bodice brushed across her breasts, a strangely erotic sensation. The last pin gave way and her hair fell heavily around her shoulders, fanning out along her back, tickling her bared shoulders.

"Don't laugh," Imogen warned.

Tentatively, she stepped out from behind the screen, her bare toes curling against the wooden boards. The skirt was just a little too long; she held it in both hands, the silk fabric sliding sensuously around her legs as she moved. She stopped, self-consciously, in the center of the room, shaking back her hair, so strangely loose and free.

Gavin was standing by his easel. At the sight of her, he stopped what he was doing, stopped and looked her up and down, from her unbound hair to her bare toes and all the curves and contours in between.

But he said nothing.

"Well?" Imogen demanded. She resisted the urge to cover one bare foot with the other. "Aren't you going to say anything?"

"I'm past words." His voice was husky. Something in it brought the color to Imogen's cheeks. He looked at her with frank admiration. "If Iseult had looked anything like that, there'd be no need for a potion."

Imogen smoothed her hands along the dropped waist of the gown, following it as it flared out over her hips. "Some say that the potion only lasted for three years. And then the effects wore off and they found themselves intimate strangers, with a kingdom at war for nothing."

Gavin closed the distance between them, gently smoothing the hair back from her face. "I prefer the other version," he said. "The one in which they love one another well and truly for the rest of their lives, risking all and forsaking all others."

His words felt like an incantation. The rest of their lives . . .

Imogen felt her throat tighten. They didn't have that kind of time. Only today and possibly tomorrow.

She tilted her head up to him, her heart in her eyes. "Even if it was all an enchantment?"

Gavin's thumbs traced the curves of her cheeks. "Enchantment or chance, does it matter how two souls come together, so long as they do?" Quietly he added, "Love is love, however you come by it."

The air in the studio felt suddenly charged and fraught, as though the very dust motes had paused in their dance to wait and listen.

Love. They didn't speak of love; it was an

unspoken rule.

There was no future for them; they both knew that. This was borrowed time, stolen time, as much of a fantasy as the dress she was wearing or the props piled in the corner, none of them made to withstand the test of time.

If only it were otherwise. If only she could slither out of her old life as she had from her stays and stand with Gavin in the sunshine, and tell him, truly, *I love you,* and know that it was a pledge and not a curse. For a wild moment, in her borrowed gown, Imogen grasped at the idea. They could flee over the hills and far away — and ruin Gavin's career and Arthur's reputation and Evie's chances of a good marriage.

The words *I love you* felt like ashes in Imogen's throat. Her love ought to be the one thing she was free to give, but it wasn't, not really, not when it came with promises and expectations and all they had was this moment, this one, suspended, moment.

She had made grand declarations of love before, and look how that had all turned out. It was a nasty, slippery thing, love, and she didn't trust it. Or maybe it was that she didn't trust herself.

So Imogen reached up and drew Gavin's head down to hers and kissed him instead, kissed him hungrily, passionately, her fingers tugging at his shirt, expressing in action what she couldn't say in words. They made love on the dusty floor, amid the paint drops and the charcoal shavings, breathless and frantic. But there was an urgency to it that sapped the sweetness from it, a chill that wouldn't go away, no matter how Imogen burrowed against the warmth of Gavin's body after, as they lay there, sweaty and sated, on the dusty floor.

Whatever it was they felt for each other, however powerfully it possessed her, their time together was limited; Imogen could feel it fragmenting like sand between her fingers, with no idea how to hold on.

How long until someone saw them? How long until Arthur found out?

Herne Hill, 2009
Julia and Nick argued all the way up to the attic.

"There's no reason to assume that the lives of the real people mirror those of the characters in the painting." Julia led the way down the second-floor corridor, to the narrow door at the back that led to the attic stairs. There was another way, from the basement straight up to the attic, but it was just a little too Nancy Drew: narrow and dark and ill lit. "You said yourself that the Pre-Raphs tended to co-opt anyone within reach as a model."

The bulb on the attic stairs was one of the sort with a dangling string. Nick obligingly reached over Julia's head and tugged it for her. "Yes, their friends and relatives. What relation does Thorne have to the Granthams?"

"Poor relation?" suggested Julia, wrinkling her nose at the strong scent of dust. She started up the stairs. "Cousin? Nephew? Illegitimate son? For all we know, Thorne might have been here for tea on alternate Tuesdays or living in a shed in the yard."

"The other makes a better story, though, doesn't it?" From behind her, Julia could hear the note of amusement in Nick's voice. "Art replicates life; the repressed Victorian housewife finds passion in the arms of an artist right beneath the nose of her stodgy husband. Not to mention," Nick added practically, "that it might bring the price of the painting up."

Julia stumbled slightly on an uneven step, closing her mouth over an instinctive denial. Of course, the logical thing would be to sell. And, given his efforts, it would be equally logical for Nick to assume she intended him to take on the task for her. And the commission.

The thought gave her a nasty sensation in the pit of her stomach. What did you expect? she demanded of herself. That Nick was doing all this for the sheer joy of discovery? Or for the promise of her inconsiderable charms? He was an antiques dealer. She had a promising antique. That was all.

Pausing on the landing, Julia said rather shortly, "I doubt you'll find Imogen Grantham's diary up here. And even if you did, she'd hardly detail her illicit affair for posterity and leave it lying around the family home."

If Nick noticed the change in her tone, he didn't comment on it. He said mildly, "Of course not. But there might be letters, account books. Anything that places Gavin Thorne in or near this house would be useful. What's in here?"

Julia looked back over her shoulder. "That's the old nursery, from the days when children were meant to be neither seen nor heard. There's nothing there. The rooms we want are around here — old servant rooms, I think."

Instead of following her, Nick opened the nursery door wider. "Someone's used this as a studio."

Reluctantly, Julia tagged along after him.

328

"Not Gavin Thorne. I don't think you'll find anything that old in here."

"Those tiles are," said Nick, crouching down to inspect the story tiles around the hearth. "Or nearly. I'd put them somewhere between 1860 and 1880."

"They don't look like Thorne's work," said Julia flatly. The tiles illustrated scenes from fairy tales: Cinderella by her hearth, Rose-Red and her bear, Red Riding Hood and the wolf. There was a stylized sweetness to them that was a far cry from the wild romanticism of the printouts Nick had shown her of Thorne's work.

"No, they don't," Nick agreed, rising easily to his feet. "Pity. It would have made a nice twist, a mad artist in the attic instead of a mad wife."

"We're the only ones who are mad here," said Julia sourly.

All her joy in exploring had been sapped by the feeling that there were price tags being appended to everything. Which was silly. That was what she had come out here to do, to appraise and sell up. But it felt like a violation all the same.

She moved hastily forward as she saw Nick prowling towards the easel. "I don't think that's anything to do with what we're looking for."

"Too modern," Nick agreed, but he was already peeling back the cloth that covered it. Julia's hand fell back, too late to stop him.

It was a watercolor, not an oil, the colors light and delicate but as clear as the day they had been painted, protected from light and grime by the cloth that had been draped over it.

"I don't think anyone's touched this since it was painted," said Nick, and Julia could only nod, her throat suddenly tight, her vocal cords not working properly.

In the picture, it was autumn, the leaves on the trees just beginning to turn, the grass still bright and green. The grounds had been better maintained then, but Julia could still recognize the view down the slope in the back. In the center of the scene, by the summerhouse, a little girl was spinning in circles, her fluffy pigtails whipping around, her arms flung wide with the joy of movement. She wore a navy corduroy pinafore over a long-sleeved blouse with a Peter Pan collar, and on her feet were a pair of shiny red Mary Janes.

Julia remembered those shoes. Big-girl shoes, like the ones the girl in the flat upstairs had. Julia had wanted them so. Her father had said, *Why not brown? They would wear better.* But her mother had just smiled and said, *Let her have her spot of color.*

So she had had her red shoes, shiny and new, with the pricked-out tracery on the tops and real buckles on the side. Red shoes. Big-girl shoes.

"Julia?" Nick was looking at her, not the painting. "Are you all right?"

"That's me." The words came out as a croak. Spinning and spinning, the wind in her hair, and Mummy, with her easel, standing halfway up the hill, laughing. "She was painting me."

Flopping on the grass, breathless, giggling, the ground cool under her back. Squirming and laughing as Mummy pounced, tickling her.

Julia stuffed a fist in her mouth, fighting to hold back the sobs that seemed to come out of nowhere, that rose up from the pit of her stomach, bending her double, a quarter century's worth of sobs stampeding their way through her.

She could remember the feeling of the autumn air on her cheeks, the slosh-crunch of damp leaves beneath her feet, the scent of cigarette smoke in the air. And not just that. Memories were flooding back. Mummy, tucking her into bed, with that horrible, battered stuffed rabbit Julia used

331

to take everywhere with her, Peter Rabbit, his coat permanently unbuttoned and one ear off. Mummy, holding her hand in the Tube, herding her through an underground tunnel on some sort of outing, a holiday outing.

That horrible crunch and those flashing lights.

Where's Mummy? . . . Mummy's left us.

Julia's entire body was trembling; she was powerless to fight it, overwhelmed by grief that had no words, no voice, the grief of the child she had been, shaking, and scared, and so painfully lonely.

There was an arm around her shoulders, a hand rubbing circles on her back, a low voice saying, "Julia?"

She didn't hear it at first; the pounding in her head was like the howling of the waves, carrying all else before it.

"Julia?" whoever it was said again, and she remembered, disjointedly, where she was and who was with her.

She took a deep, shuddering breath. "I'm all right," she croaked, keeping her eyes down, her face hidden. Breathe in, breathe out. Breathe in, breathe out. The pain was still so strong, strong enough to keep her from thinking how she'd made a fool of herself.

"No, you're not." Julia lifted her head and saw Nick, blurred and indistinct, like a watercolor that had run in the rain. One arm around her shoulders, the other holding her elbow, he guided her forcibly to the couch. "Sit," he said.

Julia sat. Heavily. The ancient springs creaked beneath her, sending up a wave of dust. She coughed feebly, a cough that turned into a hiccup. Her eyes were red and her nose was running and she felt drained, drained beyond imagining.

"I'm sorry," she mumbled. It sounded painfully inadequate. She blinked at Nick, rubbing the salt from the corners of her eyes. "I feel like an idiot. I never —" She shook her head unsteadily. "I never cry like that. I don't know — I didn't realize —"

Nick didn't push it. Gently, he said, "Who painted that?"

"My mother. A long time ago." Julia pressed her lips together, not trusting herself to say anything else.

She felt — better now. Not good, but better. "Better" being a very relative term. She felt drained and hollow and thoroughly miserable, but herself again, not a howling mass of jelly. She wondered, abstractedly, if that was what possession felt like, that sense of being so entirely swept away from oneself, from one's own thoughts and behaviors. She had always prided herself on her self-control, on her poise.

"She was an artist?" Nick's voice was soft, undemanding. His arm sat loosely around Julia's shoulders.

She nodded, not looking at him. "An art student."

The arm behind her back shifted slightly. "She was good."

Julia kept her eyes on her hands. Same old hands. Same old freckles, same old school ring. "She died. A long time ago. When I was five. That's why we moved to New York."

The words came out jerkily, painfully. She wasn't sure why she was telling him this.

"Not easy, is it?" Nick's hand dropped to her shoulder, squeezed, lightly. "Mine walked out on us when I was seven."

Julia looked up at him, so abruptly that her head nearly collided with his chin.

Nick held her gaze, nodding as if in answer to an unspoken question. "She's an actress, in LA. I used to visit her there, summers, but it didn't suit either of us."

And she'd thought she had it bad. Julia's voice came out in a croak. "I'm sorry."

"Don't be." Nick kept his voice light. "I have a trio of very interfering aunts. They made sure to take up the slack."

Julia looked back down at her hands. "I have a very nice stepmother." Somehow, saying it made Julia feel weirdly teary again. "But we're not particularly close."

Her fault, not Helen's. Thinking of all those years of tentative overtures that Julia had so blithely brushed aside made her feel obscurely guilty.

"It's hard to be, after something like that." Nick spoke matter-of-factly. He retrieved his arm from around her shoulders and sat back, looking her full in the face. "Better?"

Julia nodded, biting her lip. "Sorry to melt down on you. I didn't realize that the attic would be so — booby-trapped." She managed a wobbly smile. "I feel like I tripped an emotional land mine."

Nick tucked a loose strand of hair behind her ear for her. There was something oddly soothing about the gesture. "Do you think you can cope with going through some old boxes?"

Julia breathed in deeply, feeling the new air filling her lungs. She felt completely wrung out, but not in a bad way. More like when she was small and would come home after a day of camp, half-asleep on her feet after a day of sun and chlorine and pool water.

She considered. "As long as they're at least a hundred years old."

"Good." Nick shifted forward, and Julia thought he meant to stand up.

But he didn't. He stayed where he was, his eyes resting gravely on her face.

"I'm all right," Julia said. "Really."

"I know," he said, and leaned forward to brush her lips with his.

Sixteen

Herne Hill, 2009

Nick's kiss was light, undemanding.

For a few happy moments Julia's brain shut down, leaving her to float on sensation alone: the gentle touch of his lips, the warmth of his palm against her cheek, the heavenly sensation of being cradled, cared for, the cushions of the sofa soft against her back, Nick's shirtfront crisp against her hands.

She wasn't aware of having reached out to him until he pulled back, just a nose length away. There was a fine dusting of blond hair on his jaw, like gold dust. She wondered if she touched it whether it would be soft or scratchy.

"Hi," he said softly, not moving. His blue eyes were intent on her face, watching her, waiting for her reaction.

It would be so easy to slide her hands up from his chest to his shoulders, to lean back against the cushions and draw him with her, back into that pleasant floatiness, where neither the recent nor the long dead past mattered, just two bodies — and, from the feel of it through the thin, linen shirt, his was a very attractive body.

So easy. But she didn't trust herself right now. She felt off-kilter, unsure of her own emotions. Seizing on an easy excuse, Julia heard her own voice saying, hoarse and breathless, "What about Natalie?"

Nick blinked and blinked again. "Natalie?"

Should she take it as a compliment that he sounded quite so befuddled? "Your best friend's sister. Tall, brunette, gorgeous?" Madly in love with you?

Nick sat back. "I know who she is," he said in a tone of understandable irritation. "What I don't understand is what the — what she has to do with this."

This? Julia decided not to explore that. That way madness lay. She hitched herself up to a more vertical sitting position. "It can't have escaped your notice that Natalie has a huge thing for you. I don't want to" — Julia almost said *tread on her turf* but quickly amended it to — "hurt her."

"Trust me," said Nick flatly. "It's not her heart that would be bruised."

"That's pretty presumptuous." Julia was offended on Natalie's behalf. She didn't even particularly like Natalie. But it was easier to be offended for Natalie than tussle with her own feelings, so she waded merrily in on Natalie's behalf. "Have you seen the way she looks at you? The girl has a class A crush on you."

Nick drove his fingers through his hair. "Natalie doesn't have a crush on me, as you so eloquently put it; she has a crush on the idea of me. She wouldn't know what to do with me if she had me."

Well, then. Julia folded her arms across her chest. "You just keep telling yourself that, big boy."

Nick pressed his eyes shut and then opened them again. "I didn't mean it that way." His gaze, as his eyes met Julia's, was disconcertingly frank. "Look, I'm not even sure how to explain it."

"There's no need," said Julia hastily. She was confused enough as it was; she didn't need him going all likable on her again.

"No?" Nick arched a brow. "Andrew is the best bloke in the world — and Natalie used to be such a decent kid."

Ouch, thought Julia. Decent kid? That was the kiss of death if ever she'd heard it.

Oblivious, Nick went on. "But her mother's gone and filled her head with all these ideas about my aristocratic connections — and it's not like that," he added forcefully. "I'm not like that. My family are normal people. Barking mad, the lot of them, but otherwise normal."

Tentatively, Julia leaned an elbow against the back of the couch. "What *was* all that stuff about if you had your rights? Cousin Caroline made it sound like you were the lost heir to the royal family or something like that."

Nick smiled grimly. "Not even near something like that. One of my ancestors did a favor for Charles the Second back when he was in exile — probably helped smuggle a woman into his rooms — and was rewarded with a title for his pains. Viscount Loring."

Julia raised her brows in mock awe. "Snazzy."

"And that, as they say, was that. My ancestors went on being generally charming and not particularly interesting until the beginning of the last century, when my great-grandfather created rather a fuss by running off with an actress." Nick pursed his lips. "Which, given the origin of the family title, seemed rather an appropriate way for it to end. As James the Fifth of Scotland said, 'It came with a wench, it shall gang with a wench.' I paraphrase, of course."

It all sounded strangely familiar. Not the James V bit, but the viscount running off with an actress. Julia remembered that pile of old *Tatlers* in the back bedroom, the ones she had so guiltily devoured, such a strange and foreign world, debutantes and bolters and errant viscounts. It had been all over the front of one issue. . . .

Julia sat up so abruptly that the couch springs creaked. "Wait, that was your family? 'Viscount Runs Off with Gaiety Girl'?"

Nick looked at her strangely.

Julia shrugged, saying a little sheepishly, "I found a pile of 1920s magazines when I was cleaning out one of the back bedrooms."

"Don't you know better than to believe everything you read in the papers?" Nick breathed out a long-suffering sigh. "She wasn't a Gaiety Girl; she was an actress, from an acting family. She got her start playing Cordelia. Although she did perform in some pretty risqué comedies in the twenties. That's how my great-grandfather met her. Met her, fell for her, shacked up with her, and, eventually, married her."

It all sounded pretty tame by modern standards. "I didn't realize they could untitle people for things like that."

Nick's lips quivered. "Un-title?"

341

Julia waved a hand, feeling strangely buoyant. Something about that glint in Nick's eye . . . "Or whatever you call it."

"Whatever you call it," Nick agreed. "And they can't. There's no removing titles for inappropriate liaisons, or half the House of Lords would be out on their ear. No. It's . . . a bit more complicated than that."

Julia burrowed down into the cushions. "I don't have any snooker to watch."

Nick acknowledged the point with a nod. "It's not all that exciting, mostly just a legal tangle. My great-grandmother was something of a Bohemian. She didn't believe in marriage as an institution, love should be free. . . . So my grandfather was born out of wedlock. At some point, she must have relented, because they were married in time for my great-aunts to be legitimate, but . . . Too late for Grandfather."

Julia had hung out with enough lawyers to pick up some of the lingo. "If they were married after, wouldn't that solve the problem? Retroactive legitimation?"

"Not back then." The answer was immediate and authoritative. "The law changed in 1926, but that was three years too late for my grandfather. And all the rest of their children were girls. So the title went the way of the dodo."

"That sucks," said Julia eloquently.

Nick shrugged. "I don't miss it. I don't think my great-grandfather did, either. It saves a lot of bother from title hunters."

Like Natalie? "What about the rest of your family?" said Julia quickly. "Did they mind?"

A slight reminiscent smile curved Nick's lips. "The only one who minded was my grandfather. He was a conventional old soul, for all that he was practically raised at the stage door. In his heart of hearts, he would have rather liked to be a viscount. He wouldn't say so, of course. But he did his best to get back on the straight and narrow, married a baronet's daughter from an unimpeachable county family — and then discovered that she had a secret passion for poetry."

"Reading it?" Julia asked, charmed.

"No, writing it." She could hear the laughter in his voice, laughter and love underneath it. "Granny used to have monthly readings. Salons, she called them. She'd dress up in flowing draperies and recite, while striking positions. It was atrocious. But everyone suffered through them and would tell her how wonderful it all was, because she was otherwise such a lovely person — and she played a very good hand of bridge."

"What did your grandfather think?"

Nick's expression softened. "He adored her. If she had taken up the ukulele, he would have been the first one sitting there in the front row, applauding."

Julia's throat felt suddenly tight. "They sound wonderful," she said.

She'd never known her grandparents on either side, and while she'd never felt the lack of it before, now she wondered what it would have been like to have that kind of family. Maybe the retelling made it rosier; maybe there would have been discontent and disagreements. But it would have been nice to have known.

"And your parents — I mean your father?" she amended quickly, remembering what Nick had told her about his mother. "What's he like?"

"Dad?" Nick overlooked her slip. "He's an actor. He did some stage stuff in his youth, but now it's mostly bit parts in costume dramas. That's how he met my mother," he added. "He did a brief — and not very successful — stint in LA."

"Blood will tell?" said Julia lightly. "Your actress great-grandmother's talent coming through?"

Nick snorted. "Hardly. I bolloxed my star turn as Bottom in *A Midsummer Night's*

Dream back at school. And it's hard to make an arse out of yourself when you're already wearing an ass's head."

She laughed, as he had intended her to, but as their laughter faded their eyes met and the tension that his family stories had kept at bay rose again between them. A dozen phrases ran through Julia's mind, only to be discarded again.

"Well," she said awkwardly, just as Nick began, "Julia, I —"

They both broke off. "You first," Nick said.

Julia chickened out. She fussed with her cuffs. "I was just going to say that we haven't made much headway on the attic."

"No, we haven't." For a moment, he looked at her, and she thought he might say something more. Whatever it was, he thought better of it. In one fluid movement, he rose from the couch and held out a hand to her. "Shall we?"

"Yes, thanks." Julia put her hand in his and let him help her up.

His hand tightened briefly around hers before he released it. "All right now?" he asked softly.

"All right"? Not exactly the term she would have used. "Confused as all hell" was more like it. But he had, she thought, swallowing a slightly hysterical laugh, succeeded admirably in getting her mind off her mother.

"Yes, perfectly, fine," Julia babbled, shoving her hair back behind her ears. "There are a whole bunch of little rooms in the back, all crammed with stuff. It will probably go faster if we each pick a different room. Maybe we start at the very back and work forward? I'm guessing the older stuff is probably pushed farther back."

"All right," he said, and if he was amused he had the courtesy not to show it. "Let's split up and reconvene in — an hour?"

"Sounds good to me," said Julia. She pushed open a door at random, revealing an ancient iron bedstead and cheap chest of drawers, all piled with a depressing jumble of decomposing cardboard boxes, smelling heavily of must. She paused in the doorway, her palm against the old wood. "Holler if you find anything good."

"Who knows?" Nick's slow smile did unfair things to her nervous system. "Maybe we'll find Imogen Grantham's diary."

Herne Hill, 1849
"Vittoria, Vittoria!"

The gaslight glinted prettily off Evie's golden curls as she stood by the pianoforte, warbling an Italian aria. Sophie Sturgis, accompanying her, was at least half a beat behind, and Evie's Italian pronunciation could, at the kindest, be termed "eccentric," but the audience called for an encore all the same.

Sitting on a settee a few yards away, Imogen smiled encouragingly at Evie and then hastily pulled in her feet as two of the younger Sturgises came careening around the side of the sofa, the one in pursuit of the other.

"Gently, my loves, gently!" called Mrs. Sturgis, without leaving her own comfortable chair. For a moment, the two children, eight and six, were the very picture of innocence — before running whooping into the next room.

Imogen suppressed a smile and turned to her left, ready to share her thoughts with Gavin — only to remember that it was Ned Sturgis on the couch beside her, not Gavin.

Fortunate for her that Ned's dazzled eyes were fixed on Evie. Imogen dropped her eyes to her hands, fighting a curious sense of dislocation. It scared her how dependent she had become upon Gavin, how flat and dull everything felt without him, as though she were only alive in those stolen hours and everything else a curious dream.

When, really, it ought to be quite the other way around.

Arthur wasn't with her tonight. He had a dinner at his club, but that was no matter. Just a comfortable family party, Mrs. Sturgis had said, no need to stand on ceremony, and Ned would see Imogen and Evie escorted safely back. Imogen had no doubt Ned would, nor any doubts as to why his mother had organized the party; the young man appeared to be head over heels over Evie. Imogen suspected this evening was something of an audition, to see how well Evie would fit within the boisterous Sturgis family circle. The fact that Evie was entirely unaware of this could only stand to her credit with Mr. and Mrs. Sturgis.

Evie was in deep conversation with Sophie Sturgis over the sheet music piled high on a table by the piano.

Imogen took a deep breath and recalled herself to her duty as guest. "Your sister plays very prettily," she said to Ned Sturgis.

"Hmm, pardon? Oh. Yes, yes, she does." Poor boy, he was so obviously flustered, caught out in a moment of reverie. The whiskers he had so proudly cultivated only made him look younger still. Manfully he offered back, "Miss Evie sings like an angel."

Miss Evie sang like a not very well-trained

seventeen-year-old girl, but Imogen appreciated the accolade all the same. "Perhaps you ought to tell her so yourself," she suggested gently.

"Do you think? I shouldn't want to be forward — that is —"

His earnestness was painfully endearing. "Everyone likes a little honest praise," said Imogen encouragingly.

And Ned Sturgis was such a nice boy.

A nice boy? Imogen caught herself up short. She was thinking like a dowager, like someone's elderly mother or maiden aunt.

Well, that was what she was, wasn't she? In calendar years she might be far closer to Ned's age than to his mother's, but Imogen's position in life placed her firmly on the sidelines of the room with Mrs. Sturgis, a respectable matron with ten years of marriage behind her. Even if Imogen hadn't been behaving like one recently.

What would they say, these Sturgises, if they knew she was off cavorting with an artist when she was meant to be at the dressmaker's or confined to her room with the headache? Would Mrs. Sturgis draw back her skirt as Imogen walked down the street? That thought didn't unduly disturb her. But what about Evie? There was no doubt her reputation would be tainted by association.

Imogen should break it off; she knew that. At least, she knew that at times like this. When she was with Gavin, it was a very different thing. Then, she just wanted to burrow into his arms and never let go.

It wasn't hurting anyone, Imogen told herself, as she had told herself time and again.

At least, not yet.

Evie finished her song, a Scots ballad, to another round of enthusiastic applause. Like a cork released from a bottle, the two youngest Sturgises careened towards their older brother. "You promised you'd play tiddlywinks!"

Ned looked from one to the other, obviously torn. "But Miss Evie —"

"Is quite done singing," said Evie gaily, joining them. "I shouldn't want to keep you from your obligations."

Rising, with more alacrity than grace, Ned said, "You'll join us?"

"Perhaps by and by," said Evie, smiling prettily at him, in a way that Imogen knew meant "no," even if poor Ned didn't.

Ned suffered himself to be tugged away by his younger siblings, but his gaze was fixed on Evie, his heart in his eyes.

"What a very nice young man he is," murmured Imogen.

"Ned Sturgis?" Evie looked at Imogen in surprise. "I suppose he's well enough."

"I believe that young man is carrying something of a torch for you." Only half-jokingly, Imogen added, "Say the word and you could be mistress of all you survey."

"Ned?" Evie dismissed the idea with casual scorn. "Ned is just a boy. He won't be thinking of anything like that, oh, for years yet."

"That boy is five years older than you are," Imogen pointed out, with some amusement. "And already a partner in his father's firm."

"Oh, *trade*." The contempt in Evie's voice made Imogen's eyebrows go up. She'd never heard her sound that way before, not Evie, who never had an evil word to say of anyone or anything.

"I shouldn't have thought to hear you mocking trade," said Imogen. The Grantham import business had paid for the dress on Evie's back and the gold locket around her neck. "Your father is in the same line of work."

"Yes, but Papa doesn't really concern himself with it, does he?" Evie turned eagerly in her seat on the settee, all ribbons and flounces. "He just signs papers when his man of business brings them. He's really more of — more of a gentleman scholar!"

351

"He does rather more than that," said Imogen mildly, trying not to let her disconcertion show. "He's in the offices several days a week."

Or so he claimed. She suspected he spent a great deal of that time napping in his club.

Imogen tried another tack. "I had heard from Mrs. Sturgis," she said carefully, "that Ned was to spend some time in Lisbon to look after his father's business interests there."

"Yes, another office," said Evie dismissively. "It's all papers and accounts and nothing the least bit interesting. It might as well be Perth or Liverpool. It's not as though there would be any society there. Any *proper* society."

"Proper society?" Imogen echoed. This snobbishness was as unexpected as it was new. Their neighbors, the circles in which they moved, all were engaged in some sort of business and proud of it, many only a generation or two removed from life above the shop.

With one exception: Augustus Fotheringay-Vaughn had been full of "society" during his calls that past summer, improbable stories of this baroness and that earl and all the good and the great with whom he claimed to mingle.

"I would hardly call this improper, would you?" said Imogen lightly. "Mrs. Sturgis would be very offended to be thought anything other than the soul of propriety."

"That's not what I meant. . . ." Evie fussed uncomfortably with her skirts. "You know. Proper town society."

"No," said Imogen firmly. "I don't know." Taking a chance, she added, "Nor, I imagine, does Mr. Fotheringay-Vaughn, for all his bold words."

She knew she had hit her mark when Evie's cheeks turned a bright, vivid red. "Augustus moves in very exalted circles."

Imogen looked sharply at her stepdaughter. "Augustus, is it?"

Evie looked away. "In any event," she said hastily, changing the subject with alarming alacrity, "Ned may be five years older than I am, but he has no dignity. Just look at him playing tiddlywinks with the children!"

With glorious unconcern for the state of his trousers, Ned had folded his long legs beneath him and was sitting on the hearthrug with his siblings, a younger sister hanging around his neck, a younger brother by his side. With the firelight limning them in a warm glow, they made a charming domestic picture.

"I think it's rather sweet," said Imogen.

"Very sweet," said Evie, in tones of worldly condescension that sat comically on the lips of sheltered seventeen. "When I marry, I want it to be someone older, someone — someone with some knowledge of the world."

Someone like Augustus Fotheringay-Vaughn?

"At your age," said Imogen slowly, "I thought so, as well."

She remembered the garden, in Cornwall, her father's frail hand in hers, as he tried, so very hard, to make her see sense. She had been as oblivious as Evie, convinced that she was a woman grown and equal to anything the world might throw at her.

And Arthur, whatever his shortcomings, was a well-meaning man. She couldn't say the same of Fotheringay-Vaughn.

Evie wrinkled her nose. "I didn't mean someone old like *Papa,*" she began, and then caught herself. "Not that Papa's not lovely, of course."

No, just geriatric, by Evie's standards. How old must Fortheringay-Vaughn be? Imogen put him at thirty, at least. Not quite as wide as the gap between Imogen and Arthur, but close.

"I was your age when I married your papa," Imogen said soberly, "and your papa wasn't so very much older than various persons of our acquaintance of whom you might be thinking. He was still quite dashing when I first met him."

Evie shook her head lightly, uncomprehending, the comparison between her father and Fotheringay-Vaughn a nonsensical one to her.

How to reach her, how to talk some sense into her? Not that Imogen was exactly a pillar of good sense at the moment.

She placed a hand over her stepdaughter's, saying in a low, urgent voice, "Do not let yourself be rushed into making a too-hasty choice. Evie! Do you understand me?"

Evie was spared answering by one of the younger Misses Sturgis — Imogen never could tell them apart — who bobbed a quick curtsy, saying, all in one breath, "With your pardon, Mrs. Grantham, Sophie's agreed to play if we would like to dance and would Miss Grantham make one of our set?"

"Go on," said Imogen. It was no use pursuing the conversation now. Evie wasn't hearing a word she said, not really. "I've been wanting to speak to Mrs. Sturgis."

She hadn't really — Mrs. Sturgis was a wonderful, warmhearted woman with two topics of conversation, her husband and her children — but at least Imogen knew Evie would come to no harm romping with the Sturgis children. It might, she hoped, soften her heart towards Ned. Or at least start her thinking.

It didn't have to be Ned Sturgis. But someone kind, someone young, someone who would value Evie for herself and blush at her name as Ned Sturgis did. Not a fortune hunter. Not a Fotheringay-Vaughn.

How far had it gone? Imogen excoriated herself for her blindness. She ought to have known; she ought to have realized. All those "teas" with Eliza Cranbourne . . . Evie had never liked Eliza, not even when they were children.

If Fotheringay-Vaughn had resorted to meeting Evie in secret, it meant that he had abandoned the hope of winning her by normal means. Were they already plotting an elopement? Not that an elopement was the only possible expedient. It would be just as easy to get her with child and demand a hasty marriage as a means of hushing up potential scandal.

Just thinking about it made Imogen distinctly sick to her stomach.

As she looked at Evie, so innocently romping with the Sturgis children, it all seemed like a sick fancy. But there had been that telling "Augustus."

She would have to be more vigilant, that was all. Guilt gnawed at her like rot, eating away from the inside out. If she had been at home, rather than indulging herself in adulterous pleasures, would Evie have been spared? Imogen couldn't help but feel, obscurely, that this was somehow all her fault, a punishment for her own sins. She had tried to tell herself that no one would be harmed by her liaison with Gavin, that Arthur would never miss what he didn't want anyway, and what Evie didn't know wouldn't hurt her.

But it did. It could.

Imogen folded her cold hands in her lap, twining her fingers so tightly together that she could feel the bones through the lace of her gloves.

She would deal with Fotheringay-Vaughn first. And then —

No. She couldn't think of it. Not now.

SEVENTEEN

Herne Hill, 2009

Julia did find a diary, but it wasn't Imogen Grantham's.

She tried to be methodical, but it was hard, when her ancestors' chosen filing method appeared to be "just shove it over there." Not to mention that her mind was largely elsewhere, scuttling back and forth between the memories evoked by her mother's painting and that confusing, entirely unexpected kiss.

She couldn't figure out what to make of Nick. Entrepreneur on the make or genuinely decent guy? The way he'd held her when she'd lost it — the thought of that still made her wince — and the way he'd talked about his family both seemed to signal the latter. But then she remembered her first impressions of him and those offhand comments about value and valuations.

It didn't help, Julia thought wryly, that she had all the emotional stability of a wet dishrag right now.

It wasn't just that she felt emotionally wrung out; she was off-balance, too. She'd always taken it for granted, part of the framework of her life, that her mother had been, for lack of a better word, a flake, that she must not have really cared very much about Julia. No one had ever said as much, but it had been there in the subtext. All that her father ever said about her mother was that she was an artist or "artistic," the tone of the word subtly pejorative.

He hadn't said anything to Julia about the woman who had tucked her in at night, the woman who had painted that picture. There had been so much love in it.

Julia rubbed the heels of her hands against her eyes. Okay, now she was getting silly, attributing emotions to paint on paper. If she looked at it again, would she see and feel the same things? She didn't know. She wasn't sure she wanted to try.

Looking down, Julia realized that she had just emptied and refilled the same box without paying the slightest bit of attention to any of the contents. More slowly, forcing herself to pay attention, she went through the box again. There was a collection of records, painfully quaint in their square cardboard cases, mostly folk and rock from the seventies: David Bowie, Gary Glitter, Roxy Music. Julia set the records aside and kept digging.

Had these people ever thrown anything out? There were defunct toasters and buttoned boots and an obscure metal item that she finally identified as a primitive sort of curling iron. The photo albums were tempting, with their sepia-toned pictures of women with World War II–era hair and ludicrous bathing costumes, but far too late to be anything of the sort she was looking for.

Imogen Grantham, Julia reminded herself. Gavin Thorne. Missing paintings.

She found World War I–era letters and late Victorian journals, a whole set of them, dated from the 1870s to '90s. They were interesting in their own way, an odd compendium of recipes, sketches, quick thoughts, and personal reminders, but far too late for her purposes. If she was in her twenties, in the 1870s, Olivia Parsons — Julia checked the name on the flyleaf — wouldn't have been around in the 1840s.

It was while she was moving the Olivia oeuvre out of the way that Julia found the other, smaller book, buried beneath Olivia's larger, heavier journals. Unlike Olivia's handsome, leather-bound journal, this one had a cover of stiffened paper, patterned in what might once have been paisley but had turned with dirt and age to a murky swirl, the spine and edges protected with faded red fabric.

Evangeline Grantham, January 14, 1846, was written on the flyleaf in an elaborate, curly script.

It was the right time period, even if it was the wrong name. Imogen . . . Evangeline . . . Phonetically similar? Perhaps Cousin Caroline's family tree had gotten it wrong? Julia couldn't remember an Evangeline in there.

She flipped the book open, skimming passages at random. The paper had been cheap; it had darkened with time, crumbling at the edges, but, mercifully, the ink hadn't faded too badly. It didn't take more than a few entries for it to become clear that Evangeline couldn't be Imogen; she spoke of being moved from the nursery to a proper bedroom on the first floor, and there were many references to both "Papa," the owner of the establishment, and Papa's second wife, who appeared to be in constant tension with a character known as "Aunt Jane." Evangeline's sympathies were clearly with her stepmother, not with Aunt Jane.

Imogen? Possibly. The timing worked. Julia started flipping forward. Evangeline hadn't kept her diary regularly, just when she was particularly worked up about something: Aunt Jane being cross or a pretty length of fabric.

About two-thirds of the way in, a name leapt out at Julia. *We had guests for dinner tonight! They were all artists who had come to call on Papa and see his* — the words blurred there, but the next line was clear enough. *There were three of them: Mr. Rozzetty, Mr. Thorn, and Mr. Fotheringay-Vaughn. Mr. F-V was quite elegant and more like a fine gentleman than an artist.*

Jackpot.

Julia sat down on the floor next to the bed, in a dusty little nook between cardboard boxes, drawing her legs up to her chest as she read.

Aunt Jane was very cross at not having been told there would be that many for dinner, but the rest of us were very glad for the company. Mr. F-V was particularly amusing.

Julia checked the date on the entry. *February 1849.*

She went back and read the rest of the

entry, more carefully this time. It was mostly about Mr. F-V. Mr. F-V's witty stories, Mr. F-V's cunning watch fob, Mr. F-V's pretty compliments; at least, Evangeline thought they were compliments (was there anything more tedious than a teenager's *does he like me?*), but the evidence was there, Mr. Thorn and Mr. Rozzetty, in the house, in early 1849.

It was kind of amazing to think that Dante Gabriel Rossetti — it had to be Rossetti — had eaten in Julia's dining room.

Evangeline was disparaging of both Rossetti and Thorne. Rossetti went on and on about art, and Thorne was very quiet and when he did speak spoke only of serious things, which was really very tedious and made Aunt Jane cross, although Mama seemed to find it interesting.

"Julia?"

The sound of her name made Julia's head jerk up. Knocked 160-odd years out of the past, it took her a moment to focus her bleary eyes on the strange man in the doorway.

"Wha— oh, hi." She scrubbed the hair back from her face with a grimy hand. "What's up?"

"Success," Nick said with great satisfaction. He rested a hand against the doorframe. From Julia's position on the floor, he seemed to be about ten feet high. "In 1849, Arthur Grantham paid one Gavin Thorne the lordly sum of twenty guineas for painting a portrait of his wife."

Julia stretched her cramped legs out in front of her. Her brain felt muddled, still half in Evangeline Grantham's diary. "Lordly?" she echoed.

"Not really." Nick was clearly on a high. He paced in a little circle between the boxes. "Twenty guineas was a fair amount of money in those days, but much less than you'd find spent on comparable paintings. It seems like Grantham got Thorne at fire-sale rates. Struggling artist, grateful for patronage, needing to eat . . ."

Julia rubbed the grit out of her eyes. "But that's the portrait. What about *Tristan and Iseult*?"

"Nothing," Nick admitted. "At least, yet. I checked Grantham's account books from 1848 to 1852. No more mention of Thorne. If Grantham did commission that painting, he paid him under the table."

"So, basically," said Julia, her voice rusty, "we still have no idea how the Tristan and Iseult painting got here. Or why it was in the back of my wardrobe."

"But we do have something linking

Thorne to the household. And you, dear girl, have not one Gavin Thorne painting, but two."

"You are a poet and you did not know it," murmured Julia. "Sorry. Getting a little slaphappy here."

Unsteadily, she levered herself to her feet, one hand on the old bed frame, the other still holding the diary. Her limbs felt old and creaky.

Nick nodded at the book in her hand. "What's that?"

"This?" Julia couldn't help herself. She gave a nonchalant little wave. "It's a diary."

"You're joking."

"Nope. But it's not Imogen's," she added quickly. "It's her stepdaughter's. And, yes, Gavin Thorne was here. Don't get too excited. She mentions Thorne only in passing. It's typical teenager stuff. She's mostly interested in the things that directly concern her. New dresses. Her first big crush . . . Who, by the way, is another painter."

Nick perked up. "Does she say who the other painter might be?"

"Augustus something-or-other. Sorry," Julia said as Nick's face fell. "Not Rossetti or any of the big names. Although Rossetti was here for dinner." The thought of it still gave her a thrill. "Here." She handed the diary over, open to the relevant page.

"Hmm," said Nick, rapidly skimming. "At least her handwriting is reasonably tidy. Although her prose style appears rather . . . overwrought."

"Teenager," said Julia succinctly. "Teenager *and* Victorian. Bring out your italics." The last word was slightly muffled by a massive yawn.

Nick lowered the book and looked at her with a professional eye. "You're done in."

"It's only —" Julia checked her watch. No. That had to be a mistake. On the other hand, no wonder her legs hurt. "Is it really three thirty?"

"Sadly, yes." Nick relinquished the diary, stretching his arms up over his head, narrowly missing the single, hanging bulb. "And I should be going home."

Julia tucked the diary under her arm. "You're welcome to stay here." Realizing how it sounded, she hastily added, "It's not like there's any shortage of empty bedrooms. You can take your pick."

Empty bedrooms. Empty beds. Nothing suggestive there.

Nick pondered. Probably, thought Julia, trying to find a tactful way to turn her down.

She was on the verge of rescinding her offer — to save awkwardness all around —

when he said, "Thanks. You don't happen to have a spare toothbrush, have you?"

Herne Hill, 1849

The next time Evie left to call on Eliza Cranbourne, Imogen followed.

She watched from the window as Evie left by the front door, properly attired in a prim walking dress, and then, checking carefully to make sure that no one was watching, feinted left, around the side of the house.

Imogen ran lightly down the stairs, not pausing to collect her gloves and bonnet. Part of her was appalled at herself, snooping and spying like — like Jane. She had tried, half a dozen times over the past few days, to elicit confidences from Evie, to lead her gently to discussing the matter. Evie had said nothing.

Imogen had, she realized in despair, made the cardinal error of treating her stepdaughter as more of a friend than a child. She had never made any efforts to exert any discipline, preferring to be a playfellow rather than a parent. Yes, Evie loved her, but when she made any effort to speak to her seriously Evie only smiled and kissed her lightly on the cheek and did not heed her.

She could tell Arthur, she supposed, but

367

at that Imogen's spirit rebelled. No. Better to nip the affair in the bud with the minimum embarrassment to Evie and no one else the least the wiser. They would laugh about this together someday, Imogen told herself firmly as she reached for the door that led out into the garden, someday when Evie was safely settled with a young husband who adored her and children of her own and Augustus Fotheringay-Vaughn just a childish fancy, the bloom long since worn off.

As Arthur might have been, had Imogen heeded her own father's counsel.

"Where are you off to?" Imogen started as a voice spoke sharply from behind her.

It was Jane, standing in the doorway of the morning room, her embroidery hoop in her hand.

"I'm — taking a walk." She wasn't going to betray Evie to Jane. Jane would go straight to Arthur. She smiled determinedly at Jane. "It's such a fine day."

Jane regarded her narrowly. "You've been taking a number of walks recently. You should watch where you go. People might start to talk."

"Yes, well, it is quite good for the constitution. You might want to try it." Imogen hastily opened the door, although not in time to miss Jane's parting shot.

"Unlike some people, I prefer to stay close to home."

Yes, someone else's home. It was a churlish thought, but it was true. Not for the first time, Imogen wondered how Jane could live as she did, fetching Arthur's slippers, ordering his household, a perpetual outsider.

Except that she wasn't, not really. It was Imogen who was the outsider and had been since that first day. She had no more place in Arthur's household than she had ten years before.

If she were to leave —

Imogen nipped that line of thought before it could go further. She was meant to be looking for Evie. From the direction in which she had been heading, it seemed as though she was heading for the orchard gate, down by the far end of the garden. The very same route Imogen had used in her meetings with Gavin. Why was it that that thought filled her with such distaste?

It was all topsy-turvy. The idea of Evie trysting with Fotheringay-Vaughn filled Imogen with repugnance, and, yet, in the eyes of the world there was nothing so very wrong with two young lovers seeking a stolen moment alone, while there was something very wrong with a married woman meeting her lover. Try as she might, Imogen couldn't see it that way, though, couldn't find anything wrong or sordid about the time she spent with Gavin, except for the awful technicality of those marriage lines that bound her to Arthur.

Being with Gavin felt natural, in a way that being with Arthur never had.

It was cold among the trees of the orchard, the air acid with the vinous scent of rotting apples, fallen from the tree to decompose among the yellowing leaves. The smell seemed even more acute than usual; the combination of overripe fruit and rotting leaves made Imogen's stomach turn. The enchanted season was well and truly over. The few apples that still clung stubbornly to the tree were misshapen and worm-eaten.

Imogen nearly didn't see them. They had chosen their spot well, hard by the high garden wall, shielded by the gooseberry bushes on one side, by the trees of the orchard on the other. They made a pretty tableau: Fotheringay-Vaughn's arms about Evie's waist, her head tipped trustingly up towards his, her blond hair, confined only by a ribbon pulling back the sides, tumbling in curls down her back.

". . . soon," Imogen heard him murmur, his fingers playing with Evie's curls, his lips by her ear.

Imogen planted herself firmly before them. "What's all this?" she said sharply.

Her voice acted on them like a pistol shot. The lovers sprang apart. Imogen had the petty satisfaction of seeing Fotheringay-Vaughn skid on a patch of wet leaves before recovering himself with a hand against the rough wood of the wall. He sent her a look of pure hatred.

"Mama!" Evie's color was high, her eyes bright, but there was no shame in her face, just an expression of exalted consciousness, like Joan of Arc listening to spirits. "You remember Mr. Fotheringay-Vaughn?"

She spoke the name like an incantation, looking at him with worshipful eyes.

"Vividly," said Imogen quellingly. "What I would like to know is what he is doing in our orchard?"

Evie colored but went on undaunted. "You cannot imagine how I have wanted to tell you! But Augustus . . . that is, I . . . thought that perhaps —"

"It would be more conducive to your well-being and good reputation to meet in secret?"

"No! That is —" Evie looked imploringly at Fotheringay-Vaughn.

Fotheringay-Vaughn essayed a bored-

371

looking bow and said in his aristocratic drawl, "Madam, I assure you, my intentions towards your daughter are entirely honorable."

"That," said Imogen succinctly, "is precisely what I feared."

Evie's brow wrinkled. She stepped forward, holding out her hands in an instinctive gesture of supplication. "It's true, Mama, really it is. Augustus would never do anything to hurt me. We intend to be married!"

Fotheringay-Vaughn inclined his head in acknowledgment. "Ma'am," he said.

"Isn't this rather the wrong venue and audience, then?" asked Imogen pointedly. She directed her questions to Evie. "If all of that is true, why are you meeting in secret rather than in the drawing room? Why doesn't he go to your father and sue properly for your hand?"

Evie glanced uneasily at Fotheringay-Vaughn but rallied gamely. "We thought Papa might make objection to Augustus's profession. But once he sees us established in society . . ."

Imogen looked from Evie to Vaughn. "Established in society? Do you mean you weren't planning to tell your papa until after you were married?"

Evie looked pleadingly at Imogen. "You know how he can be! I wanted to tell you," she added disingenuously. "I knew you would understand."

Imogen's heart sank. These past years, she had prided herself on, if nothing else, having rescued Evie from the stifling influence of Jane. But what had she really done?

"What I understand," said Imogen quietly, "is that such a marriage is illegal. He didn't tell you that, did he? You cannot marry without your father's consent. Unless you intended to go to Scotland?"

From the quick look that passed between the two of them, she knew that she was right.

That Evie would even think of such a thing — that she could so coolly contemplate an elopement — Even worse, she seemed entirely unaware of the consequences of her actions. She had put herself, wholly and entirely, into Fotheringay-Vaughn's hands. Even now, she was looking to him, a quick, anxious look. Fotheringay-Vaughn gave a little shake of his head, as if to say, *Never mind all this.*

The gesture made Imogen see red. She spoke sharply to Evie. "Didn't you stop to think that such a betrayal would break your father's heart?"

"We never meant to distress Papa! Did we, Augustus?" Evie twined her hands together, so painfully, achingly, young and earnest. In slightly muffled tones she said, "I'm sure once Papa saw us moving in society "

"What society? A sordid rented room in a miserable part of town? Or did your gallant lover intend to apply to your papa for the means of setting himself up in the style he so ardently desires?"

She had the satisfaction of seeing Fotheringay-Vaughn's lips tighten. But he said nothing.

"Oh, it's not like that," Evie said quickly. "Augustus doesn't need Papa's money, do you, Augustus? He's more than enough of his own. His family —"

Imogen couldn't bear to see Evie deceived so. Gently but firmly, Imogen said, "Dearest, you've been fed a passel of lies by a man whose only interest is in your dowry."

Evie looked at her with wounded eyes. "How can you say such horrid things? Augustus doesn't need my money! He only paints portraits as a — as a vocation! Not for the money." She looked to her betrothed. "Tell her, Augustus!"

Fotheringay-Vaughn leaned back against the fence, his very posture an insult. In an insolent drawl he said, "I wouldn't dignify that sort of base accusation with a response."

"No," said Imogen, tight-lipped. "You wouldn't. Because it's true."

"But —" Evie looked uncertainly from Fotheringay-Vaughn to Imogen. "His family — the secret marriage lines —"

It was time to nip this in the bud once and for all. With silent apologies to Gavin, Imogen said crisply, "Your suitor's real name is Alfred Potts. His father was a dustman. He is no more a Vaughn than I am. If you'd like, I can prove it to you."

The last was pure bluff, but she had no doubt it was true, if she knew where to look.

"Augustus?" Evie turned wide, bewildered eyes to her betrothed, searching for reassurance. "Augustus?"

But he wasn't looking at Evie. His eyes were narrowed on Imogen, with a look of such concentrated venom that it took all her will not to take a step back.

"You sanctimonious bitch," he said.

Next to her, Evie gasped.

Imogen kept her head high, her eyes focused on Fotheringay-Vaughn. "Evie, I think you should go back to the house."

Fotheringay-Vaughn took a step forward, his usual languid pose abandoned. His hands were clenched loosely at his sides. "I suppose it was Thorne who told you, wasn't it?" His eyes flicked to Evie. Deliberately, maliciously, he said, "Was it before or after you took him to your bed?"

There was no sound in the orchard but the rustling of the leaves of the trees. Even the squirrels seemed to have ceased their industrious activity. The scent of rotting apples was strong in Imogen's nostrils.

He didn't know anything, not really; he couldn't prove anything.

Imogen could feel the patches of color rise in her cheek, high and bright, but she kept her spine straight, her voice steady. "You, sir, have made yourself unwelcome here, twice over. This interview is at an end."

She turned her back on him, her step steady on the slippery ground, but Vaughn's voice followed her. "Oh, you can dish out other people's secrets, but you can't take it, can you? Don't want your little precious knowing what you've been getting up to in the dark. In the dark, and the morning, and the afternoon . . ."

She shut her ears to his nasty words. Whatever she and Gavin had, it wasn't like that; it wasn't anything shallow and sordid. She wished she could turn and shout that back at Vaughn, toss his words back in his face. She could feel herself trembling, trembling with anger and frustration, that she and Gavin should have to hide themselves from the world, that it didn't matter at all —

That she loved him.

Imogen drew in a deep breath, trying to steady herself. Resolutely, she held out a hand to her stepdaughter. "Come, Evie. Let us back to the house."

Evie made no move to take her hand. There were twin lines between her brows, lines Imogen had never seen there before. Evie looked at Imogen with bewildered eyes, like someone in a nightmare, seeing the familiar turn strange.

In a trembling voice, she asked, "Is it true?"

"Oh, yes," said Fotheringay-Vaughn silkily. "Down to the last, sordid detail."

"Cornered rats bite," said Imogen shortly. "Come." She held out her hand again to Evie. "He's trying to hurt you — and hurt me for ruining his chances with you. That's all."

Evie took a step back, pale but determined. "You haven't answered me," she said. "Is it true — about you and Mr. Thorne?"

Something about the set expression on

Evie's face made Imogen's heart twist. The little girl whose hand used to rest so trustingly in hers, who used to run to her with her childish tragedies and triumphs. She looked all grown-up suddenly, grown up too fast.

"Evie!" Imogen stepped hastily forward and felt a rotten apple squish beneath her boot, the pungent scent filling the air. She swallowed hard. "How can you think such things? You know I would never —"

But she had. The words stuck in her throat. She couldn't say it, and she couldn't bring herself to deny it.

Behind her, she could hear Fotheringay-Vaughn laughing. It was a singularly unpleasant sound.

Despair crashed around her. What did it matter how much she loved Gavin or how much Gavin loved her? "Criminal conversation," that was the legal term for it. Criminal. As if they had stolen something that belonged rightfully to someone else. To Arthur. Never mind that Arthur didn't need her love or want it; in the eyes of the law, both it and she were his.

Then why did it feel as though she was betraying Gavin by denying him?

Her eyes on Evie, Imogen said thickly, "I would never do anything to hurt you. I love you. You know that."

"How could you?" Imogen wasn't sure whether the words were directed at her or Augustus or both. Evie pressed her fist against her lips, trying to hold back the tears. "How could you?"

"Evie, darling, wait —" Imogen reached out to her, but the girl wrenched from her grasp.

Evie's hair whipped sharply around her as she yanked away. "Don't touch me! Don't speak to me!" Her voice was wild and etched with acid, the tears streaming unheeded down her face. She turned to Augustus. "And as for you — As for you —"

Her words were lost in a sob. With an inarticulate noise of misery, she yanked up her skirts and fled, the ruffled edges of her pantalets visible beneath her skirts, her calves pumping. Imogen had a sudden, disorienting image of her, ten years ago, running up and down this same hill, her little boots sure on the slope, her hair flying behind her as it did now, calling, *Mama! Come see!*

Half-blinded by tears, Imogen started to follow. She could find her, talk to her, make her see. . . . Make her see what? Lie to her? It was an impossible situation. Vaguely Imogen began to realize the depth of the trap she had dug for herself. She could betray her love or her marriage vows. Either way, she was damned.

"That didn't have to happen," came Fotheringay-Vaughn's voice from behind her. The serpent in the garden. "If you'd let right enough alone."

Imogen knew she shouldn't, but she turned anyway. He stood by a tree, an apple in his hand. There were lines of dissipation etched in his face, and the curl of his lip was distinctly unpleasant.

"Go away," she said indistinctly. "You're not wanted here."

Fotheringay-Vaughn laughed, a low, unpleasant laugh. "Thanks to you." He took a large bite of the apple. "How d'you think Grantham will react to the news of your little trysts with Thorne?"

And with that, tossing the apple in his hand, he disappeared through the garden gate, leaving only a muddy set of footprints and the smell of rotting fruit behind him.

EIGHTEEN

London, 1849

"Shhh," Gavin said. "Augustus is all bluster."

His fingers itched to reach out and draw Imogen close, to stroke her hair and bury her head in his chest, as if he could protect her from all the calumnies of the world. But she held herself stiff and tense, buttoned from cuffs to chin in a jacket that fit tightly over her demure dress, her hands hidden in leather gloves, her face shaded by her bonnet.

They had met on neutral territory, by Westminster Bridge, far from Herne Hill, far from Grantham's offices, far from Gavin's studio. All around them, the daily bustle of London went on, the ships darting along the water, the street vendors hawking their wares. Imogen stood, looking down into the river, her gloved hands on the rail.

"What good would it do Augustus to share

his suspicions?" Gavin argued, wishing like the blazes that he believed his own words. Pure venom might be reason enough for Augustus. "That's all they are. Suspicions. He has no proof."

"Proof!" Imogen lifted a stricken face. Her cheeks were pale despite the wind, her eyes hollow. "The way Evie looked at me —"

"Shhh," Gavin said, for want of anything better. He would have settled his hand on hers on the rail, but the posture of her body forbade contact. "Shhh."

"She won't speak to me," Imogen said brokenly. "She looks through me as though I weren't even in the room."

"She's young," said Gavin, feeling helpless in the face of Imogen's grief. "These things pass."

Imogen shook her head, tight-lipped. "She feels that I've betrayed her — and I have. Gavin —"

Something about the way she looked at him, the way she said his name, sent a flare of raw panic through him. "She's probably looking for a scapegoat for her own foolishness," he said gruffly, "running about with Augustus. She needs someone to blame, and who better than you?"

Imogen stared at her hands, lightly clasping the rail, and said nothing.

Gavin redoubled his efforts. "It's been two days now. If either of them were going to say something, they would have. Neither of them can say anything without implicating themselves. Your silence for theirs, that's what they're relying upon, mark my words. Besides," he added wryly, "Augustus wouldn't do anything that didn't benefit himself. What good would he have out of destroying you?"

"Revenge?" Gavin couldn't dispute her reading of Augustus's character. Her fingers fleetingly touched Gavin's sleeve. "Will Fotheringay-Vaughn make trouble for you? He knows that you were the one who told me. . . ."

Touched by her concern, Gavin cloaked his feelings in bravado. "What can he do to me? Save remove his presence from my studio? I can pay the rent without him." In a gentler voice he said, "Don't worry yourself about me."

"But I do worry about you." Imogen lifted a troubled face to his. "I worry what a scandal might mean for your painting. Arthur knows too many influential men in the Academy. If I were to be the architect of your ruin . . ."

"You're making dragons out of clouds," said Gavin dismissively. Every instinct screamed that it was time to end the discussion now, before she could bring it to its logical conclusion.

Before she could bring them to their logical conclusion.

With false heartiness Gavin said, "What you need is some distracting. What do you think of a bit of low theater? I saw a penny gaff just down the street. There certainly won't be anyone you know there."

It was a poor feint and he knew it. For a moment, he thought she might argue, but she seemed no more inclined to press the topic than he. Her face was white and tired, dark circles around her eyes.

She bit her lip. "All right. So long as I might sit?"

"It's crude, but there are benches," Gavin assured her.

He tucked her hand into the crook of his arm. She didn't lean into him as she once would have. Instead, she held herself stiffly, moving without her accustomed grace.

"In a few days," Gavin said softly, "this will all have blown over."

Imogen lifted her face to his, her lips pressed tightly together. "Perhaps," she said wearily.

"I wish —" he began, and broke off. "Never mind. That's the theater, over there.

Such as it is."

Outside the pub, garish posters proclaimed the wonders awaiting them. *The Dastardly Deeds of Jack Sheppard!* proclaimed one, featuring a picture of the notorious highwayman, his hat pulled low over his brow and his pistol at the ready, while another promised *The String of Pearls: A Romance,* as a scantily clad lady fainted over a gentleman's arm and another man lurked ominously nearby, a knife at the ready.

"It's not Drury Lane," said Gavin apologetically.

"I believe I shall like this exceedingly," said Imogen gamely.

He felt her hand tighten for a moment on his arm, and felt a wave of painful tenderness wash over him.

For a moment their eyes met, but it was no use. There was no way either could say anything of what they felt.

"Come along in, then," said Gavin, feeling singularly useless. He wished it were Covent Garden he were handing her into, not the back room of a pub.

The small antechamber was already packed with people, many of them clustered around the refreshment table, factory girls in their scanty frocks and errand boys exchanging insults and spitballs. There was only lemonade, apples, and cake for sale at the stall, but the smell of gin was already strong in the air. As one of the factory girls held out her glass, Gavin saw the stallholder add a liberal splash of the clear liquid to the lemonade with a wink and a nudge.

He hastily paid their two pennies and ushered Imogen into the makeshift theater. The floor was sticky beneath their feet, and he saw Imogen surreptitiously lifting her skirts. Nutshells crackled beneath her boots, the detritus of the prior performance, and the air was noxious with the smell of cheap tobacco.

It had been so long since he had been to one of these entertainments that Gavin had forgotten that the seats in the makeshift gallery were segregated by sex.

"Will you be all right in the pit?" he asked. The pit was already swarming with ragged boys, tossing nuts and insults at one another. There were women there, too, ragged factory girls, probably younger than Imogen's stepdaughter, but aged beyond their years. On a bench in the middle, an older woman snored, sodden with gin. "Otherwise, we must sit separately."

Imogen picked her way gingerly down, dodging a flying walnut. "I've never sat in a

386

pit before."

"I believe this one was a cock pit before it was a theater," said Gavin drily. "This should be some slight improvement on its former use, but I can't promise how much."

Discreetly, Imogen lifted her scented handkerchief to her nose and took a deep breath. Her eyes took in the crude stage, the women jostling one another in the gallery. "I had never thought to see such a place."

Gavin turned in his seat. In a low voice he said, "Should I not have brought you? We can still leave —"

"No." Her hands tightened in her lap. "I want to see this. There is so much I want to see, and you are the only one who doesn't find it strange in me to want it."

"Probably," said Gavin ruefully, "because I am no gentleman. If I knew better —"

"I wouldn't have you be anything other than what you are. As it is —" She broke off, her lips pressing tightly together, as if she had already said too much.

Gavin's emotions overmastered him. He caught her hand. "Imogen —"

He was interrupted by a loud banging of a drum. The din of it reverberated through his head. He wanted to leap to his feet and shake the thoughtless drummer, to rip the drum from his hands and fling it in the pit.

Imogen gently withdrew her hand from Gavin's and turned her face to the stage.

Gavin cursed under his breath as the master of ceremonies, a red-faced man in a black coat gone green with wear, began his stock patter.

"Ladies and gentlemen, I regret to inform you that we ain't got Jenny Lind for you t'night. Sadly, the nightingale is engaged elsewhere."

The audience hooted its appreciation. Imogen sat silent beside Gavin, her hands folded neatly in her lap. Damn that blasted bonnet, that hid her face so entirely from his view. Was she seething within, as he was? Burning with words that couldn't be said?

The master of ceremonies yanked on his suspenders. "But I trust you'll find what we got just as much to your taste. Now — *Now,*" he bellowed, raising his voice to be heard over the shouted responses from the pit. "You may be asking yourselves why it is we don't got no carpet on these here boards and no curtain to raise."

"At yer uncle's?" shouted a voice from the gallery.

"Pshaw!" interrupted another. "His wife has gone and turned the stuff into 'er petticoat, ain't she?"

"Make 'er lift it up and show us!" contributed another.

Gavin looked uneasily at Imogen.

" 'Old yer 'orses," retorted the master of ceremonies, with great dignity. "You'll look your fill, soon enough!"

Under cover of the resulting din, Gavin leaned closer to Imogen. "Are you quite all right?"

The face she turned to him was decidedly green. She smiled with difficulty. "It is just the smell of the tobacco. I am — not accustomed to it."

It wasn't just the smell of the tobacco. As he watched, she pressed her handkerchief to her nose and took a deep breath, her entire body seeming to hunch in upon itself.

Gavin made a quick decision. "You're not well." He placed a hand beneath her arm and helped her up, feeling her sway on her feet. Her eyes were half-closed. "I'm taking you away. Now."

"Oy!" complained a woman behind them. "I can't see!"

Gavin shoved a way through, kicking a boy's sprawled legs out of the way. "The lady isn't well."

"Oh, a *lady,* is it?" The woman nudged the man next to her. "Just listen to that!"

Her companion gave a rough laugh.

389

"They're all the same in the dark!"

"If she's a lady, I'm the Queen of Sheba!" shouted someone else.

Various ribald suggestions as to Imogen's true occupation followed after her and Gavin as they made their way through the tight-packed pit and back down the corridor.

Gavin wasn't sure that Imogen even heard them. That was a small mercy. All of her attention was concentrated on picking her way, step by step, as if she were afraid her feet might not manage on their own. With his arm around her waist to steady her he could feel each labored breath as though it were his own.

When they were at last outside, Gavin said roughly, "I should never have brought you to that place."

"It's not your fault. Or — theirs." Imogen managed a sickly ghost of a smile. He could see her struggling to control her heaving stomach, every word an effort. "I'm sorry . . . to have disrupted . . . the show. Cook isn't . . . quite so good . . . at identifying fresh fish . . . as she thinks she is."

Bad fish or stale tobacco, whatever the cause, Imogen looked about ready to keel over. Gavin began to look about for a hansom cab. "We'll get you back to my studio. You can lie down for a spell. Maybe some whiskey?"

Gavin couldn't remember if he had spirits in the studio, but Augustus would. Given that this situation was, in Gavin's opinion, entirely Augustus's fault, he had very little compunction about helping himself to the man's liquor.

When Augustus deigned to return to the studio, thought Gavin grimly, they were going to be having a good, long discussion.

"No, really." The suggestion galvanized her into movement. She shrugged away from his arm. "I —"

She broke off, her face gone chalk white.

"Imogen?" Gavin caught at her arm. "Imogen! What is it? Speak to me."

"There," she said.

She lifted a trembling hand and pointed to the other side of the busy street. Following her direction, Gavin caught a glimpse of a man in a heavy overcoat and muffler entering a house across the street. Before he opened the door, he took a quick look about him and Gavin had a fleeing impression of a high-crowned hat pulled low on his brow, the only bit of his face visible a bristle of ginger whiskers.

Imogen's fingers cut into Gavin's arm. "It's Arthur."

Julia was blearily shoveling coffee into the filter when the knob of the kitchen door rattled.

Nick hadn't made his appearance yet, not entirely surprising considering that it must have been well past four in the morning by the time she had tucked him into bed. And by "tucked" she meant handed him her British Airways travel toothbrush and a spare towel, pointed the way to the bathroom, and waved him in the general direction of the nearest room with a full, working bed frame and reasonably clean sheets.

Nick had tactfully withdrawn into his room until she had finished her hasty ablutions. It wasn't until her own door was safely closed that she had heard his door squeak open and the the hall floorboards creak. Five minutes later, the process had reversed itself. There had been no late-night visitations or nocturnal ramblings. At least, not that she knew of. When Julia had dragged herself out of bed that morning, determined to be up and sentient before her houseguest, Nick's door had still been chastely closed.

She couldn't tell if he was being a gentleman or just plain not interested. Had he taken her reaction to his kiss as a rebuff? It wouldn't be surprising if he had. Or if he had written her off as a basket case. Although, to be fair, she'd gone all basket case on him before he'd kissed her.

Not that any of it meant anything, Julia reminded herself. Nick wouldn't be the first guy to kiss someone just because she was there. Usually, there was more alcohol involved, but the general principle remained the same.

Besides, the last thing she needed right now was a romantic entanglement. This was meant to be a task, not a vacation. Sell the house, go back home to New York, find a job.

Dallying with enigmatic Brits was definitely not part of the plan.

The door rattled again, but the bolt Julia had put on the door, with considerable effort and cursing, held it in place.

"Hello?" Julia said sharply.

The rattle changed to a knock. "Julia?" It was a female voice, painfully upbeat. "I was hoping you would be home. It's Natalie."

Too late to pretend she wasn't there. Julia pressed the Brew button on the coffeemaker before crossing the kitchen to unlatch the door.

"Hi," she said, doing her best to sound enthusiastic. "What brings you here?"

393

Natalie breezed past her into the kitchen, dropping her large leather bag on the kitchen table. "I happened to be in the area and I just wanted to see how you were getting on."

At ten on a Saturday morning? Hadn't the woman heard of the phone? "That's very sweet of you," Julia said cautiously. "You really shouldn't have."

"Oh, family," said Natalie airily, peering past Julia into the butler's pantry and the reaches beyond.

A nasty suspicion arose in Julia's uncaffeinated mind. Surely not even Natalie would be stalkerish enough to have followed Nick's car . . . and sat around all night waiting to see if he came out?

No. It was absurd. And Natalie was far too freshly showered for an all-night surveillance.

"Are you looking for something?" Julia asked. She devoutly hoped that Nick stayed safely snuggled up in bed.

Not that she had anything to hide; it would just be . . . awkward.

Natalie's eyes snapped back to Julia. Leaning forward, she said, "Have you found anything interesting?"

Aside from learning that Nick preferred to sleep in boxers . . .

"More of the same," Julia said neutrally. "Lots of old magazines and moth-eaten clothes. You know."

Natalie propped a hip against the kitchen table. "I felt dreadful we weren't able to stay longer last Saturday. Leaving you with all —"

She broke off as another tread was heard in the hall and a male voice carried down the hallway.

"Julia? I hope you don't mind, I used your shampoo."

Nick appeared in the doorway, looking like an advertisement for illicit one-night stands. Last night's shirt clung damply to his chest and his hair showed the signs of recent and vigorous toweling.

At the sight of Natalie he came to an abrupt halt. A brief *oh, shit* expression crossed his face before he got his features back under control. "Natalie. Hi."

"Nicholas?" Natalie looked as though someone had just kicked her in the gut. Her face a picture of suspicion and distress, her eyes slid to Julia.

All Julia could think was that they looked like the illustration from a nineteenth-century morality tale, titled "Caught in the Act" or something equally unsubtle. She had clearly been reading too many antiquated magazines.

"Nick was helping mc clear out the attic," Julia said quickly. "Being the expert and all."

"The attic," Natalie repeated flatly.

Put like that, it did sound like a rather lame excuse.

"There's a ton of junk up there," Julia babbled. "Cubic meters of junk."

She wasn't sure why in the hell she felt so guilty, but she did. Maybe it had something to do with the way Natalie was looking at her, as though she'd just stolen all of her stickers and kicked her puppy for good measure.

"Much as I would like to stay," Nick said smoothly. "I'm afraid I have to take my leave."

Way to throw her under the bus. "Let me guess," said Julia, folding her arms across her chest. "You have a lunch."

Nick's expression remained entirely bland. "How did you guess? Natalie." He nodded politely to his best friend's sister. "Tell Andrew I'll ring him later. I owe him a round of squash."

Julia politely refrained from telling Nick what he could do with his squash racket. Or begging him to take her with him.

Natalie nodded mutely, too stricken to speak.

As if matters weren't bad enough, Nick leaned over and brushed a kiss against Julia's cheek. "Thanks for everything," he said in a way that couldn't help but invite speculation. Julia narrowed her eyes at him. "You'll be hearing from me."

"Don't strain yourself," said Julia politely, and saw Nick's lips twitch in amusement.

Somehow, she got the impression that Natalie wasn't quite so amused by that little performance. The phrase "human shield" came to mind. And she was obviously it.

"I'll see you out." Julia took Nick by the arm and propelled him through the door to the butler's pantry and the corridor beyond. Over her shoulder, to Natalie, she added, "Please help yourself to coffee. There's milk in the fridge."

She didn't wait to see if Natalie took her up on it. She just hoped the other woman didn't poison the coffee while she was out. Not that she could entirely blame Natalie. It would be devastating to walk in and find the object of your adoration making himself cozily at home in the house of another woman, especially a woman who had been on the scene for all of two minutes.

If Nick wanted to send a message to Natalie, this was a pretty low way to do it.

Julia opened her mouth to express that

opinion but instead found herself asking darkly, "Do you really have a lunch?"

"I intend to eat lunch, if that's what you mean." Nick dodged the question.

"Coward," said Julia.

"The better part of valor," said Nick smoothly as they came to a stop before the front door. The weather seemed to be making up for the previous few days of rain. Sun shone through the fanlight, dappling the old wooden floor with cheerful flecks of gold.

"Wasn't that meant to be discretion?" said Julia pointedly.

"You can't deny that there's a certain amount of overlap between the two," Nick said wryly. Before Julia could come up with a suitably snarky comment, he added more seriously, "I will be in touch."

"I appreciate your help," she said formally, and then, just to be safe, "With the paintings."

Nick paused with one hand on the door, looking down at her. Through the open door came the smell of sun-warmed greenery and the sound of birdsong. "That painting of your mother's . . ." he said diffidently. "I know it's none of my business, but if you wanted to have it framed, I'd be glad to help. I do know a few people in that line of work."

"Thanks." Julia looked up at him, surprised and touched at the thoughtfulness of the gesture. "I'm not sure what I want to do about it yet . . . but thanks."

Nick touched a finger to her cheek.

"I'll ring you," he said, and slipped away down the front walk. The sunlight made the droplets of water in his hair sparkle like stars.

That had been really sweet of him. Thoughtful. Kind.

Of course, Julia reminded herself, as she closed the door behind him, this was the same man who had left her with an enraged cousin in the kitchen, so maybe she'd better postpone that petition for canonization.

But all the same . . .

She nearly caught her finger in the door when Natalie said sharply from behind her, "You just couldn't keep your hands off him, could you?"

NINETEEN

Herne Hill, 2009

Julia turned, slowly, repressing the urge to snap back, *Who asked you?*

Natalie stood in the doorway, her bag clamped under her arm. Julia didn't like to think how much of the conversation with Nick she might have heard. Not that the reference to her mother's painting would mean anything to Natalie, but it felt like an intrusion all the same.

"You've gotten hold of the wrong end of the stick," Julia said shortly. "If there were even a stick to get hold of, which there isn't."

Natalie ignored Julia's protests. She radiated wounded dignity. "I should never have brought him here. I suppose this is what happens when you try to be nice."

No, this was what happened when you repeatedly barged into someone else's house uninvited.

It was all particularly ironic considering that Julia was fairly sure that Natalie had originally invited Nick over not out of any altruistic impulse but in the hopes of impressing him with the grandeur of ye olde family homestead. Not exactly her most cunning plan.

All the same, Julia couldn't help but feel sorry for her. That sort of crush could be so painful. And who hadn't resorted to a few foolish stratagems in the pursuit of love — or something like it.

Although, as Nick had intimated last night, Julia wondered if this was less love and more a desperate attempt to feed Cousin Caroline's social delusions. If anything, that made her feel even worse for Natalie. Julia knew what it was to be the speed bump in the path of a parent's ambitions.

"Look," said Julia, extending the metaphorical olive branch, "why don't you come back to the kitchen. We can have a cup of coffee and sort this out."

"No. Thank you," said Natalie in a brittle voice. "I don't need you to rub my face in it. First you take the house, and now you take Nicholas."

"I believe he prefers to be called Nick," said Julia inconsequentially. Was that what this was really about? The house? "As for the house . . ."

"It's not fair," said Natalie tightly. Her fingers plucked at the brass ornaments on her bag. "You weren't the one who had to come visit ghastly Aunt Regina once a week. You didn't have to sit here and listen to her absurd opinions and pretend to find her horrid stories amusing."

"No," said Julia slowly, "I didn't." Quietly, she added, "I would have liked to have had the opportunity."

She was beginning to think that she had missed out on a great deal by not knowing Aunt Regina.

"It's just like Aunt Regina." Natalie was too lost in her own grievances to pay any attention to Julia. "All those hints about the family treasure — keeping us coming back week after week — when all that time she intended to leave it all to you!"

Julia opened her mouth to say she'd never wanted it when the real meaning of her cousin's words belatedly struck her. "Treasure? You think there's some sort of treasure?"

Natalie, already in the house when she got here; Natalie, so eager to help; Natalie, rattling the wonky latch on the kitchen door.

Julia looked at Natalie with the dawning

of understanding. "You didn't come here to see me this morning, did you? You were hoping I wouldn't be home."

Natalie's mouth closed like a steel trap.

It didn't matter; Julia had her answer. Disgust churned through her. She felt as though she had just stepped in something slimy and unpleasant. All of those overtures of friendship, all of that *I just wanted to see how you were getting on,* all of the tender solicitude for the long-lost cousin, all in the pursuit of some hypothetical treasure.

Julia wrapped her arms tightly across her chest. "Just what is it you think you're going to find?"

Natalie looked mutinous. "I don't know," she said finally. Her fashion model face was sulky. "It was just like Aunt Regina. She never said anything definite, just dropped hints about there being more to the family than we knew and treasures beyond imagining."

"That's crazy," said Julia flatly.

Natalie flared to life. "It's not crazy. There was real money in the family once, you know. There might be gold, jewels —" She broke off abruptly, her lips clamping shut.

So that was what it was. Julia didn't know whether to laugh or swear. "And you were just planning to walk off with it, whatever it was?" she said. "There's a word for that. It's called stealing."

"It's not stealing when it ought to have been mine in the first place," Natalie burst out. "Mummy says —"

"Mummy had better find herself a good lawyer, if that's her attitude," said Julia sharply.

For a moment, they remained locked in silent combat, staring each other down. Julia's hands were in fists at her waist, Natalie's knotted in a death grip on the strap of her bag. So Natalie thought she could just barge in and rob her American cousin blind? She'd been in finance for nine years now; she was hardly such a pushover as that. If Natalie and Caroline wanted a fight, they'd have a fight on their hands.

So much for Cousin Caroline's tender reminiscences of Julia's mother and Natalie's airy chatter about family loyalties. Julia felt a taste like acid at the back of her throat. It wasn't as though she were under any illusions about tender family sentiments; they'd all gone a quarter century without so much as a Christmas card.

At least, that was what she had told herself. But, on some level, she had thought — she had hoped . . .

"Two things," said Julia. Her voice

sounded rusty and too loud in the strained silence of the hall. Julia cleared her throat. "One, I'm pretty sure there isn't any treasure. Not the kind you're thinking about. Did it ever occur to you that Aunt Regina might have been speaking metaphorically?"

One of Natalie's shoulders twitched slightly. Okay, clearly that theory was a no-go.

Julia went on. "Two. If you'd come to me like a human being —" Her voice cracked, embarrassing her. She didn't want to show any weakness, not now, not in front of Natalie. Julia took a deep breath. "If you'd come to me and just *told* me about all this, don't you think I would have shared?"

The thought had obviously never occurred to Natalie. It might almost have been worth it to see the emotions play out across her face, surprise, confusion, and then, belatedly, panicked comprehension. Her mouth opened, then closed again; panic was replaced by speculation. Julia could see her weighing her options, preparing her pitch.

Whatever it was, Julia didn't want to hear it.

"Of course," said Julia, "it's probably better this way, isn't it? At least, now I know what I'm dealing with." Deliberately, cruelly, she added, "I'll let you know if I find any

405

diamond tiaras. I'm sure Nick will be more than happy to help me appraise them."

That was too much for Natalie. "Why do you think Nicholas has been so keen?" she asked shrilly. "Did you think it was out of the kindness of his heart?" She gave a nasty, brittle little laugh. "You can't have thought it was anything to do with you."

Her contemptuous gaze took in Julia's faded flip-flops, her unwashed hair. Natalie had to be at least six inches taller; the way she was looking at Julia, it felt more like a foot.

Julia tucked her hands underneath her elbows, trying not to feel small and plain. Hadn't she faced down Masters of the Universe twice her size? But that had been different. That hadn't been personal.

"I think it's time for you to go now," Julia said coolly. "Don't you?"

"Ask Nicholas," said Natalie. There were bright spots of color on her cheeks, showing unevenly beneath the expertly applied layers of foundation. "Ask Nicholas why he's been so keen to help. Don't you think he knows about the treasure, too? He's just found a better way of getting at it."

Her words made Julia feel dirty. Dirty, and more than a little bit uneasy.

It made her feel disgustingly naïve that

406

she'd been so taken in, that she'd believed Natalie's overtures of friendship, that she'd felt guilty about not liking her, guilty because she was family and somehow that meant Julia was supposed to like her. So much for that.

"As you've noted before, this is my house. And this is the door." Julia's hand slipped slightly on the knob, but she managed to get it open with a minimum of fuss. She felt cold straight through, the space beneath her arms clammy with sweat. "If I see you here again without an invitation, I'll call the police on you."

Shoving her bag up under her arm, Natalie stalked through the door. "Mummy always said your side of the family was vulgar and crass."

Julia was left speechless by her gall. Natalie was the one contemplating a bit of light larceny, but *her* side was vulgar and crass?

"I'm sure when you burgle, you only do it genteelly," Julia said politely.

She started to close the door, but Natalie paused on the top step, her voice like cut glass. Her shadow cast a dark pall over the sunny walk. "Enjoy your time with Nicholas — and don't come crying to me when you find out the truth about him."

"I wouldn't judge everyone by your own

standards," Julia said grimly.

Swiping her long hair out of the way, Natalie smiled at her over her shoulder, a three-cornered cat's smile. "If you think you know him so well, ask him why he had to leave the City. Go on. Do."

Julia resisted the urge to slam the door behind her. But only just.

She hated the idea of lending credence to anything Natalie said. The woman was the lowest of the low, a self-confessed would-be thief, entirely selfish and self-serving. But, despite herself, she found herself wending her way back to the kitchen and her laptop. The pot of coffee was, to her surprise, still warm. Had it only been a few minutes? It felt like far longer.

Sitting herself down at the kitchen table, she flipped open her laptop and pulled up Google.

In the search bar, she typed: "Nicholas Dorrington."

London, 1849
"It couldn't possibly be he," said Gavin, but Imogen could feel his arm tighten around her waist all the same. "Not here."

"It was Arthur," Imogen repeated.

He wasn't there now, but he had been; she was sure of it. She slipped out of

Gavin's grasp. For all she knew, Arthur might be behind one of those heavily draped windows even now. Watching them.

"But — What would he be doing in a place such as this?" Gavin's expression was a study in skepticism. He looked across the street, at the closed door, at the place where Arthur had stood, and shook his head. "It was just a man, in a muffler, that was all. It might have been any man of a similar size."

Not any man. A wave of vertigo seized Imogen, as though she were standing on the very verge of a precipice, staring down into the abyss, at the waves and the rocks below. That had been Arthur's coat, his hat, his muffler. Akin to a thousand others, it was true, but not the way he moved, the way he walked, the way he turned his head. After a decade of marriage, she didn't need to see his face or hear his voice to identify his tread.

"He must have followed us here," she said, wrapping her hands together, trying not to let Gavin see how they were shaking. She felt shaky, so very shaky, and ill. "He must have found us and followed."

"Nonsense," said Gavin briskly. "There's no reason to suppose — Imogen?"

His words receded. She could barely hear him over the ringing in her ears. Her head swam and her vision blurred. She doubled over, just in time to spew the contents of her stomach into the gutter. She was only vaguely aware of Gavin holding her by the shoulders, keeping her steady. Her stomach heaved and heaved again. All she could think of was the revolution in her body, every sense subsumed in the desperate struggle to rid her stomach of everything inside it.

She subsided, trembling, her abdomen aching, the taste of sick in her mouth and the smell of it in her nostrils.

"Here." Gavin fished her own scented handkerchief from her sleeve and handed it to her.

Imogen pressed it gratefully to her nostrils, concentrating on breathing in and out. Blindly, she stumbled along as Gavin put an arm around her shoulders, moving her away from the puddle of sick, into the relative shelter of an alleyway.

The alleyway was narrow and dark and fetid, but the rays of the sun didn't penetrate there, and for that Imogen was grateful. She rested her aching head briefly against Gavin's shoulder. Her stomach appeared to have subsided, for the moment, but she felt dizzy and weak. And scared, with a fear to which she couldn't quite put a name.

Couldn't, or didn't want to.

"I need to go home," she said hoarsely.

"I'll take you," Gavin said immediately.

"No." Imogen looked up at him in sudden panic. "The less we're seen together, the better it will be."

She didn't care for her own sake — what could Arthur do to her? Ignore her? Set her aside? He wouldn't, not if there would be a scandal. It didn't matter for her, but it mattered terribly for Gavin. Arthur had friends at the Royal Academy and among the world of collectors.

Her fingers clutched at Gavin's sleeve. "I will not see you ruined."

"And I won't see you go off on your own like this." Gavin's accent was thicker when he was being stubborn. The burr went straight to Imogen's heart. "Not when you're ill."

"Please." Imogen drew on her dwindling reserves of strength. "If you put me into a hack, I'll be all right. It's not so very far to Herne Hill."

The idea of going back to that cold and unfriendly house, to Evie's hurt and Jane's scorn and Arthur's indifference, made Imogen want to curl into a little ball. She wanted to curl up in Gavin's arms and burrow in against his chest and stay there,

411

forever. She wanted, with every fiber of her being, to stay with him, even here, in this noxious alleyway. In a cottage, in a hovel. Anywhere.

But she couldn't.

She felt as though she were on the wrong side of the gates of paradise, looking in to what she couldn't have. There was a bitter-sweet knowledge to the fact that Gavin had been right, all those months ago, when he had tried to leave and she had made him stay. It hurt so much more now, knowing what they were, what they could be.

Gavin grasped her hands. "Are you sure you want to go back there by yourself?" he said, his eyes intent on hers, and Imogen knew what it was that he was really asking. "Not that I believe it was your — that it was Mr. Grantham across the street. But if it was —"

"If I have to, I'll tell Arthur I was with someone else." Imogen mustered a shaky smile. "I'll tell him it was Fotheringay-Vaughn. That will serve the man right." Fighting tears, she said tremulously, "You've too many beautiful paintings in you for my folly to be your undoing."

"Not yours," Gavin said seriously. "Ours. And it isn't folly."

The tenderness in his voice cut her to the bone.

"Under the circumstances," said Imogen shakily, "what else can it be?"

Gavin lifted her gloved hand to his lips, uncaring of stains or smells, and pressed a kiss to the palm. Imogen felt the warmth of his lips straight through the fine leather. He looked up at her, his expression intent. "You know what I think it is."

The word hovered unspoken between them.

Imogen lowered her head, avoiding his eyes. "I — should go home." As if Herne Hill had ever been home. "Please."

Before she weakened and confessed her feelings. And what were they to do then? Especially when — Imogen shied away from the thought.

"The sooner I am home," she said quickly, "the less trouble there will be. Even if we were seen."

"All right," Gavin said reluctantly. He squeezed her hand before letting it go. "If that is really what you want?"

It wasn't what she wanted, but it was for the best.

What a miserably smug phrase that was, "for the best." And why was it that doing what was right felt so dingy and wrong?

Imogen managed an uneven nod. "Arthur will find me innocently ill in my bed."

Gavin's face was like granite. "Just so long as he doesn't share it," he said grimly, and strode out to hail a cab, his movements abrupt and angry.

The first to stop was one of the new, two-wheeled variety. Gavin spoke briefly to the driver, giving him the direction, before handing Imogen into the cab.

His face softened as he stood by the side of the cab, her hand still in his. "Don't eat any more of that fish," he said.

"I won't." Imogen leaned forward with sudden urgency. "Gavin —"

He was all attention. "Yes?"

The words caught in her throat. Imogen sank back against the seat. "Good afternoon," she said, her throat tight.

The last thing she saw as the cab pulled away was Gavin standing there, by the side of the street, two deep furrows in his brow.

The hansom cab jostled along the uneven streets. The smell of the previous occupants of the carriage clung to the cushions, stale tobacco and unwashed wool and strong perfumes. Imogen fumbled for her handkerchief, pressing her eyes shut in an attempt to shut out the sights and smells of the city beyond.

Fish, Gavin had said.

She had felt like this before, and not from bad fish.

Not the first time. The first time, it had all happened so quickly. She hadn't even known she was with child until the cramps and the bleeding had made it painfully apparent that if she had been, she wasn't anymore.

But the second time — the second time she had carried the child long enough to feel just like this. That had been the year Jane had insisted on repapering the hall. The scent of the fixative had sent Imogen fleeing to her own room, vinaigrette in hand, prey to the kind of weakness she normally scorned. Meals had been a form of torture, the sight and smell of the food a barrage on her weak senses. She would have taken toast and weak tea in her room, but for Jane's obvious scorn.

Imogen had felt then just as she did now: weak and wobbly and constantly queasy.

She could tell herself it was the fish — but how many days of fish? If she were to admit it, she had been feeling ill and tired for at least a fortnight. There was always a convenient excuse. She hadn't slept well; the fish must be off; her stays were too tight.

Her stays did feel tighter.

415

Dear Lord. Imogen clung to the strap as the cab bounced over an uneven patch of road. How long had it been since she had last had her courses? July — or perhaps it had been early August. Time blurred. She had been too happy to count the months or days. Too happy to consider the possible, practical consequences of her actions.

The carriage barreled over the river, past the spot she had stood with Gavin what now felt like a very long time ago.

Imogen closed her eyes as the carriage rumbled its way out of the crowded streets of the city, out towards the country, towards Herne Hill. She had assumed, if she had thought of it at all, that after all these years she must be barren, or close to it. She had been married to Arthur for over a year before she had conceived the first time, and that had been back in the days when Arthur's visits to her bedchamber had been expected occurrences.

They had assumed, both of them, that the problem lay with her.

The cab jolted to a halt before the house. Arthur's house. The coachman ambled down from his perch to help Imogen out of the carriage. With numb fingers, Imogen reached into her reticule.

"Keep your coin," said the coachman

laconically. "The gentleman paid."

The words had an ominous knell to them. Imogen murmured her thanks to the driver and hurried into the house.

Jane was lying in wait for her by the door. "Did you find what you were looking for?"

It took Imogen a moment to remember her excuse for going into town. "No," she said, walking quickly past Jane to the stairs. Her skirts dragged against her legs, nearly tripping her. "No. The trim we saw on Half Moon Street last week was by far nicer."

"I told you so," said Jane. Imogen looked back to see Jane still standing there, in the hall, her arms folded across her chest. "But you did have to go gadding off to town."

She couldn't take Jane's smugness, not now. "Will you excuse me? I really don't feel quite the thing."

With Jane's watchful eye on her, Imogen fled to the privacy of her bedchamber, her stomach heaving and her mind in turmoil.

Try to avoid it how she would, there was only one conclusion. She was with child.

Gavin's child.

Twenty

Herne Hill, 2009
It didn't take Julia long to hit pay dirt.

The first article to come up when she typed "Nicholas Dorrington" into the Google search bar was innocuous enough, a Sunday *Times* arts piece about his shop and some of the more interesting pieces.

The second wasn't quite so innocuous. The *Daily Mail* dealt with it rather primly:

Dietrich Bank Director Investigated in Connection with Insider Trading Scandal as FSA Clamps Down on Market Abuse.

The Sun wasn't quite so subtle.

Caught with His Hand in the Till: Top Banker's Insider Trading Scam.

Two more hits down, *The Wall Street Journal* reported:

Dietrich Bank Director Resigns After Insider Trading Scandal.

All of the articles were dated four years before, in the fall of 2005. Julia sat back in her chair. She remembered this one. She'd just started at Sterling Bates as a junior analyst. The story had been all over MSNBC and C-SPAN, a major money-maker going down due to the sort of stupid financial shenanigans they warned you away from your first week in B school. There had been a lot of self-righteous head wagging and barely concealed smugness of the "there but for the grace of God" variety and a lot of surreptitious rechecking of the relevant rules and personal stock positions. It had been all over *The Wall Street Journal* and *The New York Times* for about two weeks before the buzz had died down and the media had moved on to the next train wreck in the making.

And that had been Nick. The same Nick with the shop in Notting Hill who had brought over curry on Friday night and offered to see her mother's painting framed. Somehow, Julia couldn't reconcile them in her head: the Nick she knew with the Nick who had committed financial fraud on a grand scale.

Although, as Natalie had so charmingly pointed out, how much did Julia know about him anyway?

Not much. She'd seen only the aspects of him that he'd wished her to see. There had been the illusion of intimacy created by that discussion of his family, but it had been just that. An illusion. He'd told her all about his grandparents but nothing at all about himself.

Only that he had worked at Dietrich Bank in M&A. Until he'd inherited his great-aunt's estate and opened shop.

Julia clicked on the *Wall Street Journal* article. The details were simple and sordid. Nick had been the lead man in a major acquisition. The FSA had noticed a suspiciously heavy volume of trades in the target company's stock the week before the deal closed. They'd had little trouble in tracing it back to Dietrich Bank.

There were some mitigating details. He'd been investigated, not charged. He'd resigned, not been fired. Or, more likely, he'd resigned before he could be fired. Julia wondered what sort of deals had been struck behind the scenes, what kind of favors had been traded. She knew this world, and she knew just how scummy it could be.

Any way she looked at it, the case seemed pretty grim. It was corporate malfeasance on a grand scale, driven by pure, unadulterated greed.

So much for Nick's charming tale of an inheritance from an eccentric aunt prompting his great career change.

Maybe there had been an aunt. Maybe some of it was true. The best lies were all rooted in a grain of truth — even if it was only a lie by omission.

Julia closed the lid of the computer with a snap. She didn't need to read more. She hated that Natalie had been right. Not that she knew that Natalie was right in the larger sense — just because Nick had been involved in a major financial scandal didn't mean that he was out to bilk Julia for what he could get.

But it certainly wasn't a point in his favor.

Julia wrapped her hands around her coffee mug, feeling, suddenly, very isolated and very lonely. The old house whispered and creaked around her. Why did it feel like everyone was out for what they could get? Natalie . . . Nick . . . Everyone seemed to have an ulterior motive. There was no gesture of kindness that was untainted. She felt like a hedgehog, all rolled into a ball, prickles out, small and scared beneath her meager defenses.

Stupid, Julia told herself, pushing the chair back. Her knees creaked as she stood. It wasn't like she should be under any illusions about the goodness of her fellow man. Most people were out for what they could get in one way or another. Like the higher-ups at Sterling Bates. They had smiled and smiled and smiled at her and written her stellar reviews and told her what an asset she was to the firm right up until the day they had handed her a cardboard box and told her to pack up her pictures and potted plants — and, by the way, could she leave her badge and corporate card by the door?

The milk of human kindness had long since gone off.

Of course, she'd expected it from them. She hadn't expected it from the cousin who had professed to be so delighted at her return and the man who — well, a man who had seemed to be genuinely nice.

But that was the stock-in-trade of a con man, wasn't it? It took a certain measure of charm to gull one's victims. And what did she have to go on, anyway? A few kind words, a few family stories. She'd also seen him smoothly lie his way out of Natalie's company, not once but twice; that ought to have clued her in.

From now on, she was on her own. Nothing unusual about that. She was used to it.

Too used to it.

Julia told herself to stop the pity party. There was no reason she couldn't track down the provenance of that painting on her own, without Nick. She'd been an art history major back in the day. Somehow, at twenty-one, she'd managed a fifty-page senior essay on Isabella d'Este, court patronage, and the construction of identity.

Shouldn't this be easier? At least the sources would all be in English.

To hell with Nicholas Dorrington, whatever his real intentions; she could do this all by herself.

Nick made that resolution harder, by calling on Monday, just as he had said he would. Julia's finger hovered briefly over the ACCEPT CALL button — but the memory of Nick, blithely making up stories about his change of career, stayed her hand.

She let it go to voice mail.

When she hadn't returned his call by Wednesday, Nick texted her. *You all right? If trapped under pile of debris, text SOS.*

It would be so sweet of him — if she didn't have to worry about his motives. Life was too short to get involved with lying smootharses. She'd known enough of them back in her old job, Masters of the Universe who thought everything was coming to them, be it by fair means or foul.

Every time she thought of the way he'd touched her cheek as he left, his offer to frame her mother's painting, Julia felt more confused and angry. One thing if she could have ascribed all her feelings to lust. Lust was such an easily comprehensible emotion.

But she'd genuinely liked him, too.

At least, she'd liked the person she thought she knew.

No need for SOS, just busy with house.

Her phone bleeped again. *Curry and snooker on Friday?*

Adorably persistent? Or more evidence against him. Either way, it was a moot point. *Can't,* she texted back. *Dinner plans with parent.*

It even had the benefit of being true. Her father got into town on Friday morning for his conference. They were slated for dinner Friday night, before the conference got going.

Sticking her phone firmly under a couch cushion, Julia went back to her research. She'd been trying to remember how she had done it back in her undergrad days, before her world had narrowed to numbers and charts and a glowing screen with red and green stocks on it, back when she still worked in words instead of equations.

That, of course, had been before the ease of the Internet. She'd graduated in 2000, in the infancy of the Web, and well before "Google" became a verb. She hadn't realized just how much had been digitized over the past decade. Forget university libraries, all she needed was her laptop. The piles of old clothes she had meant to take to the charity shop remained in a dingy heap in a corner of the dining room; the e-mails she had meant to send off to potential employers remained unsent. Julia's world narrowed to the screen of her computer and the notepad next to her, on which she scribbled largely illegible notes to herself.

Rossetti bio says frequent visitor to Thorne studio. Check Rossetti correspondence? Other personal papers? Who started New South Wales story? No attribution.

The Granthams popped up once, in one of the Rossetti biographies. Of all the early Pre-Raphaelities, Rossetti really did seem to get the lion's share of the attention. Julia suspected it was because, of all of them, he looked the most like the romantic conception of an artist, all tousled hair and brooding expression. Not to mention that whole romance with Lizzy Siddal and the sister who wrote poetry.

Arthur Grantham got one line in the early pages of a 1982 biography as a collector of medieval antiquities, one of the stops along the way in Rossetti's quest for models before the era of Raphael. Imogen wasn't mentioned at all.

Julia shouldn't have been surprised. From the contemporary point of view, Imogen didn't count. She wasn't a person in her own right; legally, her being was subsumed within her husband's. Her signature carried no legal weight; she had no possessions that weren't also his. It was a distinctly chilling thought.

By Thursday, Julia had a list of potential primary sources to check out, including a cache of Thorne's letters at the National Art Library in the Victoria and Albert Museum. Not to mention five hundred volumes of Dante Gabriel Rossetti's collected correspondence. Maybe not quite five hundred, but close. The man had clearly been at no loss for words. And someone had saved all of them.

Julia made a note to check out volume 1,

The Formative Years. If there was any mention of Thorne, it would be in that collection, before Thorne had disappeared to New South Wales or parts unknown, leaving behind his painting of Tristan and Iseult, wrapped in brown paper in a wardrobe in Herne Hill.

Her dinner with her father wasn't until seven. The V&A library closed at 6:30. Julia set into town a few hours early and found her way through the crowds of tourists thronging the front hall of the V&A, along the side, and up the marble staircase that led to the art library.

It looked the way a library ought to look, with tall, arched windows flanked by bookshelves, and a ceiling that stretched up into infinity. A gallery ran around the length of the room, banded by a wrought-iron balcony, with row upon row of books above, encased in bookcases of richly polished wood.

The room smelled of leather bindings and old paper and just a little bit of feet. At the long, communal tables, more than one scholar had surreptitiously pushed off his shoes.

Julia presented herself at the reference desk and registered for her reader's ticket, which appeared to consist of nothing more than proving that she was a human with an address and promising not to scribble in, set fire to, or otherwise deface the books. Then she presented her call slip to the librarian.

The librarian took one look at the slip and shook her head. "Oh, dear."

Julia squinted upside down at her slip. "Is there something wrong?"

The little stub of pencil they had given her to write with didn't exactly make for the clearest lettering.

The librarian handed back her slip. "I'm afraid these are already checked out," she said apologetically. She peered around Julia, then pointed at the far corner of one of the tables. "To that gentleman over there."

The late-afternoon sunlight streamed through the long windows, highlighting the man's fair hair. There was a large folio open in front of him and a cardboard box beside him. His head was bent diligently over his book, but Julia didn't need to see his face to know him.

Nick had beaten her to it.

Herne Hill, 1849
Gavin waited at the orchard gate the next day, but Imogen never came.

He was back the day after that and the

day after that, but there was no one to greet him but a curious squirrel and the wind among the bare branches of the almond trees. Gavin went so far as to scout around the side of the house, but he saw no sign of Imogen, only Miss Cooper climbing into the carriage, presumably to pay her afternoon calls. Frustrated, Gavin retreated.

Fantastical speculations plagued him. Grantham had seen them, was holding Imogen prisoner. He had the right; no one would say him nay if he kept her confined to her room or clapped her in an institution, although Gavin had a difficult time imagining the genial man he had met pursuing a plan so hard and cold. Although seemingly reasonable men had been driven to far worse when they felt their honor slighted.

What did he really know about the other man? Gavin conducted some inquiries at the house where Imogen had spotted Grantham. The information he received cast the man in a whole new light, and not a very pleasant one. The house was a brothel that catered to men with a taste for young girls, girls in their early teens.

Should he tell Imogen? That would be petty. And, besides, he couldn't find her to tell her.

Having a blazing row with Augustus didn't

do much to relieve Gavin's feelings, although it did mean that the studio was now his, to work in in lonely isolation, day blending into night and night into day. During the long, sleepless nights, Gavin finished his *Tristan and Iseult,* painting in Imogen's face for Iseult, his own for Tristan, and, in a final spurt of anger, Arthur Grantham in the role of King Mark. It was a foolish indulgence, he knew. He would have to scrape the faces out and repaint them before he could present the painting to the Academy in April, but his frustration had guided his brush.

The following week, Gavin received a note. It said only:

> Domestic concerns keep me close to home. I fear I must cancel our appointment.
>
> With the warmest expressions of esteem,
> I.G.

It was in Imogen's hand, that much he knew, but apart from that, the communication left Gavin baffled and increasingly alarmed. He couldn't imagine Imogen breaking with him in such a detached and distant way. She would have met with him, at least.

Unless she was being watched. Or her hand had been forced.

Driven to the end of his wits, Gavin called at the house on the pretense of ensuring that Mr. Grantham was quite satisfied with the portrait. It was Miss Cooper who received him, telling him coolly that Mr. Grantham was not at home. Mr. Grantham came in, just at that moment, ruddy cheeked from the cold, and received Gavin with every appearance of cordiality, offering him a glass of whiskey to warm his insides before he went off again for the long walk back into town. Grantham would have invited him to supper, but his wife's health wasn't what it should be.

Grantham didn't look like a man confronting his wife's lover. In fact, he seemed just as he had been before, friendly, talkative, eager to discuss art and antiquities, full of praise for the quality of the portrait and curious to know what it was Gavin planned to display at the next Exhibition.

Trying not to display too much alarm, Gavin said that he trusted Mrs. Grantham wasn't seriously ill.

No, no, Grantham assured him. Nothing but a temporary indisposition. Was he sure he wouldn't like something to drink before he went on his way?

Confusedly Gavin assured Grantham that he had other business in the area, that it was no bother at all, and excused himself without lingering.

He remembered Imogen as he had last seen her, pale and trembling. He would have laid money that Grantham was still in ignorance of their affair — although he had thought he saw Miss Evie's ruffled flounces whisk out of the way as he came through the hall — but now the even more disturbing specter of illness haunted him. It took so little to extinguish a life. He had seen sore throats turn putrid, an upset stomach that turned out to be a tumor, mysterious wasting illnesses with no cause or cure.

How to communicate with Imogen? There was no one in the household he could trust, not the compliant maid of popular fiction, not an errand boy he might suborn with a few coins. Imogen had no lady's maid and Gavin had no reason to trust the housemaid. He couldn't hang about outside the house; he would be noticed. There was no good excuse for him to be in the area.

He went again, nevertheless, lurking on the far side of the fence, and had the limited satisfaction of seeing Imogen, heavily bundled, in the garden. She was too far away to make out her features. Before he could speak her to her, someone called to her from the house and she turned and went back inside. He thought of slipping back under cover of darkness and leaving a note for her in the summerhouse, but what if it were discovered by the wrong person? The summerhouse had always been Imogen's personal province, but there was no guarantee that she was well enough to venture that far out down the garden path. Images of Imogen lying wan in her bed, her hair damp with sweat, her eyes wild with fever, haunted Gavin.

He began to wonder if he was going a little bit mad.

It was Rossetti who mentioned the reception on Denmark Hill.

"You can't say no to John Ruskin, or, at least, you ought not," said Gabriel practically. "He can make or break you with a twist of his pen. Besides, don't you want to see his art? He's said to have a grand collection."

"I'm busy," Gavin informed him brusquely. *Tristan and Iseult* sat propped against the wall, chastely shrouded in brown paper.

It was quite the best thing he had ever

done and he couldn't bear to look at it. Every time he did, he remembered Imogen as she had been as she stepped from behind that screen in Iseult's blue gown.

"Busy," Gabriel mocked, craning his head to get a look at Gavin's latest sketches. Gavin pointedly turned the easel. "Too busy to show an old friend your work. You've turned into a worse hermit than Hunt!"

"We're not all such exhibitionists as you," said Gavin brusquely, but even as he said it, it occurred to him that Denmark Hill wasn't so very far from Herne Hill. The Granthams moved in the same circles as the Ruskins. Someone might have heard of Imogen, have some news of her. . . . It was a feeble hope, but a hope all the same.

So Gavin shaved off a fortnight's growth of beard and unearthed a fresh shirt from among the musty piles of dirty linen on the floor and made his way with Gabriel back across the bridge, out of the city, to the Ruskins' home on Denmark Hill.

The last thing he expected was to see Imogen.

At first, he thought he must have been mistaken, that the woman across the room, in conversation with the elder Mr. Ruskin, must be someone else entirely. That it must be a trick of the uncertain light or the crowded room. But then she turned slightly, her face coming more entirely under the light of the chandelier, and there was no denying it was she.

She wore a rich blue gown, well off the shoulder. There was gold at her throat and ears and wrists, and in the dark waves of her hair.

She looked . . . well. No, better than well. She was blooming, her cheeks flushed with the heat of the room, her body fuller than when he had last seen her, her bosom spilling over the discreet lace edging of her bodice.

The first rush of relief at seeing her not at death's door after all was rapidly subsumed by a poisonous brew of confusion and anger. If she was well, well enough to chat of this and that with the elder Mr. Ruskin, surely she was well enough to have contrived some way of contacting him? All this while, as he had been half-mad with fear for her, she had been dining and dancing, snapping gold bracelets around her wrists and enameled combs in her hair.

She made her excuses to Mr. Ruskin and turned — looking for her husband? Gavin seized his chance.

Presenting himself before her, he bowed curtly. "Mrs. Grantham."

"Mr. Thorne!" Alarm flickered briefly across her face before she unfurled her fan. "What a pleasant surprise."

Could she really stand here and speak to him like this, as though he had meant nothing to her? Perhaps he had, at that, although he still couldn't believe it of her, couldn't make himself believe it.

And yet here she stood, looking at him not with joy but almost with fear.

"Is it?" he asked bluntly. Looking her up and down, he said, "I was told you were ill."

She looked a warning at him. "I was. But, as you see, I am better now." Quietly, she added, "It is all for the best."

The best for whom?

Gavin's temper rose. "I wouldn't have thought you would be so quick to forget old friends."

"Never forgotten," she said soberly, her polished social smile fading. She looked at him, and for a moment he saw the raw longing in her eyes. "But circumstances change." Before he could pursue that, she asked quickly, "How is the painting coming along?"

Gavin looked at her narrowly, trying to make her out. He would have questioned her right out, but the room was teeming with people, a dozen gossiping matrons who might overhear. "I have finished my *Tristan and Iseult.* Our *Tristan and Iseult.*"

Her eyes slanted swiftly upward. "Have you — have you a new work?"

There was a vein of vulnerability beneath her question that suggested it wasn't entirely about the painting she was asking. Gavin looked at her, at that familiar, beloved face, at her pink cheeks and shadowed eyes. What in the devil had happened over the past month? What wasn't she telling him?

"I had thought, perhaps, *Lancelot Denied the Grail.*" Unobtrusively, he set a path towards the quieter side of the room, away from potential listeners. "I find myself thinking a great deal on the agony of seeing what one most desires and yet not being permitted to grasp it."

"It — it sounds like a very powerful composition," said Imogen. "There are many, I believe, who would understand the sentiment."

Gavin looked down at her. "I should have preferred to paint something happier."

"Perhaps. But not every tale has a happy ending." They came to a stop before one of Ruskin's beloved Turner paintings. Imogen made a pretense of studying the canvas. "Speaking of happy tales, have you heard that my — that Miss Grantham is to be married to Ned Sturgis?" She looked away, her voice subdued. "She decided it was time she had a household of her own."

Gavin remembered that last day by the bridge, Imogen staring out into the water. *She won't speak to me. She looks through me.* In other words, Miss Evangeline had gone and gotten herself betrothed in a huff.

Pity stirred in him, undermining his indignation. He didn't want to pity Imogen; he wanted to wallow in being wronged.

"He is a very nice young man," said Imogen, and the forced cheer in her voice cut straight to Gavin's heart. "They are to leave for Lisbon as soon as they are wed. Mr. Sturgis is to take charge of his father's business interests in that part of the world."

"I have heard that it is a charming city." Gavin couldn't bear it any longer, this dancing around the true matter. Dropping his voice, he said urgently, "Why wouldn't you meet me? Surely, you owed me that much."

"There is so much to do before a wedding." In an undertone she added, for his ears alone, "I should not wish to do anything to mar Evie's happiness."

Miss Evie, in Gavin's opinion, was well capable of looking out for herself.

"Is that what this is about?" he asked in a

low, intense voice. "Sacrificing your own happiness on the altar of hers? Did you never stop to think that it was not only your happiness, but also mine, that was at stake?"

She looked at him with wide, pleading eyes. "It is not that simple —"

Simple? Keeping a social smile on his face, he said in a rapid undertone, "I have been half-mad with worry. I thought you were sick, dying. Or that Grantham had locked you up. And then to find you here, like this —"

Imogen's hand reached out, as though she might touch his sleeve, and just as quickly fell away. "Please. Not — not here."

"Then where?" He turned his back to the room, blocking her from view with his body. "Day after day, and all I hear is that you are detained *by domestic concerns.*" He had the satisfaction of seeing her wince. "I had not thought your affections that lightly given — or rescinded."

Imogen stared into Turner's orange sunset. "They are not." Her voice was barely audible. "Do you not think I —" She broke off, biting her lip, and said very quietly, "I have missed you more than I can say. Is not that enough?"

"Easy enough to say." It maddened him that he must speak only to her profile, must keep up the pretense of polite chatter when his very soul was on the rack.

"No. It hasn't been easy at all." She shook her head in frustration. "Please believe me, if I have been cruel, it is for your benefit, not mine,"

"And why should I believe you?" he asked, his frustration rising to match hers. "You speak in riddles."

Imogen squared her shoulders. The nape of her neck looked very bare and vulnerable, the gold chain of her necklace trailing down behind. "Then let me speak plainly. There must be nothing to tie you to me, nothing to incriminate you — when the scandal breaks."

Something about the way she said it made the hairs on the backs of Gavin's hands stand up. "What scandal?"

"Have you not seen Mr. Ruskin's del Verrocchio?" said Imogen in a loud, clear voice, and Gavin was reminded, jarringly, that they weren't alone, that there was a roomful of people around them. "It is one of the prizes of his collection. It dates from the fifteenth century and is really quite the loveliest I have seen of its kind. I believe it will interest you."

Mastering his impatience, Gavin followed Imogen into the relative privacy of the alcove. The painting was a Madonna and child, a miracle of color and line, the Madonna resplendent in her blue robe, her head bowed, the child kicking his chubby legs on the ground in front of her. Ordinarily, Gavin would have been rapt. But now his attention was all for Imogen.

"What scandal?" he demanded. "If Grantham doesn't know of us —"

Imogen drew in a long, shaky breath. "He will." In the shadows of the alcove, her face looked tired and drawn. "It will soon become all too obvious to Arthur that I — that I betrayed him with someone. I would prefer, if I can, to spare you."

Gavin opened his mouth to ask why, but the answer struck him before the words could make their way from his throat to his lips.

Dry-mouthed, dizzy, he looked first to the *Madonna and Child,* the little baby on his pallet on the ground. Did she — were they —

Imogen's lips twisted in a sad little smile. "Yes," she said. "I am with child."

TWENTY-ONE

Herne Hill, 1849

"Mine," he said.

It wasn't a question.

There was no point in denying it. "Yours."

"Why didn't you tell me?" Gavin's voice was hoarse. He looked at her with something almost like horror. "Were you not going to tell me?"

Imogen pressed her eyes together, striving for control. "I — wanted to tell you."

How she had wanted to! Her body had rebelled against her; she had been ill, weak, fretful. All she had wanted was Gavin. She wanted to burrow deep into his arms, her head pillowed in that particular kink between neck and shoulder, breathing in the comfortable, familiar scent of him, of paint and charcoal and laundry soap.

A dozen times she had nearly trumped up some pretext to go to town. Each time, on the verge of ordering the carriage, she had balked, thinking of Arthur, standing across from them on that fetid street, of Gavin and his career, of all the children who had never come to term.

"But you didn't," said Gavin. He looked as though someone had struck him in the stomach, hard.

Unsteadily, Imogen said, "I did not know that I would keep it." Her hand rested instinctively on the curve of her waist, where the maid had helped her let out the seams of her dress just this morning. "I never have before. When I was younger. There were two . . . disappointments."

Disappointments. That was what Arthur had called them, blotting out the messy medical reality of it, the tears, the pain, the bloody towels. This time, she knew that a miscarriage would, in all practicality, be a blessing, making the past a nullity, wiping out the evidence of her sin. It made sense, she knew.

But the thought of it filled her with horror.

Against all reason, she wanted this child, wanted it with a fierce yearning, wanted to hold its tiny body in her arms and kiss its downy head.

Gavin stared down at the swell of her skirts. "A child," he said, and his voice was thick with wonder. "Our child."

"Our child," Imogen echoed softly.

The words were bittersweet.

She put a hand tentatively on his sleeve. Even that slight touch was a small torture, the familiar feel of his arm stabbing her with longing. "Don't you see? Arthur will know it couldn't be his. If there is — if there is retribution, it should not fall on you."

She had thought it through, again and again, hour after tortured hour. Once her condition became impossible to hide, it would be all too clear to Arthur that the child couldn't possibly be his. Current fashions helped; the widely belling skirts would hide her growing stomach for a time, but she had perhaps a month, or two at most, before it developed to a point where reefing up her top hoop would no longer serve.

Jane, Imogen was quite sure, already suspected. Suspected, but hadn't yet had the nerve to ask right out.

Of course, Jane would have no reason to know that the child wasn't Arthur's. She had been even nastier than usual the last time Imogen had been with child; it was more likely jealousy than delicacy that had stilled her tongue. She hated the idea that Imogen might present Arthur with a child.

It took Gavin a moment to make sense of what she was saying. "No, not on me," he said, his voice heavy. "Just on you and our child."

Imogen lowered her head. "I have thought about this a great deal," she said quietly. "Arthur will not want a scandal. There is every chance he will acknowledge the child as his." What other choice did they have? "What private censure he heaps upon me I can bear."

It was separation from Gavin that was the hardest part; if she could bear that, anything Arthur might say would have little power to hurt her.

"No," said Gavin. "No."

"You must see —" Imogen began, but Gavin silenced her by grasping her hand, holding it tight in his.

"Come away with me," he said.

Imogen stared up at him, her eyes searching his face. "You can't mean that."

"Can't I?" His face cleared, the lines at the corners of his mouth lifting, his pale eyes alive with sudden light. "Come away with me. Far away. We'll start fresh, together."

The words were like an incantation, like a conjurer's charm. Imogen couldn't look away. In the golden light of Gavin's eyes she could see them, frolicking together through a landscape of impossible verdure, forever enchanted, forever young.

In a Shakespeare play, perhaps, with a deus ex machina to make everything right at the end. In the real world, she was married to Arthur and he had every right to pursue her to the full extent of the law.

Ruefully, she shook her head. "It can't be done."

"Never say can't." Gavin's fingers tightened on hers. His face hardened. "What's impossible is your thinking I would leave you to stay here, after —"

"What other choice is there?" Imogen looked hopelessly up at him, feeling the weight of the world upon her. She felt suddenly absurdly tired. With an attempt at humor, she said, "Even in the old tales, it seldom ends well for the escaped lovers. Didn't they try to burn Guinevere at the stake?"

Gavin's face was set. "And didn't Lancelot rescue her? Give me the credit you would he, and more for the not being in a tale. It will take some planning, but we can do it. . . ."

She could see his mind working, sorting through possibilities and permutations. "But what of your painting?"

"Painting be damned!" he said, recklessly casting aside the one thing he had worked for all these years.

"I'll not leave you and the child to him." His voice softened. "Do you think I could just walk away from my own child? I couldn't do that any more than I could walk away from you."

Imogen struggled for self-control. "I know you think that now, but in time . . ." She forced herself to put her deepest fears into words. "What if . . . this thing between us . . . doesn't last? I have mistaken myself before."

"I haven't." Gavin grasped her hands in his. She could feel the heat of his grip through her gloves. "Trust me," he said. "Whatever difficulties may come, we'll face them together, us two."

The picture he painted was so alluring, so seductive, the two of them, hand in hand together against the world. "But. . . ."

Gavin glanced quickly over his shoulder, biting off a curse. "This is no place for this. Meet me tomorrow. In our old place."

Now was the time to nip this madness in the bud before it could go further. Imogen opened her mouth to say no, but something in his expression stayed her. His expression, and the sound of steps approaching their alcove, forcing her hand.

In a breathless voice she said, "All right. Tomorrow." Stepping hastily away from him, she said loudly, "The expression on the Madonna's face, it captivates you, doesn't it? Oh, Arthur! I was just showing Mr. Thorne Mr. Ruskin's *Madonna and Child.*"

"Quite right!" Arthur nodded genially to Gavin.

Imogen kept her eyes on her husband, trying to keep her breathing in order, hoping the high color in her cheeks could be attributed to the warmth of the room.

Arthur contemplated the painting thoughtfully. "It is very much in your line, Thorne. I ought to have thought of it myself." He gave a small, self-deprecating cough. "What would we do without the ladies, eh, Thorne?"

Gavin inclined his head ever so slightly. "Sir."

"Mr. Thorne is, as you can see, transported beyond reach of words," Imogen said lightly. She twined her arm through her husband's, tilting her head up at him in a simulacrum of wifely devotion, hoping, desperately, that Gavin would follow her lead. "I suggest we leave him to it. I believe you promised me an ice."

"And so I did." Arthur patted her hand.

Imogen could feel Gavin watching them, watching Arthur claim her.

Turning to Gavin, Arthur said pleasantly, "I hope we can persuade you to visit us again soon. My wife and I should both be pleased to see you, shouldn't we, my love?"

"Certainly," Imogen murmured. Arthur's hand felt like a lead weight on her arm.

"Thank you, sir," said Gavin, and his accent was very strong. "I do believe I shall."

Tomorrow. In our old place.

Imogen smiled brightly up at Arthur. "My ice?" she prompted.

"Yes, yes," said her husband, and with a final, apologetic nod to Gavin led her away, chattering inconsequentially of this and that.

Imogen made the right sorts of noises, but she didn't hear any of it.

All she could hear was Gavin's voice, rough with emotion:

Come away with me.

London, 2009

"I can't tell you how much longer he'll be," the librarian said apologetically. "You might want to come back tomorrow."

"That's all right," said Julia vaguely. "I know him."

She set off towards Nick's corner of the

449

room, with only the faintest idea of what she meant to say.

Are you trying to embezzle my hypothetical family treasure? was hardly a conversation starter.

She couldn't really accuse him of going behind her back when she was the one who hadn't returned his calls, but it still felt a little creepy to find him there with the very books she had intended to use.

Logically, none of her suspicions made much sense. What was the benefit of it? Sure, establishing a provenance for the Tristan and Iseult painting would probably raise the price, but even with that she doubted it would command the kind of sum that might tempt a man toward fraud.

Unless, of course, it was a man for whom fraud was a way of life, a man looking for one easy out after another. Nick certainly had charm enough. Why work when you could smile and steal?

"Julia!" Nick looked deceptively scholarly in his wire-rimmed glasses, books scattered around him. He lowered his voice as the woman next to him glared. She had the harried look of a very senior grad student or a very junior lecturer. "Did they tell you at the shop that I'd be here?"

Did he really think she'd come running

after him like Natalie?

"I just came to do some research," said Julia coolly. "I gather that you had the same idea."

Nick took in her little black dress. His brows went up. "That's quite a dress for the library. Not that I'm complaining, mind you."

Julia resisted the urge to tug on the hem. It was just a plain black sheath, nothing fancy, but in the V&A library, among all the researchers wearing jeans and T-shirts, the combination of black dress, pearls, and patent-leather sling-backs looked as exotic as a grass skirt and coconut bra.

Julia twitched the edges of her hot pink pashmina closer around her shoulders. "I'm meeting my father for dinner at seven."

Nick tipped back in his chair. "Ah, right. The man who has consigned me to a lonely evening of snooker."

Julia tipped her head towards the books. "You seem to have found other occupation."

It wasn't quite the same as Natalie letting herself in by the kitchen door, but it made Julia wary, nonetheless.

"I wish I'd thought of it sooner." If he'd realized anything was wrong, he was doing a very good job of pretending otherwise. "These papers are a gold mine."

451

The choice of phrase made Julia's hackles rise. "How so?"

Nick gestured dismissively at the cardboard box. "Thorne's papers aren't much use. You get the feeling he wasn't very comfortable with a pen. He only wrote when he had to. But Rossetti . . . That man wasn't at a loss for words. There are several references to Thorne — and," he added, with the air of a magician pulling a rabbit out of a hat, "at least three mentions of our *Tristan and Iseult.*"

Curiosity warred with caution. Curiosity won. "What does he say about it?"

Next to them, the grad student pointedly shifted two seats to the left. Julia leaned against the back of her vacated seat.

"Not much. Just the subject and that Thorne refuses to show it. That," commented Nick, with a glimmer of humor, "appears to have been a sore point for Rossetti. He liked to see what his friends were painting."

"But it means we do have a link between Thorne and the painting." The *we* came out before Julia realized what she was saying.

Fortunately, Nick didn't seem to notice. "It's not proof, but it's a damn good argument. How many Tristan and Iseults could there be from that year, in that style? But

452

that's not the best part." His eyes were aquamarine with excitement.

"No?" The curved back of the chair was biting into Julia's arms. She shifted her weight.

Nick flipped back a few pages in the book, which had been liberally dotted with white markers. "In January of 1850, Rossetti writes to William Holman Hunt that he stopped by Thorne's studio and found that Thorne had cleared out." Just in case Julia didn't get the significance of that, he added, "Paintings, drawings, clothes, all gone."

"We knew that Thorne left England in 1850. That's not a surprise."

"But this is. Thorne's landlord told him that a lady had come by to pick up the last of Thorne's things a week before. Not a woman. A lady."

Julia thought she saw where he was going with this. "You think Imogen stole the painting?" It wasn't an altogether bad idea. "If they were having an affair, she'd want the evidence hidden. . . . And that would explain how it wound up in the wardrobe."

Nick shook his head impatiently. "I don't think Imogen ran off with the painting. I think Thorne ran off with Imogen. Wait," he said as Julia opened her mouth to protest. "Rossetti's brother, William — who was also a member of the PRB, if a rather woodwork one — told his brother that he'd seen Thorne, or a man he believed to be Thorne, purchasing passage to New York. Not one passage, two passages. For a husband and wife."

"It doesn't work," Julia argued. "How did the painting get in the wardrobe? You can't have it both ways."

Nick rolled his eyes heavenwards. "Can we abandon the wardrobe for the moment? Maybe Imogen stuck the painting in there for safekeeping before they fled."

Julia looked at him closely. "You're pretty invested in this, aren't you?"

"I like a puzzle." Jokingly he added, "You do realize what a story this would make. It has BBC special written all over it. Pre-Raphaelite painter, repressed Victorian wife . . ."

Like a devil on her shoulder, she could hear Natalie's voice saying, *Ask Nicholas. Ask Nicholas why he's been so keen to help.* "Is that why you're taking such an interest?"

Nick closed the book. He looked at her quizzically. "I thought you wanted my help."

Julia's hands tightened on the back of the chair. "It depends on the price."

Nick looked up at her through those gold-rimmed glasses, looking disarmingly boyish. "If you want to buy me a drink, I won't object." When she didn't smile, his own smile faded. "What are you trying to say?"

With the memory of Natalie's words buzzing in her ear, Julia blurted out, "Did Natalie ever tell you her theories about treasure in the house?"

"Well, yes, but it's all —" Puzzlement gave way to dawning comprehension as the penny dropped. His lips tightened into a hard line. "You think I'm after Natalie's imaginary treasure?"

Put that way, it sounded idiotic.

"You never told me the real reason you had to leave Dietrich Bank," she said belligerently.

Nick pushed the book away from him. "It's not exactly something I enjoy talking about," he said shortly. He looked up at Julia. Whatever he saw in her face made his eyes narrow. "That's what this is about? You think I'm —" Words failed him. "Christ. I would have thought you had more sense than that."

Stung, Julia struck back, "You don't exactly have a reputation for probity."

Nick pushed back his chair with a scrape of wood against wood that made the grad student glare at them.

"If," he said in a tight voice, "you had bothered to investigate before lobbing accusations, you would have seen that I was cleared. It was one of the junior members of the team who was moving the stock, not I. Not that it matters."

His voice was utterly flat and without inflection. It made Julia feel worse than any display of temper might have done. It was like listening to the knell of a funeral bell.

Behind her, she could almost hear Natalie snickering.

"Nick —" she began.

He cut her off. "Since you've already tried and condemned me, there's not much more for me to say, is there? Here." He pushed the volume of Rossetti's letters across to her with a quick, impatient gesture. "You can have this."

"You don't have to —"

Nick stopped her with one withering glance. With unerring aim he struck the final blow. "That will teach me to engage in charity work."

Before Julia could gather her wits together, he was already well away, striding towards the exit.

TWENTY-TWO

Herne Hill, 1849

Gavin arrived at the orchard gate the next day armed with an arsenal of arguments in favor of flight. He had stayed up half the night, planning and replanning, parsing out his reasons with the precision of a barrister at the bar.

When he saw Imogen, all his well-reasoned arguments fled.

She was waiting for him by the gnarled apple tree at the base of the hill, the bare branches providing a rustic frame. Gavin held out his arms to her, and she came into them, resting against his chest with a little sigh of content.

They stood like that for what seemed an eternity, content just to be together, his cheek resting against her brow, her skirts rustling around his legs. The wind might howl around them, the branches might bow and shake, but they were warm and safe together, whole and entire to themselves.

Her voice rusty, she said, without moving her head, "Arthur is gone away to town and Evie is at the Sturgises'." At the moment, Gavin couldn't have given a farthing for any of them; all he cared for was the feel of Imogen in her arms, the warmth of her body, the smell of her hair. "Jane is doing something with the flowers at the church and the maids will be staying close by the fire."

"So we are safe," he said.

"For the moment." In a voice so low he could hardly hear her she said, "I have missed this so." Imogen lifted her head and looked him full in the face, her expression rueful. "I have missed you so."

Gavin lifted her ungloved hand to his lips. He could feel triumph singing in his blood, although native caution urged him to go slowly.

"You needn't sound so sad about it," he said with rough humor. "This is a gift, what we have."

Her eyes met his. "With a very high price."

"It's a price I'm willing to pay." Gavin squeezed her cold fingers. "I want us to be together. I can't say you truer than that."

Imogen's petticoats crinkled as she drew her hand away, making an anxious gesture.

"But what about all the prospects you would be giving up? You've only just begun to make a name for yourself."

He had thought all that through, the night before. "The skill is still there, name or no name. If I can make a name for myself here, I can make a name for myself elsewhere — it will just be a slightly different one." He cupped her face in his hands, resting his forehead against hers. "I'm not afraid of hard work. I've worked with my hands before and I will again, if that's what needs be. And now," he added, "I'll be working for we three. That's a powerful incentive."

He felt her shoulders relax, her eyes close, as she leaned against him. "We three," she said slowly, as though testing the words on her tongue.

Gavin ran his thumb soothingly along the long line of her neck. "A family. Our family. We'll be happy as grigs, just you see."

He could see her struggling with her conscience. "It won't be legal."

Gavin rested his hands on her waist, thicker now than it had been two months before. His child was there, under all those layers of wool and linen. The law be damned; the three of them belonged together, just as in the days of old Adam, before lawyers and clerics and the whole

459

damnable apparatus of gentility.

"What's the law, in matters such as these?" he demanded. "Your kind worries about parish registers and bits of paper. In the rest of the world, there's many a marriage dissolved by a bit of shoe leather and time, and no one the worse for it."

Imogen looked at him doubtfully, and Gavin knew that this was an idea that had never occurred to her before. She hadn't grown up as he had, in a world where such matters were more fluid, where there wasn't the money or energy to worry about such trivialities as legality.

Gavin redoubled his efforts. "What will they care for such things in America or Australia? If we say we're husband and wife, we shall be. And so we shall be," he said more forcefully, "where it matters. Can you tell me you ever felt like this about Grantham?"

The wind whistled through the bare branches around them, sere and cold. Imogen drew her heavy shawl more firmly around her. "No. It was a young girl's fancy, an illusion, and I knew it for such within the year." Her mouth twisted wryly. "I thought love was all high romance and courtly words. I never thought of all the days and days and days to follow."

From the sound of it, those days had been long ones.

"I've little in the way of courtly words to offer you," said Gavin honestly. "And even less in the way of high romance. Just my devotion and the work of my hands."

Put that way, it sounded like precious little. Gavin shifted from one foot to the other, the frost crackling on the ground beneath his feet.

But Imogen didn't turn away. Instead, she took a step forward, towards him. "You do yourself too little credit. Words can mislead, but this —" She looked up at him, her heart in her eyes. "Whenever I'm with you, I feel as though I've come home after a long journey. You are hearth and harbor to me."

A cold hearth and a choppy harbor at the moment, but Gavin wasn't about to quibble.

With a crooked smile Imogen said, "It was easier when I could tell myself that you were just another passing fancy."

Gavin felt the world go still around him. "But now?"

"You are all I'll ever want," Imogen said simply. As she spoke, her voice gathered strength. "I love you, through and through, every part of you."

Gavin could hardly speak through the lump in his throat. "Even the shabby bits?"

"Especially the shabby bits," she said firmly, and somehow they were in each other's arms, rocking from side to side, laughing with elation and fear, clinging to each other with all their might.

Gavin wrapped his arms firmly around her, resting his cheek against her brow, hardly daring to believe his luck, to have found the one woman in the world made just for him. "Then — you'll come away with me?"

Imogen glanced over her shoulder at the house, the chimneys just visible through the bare branches of the trees. "Evie will be married in a month," she said. "Once she's married and in Lisbon, my scandal can't touch her — or not enough to matter."

Fairness prompted Gavin to say, "I can't offer you anything like this, at least, not at first. You won't miss it?"

"This house?" The curl of Imogen's lip was answer enough. "This has never been a home to me." Her expression lightened. "But if I had never married Arthur, I should never have met you."

"In that case," said Gavin, "I'll try to think kindly of him — although it will be difficult until I have you safely to myself!"

His father always had said that the Lord worked in mysterious ways. Of course, he'd usually been in his cups when he said it and looking for someone to thrash, but the sentiment held just the same.

He wouldn't be a father as his father had been. No matter how they had to scramble at first, he'd see his wife — for his wife she would be, in his eyes and the eyes of the world — and child safe and well, and no matter how little they had, they would always, always know how he cherished them.

"We will be happy together," Gavin said fiercely. "I promise you that. It may not always be easy, but I will do everything in my power to make you happy." Switching abruptly to practical matters, he said, "When is your Miss Evie's wedding?"

"Soon," said Imogen. "The eleventh of January."

He hated to wait that long, but he knew better than to ask Imogen to leave before her stepdaughter was safely wed. "Then we leave on the twelfth. You'll not need to bring much with you, just what you can fit into a portmanteau. I'll see to all the arrangements."

There was a faraway expression in her eyes. "A new life in a new land," she said, testing it out. Her lips quirked in a lopsided smile. "It's rather like something out of a Shakespeare play. Without the shipwreck."

"Please God, no shipwrecks," said Gavin.

He'd never had the stomach for the sea. It didn't sing in his blood as it did with some. But it was a necessary evil to making a life with his Imogen and their child.

He placed his hand over her stomach, on the place where he assumed their child must be, beneath the wide swell of her skirts. "Whatever comes, we face it together."

Imogen set her hand lightly over his. "Together," she echoed. It felt like a pact. Reluctantly, she drew back. "It will most likely be safest if we don't meet again until then."

Gavin could see the sense of that. "We'll have plenty of time together to make up for it."

But he drew her in for a long kiss, nonetheless.

"Something on account," he said, when they could speak again, "to last us through until January." More seriously, he added, "I'll meet you at the summerhouse at midnight on the twelfth. Can you slip out of the house unseen?"

Imogen didn't think twice. "Down the back stairs."

Gavin veered between exhilaration and fear. "Two flashes of light, a pause, and one more. That's how you'll know I'm there.

Watch for the signal. I will not fail you."

Imogen lifted her cold hand to his cheek. "I know," she said tenderly. "You never could."

"One last kiss," said Gavin, "to speed me on my way."

"And speed your way back again," said his Imogen, and went willingly into his arms, their bodies and lips blending together in perfect harmony, in promise of all the years to come.

If, on the other side of the gate, someone slipped away, they didn't hear it. The crunch of the frost beneath booted feet was lost in the rustling of the branches in the breeze and the weeping of the wind.

London, 2009

Julia arrived at The Grill of The Dorchester feeling confused, cranky, and emotionally raw.

She had spent the Tube ride over alternating between anger at herself, anger at Nick, and anger at the man who really ought to have put on deodorant before deciding to ride the Tube at rush hour.

No matter how she tried to convince herself that she had been in the right, she couldn't shake the conviction that she had just behaved like a prize jerk. That realization didn't do anything to improve her mood. Guilt, she had learned, tended to make one more defensive than conciliatory. And she was feeling pretty damned guilty right now.

But what had she been supposed to think, with Natalie talking about treasure hunting, and those damning *Wall Street Journal* articles? Even Nick had to admit, he didn't exactly appear squeaky clean. Although, it was true, she could have kept reading instead of seeing a few damning headlines and instantly assuming that he was out to gyp her.

But what else was she supposed to think? Why else would he have taken such an interest?

It wasn't as though she looked like Natalie.

Charity work. That phrase still stung.

"Julia?" Her father had to say her name three times before she realized he was standing there.

"Oh, sorry." Julia gave her father the obligatory kiss on the cheek. He wasn't a tall man. In her three-inch heels she was only an inch or two shorter than he was. "I didn't see you there."

"Obviously," said her father drily.

"Did you have a good trip over?" Julia

asked as the waiter led them to their table.

The walls were patterned with a mural depicting men draped in excessive amounts of tartan, a theme echoed in the upholstery of the chairs. The chair the waiter pulled out for her was covered in an aggressive red plaid.

Julia sat with more speed than grace and contemplated the usual dilemma of how to dispose of her bag: hanging off the back of her chair, where it was sure to fall just as the waiter was putting something on the table, or by her feet, where she was sure to kick it and knock out half the contents.

She tucked her bag down by her feet and accepted the menu the waiter handed her while her father pondered the wine list with the attention he usually gave to removing someone's gallbladder.

At least, she hoped he gave that kind of attention to removing someone's gallbladder.

"How are Helen and the boys?" she asked.

It seemed that Helen was well and the boys were enjoying camp, if "enjoying" was quite the right word. Jamie had earned some sort of swimming medal and Robbie had nearly gotten himself expelled over an incident involving a flaming marshmallow. Robbie had justified it as a scientific experiment, although the camp authorities were more inclined to label it arson.

"Are you saying I shouldn't have bought him that chemistry set for Christmas?" asked Julia as she ran her eyes down the intricately printed menu, which ran heavily to food with place names.

"Sadly," said her father, raising his hand to flag down the waiter, "his incendiary propensities were already well developed. You simply provided him new means."

Her father waited until they had gotten the important matter of ordering over with before asking, "How is the 'job hunt'?" The way he pronounced the phrase made it sound as though it were in inverted commas.

Julia tore open her bread roll. "Nonexistent." She opened her mouth to make the usual excuses: the bad market, too many people out of work. Instead, she said baldly, "I'm thinking of applying to grad school. Art history."

She stabbed her knife into the butter, waiting for the explosion. Instead, her father said calmly, "You'd be applying for the fall of 2010?"

"Yes." Poised for a fight, she felt as though the stuffing had been taken out of her. "It's too late now for this academic year, and I'll need to take the GRE."

She sat back as the waiter appeared with the bottle of red her father had chosen. She waited while her father went through the ritual of swirling and sipping. The waiter filled their glasses and set the bottle in a silver bucket next to the table.

Good. She might need more of that.

"Where were you thinking of applying?" her father asked.

Had aliens kidnapped her parent? Julia eyed her father over the top of her wineglass. "What, no lobbying for med school?"

"If you had wanted to attend, you would have," he said simply, and took a tidy sip of wine.

Not his attitude ten years ago. Julia wondered how much of the change had to do with Helen and how much was just mellowing with age. "I suppose now you have Jamie and Robbie to be your future surgeons."

Her father gave her a look. "Jamie's sole interest appears to be exterminating alien galaxies. As for Robbie, we'll just be pleased if he isn't arrested for arson before he reaches the age of majority."

It wasn't true, Julia knew. For all his dry tone, her father was tremendously proud of both boys. As he had been of her.

"You threw a fit when I majored in art

history," she said tentatively.

"Well, yes," said her father, as though that were the most logical thing in the world. "I didn't want to see you throw your degree away. But this is different. You're older now. It was also," he added delicately, "quite clear that finance wasn't making you happy."

"Really?" She hadn't thought of herself as actively unhappy. Not precisely dancing on rainbows, but okay.

"Credit me with some perception," said her father. Julia decided to let that one ride. "You're old enough to make your own decisions. If you feel that a career in academia is where your ambitions lie, I certainly can't stop you. Even if there are no jobs in it."

That was more like the father she knew and loved.

"I'd thought you didn't want me doing art history because it reminded you too much of my mother."

Her father raised his brows at her frankness. "Perhaps. A little. But not in the way you mean." He set down his butter knife carefully on the side of his bread plate. "It is one of nature's great ironies that having worked to give you the advantages I didn't have, it never occurred to me that you would never need to go out and fight for them yourself."

470

Julia contemplated her wine. "Why do I feel as though I've just been obliquely insulted?"

"I didn't mean it as such."

They both fell silent as the waiter set their plates down in front of them, the food carefully arranged for the maximum impact, little bundles of baby carrots with the stems still on tied with some sort of green, a pale sauce for her father's fish, a rich port gravy under Julia's beef. Around them, there was the sound of genteel conversation and the muted clink of silver against porcelain.

"I haven't told you anything of how I grew up, have I?" asked her father abruptly as Julia cut into her filet mignon. "I've spent most of my life trying to get away from it."

This was something new. Julia looked up at her father. "It was in Liverpool, wasn't it?"

"Manchester," her father corrected her. "Six of us in a three-room flat with the loo down the hall, shared by four families. Half the time we pissed in a pot."

The unexpected vulgarity made Julia blink, especially delivered in her father's usual precise tone.

"Wow," she said weakly. Her father's current apartment had no fewer than four bathrooms, each with carefully coordinated

471

towels and tiles and Molton Brown soaps. "Not exactly Fifth Avenuc."

"No," said her father drily. "Sometimes, I would look at you, in your private-school uniform, and think how very odd it was, that there you were with no idea. But that was what I wanted for you. I wanted you never to have to feel inferior to anyone, never to have to apologize for your accent, or feel awkward because there were holes in your clothes." He stabbed his fork into his fish. "If I pushed medicine at you — well, it was because I saw a medical degree as the surest way to a decent life."

She had never really thought of it that way before. There hadn't been the same extras the boys had when she was little; the apartment had been on Third, not Fifth, one of those huge high-rises that always smelled vaguely of burnt grease, but her tuition alone must have cost a small fortune. She had always had the security that came of knowing that she had a gold-plated academic pedigree, from grade school straight through college.

"Are you going to tell Jamie and Robbie this, too?" she asked.

Her father devoted a great deal of attention to separating his fish from the bone. "Perhaps. It is, I think, less relevant for them." He looked at her, across the porcelain and silver. "You bore the brunt of it. I was . . . more raw when you were young."

It had taken Helen to mellow him. Or maybe it had just been time. Either way, Julia thought she knew what he meant.

Julia pushed a piece of meat through a sticky puddle of gravy. "Speaking of that . . . Being back in that house, I've started to — well, to remember things." It sounded pretty stupid said like that. "Just little things. Impressions. Memories I didn't remember I had."

Her father was silent for a long moment. "It's to be expected."

Julia abandoned the abused piece of meat. "You and my mother weren't happy together, were you? I have these weird memories of hiding under the table while you shouted at each other."

Her father's hand stilled on his fork. "We weren't unhappy, not at the beginning." He made another attempt. "We were both very happy to have you."

Julia took a swig of her wine. "That sounds like the parental equivalent of 'it's not you, it's me.'"

"It was all so long ago." Her father looked suddenly very tired and much older than his age, the silver in his hair pronounced in the lamplight. "I'm not quite sure what to tell you."

"Anything," said Julia. Anything would be better than nothing.

"Well, then." Her father looked down at his hands, at the wide gold wedding band that had replaced the narrower one that Julia remembered from her youth. "I met your mother on Hampstead Heath. I'd gone with a group of medical students; your mother was there sketching. A page from her sketchbook blew away and I went after it for her. And that, as they say, was that."

Her father's face softened at the memory. Julia tried to imagine them as they must have been then, her father a younger, less painfully refined version of himself and her mother as she had seen her in that long-ago photo, her black hair under a kerchief, her face alight with laughter.

"Your mother was —" He sketched a helpless gesture with his hands. "I'd never met anyone like her before. She was a creature from another world. There was — a glow about her. Everything was an adventure, an opportunity. She didn't seem to worry about mundane things like money or getting on in the world. She didn't mind that I'd come up from muck."

Julia listened, fascinated. Under her fa-

474

ther's careful BBC diction there was a hint of an accent she had never heard before.

Her father took a long sip of his wine, and when he spoke again his voice was the one she knew again. "That," he added blandly, "was one of the best things about your mother. She hadn't an ounce of snobbery about her. Your cousin Caroline looked down her nose at me, made fun of my clothes, my accent, my attempts to fit in, but Alice — Alice just didn't see it. It didn't matter to her. Whatever else, your mother had a good heart."

Julia didn't like the sound of that *whatever else.* "So what went wrong?"

Her father shrugged. "It was inevitable, I suppose. At least, I can see that now. At the time . . ." He sliced a baby carrot neatly in half before spearing it with his fork. "There was your mother, the original free spirit, and there I was, trying so very hard to make something of myself. The very things that had originally drawn us to each other became irritants — especially once there was a child involved."

"Me," said Julia.

"You." For a moment, she thought he meant to leave it at that, but, then, slowly, he went on, "We began to have rows. Just little ones at first. She was upset about the hours I put in at the hospital; I couldn't understand why she couldn't see that it was for her — for you — that I was doing it. You can imagine. We grew . . . increasingly impatient with each other."

Julia sat very still, not even daring to take a drink from her wineglass. She didn't want to say anything to derail the flow of memory. They had never spoken like this before and she deeply doubted it was likely to happen again.

Her father looked off over her shoulder, reliving events long gone by. "Your mother told me she wanted a husband, not a pile of medical books on the kitchen table; I told her that we couldn't all live in an airy-fairy fantasy world, that the rent had to be paid somehow. She accused me of being mercenary. I called her unrealistic. These art classes she was teaching, they didn't pay, not one red cent. It was all very well for her to talk about living on love alone, but we had a child to feed and clothe and I couldn't bear the thought of your growing up as I had, in shame and squalor."

The ferocity of her father's voice made Julia sit up a little straighter in her chair. "It sounds like you were coming from very different places," she said cautiously.

"Judiciously put." Her father looked at

her with something akin to amusement.

It made Julia feel, suddenly, very young and gauche. What did she know about what her parents had gone through? It was bizarre to think that, at the time, they had both been younger than she was now, even her father. Younger than she was and dealing with a marriage that wasn't quite working and a child who needed to be clothed and fed and comforted.

It made her own life feel very empty and shallow.

Her father twisted the stem of his wineglass between his fingers, saying thoughtfully, "Maybe, had we been older, more mature, we might have handled it better. At the time, all either of us could feel was that we had been wronged and the other one couldn't see it." He looked up at Julia, his eyes meeting hers across the table. "It all came to a head when you were five."

He was silent for so long that Julia began to think that he didn't mean to go on. "What happened?" she asked.

Her father picked up a bread roll and began absently tearing the contents into neat little segments. Even in distress, he was tidy about it. All of the pieces were the same size and shape.

"Your mother was teaching a class at the

local community center. I was meant to pick you up from school. Something happened at the hospital — I can't remember now what it was." He dropped the last piece of bread on his plate with something like disgust. "At the time, though, it seemed of the utmost importance."

The acid edge to his voice made Julia wince.

It was easy enough to see where this was going. "So you forgot me," she said matter-of-factly. "It happens."

"That wasn't exactly how you felt at the time." Her father took a sip of his wine. "The school called your mother. When she found you, you were shivering and crying. You had," he added in that same clinical, detached tone, "wet your pants from fear."

Julia looked down at her plate. She remembered that, or at least she thought she did, the horrible embarrassment of it. She was in a room with brightly painted cubbies, with her coat on, and they were turning all the lights off, one by one, because all the other children had gone, and she was the only one left. Even now, years later, she could feel that prickle of panic, the fear that no one was going to come for her.

"I think I remember that," she said quietly.

"It was the final straw for your mother."

Her father repositioned the butter knife on his bread plate, placing it at the mathematically correct angle. "By the time I got home, she was packing her bags. Your bags, too. She told me that if I cared about the bloody hospital more than my bloody family, I could bloody well live there and see if she cared."

Yes, she remembered that, too. The linoleum of the kitchen floor cold beneath her knees. Mummy shouting, her voice hoarse, rough. Daddy angry. She'd been put into a fresh dress and dry panties, but she couldn't stop shivering.

Her father's cool voice brought Julia back to the present. "Your mother told me that she had had quite enough. She wasn't going to risk your well-being to my indifferent care."

"What did you say?"

Her father's face twisted. "I told her to go right ahead. I told her to go on and leave. And she did."

The waiter made a sally in the direction of their plates. Julia's father waved him back.

Taking the wine bottle from its bucket, her father emptied the remains into Julia's glass. "There you have it. Your mother was leaving me when she died. And I drove her to it."

TWENTY-THREE

Herne Hill, 1850

By the evening of January 12, Evie was safely Mrs. Edward Sturgis and well on the way to Lisbon and Imogen had stowed what few necessaries she intended to take to her new life in a small portmanteau.

It was a little disconcerting, how little she had to show for her ten years in this house. Her pearl earrings and brooch she left; those had been gifts from Arthur. The locket her father had given her, the cameo set that had been her mother's, those she packed, along with warm stockings and a change of linen and two of her very simplest traveling costumes. She wouldn't need gowns where they were going.

She would have liked to bring her father's Book of Hours, but that would feel like stealing. In the eyes of the law, it belonged to Arthur.

In the eyes of the law, she belonged to Arthur, too, but that had ceased to worry her. The closer the hour came to her departure, the more sure Imogen was of her decision. She felt no regret at the prospect of leaving Herne Hill, except, perhaps, a little for the young girl she had been, who had been so sure she would find happiness within the walls of this house.

Already the room in which she had slept for the past ten years had ceased to feel like her own. It had never truly been her own. It was merely a place she had sojourned awhile. The flowered drapes and china knickknacks felt as impersonal and distant from her as a room at an inn.

She had no doubt they would stay in rougher places along the way. Gavin said he had some money saved up, the money Arthur had paid him for her portrait and nearly a hundred guineas for the sale of his *Mariana,* the painting that had brought him to Arthur's house and to her. It seemed fitting that the price of it should finance their flight to the New World.

The wretched sickness and fatigue of the past months had finally left her, and in its place came a surge of optimism, of hope. Fortunately, Arthur and Jane had attributed her high spirits to Evie's wedding, never guessing that her mind was awhirl with the prospect of passage across the seas. She knew, realistically, that New York was a city like London, that she and Gavin should find the same coal-blackened buildings and noisome streets, but in her dreams she saw the coast lying before them as it must have done for the earliest explorers, verdant and wild, a brave new land bursting with promise.

They would try New York first. Gavin was to see to a new identity for them, and he was quite insistent that their child be born in the metropolis, where they might be sure of finding a well-trained midwife. But once the child was well enough to travel, they might drift down the Mississippi to the estates of the great planters, who would be sure to want themselves immortalized in oils. Or they could take a stagecoach out west, to the new lands just being conquered, to places where no one would ever care where they had come from or who they had been. The future was alive with possibility and Imogen felt alive with it.

She curled her fingers protectively over the child in her belly. By her own reckoning, she was about four months along now, long enough that she could feel the hard curve of the baby beneath her skin, where her stomach had once been flat and soft.

As she stood there, by the window, waiting for Gavin's signal, Imogen thought she could feel a little flutter, the tiniest brush of movement.

It was fanciful, she knew, but she liked to think the baby leapt for joy.

Imogen lifted the curtain and peered outside. The glass of the window was cold beneath her palm. How many hours had she stared out at this same stretch of land? The garden lay dark and quiet, the white roof of the summerhouse a gentle shadow. The frost on the ground had an eerie glow in the moonlight, a phosphorescent clarity such as sailors claimed to see on certain haunted stretches of sea.

It was too far from where she stood to see the orchard gate, but she could imagine the scene. She could see Gavin, burdened with his parcels, slipping around the worn wood slats, making his way cautiously between the ranks of trees, his shuttered lantern in his hand. There would be a hired carriage waiting for them some several streets away, waiting to take them to the docks and the ship that would carry them to their new life, carry them far away before Arthur and Jane, flush with the success of Evie's wedding, ever realized Imogen was gone.

She had gone to bed with a headache, blaming the exigencies of Evie's wedding.

"I shan't be down for breakfast," she had told an openly hostile Jane. "And you needn't burden Anna by telling her to bring a tray. I shall sleep until I wake."

By the time anyone thought to look for her, she would be well away. The ship sailed with the morning tide.

The creak of the floorboard brought her out of her reverie.

"Imogen?" called a voice from the hall softly. And then, again, "My dear?"

Imogen let the curtain fall. Hastily she shoved her portmanteau under the bed. She couldn't be seen still clothed. She yanked up the covers and slid beneath them, trusting to the coverlet and the dark to hide her buttoned boots. As a final thought, she pulled the pins from her hair, so that the long coil unraveled into one long braid that fell over her shoulder.

She was just in time. The door opened, and a light shone in.

"My dear?" Her husband stood silhouetted in the doorway, a candle in his hand.

"Arthur?" She hoped she sounded like someone just aroused from sleep. Her body thrummed with nervous energy, her heart racing, her torso damp with sweat beneath the layers of clothes and coverlet. "What is it?"

Arthur couldn't have discovered their plans. True to their resolve, she and Gavin hadn't met again, not since that afternoon in the garden. No, it must be something innocuous and foolish: Anna had misplaced his slippers, or there was a book he couldn't find. Please God, Imogen prayed, let it be something swift and simple.

Arthur ventured farther into the room. The glare of his candle made Imogen wince. That, at least, she didn't need to feign. "Jane tells me that you are unwell," he said.

"It is nothing," said Imogen, damning Jane to the lowest levels of Dante's inferno. "Merely this ridiculous head of mine."

Setting his candle down on the mantel, Arthur seated himself, gingerly, on the chair by the side of her bed. "I cannot like these headaches."

Beneath the coverlet, Imogen squirmed with suppressed impatience. "A little rest is all the cure I need."

By the light of Arthur's candle she could see that the hands of the clock on the mantel read five minutes to midnight. Five minutes until Gavin was meant to come to collect her.

Arthur settled himself more comfortably on the chair, bracing his hands against his knees. "I blame myself."

"For my headaches?" Good heavens, did he mean to sit here all night?

Arthur wagged his head mournfully. The candlelight played along the silver and red of his whiskers. "I have left you too much on your own. An idle mind soon causes phantasms of the brain."

"I assure you," said Imogen desperately, "it is nothing so serious as — as a phantasm. Merely the headache. It is all this horrid, rainy weather we have been having, nothing more. A period of rest will see me well again."

On the mantel, the clock ticked away. The curtains were down. Even had she dared to turn her head, she couldn't have seen the signal. Was Gavin already down there waiting for her? A hideous suspicion kindled in Imogen's breast. But no. If Arthur had learned of their plans, wouldn't he choose some other means? He couldn't hope to sit beside her bedside all night.

At least, she devoutly hoped he wouldn't.

"You must be tired, too," she said, with what she hoped was the proper simulacrum of wifely concern. "It is no easy thing seeing your only child away."

"Yes," Arthur agreed. He showed no sign of moving. "How empty this house will seem with only we two left in it."

Imogen would have felt sorry for Jane had she the energy for it. As it was, the clock on the mantel read ten minutes past the hour.

Perhaps Gavin had been detained on the way — the roads were slick and muddy; the hired carriage might have got mired in mud or lost a wheel. Either way, he must know that she hadn't abandoned him. He would wait and give the signal again; she was sure of it.

Arthur was still following his own line of thought. "I must devise some plans for our entertainment," he said, "to keep us from being too sad and sorry in our beloved one's absence."

"Yes, do," said Imogen. Preferably right now. She blinked up at him with the most pathetic expression she could muster. "Perhaps we might discuss it on the morrow? My head . . ."

"Very well, my dear." She suffered him to kiss her cheek, his whiskers brushing across her face. "Sleep well. We shall speak more of this in the morning."

With any luck, she wouldn't be there in the morning.

"Yes," said Imogen demurely. "Over breakfast. Good night, Arthur."

She waited until the door had closed behind him, until she had heard his step retreating down the hall, and then she waited some minutes more, just to be sure.

Thrusting the covers aside, Imogen flew to the window. The frost lay hard on the ground; the birds had abandoned their nests; all was dark and still. Imogen strained to discern a dark shape among the shadows, but the dark boughs of the trees that had afforded her and Gavin shelter in their trysts in the summer thwarted her quest, creating their own fantastical shadows across the winter-hard ground.

There was no sign of light from the summerhouse.

Imogen waited by her post until her body was as chill as the glass of the window and her eyes were red with fatigue, but the signal never came.

Herne Hill, 2009

Julia stood in front of the painting in the attic and tried to remember the little girl she had been.

It was a good thing her father had put her in a cab home, because she wasn't entirely sure she would have been competent to navigate the train. It wasn't the wine, although she had had a good bit of that, and a good bit more after her father's bombshell. It was more the disorientation of watching the past as she had thought she had known it turn on its head and lock into a different shape, like one of those trick pictures that was quite definitely one image when you looked at it straight on but, when twisted, turned out to be another thing entirely.

She'd had no idea that her father had spent the past twenty-odd years blaming himself for her mother's death. Or that, in her own weird way, she had been the proximate cause. She could understand why her father felt guilty; she felt guilty herself. If five-year-old Julia had been able to hold it together . . .

That was absurd, of course. She'd been five. She'd been alone and scared and in a cloakroom with an impatient assistant teacher. She wasn't to know that her panic would set in train a chain of events that would upend all their lives. Who could have? It had been a perfectly logical five-year-old reaction, sniffles and loss of bladder control. That was what five-year-olds did.

They hadn't pursued the topic further over dinner. When the coffee came, black for her father, a cappuccino for Julia, they had reverted, by mutual, unspoken consent, to safe topics, impersonal topics: her father's conference schedule, the books she had been reading.

Back to the old routine. On the surface, at least.

Julia had nodded and smiled and kept up her end of the conversation with her mind circling over and over what her father had told her, restructuring the landscape of her childhood.

She'd always assumed, when she'd allowed herself to think about it, that her parents' relationship had been a great love affair, that Helen was her father's consolation prize, the sop of old age. After all, he needed someone to keep him company when Julia went off to college. But her mother would always be the Great Love of His Life. That was why he wouldn't talk about her. That was why he blamed her so for dying.

It didn't sound like that anymore. It sounded like her parents had stumbled into something too young and discovered they weren't really suited to each other at all.

But they were stuck with each other. Because of her.

Julia wondered what would have happened if her mother hadn't died in that crash, if her father hadn't whisked her away to New York, and Third Avenue, and an entirely new life. Would she have found herself in the middle of a prolonged and acrimonious divorce? She'd seen it among school friends: weekdays at Mom's and weekends at Dad's and complicated negotiations over who was going to attend which school play.

Julia looked at the painting on the easel, forever summer, the scene sun washed, the colors bright, as that other Julia, five-year-old Julia with no idea what was to come, swirled in a circle, around and around and around, until the sky and the leaves patterned themselves into a kaleidoscope around her.

It was strange to think that she and her mother had been on their way to this house when the car had gone off the road.

Julia remembered, as she had that first day back, that walk up the brick path, holding on to her mother's hand, the bricks slick beneath her beloved red Mary Janes. The memory came, as it had that other time, with a little trickle of unhappiness, a sense of remembered dread. She remembered being whiny and cranky, pulling against her mother's hand. Julia had wanted to go back home; she was tired; she wasn't feeling well. But Mummy wasn't listening. Mummy marched her onward, telling her sharply to pick up her bag before it dragged in a puddle.

Julia found herself looking down at her hand, half-expecting to find the tattered old carpet beneath her feet transformed to rain-wet bricks, and a small blue valise dangling from her hand.

She'd been so proud of that valise, with sliding latches on the top that went *click* and an elasticized blue band inside. She could practically feel the pressure of the handle against her palm, her own little blue faux leather suitcase, usually used only for transporting Barbies but that day inexplicably heavy with the weight of her own small jumpers and dresses.

Her mother had been carrying a suitcase, too. It was in her other hand, the hand that wasn't holding on to Julia's, making her gait awkward, making her jerk Julia's hand up at an uncomfortable angle.

Your mother was leaving me when she died, her father had said.

There was no reason for him to have gotten it wrong. But for the fact that she remembered that long trek down the walk, her mother's too-tight grasp on her hand, pulling her along when she would have dawdled and scuffed her soles against the bricks. There had been a row with Daddy, and Mummy had packed her things and put her in the car and told her that they were staying with Aunt Regina for a while.

Had Mummy left Daddy before? Julia didn't think so. It had sounded, from what her father had said, that her mother's packing her up and storming off had been an unusual occurrence, the culmination of months of frustration boiling to the surface.

Maybe it was wishful thinking, then. Or a patchwork of fragments of memories from other times, other visits.

Julia tried to tell herself that that made the most sense, but the more she thought about it, the more sure she was; that rainy fall day had been the same rainy fall day her father had forgotten her at kindergarten. Embarrassment at behaving like a baby had made her querulous and difficult; usually she loved going to Aunt Regina's, but that day she had been particularly stubborn and obstructive. She had wanted to stay home with Daddy and be tucked into bed with her stuffed rabbit; she didn't want to put on her shoes and go back out in the rain.

But her mother had been adamant. And her father — he hadn't said anything at all. He had just stood there as they left, his arms folded across his chest.

Standing in the middle of the old nursery,

still in her cocktail dress, Julia closed her eyes and forced herself to relive that walk down the path. The door opening. Aunt Regina standing in the doorway. The triangle of light falling from the hall out onto the steps.

They'd gone with Aunt Regina into her lair. That must have been Aunt Regina's name for the little room between the living room and the library. It came pat into Julia's head, without explanation.

She couldn't picture Aunt Regina's face. Instead, she remembered her as a collection of attributes: long, jangly earrings; the scent of cigarette smoke; the hem of a brightly patterned dress; a raspy, smoker's voice.

She remembered the creak of Aunt Regina's favorite chair as she'd flung herself down in it, her deep voice saying, *You're welcome to stay if you like.*

But you don't think I should, Julia's mother had said, her voice high-pitched, still angry.

Aunt Regina had taken a long drag on her cigarette. *You know I never give advice — no, Julia, darling,* not *that record — but . . . For better or for worse, they say.*

And her mother's voice. *I hate it when you're right.*

Hate me from a distance, then. But have a

494

drink before you go.

It was like looking into a snow globe, the scene distorted with distance and time but complete in every detail. Julia could remember sitting on the floor, sulkily sorting through Aunt Regina's records while the adults talked behind her, above her head. Sometimes Aunt Regina let Julia put a record on the turntable and position the needle, but today she had shooed her away and told her to let the grown-ups talk. Julia could remember that pattern of the rug, the prickle of the nap.

What she couldn't remember was what had happened next. It faded away, as childhood memories did, crystal clear and then gone.

Julia wandered over to the old sofa where she had sat with Nick and plopped heavily down on the worn seat.

What if they really had gone to Aunt Regina's? What if the accident had happened not on their way out but on their way home?

There must be some way of finding out for sure. Traffic records, police report? The time of the accident would be on record somewhere. Nighttime. It had happened at night, after dark. That she remembered vividly enough from a hundred nightmares, the rain greasy and wet against the windshield, the sudden flash of lights, the skid, the swerve, the crash.

She was pretty sure it hadn't been dark when they'd left her parents' flat. Or when they'd pulled up at the house at Herne Hill. It had been afternoon, a grim, gray sort of afternoon, the rain puddling along the walkway, sinking through the fretwork of her Mary Janes, when they'd arrived at Aunt Regina's.

If they had arrived at Aunt Regina's.

Before she could think better of it, Julia dug her cell out of her bag and pulled up the number of her father's hotel. The bored-sounding person at the switchboard put her through to his room without question.

It rang three times before she heard the unmistakable noise of a phone being dropped and then dragged up again.

"John Conley," he said blearily.

Damn. She'd forgotten about his usual ten o'clock bedtime. "Dad? It's me."

She heard a rustle of pillows as her father pulled himself up, his voice sharp with concern: "Is everything all right?"

Maybe this should have waited until morning.

"Everything's fine," said Julia hastily. "I just wanted to see you again before you go. Do you have time for a quick coffee tomorrow between your panels?"

Julia met her father at four the next afternoon, in a Costa Coffee around the corner from the conference center. It was soothingly generic, the same beige-upholstered benches and round wooden tables as a thousand other Costas in other parts of London.

"So," said her father, "what is this in aid of? Not that I'm not always happy to see you," he added.

He'd chosen one of the dark, straight-backed chairs instead of the cushy banquette. He scooted his chair awkwardly closer to the table, giving his cup of coffee a slightly dubious look.

Julia felt a sudden surge of affection for her father. She knew that meeting her today in the thick of Day One of his conference hadn't precisely been convenient; he'd probably had to blow off some colleagues to do so. But no matter how hard her father had worked, no matter how crazy things had been, he had always come running when she really needed him.

Julia fiddled with the ridges on her insulated cup, so different from the familiar feel of the cardboard Starbucks sleeve, and tried to think of a way to tell him without sounding like a complete nut job.

"Do you know how I mentioned I've been remembering things?" she said.

Her father started to raise his coffee to his lips, thought better of it, and put it down again. "Is this in reference to what we discussed last night?"

Ah, her father's usual warm and direct way of communicating. "Yes," said Julia determinedly. "It is."

Her father twitched his shirt cuffs down beneath his jacket sleeve. The cuff links were silver and monogrammed. "If you think I ought to have told you sooner —"

"No," Julia said quickly. "That's not it at all."

Her father waited for her to go on.

Julia wrapped her hands around her cup of coffee. "I think you got it wrong. I don't think Mummy was leaving you when she died. I think she was coming back."

TWENTY-FOUR

London, 2009

Her father stared at her as though she had just told him she had seen an extraterrestrial dancing a tango in Trafalgar Square.

In a voice that sounded like it had been scraped from the very back of his throat he said, "What makes you think that?"

Julia explained her reasoning. It sounded rather thin when voiced right out, nothing but a hodgepodge of hazy memories from twenty-five years ago. She couldn't have said why she was so sure, but she was.

"There must be some way to verify it," she concluded. She looked up at her father over the lid of her coffee. "The police reports?"

Her father's face had gone as gray as his hair. "I don't know. Maybe." His hand knocked against his coffee, and he hastily righted it again before more than a few drops sloshed over the side. "The car had spun all the way around. I never thought to question which way it was going. I just assumed —"

He broke off, taking a quick, violent gulp of his coffee.

It must have been boiling hot, but Julia didn't think it was the heat of the coffee that was making the sweat bead on his brow.

"What time did Mummy and I leave the flat that afternoon?" Julia asked.

"Four? Five?" Her father made a helpless gesture. "I went back to the hospital. When — when the call came, it took them some time to find me. They must have tried the flat first, and then the hospital. The nurse they spoke to thought I had gone back home. It took them calling the hospital again, later, before the nurse thought to look for me. I had fallen asleep in the break room."

Her father's expression was bleak as cold concrete. Julia felt as though she were opening the door to a place she wasn't entirely sure she wanted to see. But once she had come this far, there was no turning back.

"When did you finally hear . . . the news?" she asked carefully.

"The police didn't track me down until nearly nine o'clock that night." Her father's lips set in a tight, gray line. "I never saw the site of the accident. It was all cleared away by the time they got to me. Your mother was in the morgue and you were in hospital with a cracked rib and a particularly nasty concussion." His voice was taut with re-membered pain. "You saw double for days. I was terrified that there had been perma-nent brain damage."

"Well, that bit is still debatable," said Julia in an awkward attempt at humor.

Her father looked at her fiercely over the rims of his spectacles. "Don't even joke about it. I'd lost your mother and I was so terrified I would lose you, too." He laughed, without humor. "I think I may have gone a little bit mad for a time. I was convinced your aunt Regina was going to try to take you away from me."

"Was that why we left London so sud-denly?" She didn't remember much of it, just the flurry of activity, the international phone calls at odd hours, and the moving men coming and taking their things away. She'd cried when she had to say good-bye to the neighbor's cat.

She imagined the cat had been rather more sanguine about it.

"Yes," her father said soberly. "Not that I regret the move. I've been very happy there." He looked hastily at Julia. "You were happy there, weren't you?"

"I can't imagine having grown up any-where else," said Julia honestly.

It was what it was. Any life she might have had in London was purely a hypothetical.

She wasn't sure her father even heard her. He was far away, immersed in his own thoughts. "If you're right . . . Christ. All this time, I'd thought your mother had given up on me, given up on our marriage. She'd taken you away from me. You could have died in that car." His voice resonated with old rage. "I was so angry with her."

Julia traced rings with the spilled coffee on the table. "I kind of got that."

"Yes." Her father looked away, his Adam's apple bobbing up and down beneath the neat knot of his tie. "I know. Sometimes I wonder if I've done you a great disservice. Helen thinks —"

He stopped, looking guilty, and took a quick sip of his coffee.

Julia couldn't blame him. Once upon a time she would have bitten off his head for discussing the inner workings of her psyche with Helen.

"What does Helen think?" Julia asked re-signedly.

Her father pushed the stems of his glasses more firmly behind his ears. "She thinks I ought to have spoken about all of this with you years ago. She was concerned that by not addressing it, I" — he floundered for a moment, choosing between evils — "may have stunted your emotional growth, made it hard for you to develop, er, relationships of trust."

"Relationships of trust?"

"She means" — Julia's father was visibly discomfited — "that my refusal to address your mother's loss might make it difficult for you to be intimate with others. Not in a sexual way," he added hastily. "Emotionally."

Julia opened her mouth to tell her father where Helen could put her opinion. And closed it again. It wasn't just Helen. Lexie, her college roommate and closest friend, had said much the same thing. Julia had told her that she had no right to psychoanalyze her on the strength of one intro psych class.

Fine, Lexie had said. *Then go see someone who does.*

So Julia had gone, grudgingly, to the department euphemistically referred to as the mental health center. The shrink had told her, in somewhat more polished terms, pretty much what both Helen and Lexie had said.

503

Julia had made it a point not to return to that part of campus. She was perfectly functional as she was and she wanted to keep it that way, thank you very much.

Only, maybe she wasn't.

Julia grimaced at the lipgloss–stained lid of her coffee. "I haven't been particularly nice to Helen, have I?"

"You haven't been not nice to Helen," said her father helpfully. Somehow, that made it even worse. With a light sigh he sat back in his chair. "She didn't want to force you into an intimacy that might make you uncomfortable. She was hoping you would come to her on your own time. That's what she said," he added hastily, just in case Julia might think any of this was his idea.

Julia thought of all the tentative overtures over the years, the invitations to go shopping or meet for coffee or see this or that exhibit at the Frick or the Met. It was all right for Helen to suggest such things, Julia had told herself self-righteously; Helen didn't work anymore. She had time for all those frivolous ladies-who-lunch things. She, Julia, was too busy being a productive member of society.

Which was really all bull when she got down to it. She could easily have met her on a Saturday or gone up to the Hamptons on a weekend when invited. She'd deliberately held herself aloof.

When you cared about people, you got hurt.

"It wasn't so much for her own sake," her father said. Mumbled, really. He directed his attention to a scratch on the wooden table. "I believe it was more that Helen was concerned that my — er — baggage might be preventing you from developing a proper relationship. A proper romantic relationship."

He didn't exactly squirm as he uttered those last words — her father wasn't a squirming man — but his expression was that of a man contemplating a do-it-yourself tooth extraction.

"I date," said Julia defensively.

"Yes, yes," her father said quickly. If this conversation was unpleasant for her, it was probably pure torture for him. "I'm sure you do."

They sat in silence, Julia nursing her coffee, her father adjusting and readjusting his cuffs.

After a long moment, he said diffidently, "I do hope you won't hold any of this against Helen."

"No," said Julia distantly. "She means well."

What was more disturbing was that she might also be right.

When Lexie had voiced similar opinions, Julia had always indignantly retorted that it wasn't as though she didn't date. She did. She dated enough for multiple people.

It was true, though, that none of them had ever lasted long. Her longest relationship had lasted nine months, and that was probably only because it had been during her consulting days, when she had been rocketing about from project to project. She and Peter had seen each other only on alternate weekends, when she'd been back in New York. They'd never even reached the point of leaving toothbrushes in each other's apartments.

Had there been anyone serious since? Not really. She tended to break up with them before things could go too far. The two-month rule, she called it. Lexie called it something else entirely.

Julia had always prided herself on staying friends with her exes. No hurt feelings, no drunk dials. It had never occurred to her, until now, that that might not exactly be a point of pride. It had always been easy to end amiably because she'd never invested much in any of them in the first place.

She'd opened up more to Nick Dorrington in that one evening in the attic than she had to Peter in nine months.

Which was probably why she had been so quick to believe the worst of Nick.

The realization hit her like a triple shot of espresso. She tried to come up with other reasons, with excuses, but there it was, staring her in the face. Natalie had offered her an easy out. She'd wanted him to have a flaw — no, more than a flaw. She'd wanted him to be something irredeemably awful. Because then she wouldn't run any risk of growing attached to him.

Her latte tasted like ash.

She'd been an idiot. And she didn't know how to fix it. Although apologizing might be a start.

Her father checked his watch. "I have a panel in five minutes. But if you want me to stay . . ."

Julia rose, brushing the crumbs of someone else's scone from her skirt. She hoisted her bag up from the banquette beside her.

"No, that's okay." She brushed her cheek against her father's, in what passed between them for a hug. "There's someone I need to go see."

London, 1850
When a week had gone by without word,

507

Imogen sought out Gavin's studio.

She had kept vigil all that night, waiting for a sign that never came. A soft snow began to fall by morning, blurring the outlines of the summerhouse and the ground around it. If Gavin had come for her, there was no sign of it; the paths were all shrouded in snow, converted to a horrible, uniform sameness by that smooth, white blanket.

Arthur had found her outside, her hair starred with snowflakes, and insisted that she come inside and be warmed with a hot toddy, instructing Anna to see to it. True to his avowal of the other night, he kept close to Imogen for the next few days, reading aloud to her from the paper, insisting she go upstairs to rest, sending Anna on useless errands for extraneous shawls and undesired pots of tea.

She mustn't be moped over Evie's departure, Arthur told her; he was there to make sure of it.

And Imogen smiled and said thank you and secretly wondered whether Arthur's mission of mercy was quite so merciful or something else entirely. In her frustration she wondered whether it was a deliberate attempt to keep her from Gavin: Arthur's appearance in her room at the critical moment the other night, his constant presence by her side for the next three days. With Arthur, it was always so hard to tell. His countenance was as bland and genial as ever it was; he thanked her courteously for alleviating his pain at the loss of his only child and trusted that they would be a comfort to each other.

It would have made Imogen feel guilty if she hadn't been so madly worried.

Did Gavin think she had abandoned him? Surely he must know better than that. She had been by the window again by fifteen minutes after the appointed hour. Clocks varied; watches slowed. If he had been there, at all, surely she would have known, have seen.

If he hadn't been there . . .

That was the demon that haunted her nights and nipped at the edges of her consciousness by day. The age of highwaymen was over, but there were still footpads who lurked on the fringes of London's poorer areas. Every day, there were men clubbed or stabbed, dredged from the river or found sprawled in an alley, denuded of valuables. Gavin would have been carrying a substantial sum in coin, more than most laborers saw in a year, or even two.

It needn't even have been a footpad. The

roads had been slick and icy. What if Gavin hadn't been able to find a hackney? What if he had decided to walk the long way to her? All it would have taken would be one false step on a patch of ice to send him plunging into the unforgiving currents of the Thames.

His continued silence filled her with fear. If he were alive, if he were well, he would have come to her.

Perhaps he was ill. So many fell ill at this time of year. He might be lying alone in his studio, in the grip of fever, too ill to even think to pen a note. Imogen clung to that faint hope: a fever, a broken leg, a note that had gone astray.

It wasn't until the fourth day that Arthur finally went away to town, on business that, he said apologetically, could not be avoided. Looking at him, remembering what Gavin had told her, Imogen couldn't help wondering what the business might be.

But that was beside the point. Arthur was gone; she was free, at least for a few hours. She slipped out of the house and walked down to Half Moon Street, where she was able to hire a hack. Out of the habit of caution, she had him drop her several streets away from Gavin's studio, although mingled anticipation and apprehension mounted higher in her breast the closer they came, until she thought she might choke with it.

She had never been to this part of London without Gavin before, and even then only twice before. It seemed different without him, the buildings in worse repair, the streets dirtier, the calls of the street criers louder. Blundering her way to what she thought was the right street, she passed a woman leaning by a streetlamp, her bosom half-bared, the exposed skin tinged a faint blue with cold.

Imogen clutched her own pelisse closer around her and hurried on, trying to remember the number of the house on Cleveland Street, trying not to slip on the frozen bits of refuse and offal that littered the street.

She discovered it at last, a narrow building with peeling paint that might once have been better than it was. The door downstairs was unlocked. Imogen let herself in and began to climb the stairs, those same narrow stairs she had climbed with Gavin, clinging to the rail, going faster and faster, as fast as her skirts and her corsets would permit.

She knocked, quietly at first, and then louder. The sound echoed through the narrow landing, as hollow as the grave.

The door was locked; she rattled and

shook the knob in vain.

"Hey there!" A face peered up at her from the next landing down, a woman, gap-toothed and slatternly. "Who are you and what do you want?"

With heavy, huffing steps, the woman made her way towards Imogen, peering at her with narrowed eyes, as though Imogen were a wormy cabbage in a market stall. Keys clanked at the woman's waist and she brought with her a distinct reek of gin.

Imogen clutched her reticule with both hands. "I was looking for Gavin Thorne. About — about a commission for a painting."

The woman paused halfway up the stairs, leaning on the rail. "You're too late, then. Thorne's cleared out."

The words rang hollowly in Imogen's ears. "Cleared out?"

"Cleared out, run out." The woman's wrinkled face was a picture of disgust. "Left me two weeks' rent on the table and not so much as a by-your-leave."

"Did he — did he leave any mention of where he might have gone?"

The woman set her arms akimbo. "Didn't I just say 'e didn't? If I'd a known that, I could have sent his things on."

Necessity won out over pride. "Might I —

might I take a look?" Imogen asked tentatively. Hastily she fished in her reticule for a coin. "I will compensate you for your trouble."

The sight of gold decided it.

"Come along," said the woman ungraciously.

Huffing at the effort, she made her way up the rest of the stairs, pushing past Imogen on the narrow landing. The paint on the walls was peeling in long strips and the floorboards creaked ominously beneath her feet.

Unlocking the door with one of the keys at her waist, she shoved it open. "Go on," she said. "Look your fill."

Imogen glanced at her, but she showed no sign of going away. Her solid bulk filled the doorway, arms crossed and feet planted firmly in the door.

"You are very kind," Imogen said, and walked into the room, feeling like a person in a dream, everything familiar and unfamiliar all at the same time.

The blue gown still hung over the makeshift screen at the side of the room; the pile of pasteboard crowns and dusty velvet doublets occupied their usual place, but the sketches were gone from the table and the easel where *Tristan and Iseult* had rested stood lonely in the middle of the room, its supports empty.

The side of the room that Augustus Fotheringay-Vaughn had occupied was cleared out down to the last speck of dust, but that, Imogen knew, was to be expected; Gavin had told her that he, Fotheringay-Vaughn, had cleared out in a huff.

Imogen took inventory of Gavin's things, as well as she remembered them. His paints and palette were gone, only a few dried remnants left behind. The traveling easel was gone as well. It looked, in fact, as though he had packed as he had said he would, to leave with her.

Behind her, the landlady took a surreptitious bite of the coin Imogen had handed her. Finding it satisfactory, she said expansively, "The room where the gentleman slept was through that door. You might want a look in there as well."

In that same trance-like state, Imogen opened the door. She had never been in this room before; some strange relic of delicacy had kept Gavin from bringing her into his bedroom. They had made love in the meadows, on the floor of his studio, but never in his bed.

The room hardly justified the term. It was a tiny closet of a space, with little more than a camp bed, a chamber pot beneath it, a washstand to one side, and hooks on the wall for his clothes. There wasn't much left, just a forlorn nightshirt hanging from a hook and a forgotten piece of shaving soap on the washstand.

Imogen returned to the studio, where the landlady was jangling her keys.

"Do you know when he left?" Imogen asked. Her hands felt very cold inside her leather gloves.

The landlady shrugged. "Last time I saw him was four — no, five days past."

Imogen felt as though there were a fist slowly squeezing inside her chest, pressing tighter and tighter. Five days ago, Gavin had packed his things, just as they'd planned, and come to meet her. Come to meet her and never arrived.

"And if I'd known the trick he meant to play me then —" The landlady broke off. "But, no. There was someone moving around up here two nights ago. So he can't 'ave left till then."

"Two nights ago?" Imogen looked at her in surprise. "Are you quite sure?"

"Clomping around proper, he was," said the landlady, with righteous indignation. "Makes it hard for a body to sleep."

Imogen pressed a hand against the wall to

steady herself, her mind reeling. "Are you sure it was Gav— Mr. Thorne in the studio?"

" 'Oo else would it be?" the woman said. " 'Ooever it was 'ad the key."

TWENTY-FIVE

Herne Hill, 1850

Imogen felt the baby stirring inside her as she left the studio.

She paused on the steps, her hands against her stomach. Before, she had thought she felt a fluttering, but this was something firmer. She could feel the child pushing against her, struggling for space.

"You're not coming over ill, are you?" said the landlady suspiciously.

"No," said Imogen hastily, and continued her descent, holding carefully to the rail, feeling the child in her womb move restlessly, as if it could feel her distress. No, she wasn't ill. She was terrified, not for herself or for her child, but for Gavin.

If he had left, as he said he would, on the Saturday night, where was he? Nothing short of foul play would have stopped him coming to her; she was sure of that.

Someone moving around in the studio,

the landlady had said. Someone with a key.

A memory of Augustus Fotheringay-Vaughn as she had last seen him in the orchard flickered before Imogen's eyes, his elegant manners abandoned, his lips drawn back with anger. There had been something feral about him, something brutal.

Despite the warmth of her pelisse, Imogen found herself shivering, shivering with a cold that came from within.

Augustus Fotheringay-Vaughn had a key to the studio. There would be no benefit to his hurting Gavin, not now that Evie was safely married to Ned Sturgis, but Imogen wasn't sure that mattered. Kingdoms had toppled and wars had been fought, all in the name of revenge. She had shamed Fotheringay-Vaughn in front of Evie, had ruined his plans. The means with which she had done so had come straight from Gavin.

Yes. Imogen imagined Fotheringay-Vaughn would be willing to kill to protect the fantasy he had built around himself. There mustn't be that many people in London who knew about his true past. And now that Gavin was gone . . .

The word hit her like a blow. "Gone." She hadn't let herself believe it until now. He had only been delayed. Misplaced. She had harbored romantic visions of finding him in his studio, wracked with fever, of bathing his burning brow and kissing his sweat-damp hand.

Cleared out, the landlady had said. *Run off.*

Somehow, Imogen got herself into a hack and gave the driver directions, fighting with herself, trying to come up with other theories, other solutions: Gavin had fallen ill on his way to her; he was in hospital somewhere, too weak to remember his own name. Or he had found it expedient to remove to an inn before making another attempt at departure; there was a note that had gone astray, a communication to her that would arrive tattered and belated.

Perhaps he had seen Arthur's light in her room and decided to wait for another night. That would explain the sound of someone moving around in the studio. He might have gone back and stayed the night. He might . . .

As the carriage rocked on the uneven ground, Imogen's optimism faltered. It had been four days. One day she could imagine, or two, but by now Gavin would have made sure to bring her word. Somehow.

The image of the empty easel in the center of the studio haunted her. Gavin had said nothing about bringing it with him. But it would make a piece of Fotheringay-Vaughn's revenge, if that was his object. Dispose of Gavin and ruin her. He would sow their fields with salt and triumph over their destruction.

Wild plans fomented in Imogen's brain. She would call on Fotheringay-Vaughn, confront him — but to what end? She remembered that smooth, sneering face. He would deny it all and silently laugh at her behind it.

She had no recourse.

Imogen paid the driver, slowly mounting the steps to the front door of the house she had hoped never to see again, the house that felt less like a home and more like a gaol. The weather was much as it had been when she had arrived as a bride all those years before, gray and dripping. She felt that she would never see the sun again.

But this was absurd! Imogen rallied herself, fighting against the dragging sense of despair that threatened to envelop her. She owed it to their child, if nothing else. Gavin's friends, his fellow artists, one of them might know something, might have heard something. She could quiz them discreetly, pretend she was interested in a change in her portrait.

Anna opened the door to her, breathless

from running up the stairs. Imogen handed her pelisse, gloves, and bonnet to Anna, scraping her feet on the drugget that had been placed over the floor to protect it from winter mud.

Arthur's face appeared in the hall. "Ah, there you are! If I might have a word with you in my book room?"

"Yes, certainly." Imogen maintained her composure, hoping any redness about her eyes would be ascribed solely to the wind. Her skirts dragged heavily around her legs as she followed Arthur down the hall.

"You wished to speak to me?" she said as the study door closed behind her. Her face felt like a mask. She wanted nothing more than to seek the privacy of her own room, to think and pace and plan. Under her petticoat, the baby kicked and kicked again.

Unexpectedly, Arthur took both of her hands in his. She was too surprised to draw them away. "Isn't it time that these jaunts to London ended?" he said gently. Imogen looked at him dumbly. "Jane has told me about your" — he gave a little cough — "interesting condition."

Imogen's mind was whirling. "Jane takes a great deal on herself," she said tartly.

Arthur led her to a puffed and tufted settee, seating her with the care he would have employed on an elderly duchess. "She means well." He flipped back his coattails and seated himself beside her. "And she did well to tell me."

Through the fire screen Imogen could feel the warmth of the fire scorching her face. She turned in her seat, trying to find the right words. "Arthur, I —"

"Hush." Arthur raised a hand to stop her words. "No more. It was, I confess, lowering to hear such joyous news from Jane's mouth instead of yours, but the result is the same no matter the messenger. When are we to expect the happy event?"

"May, I think," said Imogen automatically. "Or June. But, Arthur —"

"I should quite like another little girl," said Arthur musingly. "Not that one could ever replace Evie, but it would be very nice to hear childish laughter in the house again, don't you agree, my love?"

Imogen looked at him full in the face, at the fine lines around his blue eyes, at the sagging jowls beneath his carefully culti-vated whiskers, at the face she knew so well and had never really known at all. A collec-tor, a patron of the arts, a doting father, a distant husband. She had lived with him for a decade, and in this moment she wondered if she knew even less of him now than she had when she was sixteen. He was a cipher to her.

Surely Arthur must realize that this child, this happy event, was no part of him. If he did, this was a generosity beyond her comprehension of him.

Generosity? Or self-preservation? a nasty, suspicious part of her mind whispered. Better to claim the child than acknowledge himself a cuckold, with a wanton wife.

Imogen found herself missing Gavin with a sudden soul-deep sense of loss. She wanted him with her so very badly, his arms around her, his cheek against her hair, not this awkward interview with Arthur in a study that was stuffy from the heat of the fire and the water dripping around an ill-fitted window.

This was all wrong.

But she was here and it must be got through. Imogen knotted her hands together. "Arthur," she said steadily, "there is something we must address."

The expression with which he regarded her was kind and — was it her imagination? — just a little bit pitying.

"Must we?" He covered her hand with his, such a very different hand from Gavin's, the fingers soft and well manicured, the veins on the back beginning to knot with age. "My dear. If this is about that other business, let us hear no more of that."

Imogen looked up at him in surprise.

Arthur smiled at her gently. "After all, that is all done with now, is it not?" Bracing his hands against his knees, he rose from the settee, looking down at her, still smiling that same smile, a smile that made the skin on the back of Imogen's neck prickle. "There is nothing to stop us from being as we were."

Imogen sat frozen, caught by a horrible surmise. It was unthinkable. And yet —

Arthur made a clucking noise deep in his throat. "You look chilled to the bone." He moved towards the door. "You stay right where you are. I shall have Anna bring you some hot tea. And biscuits. I imagine you would like a biscuit."

Imogen couldn't answer. Her tongue felt gummed to the back of her mouth. Arthur shook his head over her, the image of husbandly solicitude.

Arthur paused, his hand on the knob of the door. "After all," he said, smiling at her beatifically. "We must take better care of you now, mustn't we?"

London, 2009

The bells jangled as Julia pushed open the door to Nick's shop.

Her opening gambit, carefully refined and rehearsed, again and again, on the Tube ride over, died on her lips as she saw that there was someone else occupying the desk at the back of the room, a woman with hair in a pencil bun and painfully trendy glasses.

She hadn't considered what she might do if Nick wasn't here.

She could always pretend to be just another browser, she supposed, make a perfunctory round of the collection, smile stiltedly at the woman at the desk, and back out into the street again. Or she could put her big-girl panties on and leave a message at the desk.

The woman at the desk was already occupied. There was a customer with her, a middle-aged woman whose carefully groomed hair and matched accessories screamed interior decorator. At least, that was, if Helen and Julia's father's interior decorator was anything to go by.

Julia sidled a little closer, pretending interest in an eighteenth-century escritoire, waiting to see if the other woman would leave.

She was preparing to make her move when the door to the office in the back opened and Nick came out.

"Mrs. Mottram, I have the —" He caught sight of Julia and his face hardened. He only

525

missed a beat before turning smoothly back to the customer. "I have the clock you wanted to see. It's in the back. Tamsin?"

The woman at the desk looked up.

Nick didn't look at Julia. "Would you show Mrs. Mottram the Thomas Tompion clock?"

"Certainly." For a moment, she looked like she might question him, but something in Nick's expression must have quelled discussion, because, instead, she smiled at the customer and said, "Just this way, Mrs. Mottram. We've kept it hidden away so you can have the first look."

The door to the office opened and closed again and Julia was alone in the shop with Nick. Bach played faintly in the background, something complex and fiddly.

Julia cleared her throat. "Hi," she said originally.

Nick's face might have been carved out of the same stone as the marble bust on the pedestal next to him. "Can I help you?" he said, as though he had never seen her before.

"Um, yes." Julia did her best to make a joke out of it, although she had never felt less like laughing. But that was what she did, deflected emotion with smart comments and wisecracks. It might not precisely have worked for her in the past, but it was

526

all she knew. "Do you have anything with which I might flagellate myself? Something nice and scourge-like?"

Nick folded his arms uncompromisingly across his chest. "We don't carry anything of that sort, but there's a shop a few streets down that should be able to oblige."

Julia tried to smile, but it came out unevenly. "Would that even the score?"

Nick wasn't playing. In a low, flat tone he said, "What do you want, Julia?"

You.

The word popped into her head unbidden, and she realized it was true. She wanted him to smile at her the way he had before; she wanted his easy banter, his camaraderie, that excitement that lit his eyes when he had looked up at her over his books in the V&A.

Before she had killed it dead and made his eyes go hard and flat, as they were now.

Julia took a deep breath, her fingers locked in a death grip on the strap of her bag. "I came to apologize." She searched his face for some reaction, but his expression remained stony. "I had no right to speak to you as I did the other day. I — jumped to the wrong sort of conclusions."

"You wouldn't be the first." His face revealed nothing. He simply stood there.

Cold. Impassive.

It would be easier if he were blazingly angry; then, at least, she could fight with him. She forced herself to go on, saying, all in a rush, "It's not your problem; it's mine. If it hadn't been Natalie and the Dietrich Bank thing, it would have been something else." She was floundering, losing ground. As simply and directly as she could, she said, "I lashed out because I hated that you'd seen me at my weakest. And that wasn't fair. Not when you'd been nothing but kind."

That wasn't the whole of it, but at least it was a start.

"You needn't start the application for my canonization," Nick said briefly. In the muted light of the shop his eyes were more green than blue. She'd been wrong, Julia realized. His studied calm was just a façade. Underneath he was angry, angrier than she'd imagined. "My actions weren't altogether altruistic."

It took a moment for the meaning behind his words to kick in, and when they did Julia felt even worse than before. So she hadn't been wrong; he had been sending her vibes. But it was all in the past tense. Over. Done.

And she had royally screwed it up.

528

Julia looked up at him, trying to muster the right words. "Nick, I —"

"Nick?" called Tamsin from the desk. Her voice was professional, but there was a distinct edge of *get yourself over here.*

"Just a minute!" he called back over his shoulder. And to Julia, "Look, this is really not a good time."

Now, or ever? "Fair enough. Anyway, I just wanted to make sure you knew I — well, anyway." She hitched her bag higher on her shoulder. Years of ingrained instincts screamed at her to flee, leaving the shop bells jangling discordantly behind her. Instead, the words that came out of her mouth were, "I saw a little wine bar around the corner. I'll be there for the next hour or so if you change your mind. Just in case." And then, because the words, once started, wouldn't stop, "It's hard to make yourself trust someone when you're convinced they'll only hurt you. It's — I figured you would understand that."

Something flickered across his face.

"Nick?" called Tamsin.

"Wait here," said Nick tersely to Julia.

She felt a little surge of hope as he strode towards the desk, conferring in low tones with Tamsin before turning back to her.

"Here," he said. "This belongs to you."

Julia looked down in confusion at the manila folder he thrust in her direction. Her hands moved automatically to close over it, even as her brain protested that this wasn't part of the script.

She looked searchingly at Nick, trying to fight the growing sense of unease that was stopping up the back of her throat. "What is it?"

"Something to read over your wine," he said, and left her standing at the front of the shop, her heart on her sleeve and a beige manila folder in her hands.

As the impatient Mrs. Mottram pounced on Nick, Julia smiled unconvincingly at Tamsin, stuck the folder under one arm, and let herself quietly out of the shop, feeling as though she'd been wrung out and hung out to dry.

The wine bar was just where she had seen it last, around the corner, with red-painted walls, black mirrors, and artfully scattered black-topped tables, the super-elevated kind, designed for either the very tall or the very limber. Julia hauled herself into the one of the high, straight-backed chairs and ordered herself a large glass of Malbec. Her bag strap bit into her knee. The manila folder lay on the table in front of her.

Slowly, she opened it.

On top were color printouts of the pictures she'd taken of *Tristan and Iseult,* followed by the prints of Thorne's other four extant paintings. Under that were photocopies, black and white this time, of various letters and journal articles, all underlined and annotated in red pen, in an angular hand that had to be Nick's. His letters were blocky but legible.

He'd given her his file on Gavin Thorne.

The waiter brought Julia her wine, in a glass that looked like something Alice might have seen through the looking glass, blown up to three times normal size. Julia nodded her thanks.

Slowly, she began paging through the file Nick had given her, her chest tightening as she read his notes in the margins, some impatient, some excited, some commands to himself. *Follow up with ship's manifest? Name on tickets?* He'd set up a time line of Thorne's life up to 1850, up to the ship taking him to New York, cross-referenced with documents. He'd found a passenger list for the ship Thorne was supposedly taking to New York and begun to cross off passengers.

He must have put hours of work into it.

Julia squirmed with shame and frustration, hating herself just a little bit more with every page. While he had been putting together his dossier she had been avoiding his calls, self-righteously patting herself on the back for her good judgment in assuming that there must be something wrong with anyone who was so gratuitously helpful. With anyone who seemed drawn to her.

The wine burned like acid against the back of her palate.

She remembered Nick, in the attic, saying, so casually, *Not easy, is it? Mine walked out on us when I was seven.*

And, more fool she, she had taken him at his tone, rather than his words. His humor, his easy banter, were employed for just the same purposes hers were, and for the very same reasons. Maybe that was part of the draw — porcupine love, thought Julia, a little wildly. Two sets of prickles finding each other.

Except that she'd gone and stabbed him in his soft spot. Because she was self-absorbed. And an idiot.

The bells above the door jangled and Julia's head snapped up with a velocity that made her spine crunch, but it wasn't Nick; it was a couple, the man holding open the door for the woman, the woman laughing up at him over something he had just said. They looked so comfortable together. So happy.

In the past, Julia would have shrugged and told herself it didn't matter, that she didn't want that. But she did.

Julia took another gulp of her wine, feeling the sting of it against her tongue, her thoughts drifting to her parents. It was hard to tell what would have happened if her mother hadn't lost control of the car that night. Had her parents' differences been too large to solve? She didn't know; she didn't remember enough to tell. But her mother had been on her way back to try. She'd been willing to fight for what they had. And that, somehow, made all the difference.

The bell rang again. Two women this time, both with shopping bags. Then a man with "blind date" written all over him. The waiters began to make the rounds with matchbooks, lighting the tiny tea candles that sat in the center of each table.

Julia ordered a second glass. The wine bar began to fill up around her. She'd left her cell phone on the tabletop next to the folder. The screen was blank and still.

Biting her lip, Julia opened the text screen and pulled up Nick's number. But once there, she wasn't sure where to go next. *Come live with me and be my love* only worked for the Elizabethans. *Can we start over?* sounded hopelessly naïve. There wasn't any such thing as starting over, only building off one's mistakes and trying to make the best of them.

The wine bar was beginning to fill up. "Another round?" asked the waiter.

Another round and she wouldn't be able to get off her stool without stumbling. "No, just the check, please."

It was after eight already. Nick had probably closed up the store and gone home. Julia stared at the dossier in front of her, Nick's notes in the margins. Something struck her as off about his time line — something she had seen in Evangeline Grantham's diary, perhaps? — but her mind was muddled with emotion and wine, swimming with too many new ideas and revelations: Nick, her mother, Helen, everything. She had gotten, what, three hours of sleep last night? If that.

She suspected that Nick hadn't gotten much sleep, either.

Taking a deep breath, Julia bundled the papers back into the folder. Then, before she could think better of it, she picked up the phone and typed, simply: "Thank you." And then, after that: "I'm sorry."

Hitching her bag up over her shoulder, the file folder under her arm, she headed home to Herne Hill.

TWENTY-SIX

Herne Hill, 1850

Imogen's daughter was born in the house in Herne Hill, in the room that had so increasingly begun to feel like a prison.

The snow had melted and the weather turned, but Imogen wasn't allowed out into the garden; she was meant to have rest, Arthur reminded her, complete rest. The headaches from which she was suffering weren't feigned this time but real, a dull throbbing in her temples that was with her when she woke, that made her thoughts confused and interrupted her dreams.

Imogen protested that her head would be clearer if she were allowed out from time to time, but she was overridden and escorted gently but firmly back to her room, the windows closed, the curtains drawn. The doctor clucked over her poor color and swollen ankles and reiterated his strictures. Arthur was all solicitude, at her side to read her books in which she had no interest and to attempt to tempt her with dainty morsels she had no desire to eat.

And then there were the draughts, brought nightly by Jane, tasting heavily of spirits of wine and syrup of poppies. At the doctor's orders, she was told. They sent her into an uneasy sleep haunted with fevered dreams: Gavin, struggling in the icy waters of the Thames, holding up his hands to her in supplication as Arthur leaned from the bridge above, observing the spectacle, before turning to her and commenting brightly, *Well, my love, that's all done with now, isn't it?*

Other times, she would be walking with Gavin through a field of flowers as they had so often walked during their enchanted summer, but the sky had an odd, hectic light to it, an orange tinge, and the scent of the flowers would grow stronger and stronger, clogging her nostrils, cloying at the back of her throat, until she would find herself choking with it, gasping for breath, clawing at the fabric of her throat, and would awake, panting, alone in her room, the fire casting an orange light across the carpet, the smell of the laudanum overwhelming in the shuttered room.

She tried pouring the solution into her

slop bucket, but it was a poor, weak rebellion. There was always more to be had, and Jane stood over her as she drank, with an illusion of sympathy and a secret air of watchfulness, almost of triumph.

In Imogen's confinement, strange fantasies began to form. There were days that Imogen imagined that Jane was trying to poison her, that that gloating, watchful look was of the murderess waiting for her potions to take hold.

It's no use, Imogen wanted to tell Jane. I would have given Arthur to you gladly.

But her head ached too much to form the words.

Imogen developed an invalid's cunning, feigning sleep to avoid the administration of the draught, waiting until the others had left the house to throw up the window and inhale long, deep breaths of the cool, crisp spring air. Down, far below, she could see the summerhouse, waiting for her, taunting her. Sometimes she imagined she saw Gavin there, waiting for her, a dark figure among the fresh green buds on the trees.

It was only until her baby was born, she told herself, fighting the weakness, the lethargy, the odd slips between fantasy and reality. The drug and the loneliness and the stuffiness of the room. Once her baby was born, she would be able to build up her strength again, free from Jane's poisonous ministrations and Arthur's stifling solicitude. She tried, desperately, to clear her addled mind, but it was a difficult battle; even awake, she felt half-asleep, riddled with worries and nameless fears.

Her mind took refuge in flight. Some days, she was a girl in Cornwall again, sitting with her father in his study, puzzling out the archaic handwriting of his manuscripts under his directions.

When the pains hit her, she was up on the cliffs, watching an errant seagull fly in circles above the choppy gray sea.

"She's wandering," she heard Jane say to Arthur in low tones, and there was a cup set to Imogen's lips.

Imogen tried to turn her head, but the cup followed, and the liquid slid heavy and cloying down her throat. She coughed, weakly, and someone lifted her, pressing a handkerchief to the corners of her mouth.

"Not much longer now," said her husband, and in her fever and fear the words took on a sinister quality. She clawed at the sheet, trying to free herself, but Arthur took her hand and held it fast, stroking it, making noises that were meant to be soothing but took on the quality of strange incantations.

"Away with you now," the nurse said, and Arthur was gone, and there was the red-faced nurse with her white cap there instead, urging Imogen to push.

The waves pulsed around her, pulling at her, but the water was full of sharp shells that wracked her with pain. She clung to the broken remnants of a boat, the sea rocking her back and forth, as the seagulls cried out all around her in their high, shrill voices.

But that is my voice, she realized as she subsided, panting, against the pillows.

Her brow was damp with sweat and her hair fanned limply around her face. Her throat was hoarse from crying out. She wasn't in Cornwall at all. She was in her room in the house at Herne Hill and Gavin's child was struggling to be born.

"Water?" she murmured, and someone, a nurse, dribbled a few drops between her lips.

"So you're back with us now, are you?" said the nurse. "You were away with the fairies."

Imogen managed a weak smile, her lips stretched and dry. "I was dreaming."

And then the pain hit her again, all the worse for being awake. She clung to the sheet, wringing it between her hands, gasping for breath.

"That's it," said the nurse, and then, a little ways on, "a girl."

A tiny, damp bundle was placed in Imogen's arms. She looked down in wonder at the little creature, at the matted dark hair on her head, her wrinkled red face, her small, flailing limbs. Her daughter. Gavin's daughter. Imogen could scarcely move her head, but she leaned stiffly forward and brushed her dry lips against the baby's damp hair, trying to express without words all the love she felt for her.

The baby opened her mouth and howled.

"She's wanting feeding," said the nurse, plucking her neatly out of Imogen's arms. Imogen raised a hand to protest, but the nurse firmly drew the sheet up around her, saying, not unkindly, "And you'll be needing your rest, won't you?"

Imogen must have dozed, because when she woke the room was dim with twilight, the fire had burned down, and Gavin was standing by the bed, waiting for her.

At first she thought it was just a dream, like a hundred others she had had before. But the bed was damp still with sweat and blood; if this were a dream, surely her hair wouldn't be lying lank around her face, her nightdress matted to her chest. There was a sour smell to the room, the reek of her own sweat and the milk leaking from her breasts.

And Gavin stood there, sure as day, between the bed and the mantelpiece. She could see the window open behind him, the summerhouse pale in the twilight, the branches of the leaves waving invitingly in the breeze.

He looked just as she had seen him last, his cravat tied loosely around his neck, his dark hair cropped short, the same familiar lines around his eyes and lips.

"Gavin," she said weakly. She tried to sit up, but her body wouldn't obey her. Her limbs were weak as water.

He took a step towards her, his hand outstretched. "I told you I'd come for you, didn't I?"

"But you — but I —" Imogen struggled for words. She could feel the dampness of tears on her cheeks. "I thought I'd lost you."

"Hush, my love. No tears." She felt his hand against her cheek only as a cool breeze, like the flutter of a bird's wing. "We'll be together now. There's no power on heaven or earth can part us."

She reached for him, but her hand seemed to go through air. "Our daughter —" she began.

"Will always have us close by," he said. "But now it's time to go."

He held out a hand to her, and this time she felt the clasp of his hand, the lean strength of his fingers twining through hers. His grasp was warm and firm and she drew strength from it, strength enough to rise from the bed and wrap her arms around him as she had dreamed of doing all these months and months. His hair was soft beneath his hand, his cheek faintly stubbled. He smelled of summer and growing things, of open fields and fruit-rich orchards.

She felt his lips brush against her hair and his arm firm around her waist.

"Let's away, my love," he said, and over her shoulder she saw that it wasn't twilight at all but glorious day.

The sun streamed over the meadows and the birds sang madrigals in the trees and far down by the summerhouse a path unrolled, bathed in sunlight and lined in flowers.

"Away," she echoed, and, hand in hand, they walked together into the sunlight.

In the darkened hall, the nurse shut the door of the room gently behind her.

"What news?" Jane asked. She held the baby, clean now and dressed in one of the long white gowns that Jane had sewn for her. It was no use expecting Imogen to take care of such things.

The nurse shook her head, making the lappets on her cap wag. "Poor, motherless mite," she said solemnly.

"Nonsense," said Jane. "She has a good home and a loving papa. See that the wet nurse is brought."

"Yes, ma'am," said the nurse sullenly. There was nothing more disappointing than being balked of a good wallow.

Holding the sleeping baby firmly to her chest, Jane made her way carefully down the stairs. Arthur was in his study. He would have to be told.

She looked down at the child in her arms. It was a pity the child was dark rather than fair, but they did say the early growth of hair had a way of falling out. It might grow in lighter by and by. And, besides, the child had nice, large eyes and a rather pretty mouth.

Olivia, Jane thought. She rather liked the sound of "Olivia."

Holding the baby in one arm, she rapped smartly at the door of Arthur's study with the other.

It was time Arthur met their daughter.

Herne Hill, 2009
The next day, Julia braved the old garden shed, unearthing flowered gardening gloves

543

and a pair of slightly rusted pruning shears.

As a lifetime apartment dweller, what she knew about gardening was limited to the sorts of potted plants that would fit on the windowsill, but there was nothing like hard manual labor to distract the mind. The wilderness behind the house would have to be tidied before she could sell. Cleaning up the area around the summerhouse was one of the tasks she'd been putting off.

For some reason, without consciously acknowledging it, she'd been avoiding the outer reaches of the garden in general and the summerhouse in particular. She thought of that picture in the attic, twirling and twirling, her pigtails whipping in the breeze. Vaguely, she remembered tea parties, the sort with acorn teacups and pretend sips of invisible beverages.

Following the cracked stones of the path down the slope, she felt as though an invisible weight had been lifted off her. The idea of encountering those sorts of memories didn't bring with it fear anymore; she knew what had happened. And that her mother had loved her. The locked room in the back of her mind was open, the demons that had hounded her for so long banished.

It was just a pity she couldn't have gotten rid of them in time to stop herself from trampling all over whatever it was that was developing with Nick, she thought as she yanked doggedly at the creepers that had grown up around the pillars of the summerhouse.

It didn't matter how often she told herself it could only be temporary, anyway, that she was going back to New York once the house was sold; the idea of going away and never seeing him again brought with it an incredible sense of loss. She'd tossed and turned last night, alternately coming up with excuses and torturing herself with memories and might have beens.

There had been one positive by-product to her sleeplessness. She'd finally figured out what was bothering her about his notes. On his time line, Nick had Gavin Thorne buying tickets for two to New York on a ship that departed in January of 1850. But, according to Aunt Regina's family tree, Imogen Grantham had given birth to a daughter at the house in Herne Hill in the spring of 1850, months after the ship had left.

Had Thorne gone off without her? Julia wrapped a particularly knotty vine around her hand and tugged. It just didn't seem right. Perhaps the dates of the ship were wrong? Or their entire theory was. Just because Thorne had painted Imogen in as his Iseult didn't necessarily mean that he was her Tristan.

But Julia couldn't quite let go of the idea.

That would provide an excuse to contact Nick. Nothing needy. Just a professional query. Plausible deniability, Lexie used to call it in college.

Julia staggered as the vine gave way. The ancient floorboards protested as she stepped back heavily, windmilling her arms to avoid landing on her ass. No. No more plausible deniability. No more running away.

The sun was shining in her eyes. The temperature had dropped over the last few days, shifting imperceptibly towards autumn, but, for a moment, the sun seemed to burn down on her, and she could have sworn she smelled roses in the air, the roses that had bloomed and died by the end of July. Through the heat haze, she could see a man coming down the hill, a man in an old-fashioned black coat with a canvas satchel slung over one arm.

Sweat dripped down her forehead into Julia's eyes. Using the back of her arm, she swiped it away. For a moment the scent of roses was strong in her nose, and then she blinked and smelled only sweat and dirt and the sharp green tang of the vines that lay scattered in pieces on the warped floor.

Julia squinted into the sun. There was someone coming down the hill, but he was wearing a pale button-down shirt, not a black coat, and his hair shone golden in the late August sun. He wasn't carrying anything that she could see. He was just . . . Nick.

He paused in front of the summerhouse, looking up at her, his hands in his pockets.

"You need a strimmer," he said.

Slowly, Julia stripped off Aunt Regina's gardening gloves, playing for time, veering between hope and wariness. "I need a bulldozer."

Nick contemplated the denuded rosebushes. "It's a little late for gardening."

"I know." He had planted himself firmly in front of the steps, neither here nor there. Julia didn't know whether to go down to him or stay where she was. Was this a clearing-the-air visit? An *I want my file back* visit? Nothing in his posture said one way or another. "But I should probably do something about it before I put the house on the market."

Nick glanced quickly up at her. "You do intend to sell, then?"

Julia held up her hands in defeat. "I can't afford not to."

She leaned her palms flat against the

ancient railing, looking down at Nick. From her vantage point above she could see that his shoulders were slightly hunched, as though braced for a blow.

He was, she realized with surprise, just as defensive as she was.

She thought about all the Nicks she'd seen over the past two months. She'd thought him arrogant at first, dismissive and rude. Then almost a little too nice, too smooth. Then there had been those articles, and he had morphed in her head into the stereotype of the trader on the make, all pinstriped suit and slicked-back hair à la Gordon Gekko.

But this, in front of her. This was Nick. Not Natalie's image of the lost viscount, not Gordon Gekko, not the mastermind of an underground antiques ring. Just a man who was as lost as she was.

"I thought about renting it out," Julia said diffidently, "but it just seems like a half measure. And I'm not really sure I'm cut out to be a landlord."

Nick folded his arms across his chest. "It might be a bit difficult to manage from the other side of the Atlantic."

The mottled paint on the railings was scratchy against her palms. "Just because I'm selling doesn't mean I'm going." Even to her own ears, that sounded garbled. "I mean, it will take a while to sell, and even once I do — I don't really know what my plans are yet."

Nick leaned a palm against one of the pillars by the stairs. She could feel the charge between them like a current in the air, but all he said was, "You won't be sorry to see the house go?"

"It's just a house when all is said and done. It belongs to the past, and while I'm glad I've gotten to know that past, I don't have to live with it to take it with me." Julia drifted to a halt, feeling like a fool. "If that makes any sense."

Nick held up a hand to shield his eyes. He wore a battered signet ring on one finger, the crest so worn with time as to be nearly indistinguishable. "My aunt said something similar to me once. Aunt Edith."

"The one who walked off with all the furniture?" Julia's chest felt tight with the effort of trying to listen past what was being said. Surely the fact that he was still here, talking about his family, had to be a good thing?

"The very one." Nick looked out over the tangle of berry brambles and trees run to seed. Standing there, at the base of the steps, Julia was struck by how alone he seemed. She curled her fingers against the rail to keep herself from going down to him. "It was years ago, when I was fourteen. I'd just come back from California — for the last time, as it turned out."

Julia remembered what he told her, long ago, about the visits to his mother being terminated by mutual consent. From the expression on his face she wondered if it had been quite so mutual after all.

Nick acknowledged her quizzical look with a quick twist of the lips. "It wasn't the easiest time. I was feeling a bit rough and looking for something to hold on to. So I fastened on to the idea of the old family home. I even took one of those National Trust tours, trying to find portraits that looked like me, and sulking all the way about being done out of my patrimony. When I tried to complain to Aunt Edith about the injustice of it all, she turned to me and said, in that brisk way of hers, 'Nicholas, it's not places that count, it's people.'"

Something about the way he said it made Julia's throat feel tight. She nodded, wordlessly.

The skin around Nick's eyes crinkled as he smiled. "Of course, this was from the woman who walked off with a marble bust of Charles the Second because she claimed it had sentimental value."

"We'll never know exactly what her relationship was with Charles," said Julia in mock seriousness. In a different tone she added, "I'm sorry. I'm sorry I was such a jerk about the whole Dietrich Bank thing and Natalie's treasure stories and — well, everything."

The words were entirely inadequate to convey how she felt, but it was a start.

Nick shrugged. "Anyone would have thought the same." He angled a quick look up at her. "If you want to know what really happened —"

"It doesn't matter," said Julia fiercely, and realized that she meant it. "Natalie could have said anything at that point and I would have believed her. She could have said that you were — an intergalactic alien from the planet Zog." That surprised a chuckle out of Nick, but Julia powered on, her hands twisting together at her waist. "You were right. I condemned you out of hand. I was looking to condemn you. All because I was terrified by how much I — by how much I liked you."

Nick braced one foot against the bottom step, looking up at her with a wry smile that made her heart twist. "Pot, meet kettle." When she narrowed her eyes at him, he said, "I did come to the wine bar last night. I saw you through the window. And —" He spread his hands out in a gesture of helplessness. "I turned around and walked away."

Julia thought of him, standing outside the window, looking into the red and black interior of the wine bar. And she'd been right on the other side of the glass, never knowing.

"It was probably a wise move," said Julia in a voice that wasn't entirely steady. "I was getting pretty soused. I might even have made a pass at you."

Nick moved up one step, then another. "In that case," he said, "I was doubly an idiot to walk away."

The air in the summerhouse suddenly felt very close. Julia's throat was tight; she could feel the beating of her pulse in her throat, in her wrists. Every nerve tingled with awareness.

She wet her lips. "Nick —"

"I'm rubbish at this," he said, his voice low, urgent. The old floor creaked beneath his weight, but it held. "At relationships."

Julia gave a choked laugh. "Join the club. My normal impulse is to run screaming."

Nick's eyes met hers. "It's terrifying. Relying on someone."

Julia nodded. At least, she thought she

nodded. She rested her palms lightly on Nick's chest, feeling his heart beating under the thin linen of his shirt. "We're a mess, aren't we? Both of us."

Nick gently slid a sweaty strand of hair back behind her ear. "Like calls to like."

Julia looked up at him, at the now familiar planes of his face, the laugh lines next to his eyes, the mobile line of his lips. "I'd rather be a mess with you than without you," she said huskily. "I'm willing to take the chance — if you are?"

Twenty-Seven

Herne Hill, 2009

Nick's kiss was nothing like the one in the attic over a month ago.

There was nothing tentative about this kiss; it was hot and demanding, filled with all the frustration of the past three weeks of waiting. Nick's shirt was damp with sweat beneath Julia's fingers, the fabric molded to his skin. She could feel the heat of his fingers through the thin fabric of her dress, his hands splayed open against her back, holding her close as his lips devoured hers.

When they parted, Julia felt as though she'd just come up from a long dive underwater. She blinked at him, her breath coming fast.

Nick looked to be in a similar state. His hair was sticking up on one side, his cheeks flushed, his chest rising and falling rapidly.

He took a step back, his eyes never leaving Julia's. "If we —"

Whatever it was he had meant to say was lost as a horrible cracking noise filled the air.

It all happened in the space of a moment; Nick's eyes opened very wide and his arms flailed for balance as the floor opened beneath him, sending him lurching sideways, one leg suddenly considerably shorter than the other.

"Bugger!" he cursed. "Bugger, bugger, bugger."

Julia hurried towards him. It would have been comical if it weren't for the look of very real pain on Nick's face. One of his legs was wedged in a new gap in the boards. "Oh, God, are you okay?"

"I'm fine," he said, tight-lipped. "Just a little scratched up. Stupid. Bloody. Floor."

Lending him a hand, Julia helped him out of the hole. It wasn't deep. There was little more than a foot between the platform and the floor, but it was an awkward position for a man with one leg in and one leg out, particularly when a jagged bit of wood had caught on the back of his jeans.

Of all the ludicrous, farcical, ill-timed . . . She would have thought the ghosts of old lovers would have been more amenable to sharing their trysting place.

"If it's any consolation," Julia said, caught

somewhere between laughter and annoyance, "you hurt it more than it hurt you."

Nick pulled a wry face. Leaning over, he shook the splinters from his pant leg, wincing a bit as he did. "You might say that. There was something under there. It cracked when I landed."

"Buried treasure?" suggested Julia.

"I doubt it," Nick said, but he hunkered down by the hole all the same, moving a little stiffly. He landed heavily on his knees. "More likely just the sound of my shattered pride."

"The timing was not ideal," Julia agreed, trying to gently shift the conversation back to whatever it was he had been about to say before he went flying.

It was no use. His attention was absorbed by whatever it was he had seen down there in the dirt. He looked like a little boy, his hair sticking up, leaning over to poke at something down in the gap between the boards.

Cautiously, Julia took a step closer. She was lighter than he was; with any luck, she probably wouldn't go plunging through anything. "Nick?"

He looked up at her, and something in his face made the smile die on her lips. Slowly, he rose to his feet, gesturing Julia forward.

"Look at this."

"This doesn't sound good," she said, her eyes on his face, not the floor. She squatted down where he had been, squinting into the dark cavity.

At first, she thought it was a twig. It was brittle and brown. But twigs didn't have fingers. There was a hand lying on the packed earth beneath the floor of the summerhouse, a hand that had, until recently, been attached to an arm. Julia rocked back onto her heels, blinking against the sunlight, seeing dark spots against her eyes.

There was a corpse. In her summerhouse.

Or, rather, under her summerhouse.

Julia staggered to her feet. "That's a hand," she said unnecessarily.

Nick took her place by the side of the hole, tugging at the splintered edges of the board, trying to enlarge the gap. "You must have some tools — an ax?"

Julia hovered behind him. "Shouldn't we leave the body where it is?" she asked, with vague recollections of *CSI* episodes. "In case we're destroying evidence?"

"I don't think we need to worry about that." Nick looked up at her over his shoulder. "Whatever this is, it's been here a long time."

"Not whatever," said Julia soberly. "Who-ever."

She hadn't paid terribly much attention in ninth-grade bio class, but even she could identify a human skeleton when she saw one. The only plus side that she could see was that it couldn't have been recent; didn't it take the body some time to decompose all the way down to the bone like that? There had been no flesh on those skeletal fingers.

The thought was enough to make her feel cold in the heat of the day.

Nick had no such reservations. Working industriously away, he had succeeded in widening the gap so that about a square foot of the ground beneath the summerhouse was bared. He pointed at something next to the body. "The poor sod had his luggage with him when he died."

Gingerly, Julia knelt by the edge of the broken section. It felt curiously like one of those viewing stations at a nature museum, as if she were on a macabre sort of class trip. Mercifully, she couldn't see the skull; the section Nick had cleared revealed a torso, clad in a rotting jacket with tarnished buttons and legs in the tattered remains of trousers.

Beside him, next to his outflung hand, lay

a large leather bag. The brown leather was disfigured with patches of green mold, gnawed through in part by rodents. The contents had fared equally poorly. A smell of must and mold rose from the whole.

Julia's attention was caught by a flat, rectangular parcel. Unlike the satchel, it appeared to be largely intact, wrapped in a dark, tightly woven fabric.

As Nick tugged at the floorboards, attempting to widen the gap, Julia drew the package out of the hole, the fabric gritty against her fingers. It must have been treated with something. Wax, perhaps? It was dirty but hadn't decayed.

The wrappings came away with difficulty, revealing a large portfolio, the leather scratched and scraped with use but otherwise intact. Retreating to a relatively solid stretch of ground, Julia laid the portfolio flat on the floor, hunkered down on her haunches, and undid the string tie.

The top sketch was of a man, kneeling, his head turned slightly away, one hand raised to shield his face in a gesture of contrition or shame. It looked like the visual equivalent of someone thinking aloud, bits drawn and then redrawn. Julia could see where portions had been rubbed out and reconstituted; the man's legs looked as though they had been moved from one knee up, one knee down, to both knees on the ground. Even in the rough black and white sketch, she could tell that the man was wearing a stylized sort of armor and a helm and sword lay discarded by his side.

He looked a lot like the figures from the Tristan and Iseult painting. In style, that was. She couldn't remember that any of them had been in quite this pose.

"I'm going to find an ax," Nick said from somewhere over her shoulder. He sounded very cheerful at the prospect of getting to demolish a substantial subsection of her summerhouse. He thought about it. "Or a hammer. That would do."

Julia nodded, her attention fixed on the pictures in front of her. "There should be a garden shed," she said vaguely, and felt the boards beside her creak as Nick edged past, intent on his mission of destruction.

There was another study for the same painting, the same man, kneeling, but this time with a screen in front of him and a large chalice, floating seemingly in mid-air. The next one had a woman holding the chalice; the one after that reverted to the chalice elevated of its own accord, giving out rays of light like a Renaissance halo.

Julia flipped through, with growing excitement, marking the stages of a picture in progress, pages devoted to nothing but the set of an arm or fifteen versions of the same chalice. But it was the sketch of the woman that made her really stop short.

This wasn't the stylized lady of the Arthurian sketches. Her gown was tight waisted and full skirted, not the pseudo-medieval robe of the woman holding the Grail. She lay on her side on the grass on a blanket. A picnic basket sat open beside her, ripe apples spilling out onto the grass, giving an impression of fecundity and bounty.

Somehow, even in nothing but black and white lines, the artist had managed to convey the impression of a sunny summer day, the grass thick below, lines of light and shadow falling across the woman's supple body. She wore a demure dress, tightly buttoned to the waist, but the heavy skirts were tucked under and around her, creating an impression of softness despite the prim collar and long, fitted sleeves, a froth of petticoat showing beneath the hem of the skirt.

The woman's dark hair was soft and mussed with sleep. Her hands were tucked up under her face, and there was a slight smile on her lips, as though she was dreaming pleasant dreams.

Julia knew those features. She had seen

them, studied them, on the portrait on the drawing room wall and in the painting of Tristan and Iseult. There was none of the wild quality here that Julia had seen in those others; this woman wasn't haunted or wracked with dangerous passions. She looked peaceful. Content.

The sketches weren't signed. They didn't need to be.

Julia heard the steps creak with Nick's return. Without looking up from the sketch of the sleeping woman, she said, "Nick?"

"Yes?" Nick hunkered down next to her, a hammer dangling from his hand.

"Look at this." Julia pushed the portfolio towards him. She looked at him soberly. "I don't think Gavin Thorne ever made it to New York."

The discovery of a 160-year-old corpse in the garden of a house in suburban London caused a mild media sensation.

It was the silly season, Nick said, that was the problem. Whatever the reason, Julia found herself mobbed with inquiries from a dozen tabloids and local news stations. Had she ever felt anything strange in the house? Did they know who it was? Was the corpse only one of many?

When Julia countered all questions with a

terse *no comment,* they dredged up obscure historians with lisps who wagged their heads and talked of unsolved murder cases and legends of haunting, and, even worse, people who claimed they had once lived nearby and recounted with relish tales of odd moanings and wailings and clankings from the garden of the house at Herne Hill.

"Can I sue?" Julia fumed to her best friend, Lexie. Admittedly, Lexie did corporate transactional work in the United States, not UK lawsuits, but a lawyer was a lawyer when all was said and done. "This is not going to help with my property values!"

"You never know," said Lexie helpfully. "Some people are willing to pay a premium for a haunted house."

People were certainly eager to come and gawk. On the second night of the onslaught, Julia was woken in the night by strange noises and lights flashing in the garden, not from any spirits but from the ghost hunters who had snuck in by a gate she hadn't even known existed, all the way down at the far end of the property, by the overgrown remains of an old orchard. After seeing them off the property, Julia had grimly nailed the gate shut. She'd hung up a few handmade Trespassers Will Be Prosecuted to the Full Extent of the Law signs as well,

563

just for good measure. She had no idea what the law was in England vis-à-vis trespassers, but if one more film crew tried to sneak in at midnight for "ghostly messages" she fully intended to use it.

It wasn't all bad. Julia's father and Helen offered to fly out to help her cope with the reporters; Jamie and Robbie just wanted to see the bones. The Tate approached her about buying Thorne's paintings and sketches. A psychic offered to contact Thorne's spirit for her for the reasonable price of only five thousand pounds.

"Only five thousand pounds for the first hour and nineteen-ninety-nine for every subsequent communication?" said Julia to Nick at the end of the first week.

She was getting a bit slaphappy by then. It was more than a little surreal to emerge from her house for groceries only to find reporters with fuzzy microphones standing on the sidewalk. No wonder celebrities were so skinny; they couldn't leave their homes for sustenance. She didn't mind subsisting on the last of her stock of Tesco's frozen dinners, but she did very much mind the fact that she was nearly out of coffee.

"We can't have that," said Nick, and showed up at her door two hours later with two bulging sacks of groceries, among which were two pristine cans of illy coffee.

She hadn't seen Nick since they'd seen the bones into the hands of the local police the previous Sunday. The police had been justifiably bemused at being presented with a 160-year-old crime scene but had duly wrapped her summerhouse in crime scene tape all the same and taken the skeleton into custody. By the time they'd gotten through, it had been late, and Nick had an early flight to catch, a buying trip to various far-flung estates in France and Belgium. He'd offered to cancel, but Julia had told him it was fine, she could handle it.

He must, she realized, opening the door to him in his suit and collared shirt, a tie tucked into his pocket and an overnight case slung over his shoulder, have come straight from the airport.

"Bless you," said Julia gratefully, accepting one of the bags and hastily bolting and locking the front door behind him. "But you could have gone home first."

She wasn't quite sure what any of this meant. They'd spoken on the phone over the course of the week, but he had been in hotels and she'd been fuming over the idiocy of people who really believed you could track ghosts using a flashlight and a thermometer. There had been no time for state-of the relationship talks.

"I couldn't leave you under siege and un-caffeinated," said Nick. "Some of the report-ers might get hurt."

Instead of sitting in the kitchen, they lit the fire in Aunt Regina's old study, with its wood-paneled walls and warm carpet. It also had the benefit of overgrown shrub-bery blocking the window, as well as heavy drapes.

Delighted as Julia was to see both Nick and his overnight bag, the prospect of *The Star* having a long-lens camera looking through the window in the hopes that she might stumble on another corpse did put a distinct damper on amorous thoughts.

"How do people live like this?" Julia asked, drawing the drapes closed, thankful for whatever familial thrift had caused Aunt Regina to retain the anachronistically heavy curtains on their brass rods.

"It will die down," Nick said with author-ity, and Julia remembered that he had good reason to know. He'd been that two-week wonder once, in much more painful circum-stances.

"I don't know," said Julia. "I was rather tempted by the one who offered me a private séance with Gavin Thorne, results guaranteed. It would be nice to have a firsthand account of what actually happened out there."

In deference to their surroundings, while Nick had built the fire Julia had made a pot of tea in Aunt Regina's battered brown pot, paired, incongruously, with a set of delicate Spode cups and saucers. Among the bounty in Nick's grocery bags had been a variety of biscuits, so Julia had arranged ginger biscuits and chocolate fingers on a plate and now they sat, surrounded by crumbs and warmed by tea, on Aunt Regina's comfortably saggy old sofa, watching the flames in the fireplace snap and crackle.

Nick had discarded his jacket, which hung limply off the side of the couch. His collar was open and his feet were stretched comfortably out in front of him.

It all felt very cozily domestic, but for the reporters outside and, of course, the hole in the floor of the summerhouse where Gavin Thorne's body had lain, unsanctified, for the past 160 years.

"At least now we know that Thorne didn't run off on Imogen Grantham," said Nick. His arm stretched out along the back of the sofa, brushing Julia's shoulder. "Poor sod."

"Poor Imogen," countered Julia, allowing herself the luxury of leaning into his arm. "Can you imagine, all those months, living in this house, wondering what had happened to her lover? I wonder if she suspected, or if she just thought that Thorne had abandoned her."

Among the belongings found on the body, worn by time but still legible, had been papers and tickets for a Mr. and Mrs. Gareth Rose. Julia found it ironic that they had been bound for New York. It was enough to make one wonder about karma. If they had made it to New York — if Imogen's daughter had been born there —

Then Julia's mother would never have met her father and there would have been no her, she reminded herself. But it struck Julia strongly, all the same, that she had wound up where Gavin and Imogen had intended to be.

She curled her legs up underneath her, resting her arm against the back of the couch. "In some ways, it makes it sadder. To think that they were so close to happiness and someone stopped them."

Nick snagged a ginger biscuit from the plate. " 'Stopped' is such a tasteful euphemism," he murmured. "As opposed to 'walloped,' 'whacked,' or 'otherwise slaughtered.' "

The police had managed to confirm that the bones were of the right time period, give or take a few decades, and that the skull showed signs of fracture, presumably with some sort of blunt instrument.

"It's like a game of Clue," said Julia. "Do you think it was the candlestick in the conservatory or the fireplace poker in the library?"

"Or a gentleman's walking stick," suggested Nick. He crunched down on his biscuit with obvious relish, scattering crumbs across his knees. "There's one logical suspect in all this."

It didn't take much to figure out what he was thinking. "Hell hath no fury like a husband wronged?"

"Divorce wasn't easy back then." He leaned back, regarding her speculatively. "If Imogen Grantham was having an affair with Gavin Thorne in 1849 and her daughter was born in 1850 . . . Did it ever occur to you that Thorne might be your great-great-grandfather?"

"Actually, no," said Julia slowly. It had all seemed like a story in a book, something long ago and far away, with no practical application. Purely of academic interest. "That's . . . wow."

Nick took another bite of his biscuit, looking far too pleased with himself. "It would explain the artistic strain."

Julia narrowed her eyes at him. "I thought you were the one who said these things didn't necessarily run in families. Or what was that about your notable performance in *A Midsummer Night's Dream*?"

"Notable for being anything but notable," Nick corrected. He twisted his head to look at her. "Don't you like the idea?"

Julia leaned back against the cushions, trying to make sense of it all. "In the abstract, yes." It was kind of neat to think of being descended from one of the original Pre-Raphaelites. "But it doesn't really make any difference, does it? I'm still the same me I was before, whether I'm descended from Gavin Thorne or the dustman."

"Or William the Conqueror — if your cousin Caroline is to be believed," said Nick blandly.

Julia lobbed a small embroidered pillow at him.

He ducked neatly, saying, "But where it does matter is in terms of motive. If Grantham knew that his wife was carrying another man's child . . ."

"We don't know that for sure. Even if she was, Grantham might have been happily ignorant. Did you see those piles and piles of diaries up in the attic? Those were their daughter's — Olivia's. It doesn't sound like

Grantham ever mistreated her or neglected her or ever gave any indication that he wasn't her real father."

"He didn't have to, did he?" Nick argued. "The adulterous parties were both dead. Easier to hush it up and play the doting father."

Julia wasn't convinced. "You don't think it would have come out, somehow, in his behavior if he'd known?"

"People are unpredictable," said Nick profoundly. "What we do know is that someone killed Thorne, here, on the grounds of this house, and had the means to stick him away under the summerhouse. Who else could it be?"

TWENTY-EIGHT

Herne Hill, 1857

It was a rainy Tuesday and Olivia Grantham needed someplace to hide.

To be fair, she hadn't meant to spill ink on Miss Penbury's false curls. Penbury was terribly proud of her hairpiece, although how she could assume that anyone believed that it was real Olivia didn't know. It wasn't even the same color as the rest of her hair. The curls were a determined auburn, while the rest of Miss Penbury's hair was a rather streaky grayish brown.

Olivia had a strange fascination with those tightly rolled curls. So, when she had happened to come upon Miss Penbury's hairpiece unattended . . .

Really, she had just been looking at it. It was pure bad luck that she had happened to knock over that bottle of ink and even worse luck that Penbury had come in before Olivia had got it all sopped up. Apparently, dropping the false front into the washbasin hadn't been at all the thing to do.

Olivia had fled the schoolroom while Penbury was still mourning over her sodden curls, which were now no longer auburn but a rather greenish black. It was, Olivia had decided, safer to be out of the way until the hubbub had died down.

But where to hide? Penbury knew most of her usual haunts: behind the thick drapes in the drawing room, beneath the claw-footed sideboard in the dining room, in that curious little nook between the day nursery and the night nursery. She couldn't take refuge in the trees in the orchard; the world outside was uniformly damp and gray and Olivia had no desire to be dripped upon, even in the interest of eluding Miss Penbury and a — she had to admit — somewhat deserved scolding.

But only somewhat. It wasn't as though she had intended to ruin Penbury's false front. Although it had turned a rather fascinating color once the ink had spilled on it.

Somehow, Olivia suspected Penbury wouldn't quite appreciate that.

For want of better options, she darted into Aunt Jane's room. Papa's room was off-limits, and the room that had belonged to

Olivia's mama was too sacred to enter. Papa had kept it just as it had been when she was alive, and Olivia didn't go there. Sometimes, she would creep as far as the door and, heart high in her chest, open it and peer inside the shrouded interior — and then close it again very quickly, before she was caught.

But Aunt Jane was just Aunt Jane, and while she might be cross at finding Olivia hiding at the back of her wardrobe, she would certainly be less cross than Penbury. By rights, Aunt Jane's room was forbidden territory; Olivia wasn't meant to be fussing with her aunt's things. In practice, though, Olivia couldn't imagine Aunt Jane would scold, any more than she had scolded when she caught Olivia wearing her best going-to-church hat and one of Father's cravats as a scarf. Aunt Jane pretended to be strict, but her scoldings were usually followed with a slice of bread and jam, the amount of jam directly proportional to the length of the scolding.

Olivia had once overheard Aunt Jane telling Father that Olivia was the daughter she had never had. While she knew this was meant kindly, Olivia was secretly, guiltily, glad that Aunt Jane wasn't her mother. Her real mother was much more interesting. She knew very little about her, only that she had been beautiful — there was her portrait in the drawing room, all dark hair and big, soulful eyes — and that she had died bringing Olivia into the world, which Olivia found terribly sad and romantic.

Aunt Jane, prim, prosaic Aunt Jane, with her graying blond hair and the horrible candies that gave her breath an odd stench, just couldn't compete, although in the everyday course of things it was Aunt Jane to whom Olivia went running with scraped knees and small triumphs.

Her room also had the distinct advantage of boasting a commodious wardrobe, with plenty of room for an agile seven-year-old to scrunch in tight at the back. One side was filled from top to bottom with drawers, the other crowded with cloth-covered dresses hanging from pegs. With a quick glance over her shoulder Olivia tugged open the doors of the wardrobe and scrambled into the opening, burrowing between a wool petticoat and a scratchy thing of stiffened horsehair, only to find her ingress thwarted by something large and rectangular leaning against the back of the wardrobe, something that took up all of the valuable hiding space behind the dresses.

It wobbled dangerously as Olivia bumped

into it, and she caught at a cloth-shrouded corner to keep it from falling. The linen wrappings tugged free in her hand, revealing a corner of a brightly painted scene, like something out of a storybook.

She had only the briefest impression of a king with a crown, and a lady with a cup, and, best of all, a darling black and white dog with its paws stretched out in front of it before there was the sound of angry footsteps and someone was upon her, hauling her out backward by the collar of her dress.

"You wicked, wicked girl!" It was Aunt Jane's voice, but Aunt Jane as Olivia had never heard her before. "What are you doing here?"

Aunt Jane's face was flushed with anger; she seemed to crackle with rage, from the top of her head down to the bottom of her crinoline. Olivia felt uncertain. She had never seen Aunt Jane like this before. She hadn't thought that Aunt Jane would mind so about Miss Penbury's curls.

Dropping her head, Olivia scuffed the toe of her buttoned boot against the carpet. "Miss Penbury —"

Aunt Jane grabbed her ungently by the arm and hauled her forward. "You can imagine I shall have a word with your Miss Penbury! Allowing you to run wild — like a little savage! — what your father will say . . ."

Olivia pulled back against Aunt Jane's arm, too curious to be wise. "But, Aunt Jane, what about the picture?"

Her aunt stopped abruptly. Her hands descended on Olivia's shoulders like talons. "There is no picture," she said.

"But there was," Olivia began stubbornly. In her short life she had seldom been contradicted and thwarted, and certainly not by Aunt Jane, purveyor of jam and bread. "It was the prettiest —"

Olivia's teeth rattled in her mouth as her aunt shook her hard enough to make the ribbon slide free from her hair. Olivia looked up at Aunt Jane in shock and indignation. What she saw in her aunt's face scared her, scared her into silence.

"There is no picture," Aunt Jane said savagely. "Do you understand me?" Another shake. "There is no picture."

Despite herself, Olivia nodded. This was worse than Miss Penbury, worse than the discolored curls. "Aunt Jane . . ."

"Come along." Taking hold of her arm, her aunt propelled her forward. "You're going back to the nursery and you'll stay there while I tell your Miss Penbury what I think of her notions of discipline."

Meekly Olivia obeyed, although she couldn't resist taking one last look over her shoulder as her aunt tugged her through the door of the room. But it was no use. The angle of the wardrobe door hid any sign of the picture within.

There had been a picture. She had seen it; she had touched it. But she knew enough not to press the point. Aunt Jane had never raised a hand to her in anger before, had never called her wicked. The words stung.

Olivia was confined to the nursery for a week, a long week with an indignant Penbury, still furious at Olivia over the destruction of her beloved hairpiece and even more outraged over the dressing-down she had received from Aunt Jane over Olivia's conduct. Olivia was set to writing out lines. *A young lady must never . . .*

There were to be no walks in the garden until she showed herself capable of behaving like a young lady, and she was forbidden the use of her watercolors for a month.

Inwardly Olivia seethed at the injustice of it all. She didn't understand why Aunt Jane was so angry. It wasn't as though Olivia had meant any harm, and didn't the vicar always say it was intentions that counted? And there had so been a picture.

The idea of the picture haunted her. At

night, she lay in her narrow bed in the night nursery, with Penbury snoring in her little room just beyond, and tried to reconstruct the scene from the little bit she had seen.

Bit by bit, life fell back into its normal patterns. Penbury bought herself a new cap and seemed resigned, if not reconciled, to the loss of her curls. Aunt Jane indicated her forgiveness by allowing Olivia to wind her wool, despite Olivia's tendency to get it into tangles. The weather cleared enough to permit the walks that Miss Penbury loosely termed "instruction in natural history."

It was several weeks before Olivia had her opportunity. She waited cunningly until Miss Penbury was laid up with a toothache and Aunt Jane had been called away to a meeting of one of her benevolent societies. Having assured, via a visit down the back stairs, that Anna and Cook were engaged in a comfortable coze in the kitchen (and secured herself a biscuit in the process), she crept into Aunt Jane's room.

The wardrobe, that object of desire, stood unattended at the far side of the room. On stockinged feet, Olivia crossed the floor. She carefully wiped her hands on her pinafore to remove any trace of biscuit crumbs before curling her fingers around the brass handles.

Her chest tight with anticipation, she pulled open the doors — and saw nothing.

There were only Aunt Jane's dresses, ghostly in their linen wrappings, with the cloak she kept for best hanging from its own peg. Olivia pressed with her hands against the back of the wardrobe, but nothing met her palms but a flat expanse of wood.

There was no picture.

Thwarted and confused, Olivia retreated to her favorite tree in the apple orchard. Perhaps Aunt Jane was right; perhaps there had never been a picture. It had appeared so vivid — but she must have imagined it. Mustn't she?

She and Aunt Jane never spoke of the matter again, and by the time spring had blossomed into summer Olivia, with the resilience of her age, had forgotten the matter entirely.

If she sometimes dreamed of a brightly patterned scene featuring a king at his high table and a dog panting in the rushes, the memory of it was always gone by morning.

Herne Hill, 2009

"Does it matter now who killed Thorne? Other than for pure curiosity's sake," Julia amended.

On the other side of the closed doors to

the drawing room, the portrait of Imogen Grantham still hung, with Gavin Thorne's signature on the bottom, the lovers united on the canvas if not in life.

"Whatever happened then, it's comforting to think that they're together now, wherever they are." She wrinkled her nose. "Does that sound soppy?"

Nick donned his most superior expression. "Very soppy. But rather sweet." Nick's voice was carefully neutral as he said, "Once the media show dies down, what do you mean to do?"

Between the police station and fighting off the media and then Nick's business trip, there'd been no chance to talk since last Sunday. Not about them.

Corpses could be very distracting. Especially when both parties had a long-ingrained habit of avoiding tough conversations.

Avoiding Nick's eyes, Julia said, "I'd like to see if I can get Thorne buried next to Imogen. It seems only right that they should finally be together."

Nick captured her hand, twining his fingers firmly through hers. "I didn't mean about them. I meant about you." He paused for a moment and said with an effort, "Do you mean to stay or go?"

Julia thought of Nick's mother, leaving him in London and traipsing back to LA. The visits that were meant to happen but stopped. If they werc going to have a chance of being together, long-distance wasn't really an option, at least not at the beginning.

Julia pulled herself slowly up against the cushions. "I've been thinking about it. A lot."

She thought about her life in New York. There wasn't much there that she would miss. Her father and Helen and the boys, yes. Lexie. But she spoke with them all on the phone more than she saw them, anyway. Her apartment could be rented or sold. If she went back, it would only be because she was afraid to stay here.

There were ways she could maneuver staying in England — if she knew that Nick really wanted her there. If she weren't so terrified that it might not work.

Julia thought about Gavin and Imogen, and the life they might have had together if someone else hadn't intervened. They had been willing to risk all they had for love. She had nothing at stake but her own fears.

Keeping her eyes on the tarnished silver tea strainer, she said, "If the Tate buys *Tristan and Iseult,* I can afford to stay here for a year while I get my grad school applications in."

She felt the couch cushions move as Nick shifted beside her. "You don't mind letting the picture go?"

"It belongs in a museum where other people can see it." Julia took a deep breath. "And it would be nice to stay here a little bit longer. As long as you want me to?"

She felt his hand tighten on hers. "If you need a part-time job for your gap year, there's a shop that could use your assistance. I hear the shopkeeper's not a bad sort."

Julia felt a wave of giddiness wash over her. Or maybe it was just Nick's proximity. He smelled of aftershave, tea, and ginger biscuits. "Is this your way of trying to drum up some cheap labor?"

"I wouldn't call it cheap. If anything, I would say it was rather dear." His arms went around her, and she heard his voice half-laughing, rough with relief, in her ear. "No. Scrap that. Very dear."

Julia rubbed her cheek against the wilted linen of his shirt. "Were you planning to seduce me between the Chippendale and the Sheraton?"

"No," said Nick reproachfully. His breath traveled from her ear, along her cheek, towards her lips, sending little tingles down Julia's spine. "I was thinking more the couch in the back room."

"Sketchy," managed Julia, "hitting on an employee."

Somehow, she wasn't quite vertical anymore. Nick might be rubbish at relationships, but he clearly had some experience on the seduction front.

"It's a good thing you aren't one, then," he murmured.

It was some time before they came up for air, long enough for the shadows in the room to have shifted and the last glowing embers on the hearth to have fizzled into ash. Julia nestled comfortably in Nick's arms. The couch wasn't really big enough for both of them to lie side by side, but neither was complaining.

She could feel Nick's voice start deep in his chest. "I was thinking," he began, and Julia automatically stiffened a bit. This whole trust thing didn't come easy.

Baby steps, she told herself. Baby steps.

"I was thinking," Nick said meditatively, "that since tomorrow is a Saturday, and Tamsin is still in the shop . . ."

Julia levered herself up on an elbow, her hair swinging down over her face as she looked down at him. "Are you inviting yourself over, Mr. Dorrington?"

"Purely to protect you from reporters," he said smoothly. "Although, just to be safe, I should probably stay in your room. In the event of invaders under the bed, of course."

"Of course," Julia agreed. "And when the media invasion is over?"

Nick smoothed the hair away from her face. There was a roguish glint in his blue-green eyes. "Didn't I promise to inspect your artwork?"

ACKNOWLEDGMENTS

Some books are easy and flow lightly off the pen. Others don't. This book fell squarely in the latter category.

Huge thanks go to my editor, Jennifer Weis, for her insight and her patience; to my sister Brooke, who played plot doctor when I needed it most; and to the entire team at St. Martin's Press, for providing suggestions, okaying extensions, brainstorming titles, and designing and redesigning the cover. Thanks also to Joe Veltre, for being my cheerleader through the rough beginning of this book, and to Alexandra Machinist, for putting a fine polish on it at the end. Every book is a team effort, and this one even more so than usual.

Thank you to the regulars on my Web site and Facebook page, for your suggestions, your encouragement, and your enthusiasm. I feel so fortunate to be blessed with such a warm and creative community to turn to on those days when the blank page is particularly blank.

A special shout-out goes to Kristen Kenney, for postcards from the Tate, countless visits to the Burne-Jones exhibit at the Met, and freshman afternoons at the BAC. Whenever I think of Pre-raphaelites, I think of you.

As always, so much love and gratitude to my husband, my parents, and my siblings, who make this book and all others possible by putting up with the author during the writing of them and providing emergency cupcakes when necessary.

Last, but not least, thanks go to my daughter, Madeleine, for graciously waiting until after revisions on this book were handed in before making her appearance in the world, as well as for condescending to nap most of the way through copyedits. Both of these courtesies were greatly appreciated, and have been forwarded on to Santa for future reference.

ABOUT THE AUTHOR

Lauren Willig is also the author of the *New York Times* bestselling Pink Carnation series and a RITA Award winner for Best Regency Historical for *The Mischief of Mistletoe*. She graduated from Yale University and has a graduate degree in English history from Harvard and a J.D. from Harvard Law School. She lives in New York City, where she now writes full time.

The employees of Thorndike Press hope you have enjoyed this Large Print book. All our Thorndike, Wheeler, and Kennebec Large Print titles are designed for easy reading, and all our books are made to last. Other Thorndike Press Large Print books are available at your library, through selected bookstores, or directly from us.

For information about titles, please call:
  (800) 223-1244

or visit our Web site at:
  http://gale.cengage.com/thorndike

To share your comments, please write:
  Publisher
  Thorndike Press
  10 Water St., Suite 310
  Waterville, ME 04901

BOCA RATON PUBLIC LIBRARY, FL

3365640012734

LARGE TYPE
        Willig, Lauren
        That summer

    JUN   2014